THE SAGA
OF CUCKOO

THE SAGA OF CUCKOO

FARTHEST STAR
WALL AROUND A STAR

Frederik Pohl and Jack Williamson

Nelson Doubleday, Inc.
Garden City, New York

CONTENTS

THE SAGA
OF CUCKOO

FARTHEST STAR

PART ONE
Doomship

ONE

The place was called Sun One. It had begun as an asteroid, circling a young blue-white giant in the great dense cloud called the Orion Nebula. Over centuries it had been built upon, sheathed, and tunneled; and what it had become was the closest thing there was to a central headquarters of the loose association of intelligent races in the Galaxy that had made contact with one another.

In one of the inner shells two members of a very junior race were meeting. They came from Earth. They loved each other. They were young. They planned to marry. All these things made them curiosities to the races that possessed personal curiosity, and they were widely watched, heard, or sensed as they came toward each other. They didn't mind. Ben Charles Pertin saw the girl and launched himself in a shallow three-percent-gravity dive over the heads of a thing like a dragon, a creature composed mostly of a single great blue eye, and a couple of scurrying collective creatures from one of the core stars. "Sorry," he cried down at them, caught the laughing girl's hand, and stopped hard beside her.

"Ouch," she said, releasing a holdfast with her other hand. "I'd appreciate a little less enthusiasm next time."

He kissed her and took her arm. "It's part of the image," he said cheerfully. "You know what the chief of delegation says. Make them know we're here. Earth may be the newest planet in the association but it isn't going to be the least important. We have a duty to Earth to make ourselves known throughout the Galaxy, and a duty to the Galaxy to contribute our strength and our know-how."

"I think," the girl said, "that if you're going to talk like that you'd better buy me a drink."

At this shell of Sun One the curvature of the spherical surface they walked on was noticeably sharp. They found it was easier to leap than to stroll. To travel arm in arm, which is how Ben Charles Pertin chose to walk with his girl, required practice and a lot of discomfort—not only to them but to the other sentients in the concourse. Pertin and Zara shifted grips, so that each had an arm around the other's waist; then Pertin caught the holdfast webbing with his free hand and partly tugged, partly kicked them into the air. They shot past the dragonlike creature, narrowly missed a steelwork vertical strut, touched down again next to something that looked like a soft-bodied beetle with three dozen legs, and were in sight of the little refreshment platform they liked.

Pertin said "Hi!" to a thing like a green bat as it flapped by. It hissed something shrill that his personal translator repeated into his ear as, "I recognize your identity, Ben Charles Pertin." The girl nodded, too, although all members of that particular race, which was called the T'Worlie, looked alike to her, and in any event the T'Worlie did not have the custom of nodding since they had no more neck than bats.

As they waited for traffic to clear, the girl said, "How did your meeting go?"

"About as usual. Things are all fouled up on the probe." He was watching a tumbling boxlike robot that was coming toward them on a tangent, correcting its course with methodical jets of steam from the faces of its cubical body; but the tone of his voice made the girl look at him sharply.

"What is it, Ben?"

He gave her a caught-in-the-cookie-jar smile. "I'll tell you about it when we sit down."

"You'll tell me now."

"Well—" He hesitated, then cried, "All right, we can make it now!" But the girl wrapped her fingers around the webbing of the holdfast.

"Ben!"

He relaxed and looked at her. He didn't say anything, but he didn't have to.

"Ben! Not again!"

He said defensively, "I have to, Zara. The other one's dying. There's nobody from Earth on the probe now to represent us. So I agreed to carry the ball."

He looked appraisingly at the traffic of aliens, then back at her; then he looked at her with a sudden shock of surprise. The girl looked as if she had come very close to crying.

"Oh, Zara," he said, half-touched and half-annoyed. "What are you making a big thing about? It's nothing we haven't done before."

"I know," she said, and blinked hard. "It's only—well, it's sort of silly. But I hate the idea of your dying out there while we're on our honeymoon."

Pertin found that he was blinking himself; he was touched. He patted the girl's hand and said seriously, "Honey, one of the traits I like best in you is that you're not afraid to be sentimental at the right time. Don't knock it. I love you for it. Now let's go get that drink."

The little café was nearly empty. That was one of the things they liked about it. It had actual waiters, Purchased People. They didn't have much personality to display, but they were actually human, genetically speaking. Pertin and his fiancée enjoyed ordering in their rudimentary Italian—not their own language, to be sure, but at least a human language, and one for which they did not need the Pmal translators.

Pertin pulled his feet up, crossed them in air, and settled gently onto his chair. They looked about while waiting for their drinks to be brought. Pertin had been on Sun One for more than two years now, the girl for several months. Even so, familiarity had not dulled their interest in the place where they were stationed or in the work they did there. The girl was a newswriter, broadcasting to Earth every week on the stereostage. Pertin was an engineer. His job on Sun One didn't involve much engineering. It did involve an interesting mixture of skills. He functioned partly as a sort of legalized spy and partly as a goodwill ambassador from Earth to the rest of the Universe.

The mere fact that a job like his existed was still secretly thrilling to Ben Charles Pertin. He was not yet thirty. Even so, he was old enough to remember the time when the human race thought it was alone in the Galaxy.

Space travel itself was not new. The old "nations" had put up their chemical rockets and sent them chugging to Venus, Mars, and the Moon in his grandfather's time. They had looked for life, and come up empty every time. Nuclear probes a generation later investigated the outer planets, the satellites, and even the asteroids, with the same result. No life. By the time Ben was twelve years old, the juice had run out of space travel.

There were still a lot of ongoing projects, such as the close-orbiting satellites that photomapped the Earth and relayed TV programs from Rangoon to Rochester and back. An occasional plodding probe was sent out to sample a comet's gases or measure the solar flux. And of course there was always the Farside base on the Moon, where radio astronomy had retreated when the world's communications systems had ruined reception for every ground-based dish. But no excitement was generated by any of that. There was not even any interest. If some pollster had sampled the Earth's billions with a question like, "Do you think intelligent life exists elsewhere in the Universe?" he would have been likely to receive as a general response, "Don't know; don't care."

Then came Contact.

It happened just as Ben Pertin was turning thirteen. Something had been found on Pluto. An artifact, half buried under Pluto's mirror of ice. The Earth suddenly looked outward again. The stereostages were full of it: the first fumbling attempts to patch it together, the first daring experiment at putting power through it. Everybody talked about it. Ben and his parents watched the glowing figures on their stage, enthralled. Their evening meals grew cold because they forgot to eat. In school, the kids made the discovery the main subject of every class.

And when the ancient communicator came to life and the first alien face peered out of its screen and looked into the face of a human from Earth, the world went mad.

"I don't want to hear any more of that cockamamie Earthman's Burden talk," Zara Doy said. "I heard too much of it when I was a kid. I don't *want* you going out to die. Stay here with me."

Pertin said fondly, "You're sweet, Zara. But this is important. The situation on the probe is exploding; the beings are fighting. They're dying uselessly. I can't back out just for some sentimental ideas of—"

"Sentiment be damned! Look. When we get married I want you right in bed with me, all of you. I don't want to be thinking about part of you dying way off in nowhere!"

"I'll be with you, honey. All of me."

"You know what I mean," she said angrily.

He hesitated. The last thing he wanted was to quarrel with his fiancée two days before they were to get married—and less than two days before he kept his promise to go to the probe ship. He rubbed his troth ring and said, "Zara, I have to go to the probe. First, I said I would; and the boss has passed the word to all the other top brass on Sun One. Second, it's important. It's not 'Earthman's Burden.' It's simple logic. We're new and pretty far behind, compared to the Scorpians or the methane crowd or the T'Worlie. But look what we've done already. We have Earth people on every major planet, working in every big project, taking part in everything that's happening. The others are getting used to us. They consult us now. If I back out, who else is there to go? Earth won't be represented—"

"I don't care."

"It's not as if I haven't done it before—"

"The other time you went we weren't going to be married," the girl responded fiercely.

"All right, that's true. Now I owe you something. But I owe our planet something, too. We're just *beginning* to contribute our share of leadership in the Galaxy, Zara. I mean, look at that waiter! Half the Purchased People around are human beings, now. When the nonviables edit a copy for Sun One, say, what shape do they copy? Human! The human shape is as familiar in the Galaxy now as the Sheliaks—and all in twenty years!"

Zara sucked at the last of her drink and put it down in its cage. She stared at the waiter, who was smoking a cigarette and thinking whatever thoughts a blanked-out personality was allowed to think; then she shook her head.

"I'll lay it out nice and orderly like an engineer for you, Ben," she said. "First, if they copy human shape, is it because they respect us or because they have some crazy methane sense of humor? Second, if they buy our convicts for Purchased People, likely enough it's because we have more criminals to sell. Third, I don't like the whole idea of Earth trying to dominate the Galaxy. Fourth—"

"Dominate! I said 'leadership.' It's not the same thing at all."

"It's a prerequisite. Not sufficient, but necessary. Fourth, I still hate it all on personal grounds, and I'm not talking about idealism, I'm talking about sex. I'll get over it. I know that. But it's going to take some of the joy out of going to bed with you, Ben, thinking that at the same time somewhere else you're getting eaten by a Sheliak or dying of radiation burn. I'm sorry it's so, but it's so."

Ben said doubtfully, after a moment, "Would it be better if we postponed the wedding a little bit?"

"I don't know. Let me think."

He waited, finished his drink, looked cautiously at the girl. There was no anger or misery on her pretty face; she was simply staring thoughtfully out at the other beings in the concourse.

Pertin beckoned to the waiter and paid the check. "They thank you," said the waiter, staring appraisingly at Pertin and the girl. "Will there be anything else?"

"No, we're going." But still the girl sat there. Then she sighed, and smiled at him.

"Well. You want to go pretty badly. Feeling the way you do, I suppose you ought to go. I won't stop you, Ben, and it's silly to put off getting married. But there is one thing I want you to do."

He waited warily.

"Give me your ring. No, just to hold. When you're finished going to the probe I'll give it back to you. But I don't want you wearing my ring when you die."

Last-minute briefing was in the tachyon transport chamber, out at the far shell of Sun One, and heavily shielded. Dr. Gerald York Bielowitz checked Pertin out himself. He was a methodical man—one of the reasons he was head of the mission to Sun One; and he read from a soundscripted list.

"We've got about ten minutes, Ben Charles. Let's see. Object Lambda. You know as much about it as I do: it's anomalous, it's exciting, the only way to find out about it is this probe, and it's in Earth's interest to make the probe succeed."

He dropped his eyes to the page and went on: "There's no possibility of survival on the probe, of course, and this has undoubtedly had some effect on the psyches of all the beings there. To the extent they have what we can map as psyches, I mean. But in my opinion, the physical problems have caused the trouble. Some of the beings are dying—your predecessor among them, of course. Others are functioning poorly, probably because of ionization interference with their nervous systems—or whatever corresponds to nervous systems.

"At any rate," he said, checking off another point, "the beings on the probe no longer constitute an orderly system. There's violence. Some of the deaths are from fights or murders. This is seriously interfering with the operation of the probe, and threatening its very success. You know how important that is. If we blow this, it's more than a hundred years before we get another chance.

"And finally," he said, folding the list and putting it in his sporran, "your account here will be credited with double-rate pay for your services on the probe. Your equipment will follow, along with Doc Chimp here." He nodded civilly to the hairy little handyman who crouched next to Pertin. "And good luck to you both!"

"Thank you, Gerald York," Pertin said gravely. He stepped up to the transport portal, waited for the signal and entered, giving a half-wave to Bielowitz as the door closed behind him.

This was the fourth time he had found himself in a tachyon-transporter box, or at least the fourth time that he remembered, or that it had actually happened to *him*. They all looked about the same. On the inside they were featureless except for what looked like studded nailheads almost completely covering each of the six interior surfaces. He stood there for a moment, and felt nothing.

But something was going on. The sensors were counting, locating, and identifying every atom in his body, measuring their bonds to adjacent atoms, charting them in a precise three dimensional matrix. The information obtained they encoded into a string of binary numbers; whereupon the great tachyon generators glowed into life, transmitting the numbers at a billibit per second in the direction of a point outside the farthest spiral arm of the Galaxy. It took only moments.

Then Ben Charles Pertin stepped out of the box and shook hands with his head of mission. "You're the best man I've got," Bielowitz said solemnly. "Thanks."

Pertin then went back to his office and worked through the rest of the afternoon. He left a little early to meet his fiancée and take her to dinner. Over the coffee she returned his troth ring to him.

TWO

At about the same time that Ben Charles Pertin was putting his ring back on his finger, as much as time at two points separated by relativistic distances and velocities can be called the "same," Ben James Pertin pushed his way out of another, almost identical box on the probe ship.

He stopped just outside the portal, moving slightly to allow it to close behind him. His expression was grim. "Lucked out," he said aloud, looking around the unfamiliar chamber.

There was no one to hear, or to see the bitter and despondent look on his face. The chamber was deserted. The probe was in free-fall, and Pertin floated slowly away from the transport; but nothing else was floating in the room. There was no litter, no sign that any other being of any sort was within thousands of light-years and, as he listened, not even any sound.

He swore softly to himself and twisted his body around to face the crated personal effects that were nudging their way out of the box. There wasn't a great deal to come: some tapes, some changes of clothing, personal items. All his belongings were in a couple of crates, and at the end of the string of transmissions came his companion on the mission, Doc Chimp.

Doc Chimp thrust out a long arm and caught the handle of the door as he went by. He hung there for a moment, staring at his environment with an expression that was a parody of Pertin's own. "Oh, wow, Ben Charles," he said sadly. "What a place."

"It'll be 'Ben James,' I think," said Pertin.

"Sure," Doc Chimp said dismally. "Me, I'm not going to bother. If you want to call me something different, call me stupid."

Doc Chimp was Earthborn, but he was not human. He was five feet three inches tall, weighed more than two hundred pounds, and, in high-G environments, habitually walked on feet and knuckles. His parents had been chimpanzees, but Doc Chimp was something different.

For one thing, he had a sense of humor. He reflected it in the clothes he wore. Over his hairy barrel chest he wore a little red vest, open, with the coarse black fur sprouting through. He didn't need it for comfort or for modesty; he wore it to please his own sense of the comic, and for pockets to hold his automatic translator, the key to his private suitcase, and a supply of macadamia nuts, of which he was very fond. For modesty he wore shiny brown lederhosen. On his head he sported a kepi with a sand veil around sides and back, and over its visor a bright green plume.

Even the plume was sagging dejectedly as he said, "I think I'm going to hate this place, Ben James."

"We didn't come here to have fun. Where the hell is everybody?"

"Don't know, Ben James. Can't say."

"Stow our stuff then. This thing won't stay in free-fall long; we'd better find somebody before it starts firing again."

"Certainly, Ben James. But there's somebody coming now."

Pertin said, startled: "I don't hear anything."

"Neither do I. But I smell it. It's a T'Worlie, coming fast."

The probe ship was T'Worlie property, but fortunately for the other races of the Galaxy the T'Worlie didn't have a very strong territorial imperative.

They had been civilized for a long, long time. They were an inquisitive race, in their unhurried way, and no doubt that was why they had been sending their probes out for hundreds of generations. Little T'Worlie rockets had radiated in all directions from their mother star, some of them aimed at other stars, some at nothing closer than the Great Nebula in Andromeda, ten million years' travel time away.

Only a race like that, deploying probes as lavishly and patiently as it had, could have discovered the curious astronomical object called Lambda. No other race would have been in a position to do it. Sirians, with their limited time-binding capacities that reached no more than a week into the future, wouldn't have bothered. Nothing that promised a remote payoff interested the Sirians at all—which made them unattractive partners, but inoffensive foes. Humans of course had no chance; their technology wasn't up to the job, and the farthest terrestrial probe was still climbing toward the turnover point on its now senseless journey toward 40 Eridani A.

But the T'Worlie thought long, slow thoughts, and they were gently but persistently curious about everything. If their race lived long enough it would learn everything there was to know. None of them seemed to mind that no T'Worlie now alive would be present to learn it.

Lambda had been discovered first by an unmanned T'Worlie scoutship and reported in a routine synoptic survey. It attracted no attention at all. When first observed, its great distance and low luminosity put it at the very threshold of detectability, and the traits that made it unique had not been noted.

Subsequent observations attracted more attention. Its weak spectral lines seemed to shift toward the violet, rather than the red—which is to say, it was moving *toward* the Galaxy instead of away from it. Curious. But the lines were so very weak, the point so very distant, and the orderly T'Worlie had many other things on their agenda to investigate.

Then, by accident, another scout turned up the same object in a survey.

It might not have been recognized if the computers of the T'Worlie had not been so patient and painstaking. The second scout had been launched five thousand years earlier, its vector several degrees away. From its point of view, Object Lambda was in a wholly different part of the sky, and its rate of approach, indicated by the spectral shift, quite different.

But the computers had sensed a possible match and had clucked over the figures until they confirmed it. There existed a specific, if hypothetical, orbit and velocity, which, seen from those two scouts at those recorded times, would have given exactly those readings.

From the estimated elements the computers made a prediction. They requested a special observation from still a third unmanned scout. Lo! It turned out as they had predicted.

Object Lambda was not more than twenty thousand light-years from the edge of the Galaxy, and was approaching it at about one-sixth of light-speed.

At this point the T'Worlie announced their discovery to the galactic civilization at large, and began a study of their existing drones in that general part of space.

The T'Worlie drones were as small as interstellar probes can be made: a scoop, a hydrogen ram, some instruments, and a tachyon installation. The T'Worlie had been launching them, thousands at a time, for tens of thousands of years. As they had never invented war, they were able to accumulate large quantities of surplus capital, and so the probes were not at first a particularly expensive project for them. Like most early-industrial races, they had energy to burn. They burned it. Their planet was largely water-covered; though they looked like bats, they were somewhat more analogous to flying fish. Their water was rich in D_2O, and they spent its fusion energies profligately.

The T'Worlie drone model was standardized early. A program was set up under which each drone, upon reaching a point suitably distant from all others, flashed a tachyonic signal to the T'Worlie planet, whereupon the tachyon transmitters scanned, encoded, and transmitted whole new drones to the mother drone's unit. As each new drone flashed into being, it signaled in to the T'Worlie planet, was given a course and program of its own and went onward. The effect was that of an enormous globe of drones, at the end thousands of millions of them, expanding outward like the shell of a dead supernova.

The program was fully automatic and economical of everything but the energy eaten up by the tachyon transmitters, and for ten thousand years there seemed to be an endless supply of that.

In the end even the T'Worlie began to realize that their energy resources, though huge, were not infinite. The drone program was cut to a trickle. But it was never stopped, and the great swelling bubble of drone ships expanded out, into globular clusters, out toward the neighboring galaxies, along the spiral arms, in toward the core of the Milky Way itself. It was a T'Worlie drone that had buried itself on Pluto and been found by the exploration from Earth. In fact, T'Worlie drones had brought into the galactic society at least a hundred races at one time or another, almost half of the total so far located. Another race might have thought of using that fact to establish dominance for itself, but the T'Worlie didn't think that way. They had never invented empires, either.

So when the T'Worlie began to be deeply interested in Object Lambda it was easy enough to find some hundreds of drones on courses and at points that were not too remote from it.

The next job for the T'Worlie computers was calculating which of these drones was on the course that would involve least time and energy in diverting it to the neighborhood of Lambda, with its huge Galaxyward velocity. Fortunately a handful of drones in that section had been redirected inward long before, to fill gaps in the global screen. Among them was one that was, by the best of luck, on a course that could match Lambda in less than five years.

After that there was no problem. The drone's matter receiver was put to work giving birth to automatic tools, hull sections, drive units, instruments, finally people. The tools went to work, assembling the hull sections, installing the drives, making room for the people. What had been a tiny kick-ram, no bigger than Earth's early Apollo capsule, was transformed and expanded into a thousand-meter vessel with room for a crew of several hundred.

There was, to be sure, one problem.

The rebuilt T'Worlie ship, now named *Aurora,* was big; but it needed to be big. It did not possess a great deal of surplus mass.

The ship was driven by the sequential explosion of hydrogen fusion charges, directional in a cone-shaped blast against a great battering plate at its base. Not much of the ionizing radiation from the fusion explosions seeped through the base plate, but enough did so that the members of the crew were constantly bathed in it.

T'Worlie and Sheliaks, Purchased People and Boaty-Bits, robots and humans—all responded to this in their individual and idiosyncratic racial ways. But few complex chemical or electronic processes can operate without damage in the presence of ionizing radiation. It didn't matter who they were. In the long run it came to much the same for all of them. They died.

Pertin and the chimp scrambled to the corridor entrance and peered out. The vinegary T'Worlie smell was strong now, and they could hear the sounds of something happening outside: a puncture-tire hiss, a faint high-pitched singing.

A circus procession was sailing toward them down the center of the corridor. First was a T'Worlie, a bat's head on butterfly body, no bigger than a pigeon but strong enough to be dragging with it a kitten-sized furry creature with enormous saucer eyes as it flew with powerful strokes of its green-spotted filmy wings. Behind the T'Worlie and the being it carried was a glittering cloud of steel-blue particles, like a swarm of gnats in the sun; and behind them, coming fast but decelerating strongly because of its mass, the square-edged form of a Scorpian robot, all fore jets pumping reaction mass.

The T'Worlie made its shrill whistling sounds, and the Pmal translator on Pertin's shoulder rattled into life. "I identify you as a Pertin," it said with mechanical precision. "I propose you transfer at once to high-G accommodations suitable to your structure, mode urgent."

"Why, Nimmie!" cried Ben James, suddenly, inexplicably, foolishly glad. "It's good to see you."

The T'Worlie braked with its filmy wings, and the five patterned eyes studied Pertin. "Verify your statement of identity," the Pmal translator rattled in his ear. "Query implications. Request clarification."

"Why, it's me, Ben Ch—Ben James Pertin. From Sun One. Why, just yesterday I saw you in the social concourse, remember?" But he stopped; this copy of the T'Worlie he had known would not remember.

The T'Worlie hesitated. It was some Nimmie or other, Pertin was sure; the key to recognizing T'Worlie was not the five eyes, or the small sphincter mouth with its cat's-whisker vibrissae, but the patterns on the wings. Green spots predominating on a pale yellow background; five of the bigger spots arranged in a sort of wobbly letter W, like the constellation Cassiopeia from Earth; yes, it was Nimmie, all right, Pertin knew. But perhaps a Nimmie he had never met, in some different line of descent.

The vinegary smell deepened; it was a sign of polite cogitation in a T'Worlie, like a human being's *Hmmm*. But Nimmie did not respond exactly. He was distracted by the swarm of tiny beings, who swept into the tachyon-transport room, swirled around Pertin and the chimp, and reformed under the T'Worlie's wings.

The kittenlike creature spoke, with a voice like a purr. The translator rendered it as: "No time kidding around, get hell out!" And the T'Worlie concurred:

"Mode urgent. Accept transportation via robot. Your physical safety at risk!"

Doc Chimp chattered: "I told you I wasn't going to like this place, Ben James. It isn't safe. Of course, I'm only a monkey, so it doesn't matter much about me. It's you I worry about."

"You're an ape," Pertin corrected automatically, his brain concentrating on what the T'Worlie had said.

"Sure, but an ape that knows what isn't safe. Come on, Ben James! Let's do like Bat-Ears says and split!"

Suddenly, the decision was taken from Pertin. The Scorpian robot hissed slowly by, still decelerating, came to a stop, reversed itself, and began to pick up momentum for the return. And as it passed Pertin and Doc Chimp it simply caught them up, each under a silvery tentacle, and bore them away. In reverse order the procession steamed away: first the robot with the two terrestrial primates, then the swarm of Bit-creatures, then the T'Worlie and its passenger.

The probe was powered by huge nuclear thrusters; the power was only off for short periods, long enough to permit instrument readings or other work that could not be carried on during deceleration times, and the rest of the time the entire environment suffered under a surging uneven pulsing drive that averaged nearly seven gravities.

The welcoming-and-transport committee barely got them to a place of refuge before the thrusters started again. The Boaty-Bits had darted away at the first warning white-noise blast; they could not operate at all under thrust and had to find safety lest they be stepped on. The T'Worlie and his passenger were next to go, leaving only the robot to see to tucking Pertin and Doc Chimp in. The robot had no particular objection to high gravity—Pertin had noticed that on the trip from the tachyon chamber; when the robot had to change direction it simply braced itself with a few of the steel-coil tentacles, stopped against whatever was in the way, and pushed off in another direction. The sensation for Pertin was like being tossed around at the end of a cracking whip, but he survived it.

The thrusting started before the robot had finished sealing their cocoons, and it was even worse than the ride. The cocoons, meant to protect them against the thrust, were tailor-made to their dimensions, equipped with the best of springing devices and every comfort. But there was no such thing as antigravity, and that was what was needed.

The robot tarried for a moment. It could no longer jet about, but its tentacles held it easily off the floor, octopuslike. As the thrusts came the appendages gave gently, then returned to position.

The robot seemed to be trying to communicate. Pertin, looking out of the cocoon faceplate, shrugged and spread his hands. One Scorpian looked like another, but if this one had come from Sun One it might recognize the human gesture. The trouble was, there was no way to tell whether it was responding to it.

Then the Pmal crackled into life: "—not move. Prerequisite explanations to you. I am repeating this on all comm frequencies, will. Imperative you not move. Prerequisite—"

The Pmal faded again, as the robot evidently shifted to another possible frequency. "All right," said Pertin, "we'll wait." But whether the robot understood him or not he could not say; it rested there on its tentacles, swaying under the thrust for a few moments more, and then slithered undulatingly away.

The probe was decelerating furiously now; a rollercoaster ride, multiplied by a hundred. There was a lot more noise than Pertin had expected, both the distant rumble of the nuclear explosions and the screeching of the torsion-bar shock absorbers that did their best to level out the thrust. But the cocoon was designed for it.

"Doc!" he called. "Can you hear me?"

The chimp's cocoon was only yards away, but the thuuud-*screech!* drowned out all other sounds. Pertin stared around. The room was half machine. Bright metal valves, gray plastic tubes coiling like dead entrails, colored screens where enigmatic symbols flickered and vanished. The walls were a sick, off-color green. No human would have designed a room like this, but of course it had not been designed for humans in the first place. It was a standard T'Worlie cocoon container, modified to take terrestrials; and the T'Worlie merely allowed them to use it.

The thuuuuud-*screech* went on and on. Experimenting with the cocoon, Pertin discovered that it would meter an anesthetic dose into his veins, or even a selective analgesic to deaden the auditory nerve for a time to block out the remorseless nuclear thunder. But he didn't want to sleep, and he wasn't tired; he wanted to get about his business. When your time is running out, he thought, you don't like to lose any of it.

Then he discovered that the cocoon had a built in stereostage.

The apparatus was not wholly familiar, but with any luck he should be able to reach Doc Chimp, at least. His first attempt was not a success. He gently turned a knurled pointer under the hollow silver hemisphere of the stage and was delighted to see it fill with the shining silver mist that indicated it was operating.

But when the mist abruptly condensed it was to show the image of a nude blond girl. "Mr. Pertin, sir," she caroled sweetly, "welcome aboard! Tonight for your entertainment, sir, you may watch me star in *The Belle of Bellatrix.* A thriller-drama of the love of a human beauty for a mutated alien and its fatal consequences. Feel the fear of the terrified girl! Share the wrath of her human lover! Feel the coils of the monster around her! Taste its dying blood! All these available by using the sen-sat foils in the small cabinet by your right hand. We have many other stereostage fiches, Mr. Pertin, and—"

He finally got that fiche turned off, and the nude blonde vanished, still smiling. She dissipated as the camera zoomed in at her until at the end all that was left was a Cheshire-cat smile and the memory of her pale, slim figure.

Then the stereostage blinked, swirled with color, solidified, and Doc Chimp's homely face was staring out at him.

"Got you first time," Pertin cried, pleased. "I didn't think I would be so lucky."

"You weren't," the chimp said. "I called you. I want to volunteer for something." The chimpanzee face looked subdued.

Pertin said, "What?"

"I think I ought to take a look around," Doc Chimp said sadly. "God knows I don't want to. But most of the beings will be tied down to pressure cocoons and I'm not. Quite."

"Good idea," Pertin said, a little surprised. He hadn't known the chimp well on Sun One—it wasn't that he was prejudiced against mutated animals, but of course they didn't have much in common. But he had an impression of Doc Chimp's personality that was at variance with the act of volunteering for a solitary excursion into what might be trouble. Humorous, pleasure-seeking, a little lazy—that's how he would have described the chimp. "And thanks," he added. "Meanwhile I'll just send back a report to Sun One, if I can figure out how to use this stereostage."

"Ah," said Doc Chimp, the mocking light in his eyes again, "allow me to instruct you, mighty human. You know, I figured you'd be too involved with high-level considerations to take much interest in hardware. So I checked out all the instrumentation with the T'Worlie on Sun One before we left."

Pertin needed only a few minutes to learn to operate the component in his cocoon; it was not, after all, anything but a stereostage, and they were common all over the Galaxy. Then he lifted himself on one elbow against the surging thrusts of the drive, the cocoon's self-adjusting circuits buzzing busily to try to compensate for his unusual position; and he watched the chimp cautiously lever himself over the side of his own cocoon—timing his movements to the surging of the drive—drop clumsily to the floor, mutter to himself angrily for a moment, and then slowly, painfully lumber off on all fours. He did not look back.

Pertin felt curiously better, as if he had discovered a friend where he had expected only an inadequate tool. He worked the controls of the stereostage, got himself a circuit through to the recording fiches of the tachyon communicator, and spoke:

"This is Ben James Pertin," he said, "reporting in to Sun One. Doc Chimp and I have arrived safely. There was no apparent problem from the transmission; at least, we look all right, we're breathing, our hearts are working. Whether our brains are scrambled or not I could not say. No more than when we volunteered for this, anyway, I'd guess. We have seen very little of the probe, have contacted only a few of the personnel; but in general the situation appears much as we understood it. At present I am in an acceleration couch, waiting for the next period of free-fall for further investigation. Doc Chimp, who is performing very well and deserves credit, has voluntarily left on a scouting mission.

"I'll report again when I have something to say," he finished, "and —personal to Ben Charles Pertin: Have a good time on my honeymoon."

He snapped off the stage before he could decide to erase the last part of the message.

In spite of the best efforts of the cocoon, his kidneys were beginning to feel bruised. The noise was even more of a problem. Efficient soundproofing kept it out of the cocoon as noise—at least, as airborne vibrations—but there was too much of it, the amplitude too great, to be shut out entirely; and it seeped through as a continual thunder and squeal.

Pertin shut it out of his mind, thought of sleep, decided to brush up on his knowledge of the "hardware."

His first attempt at the fiche library of the stereostage was only half successful. He just managed to avert the appearance of the bare-skinned blonde and found he had secured a record transmitted by another member of the crew—race unspecified—apparently for a sort of public stereostage broadcast on its home planet. He shut out of his mind the public broadcaster he should have been getting ready to marry about this time—some thousands of light-years away, *was* getting ready to marry—and discovered that the name of the vessel was the *Aurora,* or *Dawn*—the sound was of course different in the T'Worlie tongue, and they had named it; but it had the same shared meanings of new day and bright glowing promise. He discovered that it had only limited facilities for recreation—well, he had known that. There were tape-fiche libraries for almost every known race and some special high-pressure atmosphere chambers for a few of the exotics. That was it.

This was not exactly what he wanted, so he tried again. But instead of getting a fiche on the ship itself, he got one on its mission, evidently a briefing record dubbed for humans. The narration was by a man Pertin recognized, about sixty, plump, freckled; he had been a minor functionary on Sun One. He spoke in a high-pitched voice, smiling emptily at the stereo pickup:

"We will show you all that is known about Object Lambda. First we will locate it, as it would be seen from Earth if visible at that distance."

Behind him another stereostage tank glowed, shimmered, and filled with a universe of stars. Two of the brighter ones pulsed to call attention to themselves as the man spoke.

"Those stars are Benetnasch, in Ursa Major, and Cor Caroli, in Canes Venatici. Those faint stars over there"—as he spoke a faint line of light ran around an area of the tank, enclosing it in a square—"are in Coma Berenices, near the north galactic pole. Now we'll take a closer look."

Benetnasch and Cor Caroli swam aside. The faint stars of Coma Berenices grew brighter, spreading apart, as the whole field of stars seemed to move. To Ben James Pertin it felt as if he were plunging head-on into a sea of stars. The bright points fled out of the sides of the stage, and the few remaining ones became brighter, until only a few were left, and beyond them ghostly faint blurs that were no longer part of the Milky Way but galaxies in their own right.

Then the illusion of motion stopped.

Another square of light formed around a patch of blackness in the center of the stage, indistinguishable from the emptiness around it.

The man said, "Now we've reached the limits of Sol-orbiting instruments. Object Lambda is at the center of that square, but it is invisible. It is slightly better in the far infrared."

The pattern of stars shimmered; some became brighter, some dimmer, and in the center of the square there was what might have been a faint and shapeless glow.

"This is not instantaneous," explained the lecturer. "It's long exposure and image-intensified. It would never have been detected in routine sweeps from Sol-based instruments. Even the T'Worlie scouts first detected it only because of the chance occultation of some stars in the Milky Way itself, seen from beyond. What we will show you next is not an actual observation but an artifact as it would look from Earth, as deduced from all available observations."

The object brightened half a dozen magnitudes as he spoke.

"As you see, it has a sort of tipped-disk shape, like certain classifications of external galaxies. However, that's not what it is. First of all, it is far too small, perhaps only two or three A.U. Second, its spectrum is wrong.

"At its apparent distance, as determined by its angular diameter— as if it were indeed a galaxy—it should be receding at a major fraction of the speed of light. Of course, we know from triangulation from the T'Worlie ships that that distance is wrong by a good many orders of magnitude. But according to its spectrum displacement, it is actually approaching the Milky Way at nearly relativistic speeds."

The image blurred and disappeared, and the plump human was standing there by himself. He said with satisfaction, "The T'Worlie scout has confirmed the speed as accurate, in the range of fifty thousand kps. Its position, relative to Earth, is some thirty thousand light-years from Sol, in the direction of a point near the northern fringe of Coma Berenices. It is not an object from our galaxy. There are no spiral arms in that direction, nor many isolated stars or clusters much nearer than Sol itself.

"The T'Worlie backplotted its position from all observations of their drones, as recorded over the past several thousand years. Most of the data are ambiguous, but they did establish a probable line of flight. Their hope was to find a galaxy from which the object might have been ejected, and then to try to discover the reason for its high velocity. The T'Worlie were only partly successful—I should say, only *possibly* successful. No such galaxy was detected. They did, however, find scattered star swarms which they believe to be the fragments of a galaxy that collapsed and then exploded more than half a billion years ago. It is the present working hypothesis that Object Lambda was ejected from that galaxy—by what means we cannot say."

The man's expression became enthusiastic. "Because of the anomalous nature of Object Lambda," he said, "the all-race conference on Sun One determined to transmit a full size scoutship through the drone equipment, and to staff it with a crew of volunteers of all races." *Volunteers!* thought Pertin, grimacing. "And after considerable effort in negotiating, it was agreed to include Earth humans as part of the crew. The political implications of this step are of enormous consequence and reflect the true coming of age of Earth humanity in the Galaxywide confraternity of civilized peoples. Thank you," he said, bowed, smiled, and disappeared as the fiche came to an end.

Not a minute too soon, thought Pertin. A little more of that and he would have been ill. The cocoon had a fine built-in waste-handling system, but there was no sense in overloading it.

He began to see what Zara had been talking about when she accused him of an "Earthman's Burden" complex. It sounded pompous, stupid, and faintly threatening, he realized, at least as expressed by the man in the briefing fiche. Pertin tried to get his mind off that track—because he didn't want to question the cause for which he was eventually going to die, and because above all he didn't want to think about Zara Doy. He was in the middle of trying to get *The Belle of Bellatrix* back on the stage when he became aware that something was scratching angrily at his cocoon.

For a moment he thought he was dreaming. He glanced back at the fading nude on the screen, then outside at the nude girl who stood there.

But Pertin was a pretty superior type, and he oriented himself quickly. It was no girl. It was not even human. It was a female young Earth person in shape, but the stuff of which the shape was constructed was not flesh and blood. It was silvery and bright, with a metallic hue. The eyes were orange and glowing. The hair was not separate tendrils; it was a single solid piece, sculptured slightly for cosmetic effect. The creature was, he realized, an "edited" version of some methane-breather or one of even more exotic chemistry, some being who was structurally nonviable in oxygen-bearing air and had had itself transmitted in an altered form to take up its duties on *Aurora.* And it was holding a scrap of what looked like paper.

It was not right-side up. Pertin gestured, and finally the "girl" understood and rotated what she held until he could read its message. Then he signaled her to stop. It said:

Sorry, Ben James, but you've got to get out of there. Things are worse than we thought. Aphrodite here will carry you to me. They guarantee she won't drop you and squash you; and, actually, Ben James, it seems to be a matter of life and death.

Doc

The girl did not speak, but the orange eyes blazed imperatively, and the hands beckoned.

Pertin sighed, and opened the lid of his cocoon. "Okay, Aphrodite," he said. "Carry me off."

Astonishingly, being carried by the pseudogirl was actually worse than being toted by the robot; but this trip was slower, and Pertin had a chance to see something of the *Aurora.* It was roughly cone-shaped. At the nose and through the midsection were living quarters for the several score individuals who manned the ship. Since the crew varied widely, they needed a good deal of room. Space had been provided for methane-dwellers, space-flyers, and cold creatures, as well as for the more common forms based on carbon, oxygen, and water. However, most of the nonviables either stayed home or sent proxies or edited copies, so these spaces were mostly empty. "Below" the living quarters and the space for the exotics were the hardware-instrument sections. Below them still—in the sense of being sternward, toward the thrusters—was a layer of dense liquid for a radiation shield. It wasn't very effective; but of course, Pertin thought, the shield didn't have to be effective enough to keep them alive forever, since there was neither hope for nor point in that. Below the shield was the tachyon-transmission deck, where Pertin and the chimp had arrived. And beyond that deck, the shock-absorbing gear and thrusters. Since the *Aurora* was decelerating, it happened that the "stern" of the ship came first in line of flight; but that made little difference to anyone aboard. It was "down." And down was the direction they were going. The pseudogirl had wrapped Pertin in a thick blanket of something like heavy-duty plastic foam. It was not as good as his cocoon by a long shot, but it kept him from dying of the ceaseless grinding changes in gravity as the thrusters shoved and the "girl" levered herself down a ladderlike series of projecting rods. She did not speak, nor acknowledge Pertin's efforts to speak to her. Either there was something wrong with his Pmal translator, or she simply was not a conversationalist. But she was considerate enough, and when they reached the instrument deck Pertin was bruised and sick, but alive.

"Ben James!" cried a familiar voice. "I told you Aphrodite would get you here all right!"

Doc Chimp, thin lips grinning widely, scrambled over to help the silvery girl put him down, propping him against a sloping bulkhead so he could look around. They were worth looking at, a nightmare crew if he ever saw one. Besides the pseudogirl and the mutated chimp, there was a Sheliak in its high-G mode, looking like a flattened baker's bun on the deck, another web of plastic foam that hid an apparently human-sized figure, and a row of small cocoons. Two were empty; the third contained a T'Worlie. From a speaker outside the cocoon a T'Worlie voice whistled a greeting, and Pertin's Pmal translated: "I recognize your identity, Ben James Pertin. It is advantageous to all of us that you are here."

"Thanks, Nummie," Pertin said, but he was staring at the other plastic wrappings. A human being seemed to be concealed in them; but apart from himself he knew of only one human being on the *Aurora*, one he didn't really want to think about.

He said aside, "Doc, who's over there?"

Doc Chimp said, "Who? Her? Oh, I don't know her name. She's Purchased People for some low-G type or other. But she's on our side." The web stirred and a face peered out. It was human enough as far as features went, but the emptiness in the eyes told Pertin that Doc Chimp was right. "Anyway," the chimp chattered, "I better fill you in. Hell's really broken loose, Ben James. A bunch of beings tried to wreck the telescope. Not sure but what they've done it, too; the

Scorpian's trying to see how much can be salvaged. If it and Aphrodite here hadn't come along, we'd be out of business until they could send new instruments through—and by then it would likely be too late."

The thuuuud-*screech* was a lot closer here; apart from everything else, it was making Pertin's head pound. "What beings?" he managed to croak.

"Didn't see them. I just saw somebody disappearing into a passage, and then the Sheliak here came hellfire-fast after him and saw me. For a minute he thought I was them." Doc Chimp cocked his head ruefully. "You could've found yourself short a monkey right there, Ben James, if I hadn't talked fast. Then the Sheliak commandeered me to help, and we came down here to hold the fort. Oh, how sore my soles and knuckles are, Ben James, against the pounding of those rockets! But I did my duty. Then we got the observatory deck sealed off—they'd used a chemical explosive on the telescope and sprung a port—and then I happened to think of my human master, off there watching *The Belle of Bellatrix* without a care, and I persuaded Aphrodite to fetch you."

Pertin frowned. "I don't quite see why," he objected. "I can't help."

"You can stay alive," the chimp declared. "I didn't tell you all of it. When they came for the telescope they had to get past the T'Worlie here. Well, you know T'Worlie can't do much against any being that can operate in high-G. But they tried to do what they could. And two of them got killed."

That was a shocker if ever there was one; the one cardinal rule among the races of the Galaxy was that no race could ever kill or seriously maim a member of another. Even on Sun One, what disciplinary problems arose were handled within the delegation of the race that produced the problem; there was some provision for a body of other races sitting in judgment if the offending race failed to deal with the problem, but that law had never had to be invoked. Pertin would hardly have believed the chimp if Nummie hadn't confirmed it.

"They're crazy, then," Pertin said. "All right. We'll have to get a report back to Sun One. Nummie, is your stereostage operating?"

"Confirm that it is operative," the Pmal sang in his ear. "State that such a transmission has already been sent."

"Good. I'll have to send one too, and I think the rest of us should;

but that can wait." Pertin tried to shift position as the floor surged particularly viciously, suppressed a groan, and thought: Since we're here, they probably won't try anything right away. Then he said, "What we need is a comb-out. Get every being on board to account for his whereabouts and try to identify the ones who did it. For that we need a little free-fall. Can we arrange that?"

The silvery girl spoke at last. Apparently she had heard everything, had simply seen no need to comment. "We can have a little free-fall. We can have a little comb-out. But we probably won't need to arrange it right away as the next observation period is only—" A meaningless squawk, but Doc Chimp filled in:

"She means about fifteen minutes away."

It took a moment for Pertin to realize that the girl's words had been in English. He looked at her curiously, but there was no time to think about that. "Fine," he said. "How many were involved in the bombing?"

"Not less than three nor more than eight," piped the Pmal translator, responding to the T'Worlie's whistle.

"Out of how many in the crew?"

The T'Worlie hesitated. "There are in excess of three hundred thousand beings at present existing within the ship's hull. Of these, a large number are collective creatures."

"Not counting the Boaty-Bits, I mean how many individuals?"

"There are not less than two hundred forty nor more than two hundred fifty."

Pertin said, "So the troublemakers are a tiny fraction. That's good. We'll broadcast a shipwide alarm. Most of the crew will cooperate—"

He stopped, staring at the silver pseudogirl. "What's the matter?"

She had stretched out her fingertips toward the entrance port, almost in the traditional pose of a human sleepwalker. "The matter," she said in her incongruous colloquial English, the tones as deep as Pertin's own, "is that the tiny fraction of troublemakers is coming back."

A moment later no one needed the silvery girl's fingers to hear for them; the sound of a rush grew rapidly louder: a crackling electrical sound, like the patter of a collapsing charge field. Into the room burst what looked at first like a single huge blue eye. "Sirian!" Doc Chimp howled in terror, and tried to leap out of the way. But not even his simian muscles had the strength to leap, and the surging G-force of the rockets made him stumble and fall heavily on his side against the silvery girl. At one stroke, two-thirds of the beings able to move at all in the high-G field were immobilized; the T'Worlie, the Purchased Person, and Ben Pertin himself were wholly useless while the rockets were on. The Sirian, moving by electrostatic forces, was immune to mere ten- and twelve-G thrusts; and he bore with him something that glittered, carried under the great forward eye in a pair of crablike pincers, tiny and almost invisible.

Pertin, laid heedlessly just inside the portal, was first in the creature's path. He did not even have time to realize he was in danger before the Sirian was upon him. Then, queerly, the great eye stared at him and the Sirian paused, hesitated, and turned away. It propelled its glittering metal object at the bulkhead and at once reversed its field and sped away.

If that was another bomb, Pertin thought, they'd all had it now; beyond that bulkhead was empty space from the last attack. The rest of the ship might be saved if the automatic seals worked fast enough, but they would be boiled into outer space—himself, the Purchased Person, Doc Chimp, and the T'Worlie, at least.

Pertin had forgotten the Sheliak. The soggy baker's bun that slumped on the deck and had taken no part in the conversation was still in fact an able and intelligent being. It acted faster than Pertin would have believed possible. The bun shape elongated itself into a sort of stemmed sea anemone, flowed like lightning up and down around the bomb, surrounding it, drowning it in alien flesh.

It exploded.

The only sign the rest of them could see was a quick convulsive shudder of the Sheliak's tissue. Even the noise was muffled and almost inaudible, in the constant thunder of the rockets.

But the Sheliak glowed brilliant gold for a moment with a flash of the last light of its life, and died.

They had defended themselves, but at the cost of one of their allies.

As if on cue, the thunder of the rockets stopped, and they found themselves blessedly free of the crushing G-forces. Doc Chimp, struggling to untangle himself from the silvery girl, went flying across the chamber, ricocheted against a wall, and was brought up short next to where Pertin was struggling to disassociate himself from the plastic foam.

"Are you all right, Ben James?" Doc Chimp yelled.

Pertin pushed himself free and caught the outstretched chimpanzee arm for stability. He ached in every bone and muscle, and he was drenched in sweat—from the heat of the plastic wrap or from fear, he could not say which.

"I think so," he said. "Why do you suppose he did that?"

"What? Who? You mean the Sheliak? Why, I guess it's their nature, Ben James—"

"No, not the Sheliak," Pertin said, but he didn't say out loud what it was that was perplexing him. He only thought it to himself. Why had the Sirian looked at him with death in his eye, then stopped and turned away?

THREE

It turned out there were two things wrong with Pertin's calculations. First, the odds weren't quite as favorable as he had guessed; he had not remembered that the bombers might have allies who were as gravity-bound as himself, and so hadn't put in an appearance. Second, he had not realized that a large proportion of the beings aboard the *Aurora* simply didn't want to be bothered. They were apathetic, hopeless, detached, or in some exotic mood with no human analog; or perhaps, here and there, they just weren't about to take orders from an upstart biped jackanapes from—what was the name of it?—Earth.

The other problem was that the work of the *Aurora* was in observing Object Lambda, not in tracking down aberrant entities. Not even the fact that beings of one or two races had killed beings of another race could change their minds. The Scorpian robot, when it returned from patching together what it could of the damaged optical equipment, would not even take time to talk to Pertin; it went at once to its assigned place in the instrument chamber and began to oversee the series of observations that was what the thrust stoppage was for.

Pertin could not even get the free-fall period extended to permit a full-scale search of the ship. The T'Worlie pointed out to him, reasonably enough, that as they were all going to die anyhow the first priority was the errand for which they had all undertaken to give their lives: to complete the observation of Object Lambda. And the laws of celestial dynamics were remorseless. A certain quantum of delta-V had to be applied to *Aurora*'s course. There was only finite time in which to do it. If they failed to put in the necessary velocity change the probe would fly by Object Lambda too fast to accomplish the mission to which it was assigned. So the T'Worlie were going to work on their instrument observations and nothing else, although they certainly wished him well, they indicated, in his search for the guilty ones.

The search team turned out to be a party of five: Pertin, Doc Chimp, the pseudogirl, the Purchased-People woman, and the little kittenish object who had joined the party to greet them on arrival. They couldn't even recruit the Boaty-Bits to their cause. As soon as the collective creatures had learned of the bombing attempt they had departed en masse to swarm in some obscure corner of the vessel and unite all of their intelligence in the problem of deciding what to do about it.

Pertin saw a great deal of the ship, but found no criminals. The one being they had certainly identified, the Sirian, eluded their search. If a being the size of a horse, emitting an electrostatic crackle every time it moved, could avoid the searchers, what chance had they for locating a party of unidentified marauders? No chance, answered Echo; and they found nothing.

About all they really accomplished was to move the acceleration cocoons for the low-G beings they had come to think of as friends close enough together so that they could watch out for each other when the delta-V thrust immobilized them. There were many such periods. By the nature of things, there had to be. It was thuuuuud-*screech!* at least eighty percent of the time, cut up the individual portions as they would. The *Aurora* had thousands of kps of velocity to shed as it overtook Lambda, if they were to avoid overrunning it too fast to orbit their package. It made little difference how it felt to the members of the crew.

To Pertin it felt like being kicked in the kidneys four or five times a minute, for hours on end. With allowances for variations in anatomy, it felt very much like that to most of the beings. Frail little creatures like the T'Worlie were particularly hard hit, or would have been if not for the fact that the *Aurora* was their own design, cocoons and all, and many thousands of years of thought had gone into reducing the damage to a T'Worlie frame in a cocoon. It was an advantage of a sort, but against it was the overpowering debit that on their native planet the surface gravity was less than a quarter-G. They were not creatures designed for strain.

It was the unfelt pain that was the worst. Every explosion produced noise and thrust, but it also sleeted a few more curies of radiation through their bodies and brought them a few hours nearer to death.

As it was not felt, and as there was nothing that could be done about it, they seldom spoke of it to each other.

For half a dozen periods there was no further violence from anyone on board, and the *Aurora* went on about its business. Pertin reserved the time in the cocoon for taping his endless reports to Sun One, and for inspecting and studying the observation results on Object Lambda. When there was the blissful floating surcease, for half an hour or so at a time, he used it to roam around the ship. His announced purpose was to watch out for trouble. As time passed and trouble did not come, he stopped talking about it, but continued to roam. He was interested in the ship on its own merits. Simply by its novelty it helped take his mind off the growing number of things he didn't want to think about. This was the first real spaceship he had ever seen. That seemed strange to him, when he considered how many tens of thousands of light-years he had traveled since he volunteered for tachyon transmission from Earth. It was normal enough, though. Sun One was thick with beings who had crossed and recrossed the Galaxy a dozen times, and never seen a spaceship at all.

Object Lambda was getting perceptibly closer—not to the eye, to be sure. No eye on the ship was in a position to see it anyway. But the cameras were able to make out more and more detail—not easily or well, because its intrinsic luminosity was so very low, and in the low-energy long-wave part of the spectrum at that. They had even discovered that Lambda was not alone in space. Huge as it was, nearly two A.U. in diameter, it carried with it little orbiting fleas. The biggest of them was not much more than a mile through and the distance was still enormous; but the T'Worlie instruments managed to detect them, even identify them. The longest periods of free-fall were when the T'Worlie deployed their photon mirrors at the end of a tether, far from even the vibration of a footstep or shifting weight of robot mass in the ship; then their optical emulsions greedily drank up the scant flow of photons from Lambda and converted them into images.

If they had had a great deal of time, they could have answered all questions from there, or nearly all. They were in intergalactic space, and there was no such thing as haze, beyond the advance scattering of their own rocket ejecta. But they had no time: the delta-V equation still ruled them, and one of its tricky parentheses said that deceleration early was worth twice as much deceleration late, since it gave them more time for deceleration before they reached the neighborhood of Lambda. And then there was the mere fact of their rapid approach. The image did not remain still in the T'Worlie mirrors. It grew. Minutely, to be sure, but enough that an exposure for more than an hour or so began to fuzz.

Even so, they learned. The nearest thing to pleasure Pertin ever found in a T'Worlie was when a particularly fine series of photographs had been taken, and it was discovered that they showed a hint, a shadow, finally an orbital line for the biggest of the objects that circled Lambda. The pleasure was spoiled for Pertin when the calculations of orbit and time turned out to be impossible; Lambda would have had to have the density of the solar wind to have so slow a satellite. But the T'Worlie didn't mind. Explanations would come. If not then, later. If not to the present generation, to the next. Meanwhile they were accruing information.

Between the hours of thudding acceleration and the briefer periods of frenzied activity, darting about the ship, Pertin was nearly always bone-weary and aching. Sleep did not rest him. Communication with Sun One was more and more an effort. The twelve-hour wait between transmission and reply—often it was more, when the other beings on the ship had queued up for their own transmissions—destroyed the rhythm of the communication; by the time he had a response to his report of the attack on the instrument chamber, he was already relaxing in the continued comfort of the experience that the attack had not been repeated. Once it was himself, or anyway that other self named Ben Charles Pertin, who reported to him. That put him in a tailspin that only a carefully metered dose of tranquilizers from the cocoon's store could deal with. From the expression on the other Ben Pertin's face, it was some strain for him, too. But the worst from Sun One was not from his other self, it was from Gerald York Bielowitz, who acknowledged a report, suggested some additional instrument readings that would be desirable, started to sign off, hesitated, and then added: "Oh, you'll be interested, I think. Zara Doy and Ben Charles were married three hours ago."

Pertin did not remember cutting the stereostage or seeing the little figure collapse. He lay there for a long time while the cocoon stroked and soothed him, lifted him, lowered him, gently massaged what pains it could from his limbs. At some point he fell asleep. In his dream Ben

Charles Pertin married Zara Doy, but he was Ben Charles, and the two of them, intoxicated with the wine they drank and with each other, spoke sadly and wistfully about the other Ben Pertin who was busy about the task of dying on an alien spaceship a Galaxy away. When he woke up and discovered he was the other Ben Pertin he was in an instant unfocused rage.

It was Doc Chimp who woke him. "Boss," he whined. "Listen, wake up. I've been limping around this hellhole of a ship looking for the Scorpian robot, and—"

"Shut up," Pertin snarled through the outside communicator of his cocoon. His tone took the chimp aback. He slumped on his haunches, staring at Pertin's cocoon. He was in bad shape, Pertin saw, unwilling to care about what he saw: the bright green plume was sagging under the thrust of the rockets, the paws and knuckles were scarred and stained. That was why he was there, of course: feet and paws, he could withstand the constantly varying G-force of the thrusters with only a good deal of pain, so it was his job to do what Pertin could not when he was bound to the cocoon. A part of Pertin's brain told him that if he tried he probably could find ways of making the job easier.

The chimp's expression was no longer woebegone, it was angry. "Sure," he said thickly, "I'll shut up. Why not? We'll all shut up before long. Dead beings are all pretty quiet."

Pertin fought to control his own anger. "We'll be dead all right. What difference does it make? Do you think this is a real life, what we're doing here? Back on Sun One we're alive and well; this is only a dream!"

The chimp wailed, "Ben James, I'm tired and I hurt. I'm sorry if I said something wrong. Look, I'll go away and come back, only—"

"Do that," snapped Pertin, turning off the outside communicator.

The agitated hairy face stared dolefully in at him. Doc Chimp was by no means a jungle primate. The shape of his skull was different, the structure of his respiratory system was different, the very chemicals that flowed in his blood were different. But he was not human, either. Doc Chimp—his formal name was not that, but it was all Pertin had ever called him—was one of the mutated animals who had been constructed for special purposes in the molecular biology plants on Earth. His quadrudexterous hands and feet made him particularly useful even in free-fall, where he could fling himself about with perfect ease from toe rest to handhold, while humans like Pertin clumsily sprawled and spun. But he had his drawbacks.

A chimpanzee is simply not a human. His physiology is one count against him. He cannot develop the brain of a human because his skull is the wrong shape, and because the chemistry of his blood does not carry enough nourishment to meet the demands of abstract thought. He cannot speak because he lacks the physical equipment to form the wide variety of phonemes in human language. The molecular-biology people knew how to deal with that: things like widening the angle of the cranium called the "kyphosis," thus allowing the brain to round out full frontal lobes, restructuring tongue and palate, even adding new serum components to the blood like the alpha$_2$-globulins that bind human hemoglobin.

In practical terms what had been done to Doc Chimp and his siblings was to speed up evolution. But that was not quite enough. Two generations back Doc Chimp's ancestors could form only one or two of the simplest words and learn rote tricks; they lacked conceptual thought entirely. Doc Chimp had capacity. He did not have background or tradition. His sixty-degree kyphosis was close to the human average, so that his skull was domed; he possessed a forehead; he could remember complicated instructions and perform difficult tasks; he was capable of assimilating the equivalent of a trade-school education in skill and of conducting the equivalent of cocktail-party conversation in performance. What he lacked was ego. His psychological profile was high in cyclothymia but also in ergic tension; his moods shifted drastically, and he was always adventurous, always afraid. His emotional index was about equal to that of a human five-year-old. Frightened, he ran. Angered, he struck out. Baffled, he wept.

Staring back through the cover of the cocoon, Pertin relented. "Sorry," he said, snapping the communicator back on. "What were you trying to tell me?"

"I've lost the Scorpian," the chimp wailed.

"Well? Are you supposed to be his keeper?"

"Be easy on me, Ben James," the chimpanzee begged. "I hurt all over. The robot was supposed to be getting ready for some new instruments that were coming in. He isn't there. The stuff's piling up in the transmission chamber and nobody to do anything about it. I'm afraid it'll get damaged."

"What about what's-her-name, Aphrodite? Can't she store it?"

"She is trying to, but the Scorpian is a specialist in this stuff and she isn't. None of the other high-G creatures is, as far as I can tell, and, oh, Ben James, I've traveled so far trying to find someone who can help!"

He was a pitiable sight, his fur unpreened, his gay clothes smudged and wrinkled. Pertin said, "You've done your best, Doc. There's nothing I can do until the thrust stops—half an hour or so. Why don't you rest up for a while?"

"Thanks, Ben James!" the chimp cried gratefully. "I'll just take a few minutes. Wake me, will you? I—I—"

But he was already clambering into the cocoon, his spiderlike arms shaking with strain. Pertin lay back and closed his own eyes, allowing the cocoon to do its best, which amounted to increasing its rate of stroking his back muscles, trying mindlessly to calm him down.

It had seemed very easy, back on Sun One, to volunteer for a task even though the end of it was his certain death. He had not counted on the fact that death did not come like the turning of a switch but slowly and with increasing pain, or that he would be watching friends die before him.

Pertin didn't wake the chimp when he could finally move; he thrust his own way to the tachyon-transmission chamber, hurling himself down the corridors carelessly and almost diving into what turned out to be the silver pseudogirl. He didn't recognize the creature at first, for she had unfurled enormous silver-film wings and looked like a tinsel Christmas-tree angel as she drove past him.

In the tachyon chamber he found Nummie supervising an octopoidal creature from one of the Core stars in transporting crated equipment to an empty chamber. "What's happened? Where did Aphrodite go? What's this stuff?" he demanded, all at once.

Nummie paused and hung in the air before him, balancing himself against stray currents of air with casual movements of his wings. He whistled a methodical answer, and the Pmal translator converted it to this stately and precise form of speech in English: "Of those events which have occurred, that which appears most significant is the arrival of eight hundred mass units of observing equipment. A currently occurring event is that this equipment is in process of being installed. A complicating event is that the Scorpian artificial-intelligence being has elected to engage his attention in other areas. There are other events but of lesser significance. The being you name Aphrodite has gone to bring the Beta Boötis collective beings to assist in the aforesaid installation. The reason for this is that they are catalogued as possessing qualification on this instrumentation similar to that of the artificial-intelligence Scorpian. The precise nature of the stuff is tachyar observing equipment. I offer an additional observation: the purpose of it is to map and survey Object Lambda. I offer another additional observation: it will add to the radiation load by a factor of not less than three nor more than eight."

The T'Worlie hung silently in front of him, waiting for him to respond.

It had a long wait. Pertin was trying to assimilate the information he had just received. *A factor of not less than three.*

But that meant that his life expectancy was not a matter of months or weeks. It might only be days!

Tachyar was simple enough in concept. It was like the ancient electromagnetic radar sets of Earth; the difference was that it used the faster-than-light tachyons to scan a distant object and return an echo of its shape and size. It was expensive—all tachyon transmission was expensive. Its only justification was that it was indispensable.

If you wanted to get a man, or an instrument, from one point in the Universe to some other point across interstellar distances, you had only two choices. One was to build a rocket—preferably fusion-powered, like the *Aurora.* You then had to launch it, set it on its way, and wait anywhere from a decade to a geologic era for it to reach a nearby star. If you wanted to go farther than that, you would wait forever. A voyage from a spiral arm to the Core, or from any point in the Galaxy to the deeps of intergalactic space where they now were, was simply out of the time consciousness of any race but the T'Worlie.

The other method was faster. It dispensed with attempting to transport matter at all. Instead of sending an object, you sent a blueprint of the object, and had it built from plan at the destination.

It was not a simple procedure. It required enormous expenditures of energy to generate the tachyon stream that carried the blueprint. It required complex scanning devices to measure every atom and molecule in the object to be transmitted, and to encode positions and relationships for transmission. Above all, it required a tachyon receiver at the point to which you wanted to go.

But granted all those things, you could "travel" at the speed of the tachyons, those particles whose *lower* speed limit was the velocity of light, and whose upper limit had never been measured.

Of course, the original object remained behind. It was scanned and its blueprints were encoded, and then it was returned unharmed. The man who volunteered for a tachyon trip also stayed at home. What flashed across space was a description of himself, and what emerged from the receiving chamber at destination was a new-built identical copy. There was no detectable difference between original and copy. It would have been a foolproof method of counterfeiting or of duplicating rare art objects—if it had not been so expensive in terms of power consumption that there was little worth the cost of duplicating.

Tachyar was only one use of tachyons. Like ancient radar and sonar, it generated a beam and measured reflections. The problem in using tachyar was the magnitude of the beam. Vast energies were used, and the fraction that was wasted because of the natural inefficiency of the process produced ionizing radiation in large amplitudes.

Sun One must be taking the question of Object Lambda's satellites seriously if it was sending tachyar equipment to study them. The cost was high. It would be paid in the lives of those aboard.

The single planet of the golden-yellow star Beta Boötis was like a cooler, older Venus. Because it was farther from its sun, it was spared the huge flow of heat that cooked Venus sterile; but it possessed the same enormously deep, enormously dense atmosphere. It was spared the loss of its liquid water, and so its surface was covered an average of thirty miles deep in an oceanic soup. That was where the Boaty-Bits had evolved. Aquatic in origin, they could survive on Sun One or the probe ship only in edited forms adapted for air-breathing; they could not live on high-gravity planets at all, since they had only the feeblest mechanisms for propelling themselves about their native seas. An individual Boaty-Bit was about as useful as an infant jellyfish, and not much more intelligent. That didn't matter; the Boaty-Bits never operated as individuals. Their swarming instinct was overpowering, and once linked together they had a collective intelligence that was a direct function of their number. A quarter of a million Boaty-Bits equaled a man. On their home planet they sometimes linked up in collectives of four or five million or more, but those groupings could be maintained only briefly even in their oceans and were never attained in their air-breathing edited forms.

When they arrived in the tachyon-receiver chamber, they immediately took command. They were not specialists in tachyar gear. They were generalists. The skills required to assemble and install the crated instruments were built into their collective intelligence. What they lacked was operating organs, but the T'Worlie, his octopoidal assistant, Ben James Pertin, and every other being who came nearby were conscripted to be their hands and legs. It was slow work that would have been impossible in a gravity field for the T'Worlie, or even for Pertin himself; but in free-fall they were able to tug and guide the components into place, and the T'Worlie had mass enough to make the connections and calibrate the equipment. When they were nearly done Doc Chimp turned up, angry because he had been left behind, and his muscle finished the job quickly.

As they were finishing up, there was a blast of white sound from the tachyon-receiving chamber and warning lights flashed. Doc Chimp spun around, his wide jaw gaping. "Something important coming in?" he guessed.

"I don't know, but let's go look." They thrust themselves toward the chamber, got there just as the portal opened.

Three Sheliaks emerged.

They flashed out of the lock with a hollow hooting, long black shapes that rocketed toward the watching terrestrials and bounced down on the green metal surface of the chamber. They clung in spite of the lack of gravity, and flowed abruptly into a new shape, black velvet globes, thigh high.

Three more emerged, and three more. When fifteen had come to rest on the floor of the chamber the transmission stopped. Without a detectable sign, all of them moved in synchronization. From flattened spheres, like baker's buns set in a tray, they suddenly turned luminous, flowing with patterns of soft color, then elongated themselves and stretched up tapered necks that rose as tall as a man.

The tallest of them, the first through the chamber and the nearest to Ben James Pertin, made a noise like escaping gas from a compressed-air cylinder. In Pertin's ear his Pmal unit translated for him:

"Take notice! We are under the direction of the collective council of

Sun One. We are to take command of this vessel, and all other beings aboard are to follow our orders!"

Pertin's curiosity was suddenly transmuted into anger, a radiant rage that flooded his mind and overruled his inhibitions. "The hell you say!" he shouted. "I've had no such instructions from the Earth representatives, and I deny your authority!"

The Sheliak paused, the long neck swaying back and forth. "Your wishes are immaterial," it stated at last. "We can destroy you."

Doc Chimp chattered nervously, "Don't make him mad, Ben James. You know how Sheliaks are." Pertin did; they were among the few races that had built-in weaponry. On the infrequent occasions when the Galaxy found itself troubled by unruly barbarians, it was usually Sheliaks who were employed to quiet the opposition; they were the Foreign Legion of the Galaxy.

The long neck swayed toward the mutated chimpanzee. From the narrow orifice at its tip the sound exploded again, and the translators shouted at the chimp: "Your name! Your function! Reply at once!"

"I am Napier Chimski, technician," the chimp replied bravely.

The vase shape swung toward Pertin. "Your name and function!"

"Oh, Ben James Pertin," he said, distracted by hearing Doc Chimp's real name for the first time. "I'm an engineer. But don't go so fast! I've just come from Sun One myself, and I know there's no authority for one race to impose its will on another. I will certainly report this at once!"

The Sheliak swayed silently for a moment, toward him then away. At last it said, "No orders for you at present. Go about your business."

Pertin drew himself up, holding to a wall brace. "You're my business!" he shouted. "There are murdering beings aboard this ship. If you're here by order of Sun One, as you say, why don't you go find them and leave us alone?"

The Sheliak did not reply. All fifteen of them were swaying silently now. Perhaps they were conferring with each other, Pertin thought; Sheliaks had learned vocal sound only to talk to other races of the Galaxy, and the riddle of how they communicated among themselves was still unsolved.

"I certainly will report this," Pertin added.

There was still no response. The pointless confrontation might have gone on, but it was interrupted by the bright thrice-repeated flash of white light that meant the thrusters were about to go into operation again.

"Oh, hell," Pertin groaned. "Doc, we'd better get back to our cocoons."

"Never too soon for me, Ben James," agreed the chimp fervently, staring at the Sheliaks. "Let's go!"

They raced for the cocoons. The warning had caught others short; the corridors were full of low-G beings hurrying back to safety before the fusion rockets began again. The Boaty-Bits arrowed past them at top velocity, like a cartoon drawing of a swarm of wasps. The octo-poidal creature launched itself from a wall at the end of the corridor with a multiple thrust of its legs and spun, tentacles waving crazily, past them. There was a thundering roar, and three Sheliaks raced past them, then another three and another, in Vees. A being like a six-legged spider monkey bounced back and forth, scratching and clawing for footholes, whining irritably to itself in a high-pitched tone. And abruptly:

"Ben James! Look!"

Doc Chimp was staring down a broad transverse corridor as they soared by it. Pertin looked, saw a creature like an enormous blue eye, at least a foot across. It swerved as he looked, revealing the body behind it, a tapered torpedo shape, glittering with patterned scales like blue glass. A stubby wing spread on each side, the leading edge thick and scaled, flowing smoothly into the body, the thin trailing edge a flutter of blue. And beyond it was something bright, metallic and angular.

"It's the Sirian, Ben James! The one that tried to kill us all. And wasn't that the Scorpian robot with him?"

Pertin reached out, grabbed a handhold, and checked himself. The chimpanzee reacted a moment later and also stopped himself, a yard or two farther down. "What are you doing, Ben James?" he chattered.

"I'm going after them!" Pertin snapped. "The Sirian's one of the murderers. And the robot's up to something, too."

"No, Ben James! You can't take the G-force. Let's let the Sheliaks take care of them, that's what they're here for."

The featureless green light of the corridor faded and changed to a dull crimson glow. That was the short-term warning; they had less than thirty seconds now before the rockets began.

Pertin cursed. The chimp was right, of course, and he knew it; it didn't make it any more enjoyable, though.

"Oh, hell," he groaned. "All right, let's go!"

They made it—not with any time to spare. They rolled into their cocoons just as the first giant thrust struck, and a moment later the regular repeated sound of the rockets reached them. The webbing spread itself over Pertin; he fell into the warm, receiving shape of the cocoon, but he resisted its comfort. While it was still adjusting to his shape, he was already stabbing at the controls of the stereostage, trying to summon all the cocoon-bound beings on the ship into a conference call. The automatic dialing circuits were equal to the job; it was not something that was often done, but the physical capacity for it existed.

But not this time. All lines were busy. Every being on the ship, it appeared, was already using his stereostage for purposes of his own— most likely for trying to transmit a tachyon message to his own people at Sun One, Pertin knew.

He fell back and let the cocoon massage him as soothingly as it could.

Thuuuuud-screech. Thuuuuuud-screech. The thrust felt more powerful than before, the tempo a bit faster. The thunder and groan of the drive made it nearly impossible for Pertin to think, but he had to think.

The problem on his mind was not any of the obvious ones: what to do about the Sheliaks, how to deal with the murderers, the completion of the mission. His mind worried at those a moment at a time and then let them go; they required action, not thought, and action was not available to him while the fusion rockets roared.

Instead, he thought about an unpleasant discovery. The discovery was that there wasn't much in being a hero. His heroism had been entered into lightly enough, but he supposed that was not in itself rare; how many soon-to-be Medal of Honor winners had volunteered for combat patrols simply because they were bored with sitting in foxholes, and found themselves caught up in events that made them immortal reputations?

But his heroism was not even going to get him a medal. No one would ever really know what was happening on this ship, because it was absolutely certain there would be no survivors. Either *Aurora*'s mission would succeed, in which event the Galaxy at large would accept their sacrifice complacently, or it would fail. Then they would all be thought of, when they were thought of at all, as that sorry bunch that wasted themselves for nothing.

With the thud and rasp of metal roaring at him, his cocoon seesawing to the violent deceleration of the rockets, tired, half-sick, angry, and hopeless, Ben James Pertin faced the fact that there was nothing left in his life anywhere that would give him one moment's joy.

Another Ben Pertin tens of thousands of light-years away was trying to soothe his bride. He said, "Honey, I knew what I was getting into when I volunteered. I was willing to go through with it. The other me on the ship doesn't feel any different about it."

Zara Pertin said harshly, "That other you is going to die, Ben Charles."

"But I'll still be alive!"

"And he'll be dead. Don't you understand me? *I love you.* And he is you, and I don't like to think about what is happening to him." She turned over, giving her back a chance to collect some of the UV tan from the lamps overhead, and took off her goggles. She said, "What's it like there now, Ben?"

"Well—" he said.

"No, I want to know. Tell me."

Ben Charles looked around the little simulated beach beside the great water tank that was their "ocean." There was no one around but themselves. They'd come here for that reason, but Ben Charles found himself wishing for an interruption. She turned her head and looked at him, and he shrugged.

"All right. It's bad," he said. "The sensors in his acceleration cocoon report some destruction of the white corpuscles already. Pretty soon he'll start having nosebleeds, then he'll bleed internally. He'll be getting weaker, running a temperature, and before long he'll die." He paused, then answered the unspoken question. "Probably within a week."

He propped himself up on one arm—easily enough; even here the effective gravity was only a fraction of Earth-normal. He looked out at the thousand-foot cusp of water, curving upward to meet the bulkhead at its far end, and added:

"That's if he dies as a result of radiation, but he might not last that long. Some of the beings are getting violent. The electronic ones are malfunctioning, because the radiation affects their synapses. Insane, really. A lot of the organic ones are sick. All of them are scared. There —there have been deaths."

"I should have gone with you," Zara said thoughtfully.

"Oh, now, really! That's stupid! What would be the point?"

"I would have felt better about it, and so would you. He." She stood up, smiling, her mind made up. "If you have to go again, dear," she said, "I'm going too. Now I'm hungry. Race you back to the apartment."

FOUR

The tachyar verified the orbits of the little bodies orbiting Lambda; the mass estimates were right, thus the density estimates were right. Object Lambda's average density was about that of a high vacuum. Nevertheless, it appeared to have a solid surface.

Pertin greeted the news with apathy. There were more immediately important developments on the ship, and the ultimate purpose for which the ship existed didn't seem particularly interesting anymore.

For one thing, the tachyon-transmission chamber was shut down. For better or for worse, there would be no more imports, no additional beings, no new crew members, no nothing.

Its last function had been to bring in new structural members and drive units. Inside the former receiving chamber of the *Aurora* they were being assembled into a new, small ship. It took form as a squat, dense object, all fusion drive and instruments, with no living space for a crew. It would have no crew. It would carry nothing but itself, and the tachyon-receiving crystal that had been the *Aurora*'s.

Pertin had no part in the construction project. The Boaty-Bits directed it, and the metal pseudogirl and a few other high-G types carried it out. He looked in on it once or twice. Besides the new members brought in on the tachyon receiver, before it was rehoused in its new body, the small ship used bulkheads and beams from *Aurora* itself. It seemed to Ben James Pertin that vital structural parts were being seriously weakened. As an engineer, that interested him. As a living human being whose life depended on the structural integrity of the *Aurora,* he didn't even think it worth mentioning. Whatever was happening was planned. If the life of the *Aurora* was being shortened thereby, it was because the beings doing the planning had decided the ship was wholly expendable.

The only nonexpendable part of the *Aurora* now was the little drone being put together in its belly.

The drone comprised only three elements: a tiny tachyon-receiving unit, built around the crystal from *Aurora*'s own, in a globular body fitted with weak handling propulsors, suitable only for correcting minor errors in the elements of an orbit. A thick half-shell of metal-bonded ceramics on one side, an ablation shield designed to flake and burn away, disposing of excess heat. And, outside the ablation shield, the enormous fusion-propulsion engines.

It was a high-deceleration drone. It would be launched from the mother ship at some point near Object Lambda. Its fusion jets would slow it radically. Stressed as it was, with no living creatures aboard, it could endure hundred-G delta-V forces. But Pertin's engineer's eye recognized the implications of the design. Even those forces would not be enough. The drone would make use of Object Lambda's enormously deep atmosphere as well. It would dip into it, shedding velocity by burning it off as friction, blazing like a meteorite from its ablation surfaces. That frightful crunch would slow it to manageable relative speeds; as it came out of its first skip into Lambda's air it would be near enough to orbital velocity for capture. Then its handling propulsors could take over the simpler job of neatening up the elements of the orbit, and a tachyon receiver would be in place around Object Lambda.

What about the mother ship?

All the evidence Pertin needed was there in the construction of the probe. If such forces were needed to put the probe in orbit, there was no hope that *Aurora* could join it. Its kilotons of mass were simply too great for the forces available to deal with. Even if the forces were available, its living cargo would be pulped by the delta-V.

Aurora would drop its cargo, flash by Object Lambda, and continue through intergalactic space. It would no longer have fusion mass for its reactors. It would stop decelerating; to all intents and purposes, it would be only another chunk of intergalactic debris on a pointless orbit to nowhere.

Its course would continue to take it toward the Galaxy itself, and in time, perhaps, it would approach some of the inhabited worlds within mere light-years.

But that time would be too late to matter to anyone. It was a matter of thousands of years from even the fringe stars of the Galaxy, and by then there would be little left of even the dust of its crew.

They had been written off.

Meanwhile, the deceleration phases were getting longer, the zero-G pauses for observation shorter and less frequent. Sun One had lost interest in the observations that could be conducted from *Aurora*. They were only waiting for the probe to go into orbit.

All through the ship, the living crew members were showing the effects. They were weaker and less rational, less capable of fine distinctions. The automatic machinery was running the ship.

As it poured the last of its fuel reserves into space to brake its flight, it manufactured enormous clouds of radioactive gas. They were not a hazard to the ship's crew; it was too late for such trivial affairs to matter to the doomed beings. But they had caused some concern to the planners on Sun One. A thousand generations later perhaps they would be a pollution problem, as the newly manufactured clouds of gas preceded the ship in entering well-traveled portions of space. But by then some of the deadlier elements would have burned themselves out, their short half-lives expended. In any case, that was a problem for the thousandth generation—by which time, no doubt, tachyon transport would itself have been superseded, and no one would any longer trouble with such primitive concerns as the crude slower-than-light transport of mass.

The gas clouds as they departed did leave some trace of ionizing radiation, added to the larger increments from the blasts themselves and from the tachyar. The combined radiation was a witches' brew of gammas and alphas and betas, now and then primary particles that coursed through the entire space of the ship from hull to hull and did little harm, except when they struck an atomic nucleus and released a tiny, deadly shower of secondaries.

It was the secondaries, the gammas, that did the dirty work. They interfered with the electronic functions of the computers, robots, and metal beings. They damaged the instrumentation of the ship. Above all, they coursed through the organic matter they encountered, knocking out an electron here, loosening a molecular bond there, damaging a cell nucleus, making a blood vessel more permeable. The whole organic crew was on hourly doses of antirads, giving support to their internal workings. It was not enough. Still the radiation soaked in and struck at them. Blood, ichor, sap, or stew of exotic biologies, the fluids that circulated in their bodies changed and grew less capable of supporting life. Physically they grew weaker. Mentally they became cloudy.

Taken out of the environment and rushed to an antirad clinic, like the victims of an industrial accident, most of them still could have been saved.

There was no hope of that. There was no place to take them. No part of the ship was free of penetrating ionizing radiation now, and every hour more and more of the chemistry of their bodies was damaged.

"Ben James, Ben James," sobbed the voice of Doc Chimp.

Pertin roused himself. The thud and screech of the drive was still loud in his ear. Every time the floor drove up to meet the cocoon the single huge bruise that his body had become screamed with pain. Inside his chest his lungs felt as if they had broken loose and were being beaten sore against the inside of his rib cage.

He peered blearily out of the cocoon. The chimp was staring pathetically up at him. The great green plume of his hat was broken, his fur splotched with dirt and blood. The rubbery features of his face looked almost as they always had, except for an open cut along the flat, sculptured nose.

"What?" Pertin demanded thickly.

"I have to hide, Ben James. The Sheliaks are after me."

Pertin tried to sit up and could not. "They're not here to hurt you," he pointed out.

The chimp whimpered, bobbing on all four limbs as he braced himself against the rocket thrust. "They will! They're mad, Ben James. They killed the T'Worlie. For nothing, just killed him. And they almost killed me."

"What were you doing?"

"Nothing! Well, I—I was watching their mating ritual. But that wasn't it . . ."

"You idiot," Pertin groaned. "Look, can you climb in here with me?"

"No, Ben James, I don't have the strength."

"It's either that or let them catch you."

The chimpanzee whimpered in fear, then abruptly, on the upsurge of the ship against its shock absorbers, sprang to the side of the cocoon. Pertin grabbed at him and pulled him inside just as the next thrust caught them. Doc Chimp weighed some two hundred pounds at Earth's surface. The delta-V gave him a momentary weight of nearly half a ton, all concentrated on Pertin's shoulder and chest. He grunted explosively. The chimp was caught with part of his side still across the metal lip of the cocoon, but he made no sound beyond the steady sotto-voce mumble of fear.

Pertin tried to make room behind him, in a place where the cocoon had never been designed to take a load. It tried its mechanical best to give support to the double mass. It was not adequate to the job. Pertin discovered when the next thrust came that his arm was still caught under the chimp. He yelped, managed to free it on the upsurge, discovered it was not broken. He slammed down the privacy curtain, hoping the Sheliaks would not look inside if they came.

"Now," he panted, "what did you say about Nummie?"

"He's dead, Ben James. They killed him. I didn't mean any harm," the chimp sobbed. "You know how the Sheliaks reproduce—by budding, like terrestrial plants. The young ones sprout out of the old ones, and grow until they're mature enough to be detached."

"I know." Pertin had only the vaguest acquaintance with Sheliaks, but everybody knew that much. They didn't have sexes, but their conjugation provided a union that shuffled up the genes.

"Well, that didn't look like fun to me, but I wanted to see. Nummie told me to go away. He couldn't; he was in one of the spare cocoons and couldn't move. But he said they'd be mad." The chimp switched position and Pertin shouted in pain as his upper thigh took part of the chimp's weight on a rocket thrust. "Sorry, Ben James. It was disgusting, the way they did it! Any two of them can get the urge. They sort of melt down and flow together like jelly. All the body cells migrate, pair off, and fuse. Finally they form again into a sort of cactus-shaped vegetable thing that buds off haploid, mobile creatures. Those are the Sheliaks we see."

"You wanted to watch that?" asked Pertin, almost able to laugh in spite of his discomfort, in spite of Nummie, in spite of everything.

"Yes, Ben James. Just for curiosity. And then there's my friend,

Fireball. He's the Sheliak who was here all along. He was nice, Ben James. I miss him."

"I didn't know you knew any Sheliaks."

"Not well. But he was with me, helping to guard all of you, and we talked."

"You sound as if he's dead, too."

"Might as well be. That union is a sort of individual suicide. It's something you do for the race, and because your glands push you that way. But it's the end for the individual. It wipes out all conscious memory and individual personality. I guess that's why Fireball couldn't understand our notions of sex.

"Anyway," he said, "it was all right while Fireball was here alone. He wasn't lonely; or anyway, he didn't want any other Sheliaks around. When they're in danger, you see, they can't help conjugating. It's a survival mechanism. The radiation was danger, and he knew that the only way for him to keep alive was to stay away from his own people. When the new ones came aboard he was actually afraid of them. He knew when they came close they were likely to set off a biological process they couldn't control. And when it was over—"

The chimp swallowed. He thrust himself up on an elbow, regardless of the pain, and stared into Pertin's eyes.

"He didn't know me, Ben James! The two new ones that were half him, they came after me. The T'Worlie saw what was happening and tried to stop them—and that's how I got away, while they were killing him. So I ran. But where is there to run to, in this ship?"

When they could move again they found the T'Worlie easily enough. He was floating upside down, purplish drops of blood, perfectly round, floating beside him. The little vibrissae around his sphincter mouth, more like cat's whiskers than anything on a proper earthly bat, were perfectly still. Nummie was rigid. The pattern of five eyes was unmoving. The intricate pattern of blotches of color on his filmy wings was fading.

There was no one else around. "What'll we do with him, Ben James?" the chimp chattered.

"Throw him out into space, I guess," Pertin said harshly. Normally the mass would be useful in the tachyon receiver, but there were to be no more incoming tachyon transmissions.

It didn't do to think of that. He stared at the T'Worlie. A slow incrustation of thick gel was matting the fluffy surface of Nummie's

chest, and where it had once protruded sharply, like a bird's wish-
bone, it was crushed and concave.

Pertin felt the muscles on his face drawing taut, perhaps partly
because of the intense vinegar reek. He said, "Why would the Sheliaks
break up equipment?"

The chimpanzee stared at the mess in the room. Bright green and
orange transistors and microchips were scattered like jigsaw pieces in
the air. "I don't know, Ben James! None of that was that way when I
ran out of here. Do you suppose they just lost their temper?"

"Sheliaks don't lose their temper that way. They broke up instruments on purpose. What was coming in before you decided to play
Peeping Tom?"

"Oh—" The chimp thought. "More reports on Object Lambda.
The density was confirmed. Very low. Like a sparse cloud of interstellar gas."

"We already knew it was Cloud-Cuckoo Land. That couldn't have
had any effect on them."

"Something did, Ben James," the chimp cried. "Look, we've got to
do something. They'll be looking for me, and—"

"Unless," Pertin said thoughtfully, "it wasn't the Sheliaks who did
it. The robot was up to something. And there are still a couple of
Purchased People not accounted for. And—"

"Too late!" the chimp howled. "Listen, Ben James! Somebody's
coming!"

But it wasn't the Sheliaks who came in on them, it was Aphrodite,
the silver pseudogirl, the heavy-planet creature in human form. Her
fingers were outstretched toward them, listening, as her great foil
wings drove her forward.

Behind her was the Scorpian robot.

They made an eerie pair, the striking orange-eyed girl with her coif
of metallic hair and steel-bright body hues, and the mechanical creature shaped like a metal octopus. Its central body was a massive disk,
the color of the pseudogirl's flesh, and its silvery tentacles made a
fringe of snakes around it. A greenish membrane that bulged above
the upper surface of the disk fluttered, producing a drumroll of sound.
Pertin's Pmal translator obediently turned it into recognizable words:
"DO NOT RESIST. WE WISH YOU TO COME WITH US."

"Where?" he demanded.

There was no answer, at least not in words. Pertin was caught in something like a metal whip that stung a trail of fire around his waist. It was one of the robot's tentacles that had caught him; it pinned his arms, and the pseudogirl launched herself at him, her metal fist catching him full in the face. Floating as he was, the blow was robbed of some of its force, but it doubled him, flung him back against the robot's lash, dazed with pain and sobbing for breath.

He heard a cry of anguish from Doc Chimp, but could not turn to see what was happening. The vinegary smell of the dead T'Worlie penetrated his nostrils, mixing with the tang of his own blood.

"Why?" he croaked, and tried to raise his arms to defend himself as the girl dropped toward him again. She did not answer. She was on him like a great silvery bat, metal feet kicking, shining fists flying. The lights went out. He lost touch with space and time.

Pertin was not wholly unconscious, but he was so near to it, so filled with pain and confusion, that he could hardly remember what happened next. He had a fugitive impression of great shapes whirling around him, then of being carried away while someone behind him sobbed his name, the voice diminishing in the distance.

A long time later he opened his eyes.

He was alone, in a part of the ship he knew only sketchily. A large open cocoon hung from a wall, and inside it was what looked like one of the Purchased People. Pertin's face was swollen and his eyes not focusing well at all; he squinted, but could not make out the features on the person in the cocoon. It appeared to be male, however, and it appeared to be in the last stages of dissolution.

It moved and looked toward him. A caricature of a smile disturbed the weeks-old beard, and the dry tongue licked the lips. A cracked voice muttered something, the tone hoarse and indistinguishable.

"Who are you? What do you want?" Ben James Pertin demanded.

The figure rasped a sort of hacking cough, that perhaps was meant for a chuckle. It tried again, and this time its words came clear enough —clear, and familiar, in a way that Pertin had not expected.

"I want to talk to you, Ben," it croaked. "We have a lot in common, you know."

Pertin frowned, then his swollen eyes widened. He pushed himself toward the swathed figure, caught himself at the lip of the cocoon, and stared down.

The eyes that looked up at him were pain-filled but very familiar. He was looking into his own, battered, obviously dying face.

Pertin remembered a time, months ago.

He had gone to the tachyon transmitter and lightheartedly enough given his blueprint to the scanners and allowed one self of him to be beamed to the *Aurora*. It had not seemed like an important thing to do. At that time, it was not clear that the *Aurora* was a doomed ship. At that time, he had no one to consult but himself; Zara Doy was still only a casual acquaintance, the new girl from Earth with the pretty face.

"Ben Frank," he whispered.

"Right as rain," croaked the ghastly voice. "And I know about you well enough. You're Ben James Pertin, and you've been aboard two weeks now. Not very thoughtful of you, failing to visit a dying relative."

"But I thought you were dead already! They said—I mean, I wouldn't have had to come, if—"

"Blaming me, Ben James? Well, why shouldn't you? How often have I lain here, blaming you, and me, and all the Ben Pertins there ever were." A spasm of coughing racked him, but he talked right through it. "I wanted them to think I was dead. Only fair, isn't it? They were killing me, and now I've killed their Project Lambda."

"You?"

"With a lot of help. My Sirian friends were the first and best, but there have been plenty since. It was the Sirians who told me you were aboard; you gave one of them quite a start, when he saw you in the instrument room. Wrecked his mission, you did."

Coughing drowned the voice out; the other Ben Pertin convulsively clutched at the cocoon monitor controls. A warning panel lit over the bed. He was very near death; but the cocoon was not yet defeated; it metered colored fluids into the external blood supply that was trying to replace the destroyed blood cells.

"I only have a few minutes," Ben Frank Pertin gasped. "I don't mind. But I'm not finished, Ben James. You have to finish for me. Destroy that probe! I don't want it to succeed; I don't want Sun One to get its orbiting body around Object Lambda."

"But then we— Then we'll all have died in vain!"

"Of course it is in vain! What's the use of it all? A chunk of useless matter—thousands of light-years from anywhere—going nowhere! Do you know how many lives it's cost? I want you to wreck it for me, Ben James, so those fools on Sun One will know better than to try this same stunt another time!"

"But it's not a stunt," Ben James Pertin objected. "It's important. That object is something special, solid but like a cloud—"

"Cloud-Cuckoo Land! It's not worth a single life. Anyway, it's done already, Ben James, my friends are wrecking the probe right now. I only called you here because—"

He paused, coughing terribly. The face that was so much like Ben James' own was aged with the weary agony of radiation death.

"Because," he gasped, "I want some part of me to stay alive. If you keep the tachyon receiver you can live, Ben James. Weeks—maybe months! But once it goes there will be no more food, no more air, no more fuel. I want—"

But what he wanted to say at the last Ben James Pertin would never know. His duplicate suddenly gasped for breath, made a strangling sound and was still.

After a moment Ben James pulled the privacy screen over the face that was his own face and turned to leave.

Halfway to the launch chamber, he ran into the Sheliaks.

They were in pursuit of two beings, one of them the Purchased People woman, the other Doc Chimp. The Sheliaks looked strange, and in a moment Pertin realized why. They were smaller than they had been; essentially they were children now, some of their mass lost when they budded. But their behavior was childish only in its reckless disregard for consequences; it was lethal, as far as their quarry was concerned.

Pertin did not pause to speculate on issues. Doc Chimp was in danger, and he dove to the rescue.

He collided head-on with one of the Sheliaks. It was like tackling a six-foot lump of chilled, damp dough. No bones, no cushioning fat, just a great dense mass of muscular fiber. The Sheliak automatically cupped around him and, linked, they went flying into the wall. The corridor spun around him, a nightmare of blue-green light and red-black shadow and corpse-colored beings.

"Stop!" Pertin roared. "Wait! Listen to me!" But no one wanted to talk. They were all on him, thrusting, striking, crushing, with whatever offensive weapons their mobile anatomies gave them. He fought back, using a skill he had never known he had. His hands were black and slippery with blood, no doubt much of it his own. Bravely the woman and Doc Chimp had turned back to fight, but it was three of them against more than a dozen Sheliaks, and the issue was not in doubt.

What saved them was Aphrodite, the silver pseudogirl. Her carven face remote as an angel's, she drove toward them with great sweeps of her wings. Coronas of electrostatic fire haloed her fingers and wing-tips; something gun-shaped and deadly was in her hands. The She-liaks, all at once and in unison, turned to meet her. The gun-shaped thing hissed and a white jet cracked toward them. It passed near enough to Pertin for him to feel a breath of icy death, but it did not strike him; it grazed the Sheliak who held him, and at once the being stiffened and began to drift. Behind them, where the jet had struck, the wall was hidden with a broad patch of glittering frost. A cloud of white vapor billowed out around it.

In the haze Pertin caught sight of Doc Chimp and the Purchased People woman, momentarily forgotten as the Sheliaks turned against the stronger foe. The woman was badly hurt; Doc Chimp was helping her, his hairy face turned fearfully toward the Sheliaks. Pertin joined them and the three of them moved inconspicuously away.

When they were two corridors away and the sounds of battle had diminished they paused and inspected their injuries. Pertin himself had only added a few bruises to a total that was already too large to worry about; the chimp was even more battered, but still operational. The woman was worst off of any of them. She was bleeding profusely from, among other places, a gash on the upper arm; her face was grotesquely puffed, both eyes blackened; and one leg was bent at an angle anatomically impossible to a whole bone. But she did not appear to feel pain. When Pertin spoke to her, she answered in English: "They don't consider it important. It will not prevent moving about and performing necessary functions."

Doc Chimp was groaning and sobbing in pain. "Those Sheliaks!" he cried, feebly trying to groom his matted fur. "They're wholly out of control, Ben James. They tried again to wreck the probe—may have done it by now, if they've got enough power of concentration to remember what they were doing when we diverted their attention. And if Aphrodite hasn't killed them all."

Pertin said, with a confidence he didn't feel: "She'll stop them. As long as we've got her on our side—"

"On our side!" Doc Chimp cried. "Ben James, you don't know what you're saying. She's worse than they are!"

"But she tried to rescue you."

The Purchased woman said calmly, "That is wrong. She merely wanted to kill the Sheliaks."

"That's right, Ben James! She's against all organic beings now. She's not ionizable. Radiation is only an annoyance to her. The only thing that can kill her is deprivation of energy sources, and that means the tachyon receiver; once it's gone, she will die as soon as the fuel runs out."

Pertin said slowly: "Is it the same with the Scorpian robot?"

The battered face nodded, the stub of the green plume jerking wildly.

"Then," Pertin said, "that means we have to assume all nonorganic beings will feel the same and try to prevent the launch. What about the other organics?"

The Purchased woman recited emotionlessly: "T'Worlie, all dead. Boaty-Bits, more than half destroyed; the remainder too few to make a collective entity intelligent enough to matter. Sirians and Core Stars races, not observed in recent hours and must be presumed dead or neutralized. Sheliaks, destructive and purposeless."

Pertin absorbed the information without shock, without reaction of any kind, except a strange impulse to laugh. "But—but who does that leave to see that the launch occurs?"

"Nobody!" Doc Chimp cried. "Nobody at all, Ben James—except us!"

FIVE

They reached the launch chamber ahead of the Sheliaks after all. There was no one there.

The capsule, with its tiny bright tachyon crystal at its heart, lay silent and unmoving, connected to the main bulk of the ship only by a jettisonable canopy now. There had been destruction all around it, but it was still intact.

There was less than an hour until launch.

"We'll build barricades," Pertin said. "Anything. Those wrecked instrument boards—the spare plates and braces. Whatever we can move, we'll put it up against the entrance. All we have to do is delay them—"

But they had barely begun when bright silver glinted in the approach corridor, and the silvery pseudogirl came toward them, followed by the tumbling form of the Scorpian robot. They brought up short at the entrance, the robot with one slim tentacle coiled caressingly around the silver girl.

Pertin put his weight behind the channel iron he had been about to emplace at the door and launched it toward the pair. The pseudogirl made a sound that was half a laugh and half the singing of a single piercing note, and the Scorpian uncoiled a long silver sting as they moved aside, easily dodging the missile. The sting reached out and touched Pertin. A blinding light stabbed from it, jolting him with a strong electric shock.

The girl glided in, spreading her now-tattered wings. The stirred air bathed him in a strong scent, ether-sweet, with undertones like the pits of peaches. Pertin searched the bright silvery face and found no expression. It was no more human than a doll's. The Scorpian's silver tentacles thrust away the pitiful obstructions, making a sound like an enormous gong, which Pertin's Pmal refused to translate.

The Purchased woman intervened, hurling herself toward the robot, and was brushed heedlessly aside. She struck against the side of the probe ship, a blow that must have been agony to her human nervous system, but she did not cry out. Awkwardly she tried to project herself again into the fight. Pertin, his muscles beginning to relax their spasm, forced himself to join her.

A birdlike trilling from outside indicated that others were coming, and behind the great winged hulk of the pseudogirl Pertin could see black shadow-shapes moving across the dimly lighted shaft, growing rapidly as they approached.

"Oh, no!" Doc Chimp moaned. "Sheliaks and a Sirian!"

The robot's single-minded purpose was not deflected; it floated toward Pertin, green dome pulsing. An elongating tentacle struck out at Pertin like an endless silver snake, not to sting this time but to snare. It wrapped him in slick, chill coils. He fought free, was caught again, and then at last the Scorpian turned to confront the other beings. It arched its stinging jet, but held poised, waiting.

The Sirian was first into the launch chamber, a tapered, blue-scaled torpedo shape fifteen feet long, all pliant wing and shining eye. With a ripple of trailing edges it flashed at the Scorpian.

The sting coiled, jetting white light into the wide blue eye. The Sirian was not defenseless; its own forces gathered the robot's charge and repelled it, sending the jet back at the robot, reinforced and multiplied.

The pseudogirl turned with great strokes of her wings, her three-fingered hand coming up with the gun-shaped something that had killed Sheliaks. Desperately Pertin twisted to intercept her. Her wings were sadly battered now, but still gave her superior mobility; he missed her on the first try and crashed against a wall. Half blind with his own blood, flowing ink-black in the greenish light, he doubled his legs under him and launched himself at her again.

The gun-shaped thing swung to meet him. It clicked in the pseudogirl's bright silver hand, and the white jet hissed at him. He heard a brittle crackling sound in the air, and felt the cold breath of death.

But the jet had missed, and he was on her. With one hand he swung at her wrist. It was like striking a crowbar with his bare hand, but it jarred the weapon loose; and just then the battle between Scorpian and Sirian reached its climax.

The Sirian's triply potent return jet struck a vital place in the great green dome of the robot. It exploded. The mellow booming sound the robot made became a hollow jangle. The tentacles writhed and recoiled. It sprawled in the air, a grotesque huddle of tortured metal, spilling green fire and drops of an acid that sizzled and burned where they struck.

If robots have life, that life was gone; it was dead.

The silvery girl abandoned the fight with Pertin. With a great stroke of her wings she propelled herself to the robot, hovered over it, wailing an unearthly sound.

And the great blue eye of the Sirian turned toward Pertin. Behind it the Sheliaks, late on the scene but ready for battle, were elongating their wrinkled necks toward him.

Pertin cried desperately: "Wait! They—they were misleading you. They were trying to prevent the launch, to save their own lives!"

The eye hesitated.

"We're dead already," he croaked. "Nothing can help us now, not any organic creature. The radiation will kill us before long, even the Sheliaks. But the robot and the girl—"

He could hear his voice translating and hissing or singing out of the aliens' Pmals.

"The robot," he repeated, "and the altered copy that looks like a terrestrial female—they weren't radiation-vulnerable. They could go on indefinitely. But the rest of us—if we let them succeed in stopping the launch, then we will die for nothing!"

The eye paused, irresolute.

Then the foremost of the Sheliaks cried: "Fool! We too are not radiation-vulnerable! We simply need to conjugate, and be born again. But we must have the tachyon receiver, and if you try to keep us from it you must die!"

And the three tapered teardrop shapes, like a school of sharks in formation, plunged toward them, blazing with their own crimson light.

The Sirian eye irresolutely turned toward them, then back toward Pertin; then, with decision, whirled to confront them.

Contemptuously the Sheliaks changed course to meet it. The leading Sheliak widened a ruff of flesh like an instant air brake and stopped in the air, flowed with a dazzle of color, narrowed a neck toward the Sirian eye.

The thin neck spat a stream of yellow fluid. It struck the Sirian eye and clung, acid, adhesive, agonizing. The Sirian made an unearthly wailing noise at the sudden pain of the attack against which it had no built-in defenses. The great blue eye turned milky white; the horse-huge body knotted itself in agony.

But it still had strength for a final blow. It fired the jet of energy that had destroyed the robot against the Sheliaks.

Electrical energy paralyzed their muscular systems; heat seared the life from them. They died instantly, all three of them. But it was the last effort of the Sirian. All its stored energy had gone into that pulse. The reflected cascade of burning energy came bouncing back upon them all, bathed the silvery girl and sent her reeling soundlessly into a wall, to collapse into an ungainly contorted mass that didn't move. Pertin was farther away and partly shielded by what was left of the robot; even so, it lanced his skin with pain.

But he was alive.

Slowly, and very painfully, he caught a holdfast on the wall, steadied himself while he looked around.

The Purchased-People woman was dead, either bled empty or caught in that last furious bolt. The Sirian eye floated aimlessly, broken and no longer moving, a milky ooze coming from its body. The robot was destroyed; the pseudogirl was drifting impotently away; the Sheliaks were cinders.

The chamber was filled with the stench of many different kinds of death, but Pertin was still alive.

Suddenly remembering, he cried, "Doc Chimp!"

The ape was out of sight. Furiously Pertin ransacked the chamber, and found him at last, wedged between the wall of the probe and the ship's canopy, not quite dead but very unconscious.

Pertin looked down at him sadly and affectionately. It was nearly time to launch the probe, and the question in Pertin's mind was: Is it better to wake him up, or to let him sleep as the probe is launched, the canopy jettisoned, and all the air in the chamber puffed instantly and murderously away into space?

The question was taken out of his hand as the ape stirred, moaned softly, and opened his eyes. He looked up at Ben James Pertin and said thickly, "The probe?"

"It's all right," Pertin said. "We'll have to launch it by hand."

"When, Ben James?"

Pertin checked the time. "Just a few minutes now," he said.

The ape grinned painfully. "That's good to know, Ben James," he said. "No more problems. No more aches and pains. I always thought I'd be afraid of dying, but you know? To tell you the truth, I'm kind of looking forward to it."

The process that animated the body of the silvery pseudogirl was more like electrophoresis than chemistry, but it was vulnerable to attack. It was damaged now.

But she was not dead. The great wings were broken and useless, but her limbs still moved, the inappropriate angel face still showed its bleak, proud expression.

She was in great pain; that is to say, all the sensory nets of her edited body were transmitting messages of malfunction, damage, and warning. She did not perceive them as a human perceives a toothache, a sensation so blinding that it can lead to suicide; but they did not interfere with the few pleasure-bound processes left to her: reminiscence, forevision, contemplation. In the sense that these messages were pain, she had experienced pain from the moment she floated out of the tachyon receiver on *Aurora*. All edited members of her race did. There was no way to rearrange their structures into forms viable in atmosphere and low-G that was comfortable for them.

Time was when Aphrodite had experienced pain only infrequently, and in ways that were soon mended. Time was when she had lain with her sisters in the icy methane slush of her native planet, absorbing energy from the radioactive elements that swam about them, growing, learning from the tutorials of her orthofather, competing in the endless elimination battles of her race that finally won her her choice of assignments, and ultimately led her to the *Aurora* and its imminent doom. Her race was not greatly interested in astronomy; they had known almost nothing of it until the first T'Worlie probe survived the crushing pressures of their atmosphere and brought them into contact. From the surface of their enormous planet, there were no stars to be seen. Even their aircraft never reached an altitude beyond dense yellow-gray clouds.

What brought her to *Aurora* was the trait that her whole upbringing had trained into her: the competitive need to go farther and do more. It was not goal-oriented. It gained nothing from victories except the opportunity for further victories. And the only victory now open to Aphrodite was to survive; and there was but one way to do it—by preventing the launching of the probe.

She calculated she had strength enough left to destroy the two organic creatures in her way, but only just; and only if she acted now.

It was Pertin who saw her first: he froze with his hand on the release lever, and it was Doc Chimp who acted. He flung himself on the pseudogirl. "Hurry up, Ben James!" he shouted. "She's too strong for me—" And his voice stopped, punctuated with a screech of pain as the silvery arm thrust him away like a cannon shot. The chimp went flying into the floating wreckage of the Scorpian robot. The soft, frail dome of the skull, so cleverly mutated nearly into the shape of man's own, impaled itself on a steel shard, and the thoughtful, considering brain was destroyed.

Pertin hardly even saw it. He was past the point for sorrow. It would be easy to let the pseudogirl destroy him. At least one life would be saved, her own. His no longer counted. He could hope for a few days, a week or two at the most, of being able to move and breathe. But what would it be like? Increasing pain. Hopeless fear. Regret. Envy—

He pressed the lever just as her fingers touched him.

The instant sharp slap of the explosion was the last sound he ever heard.

At the second Ben James Pertin pressed the release, explosive shears cut the aft end of the ship free. The canopy flew out and away. The air puffed into emptiness. The probe rocket dropped free and began to align itself with the now near great disk of Object Lambda.

The first thing Pertin felt was the sharp pain of the explosion, then the second, longer, more deadly pain as the air pressure dropped to instant zero and his own blood and body fluids, the air in his own lungs, the gases dissolved in his blood tried to expand to fill the enormous emptiness all around. He caught a glimpse of the silvery girl, arms, legs, and broken wings flailing, as she shot past him, careened off the jagged edge of metal where the shears had cut the probe satellite free, and ricocheted out into emptiness. If she made a sound, he could not hear it. There was no longer a way for him to hear sound. There was no longer a continuous medium of air to carry it.

He had just a glimpse of the huge near surface of Object Lambda— the body he had called "Cuckoo"—as it hung like a great dull circle in the empty sky, cutting off one spiral limb of his own, eternally lost, Galaxy.

He did not see the orienting jets of the satellite spurt carefully controlled measures of flame to position it for its final thrust. He did not see the great violet flare of the fusion rockets that began to slow it. He could not see any of that, because by then he was dead.

Neither he nor anyone else in the probe ship saw the great series of flares as the satellite fought to slow itself. *Aurora* flew on, back toward the Galaxy, without power, containing only the least flickerings of life for a few of its beings. The probe left it as it drew more and more rapidly away. The distance between them was millions of miles before the satellite made its first meteoric contact with the outer layers of that anomalously thick atmosphere around Cuckoo.

It was a spectacle worth watching, if there had been eyes left in *Aurora* to see. The satellite plunged through a carefully planned chord of the atmosphere. Its ablative surface burned and tore away in a flare like all the Fourth of July fireworks in man's history going off at once. But there was none to see, not Sirian eye nor Sheliak sensors, not T'Worlie or Earthman or alien of any kind; where life remained at all, it lacked strength for curiosity, and it would not remain very long.

Fifty thousand years later *Aurora* might pass near some sun of an outstretched spiral arm. But by then it would no longer matter to anyone, except as a historical curiosity from a time about which no one cared any longer.

SIX

Some days later, the sensors on Sun One reported that the probe was in a stable orbit. The beings on Sun One responded with pleasure; everyone was delighted that the project was a success.

Now stable, the probe began to do the work for which it had been designed.

The complex H-bomb sequencing units and the small, strong pressure-plate shock absorbers fell away, responding to remote controls from Sun One. They would never be used again.

The tachyon-receiving unit began to emit a stream of tiny metallic shards, none larger than a few inches in its greatest measure.

When some hundreds of them were through, floating like a metallic mist around the drone, a quick small machine came through and began to catch them and link them together. Time passed, hours and then days. A queer boxlike shape took form and became a larger tachyon receiver, ready for action.

From tens of thousands of light-years away an angular, crystalline machine flashed along the tachyon patterns and emerged in the new receiver. It was not alive. Was not even a robot, or a proxy like the Purchased People. It was simply an automatic machine that sensed certain potentials and charges, double-checked the strength of the materials and the solidity of the joints, directed the hummingbird-sized construction machine to correct a few faults, and then reported that Cuckoo Station, the orbiting body around what had been called Object Lambda, was now ready to be built.

A few hours later the first girders of a thousand-meter revolving wheel were being joined together.

Plates appeared to surround the girders with an airtight sheath. Machines arrived to be stored in them. Atmosphere was pumped through to fill the chambers. The handling machines were busy, taxed beyond their capacities; more handling machines were sent, and soon the orbiting station was whole, supplied, and being-rated.

The first living beings appeared. A Sheliak, naked to the cold of intergalactic space—but for the brief time of its transition to the orbiting wheel unharmed by it. A dozen T'Worlie in a single elastic air bubble, scurrying into the protection of the orbital wheel. There were Sirians, reptilian Aldebaranians, a hive of Boaty-Bits, and, at the last, a couple of humans.

One of them was named Ben Linc Pertin.

He floated out of the tachyon receiver in his pressure suit, his thruster unit ready in his hands.

He did not use it at once; he paused a moment, to look around.

The first thing he did was to stare down at the enormous flat surface of Cuckoo, so near, so huge, so incredible as it hung like an endless shield in the sky.

The second was to look back to where the Galaxy lay, sparkling like the sea of stars it was.

He could not see the doomship, but he knew it must be somewhere in his line of sight. There were no signals from it anymore. There was no way of detecting it, and would not be for tens of thousands of years.

He stared for a moment, then half shrugged. "Poor bastards," he whispered, and turned and drove toward the wheel awaiting him.

PART TWO
The Org's Egg

ONE

The mountain was a friendly mountain. It had been growing for half a billion years, as mountains naturally did. Its slow cells fed on rain and air and wind-blown dust, compacting them into a core of solid quartz.

On other planets, Earth for example, mountains also grew, but in a different way. Terrestrial mountains were thrust up from below by the slow violence of shifting continental crusts and the shock of volcanic eruptions. Here mountains grew more gently.

A boy, whose name was Fifteenth, lived on this mountain with his people. When he was little it was his whole world and he had not imagined anything beyond it. Now he was nearly grown. From time to time he looked beyond the mountain, but always came back to it. It was home.

It was not all hospitable. Its summit was a rounded crown, carved with winding fissures, glowing with a blue bioluminescence brighter than the storms that often boiled around it. Lower down, where the winds were now too warm and dry, its surface film of shining life was tattered into drying shreds. With the life-coat dying, the age-eaten stone beneath was caving away from the vertical cliffs, adding black and shattered masses to the boulder slopes below, where the wild orgs nested. The boy never went that high. It was too dangerous.

But lower still, there was home! The dead stuff of the mountain had rotted into rich black soil that spread in delta-plains and marshes all around its foot. Floods from its stormy heights ran down to water the forests and mosslands that reached all the way to the grassy flatland where the people ranged to find food and trophies, and bring them back to the sweet slopes of the mountain.

Fifteenth's people were nomadic wingmen. From the heights on the side of the mountain they could launch themselves into always-present orographic updrafts, and spiral out of them to overfly the green rainpaths of the plain. There were roots and fruits, waterholes and game. When they found what they wanted they swooped down and possessed it. It was a good life. It was the only life Fifteenth had known, but it was not good enough.

And when he was just coming bearded, he looked around the camp of his people and sat in thought for a long time, testing a thought that had come to him. He looked out across the flat plains to that other distant, seemingly barren mountain that his people called Knife-in-the-Sky. It was hard to see in the uncertain light from the plains and the few forested parts of its slopes. The boy's people had never seen daylight, or for that matter night; they marked the passing of time by their own body cycles or by changes in the trees and animals, since they had no other clock on a world that showed nothing in its sky but clouds and, rarely, some faint misty distant gleam that looked like a swirl of muted silvery fire. But even when they could not see Knife-in-the-Sky they knew it was there. For every org on the boy's own mountain there were a thousand on Knife-in-the-Sky. On his own mountain their clutches were scant, and often the eggs produced weaklings; but always there were new orgs coming from Knife-in-the-Sky to replenish the stocks. The boy sat staring at the distant jagged peak for many thousands of breaths, and then he went to tell his brother that he had resolved to leave his people, to cross the plain, to climb Knife-in-the-Sky and steal a wild org's egg.

"You are young," his brother said wearily and fretfully, "and you are foolish. Other youths have gone org-hunting. They do not come back."

Fifteenth stood stubbornly silent, hanging his head. His brother was the head of his clan, the clan in which fourteen other males were older and therefore more powerful than himself. The boy did not want to show disrespect to his brother by disagreeing, but he could not make himself promise to give up his plan.

"Only those whose minds are on the ground hunt orgs," his brother warned.

The boy still did not speak. They were standing outside his brother's new tent, pitched in the yellow light of a clump of fire-trees. His brother's new wife was singing in the tent, grinding grain for their next meal. From beyond the fire-trees the slow clang of a blacksmith's anvil rang; that was the boy's cousin, Second.

The brother carefully worked his awl through a double thickness of leather before speaking again. Then he looked up. "If you stay with us, I will share my skills with you," he offered.

The boy showed his astonishment. Their father had been a wingwright. As was proper, his skills had come down to the eldest of his sons. With a new wife, First would surely have sons of his own before long, and to give wingwright skills to Fifteenth would be depriving his own get of what was rightly theirs. "I thank you," the boy said. "But I will go."

"Knife-in-the-Sky is farther than it looks," his brother said. "Why go there when there are orgs here, if you are determined to die?"

"There are better orgs on Knife-in-the-Sky. I have never seen their lairs there. I know what they are here."

"From your mother," First said gloomily. "Of course. But there are more orgs and stronger orgs there, and they take care of their eggs. Besides—"

He looked up from the harness he was mending and scowled across at the jagged distant mountain.

"Besides the orgs, there are the Watchers."

"Why should the Watchers bother me?"

"They do not tell us why!" His brother looked up angrily and incautiously, pricked his finger with an awl, and grimaced with pain. He put the finger in his mouth and said around it, "They live beyond the mountains. They ride in the sky in machines the size of twenty orgs, and attack all creatures that don't obey them. And there are new Watchers now. Little ones. No one knows what they may do."

"I've never seen a Watcher," the boy said.

"Not on the mountain. But to get to Knife-in-the-Sky you must cross the plain and marshland. You cannot do it all by wing. You must walk for many sleeps. I'm afraid the Watchers will find you."

"But if they do not," the boy said, "I will come back riding an org."

"You—riding an org!" The brother took his finger out of his mouth and spat blood. "You've never seen an org close up."

"My mother did," the boy said.

He turned and scowled across the plains toward Knife-in-the-Sky. He was a strong young man, tall even among his people, who averaged better than seven feet in height. If he had been on Earth he would have weighed no more than a hundred and sixty pounds—here much less—he looked not like a reed but a whip.

He looked a great deal like his mother—his father's second wife, whom his father had stolen away from another band. She had been a First Man's daughter, and her father had pursued them on a tamed org, until the fleeing couple set fire to dried grass and escaped under the smoke. She had handed on her lore of org-training to the boy: where the eggs were found, how the hatchlings could be tamed.

The time had come for him to use that knowledge, because he was of an age to use it—and for another reason. For the girl who had become his brother's new wife had been the girl Fifteenth himself had wanted.

The brother picked up his awl again. "If you have to be a fool—" He shrugged and suddenly grinned. "I'll make a new harness for you."

And so, for many meals, the boy hunted meat while his brother made the harness. The dark-eyed girl who had become his brother's wife helped him smoke the meat, and if her presence near him was a steady pain he never showed it, and if she knew she never told.

When the harness was finished and fitted he loaded himself and the three of them trudged up the friendly mountain toward the finest of the launching places. There where the slope fell steeply away for a thousand feet, the gentle, cradling updraft never failed. From this cliff edge one could circle and soar more than a mile into the thick, sweet air of their world, and launch oneself many sleeps away across the plain in a single flight.

They stood and stared at Knife-in-the-Sky, and then the dark-haired girl caught her breath and cried, "A fire in the clouds! Look!"

Before them, even higher than Knife-in-the-Sky, a lance of silvery light was extending itself in a soaring arc down through the bright, living clouds. Neither the boy nor his brother was frightened, although it was a strange thing to them; their world knew nothing of meteorites, since near them there was nothing small enough to fall into their air. It was not unique. It was rare.

The brother muttered, "There was such a flame a hundred sleeps ago, and after that the small Watchers appeared."

"Has anyone been harmed by a small Watcher?" the boy demanded.

The brother shook his head no, though what he meant was "not yet."

"Then I will not fear if there are more. Good-bye," the boy said, kissed them both, grasped his buttocks with his hands, and leaped headfirst into the air. When he was well clear of the rock he swept his arms up in the sinuous stroke of the wingman, extended the filmy wings of scraped leather, and flapped and soared until his brother and the girl were all but invisible to him, tiny, staring figures no larger than pebbles.

And then he turned out of the updraft and stroked through the air toward Knife-in-the-Sky.

He did not look behind him.

Even if he had looked, he might not have seen that something shared the air with him, a cube of metal, bright on all its faces, brighter still with lights and lenses on the face toward him. It was no larger than Fifteenth's fist and a long way behind as it stolidly punched a passage through the air, borne on magnetic forces of which none of the boy's people had ever heard. The boy did know it was there. He was not meant to.

TWO

A long distance away in terms of the boy's world—but only a step in astronomical distances—a man named Ben Linc Pertin watched a holographic virtual image of the flying boy and turned away, shaking his head. "They're skinny and funny-looking," he said, "but by God they're human. Figure that for me, Venus."

The girl beside him was not a girl. She did not look like a human girl except in the way that a statue does; she was silvery metal, thixotropic, anisotropic, tamed by the science of her people to flow and move like flesh. On her home world Venus had not looked human at all; for that matter she had not been female, because her race had not bothered with sexual distinctions in its development. She said, "Not only human beings live on Cuckoo, Ben Linc. We have already found Sheliaks and Boaty-Bits, or beings genetically parallel to them. And we have only begun to look."

"None of your folks, though," Ben Linc observed cheerfully. "Guess you weren't popular."

"As to that, Ben Linc, how could you tell?"

He grinned. Venus was an edited form, specially tailored to operate well in the near Earth-normal environment of Cuckoo Station.

"Well," he said, "I suppose we might as well retransmit these tapes. I think we need help, Venus. More equipment, more survey scouts. And more beings. I think it's about time we sent people down to Cuckoo. What do you say?"

The silvery girl was silent for a moment. Ben Linc knew that, through her Pmal translator, she was communicating with FARLINK, the computer that processed all the manifold information-handling procedures on the orbiter called Cuckoo Station.

FARLINK was the station's nerve center. It processed the tachyonic transmissions that replicated new personnel for the station. It coordinated the reports from the drones they sent down to the surface of the strange object itself. It stored their cumulative data and solved their research problems; and it sent their findings—such as they were— back to Sun One.

Its main terminal was a ring-shaped console inside the hollow hemisphere where Pertin, the silvery girl, and other beings were working. The beings on duty sat inside the console, or rested or clung or stood there as their anatomies dictated, with input devices within reach of their manipulative organs. The output flashed and shimmered on the screens that lined the dome, translated into the visual symbols of half a hundred cultures.

Ben Linc became impatient. "What's the matter, Venus?"

She did not move but her expression, as far as she could be said to have one, seemed to cloud. "There is difficulty," she said.

"Difficulty?" That seemed unlikely! FARLINK was as close to perfect as any machine ever made. Many tachyonic channels linked it to the banks of the even larger computers and research teams back on Sun One, and it had its own built-in power sources. And yet—

And yet abruptly, before his very eyes, the myriad screens suddenly flickered and went black!

There was an instant rumble of consternation. Cries and hoots and clangs of shock rang out all around the ring. From the console position nearest his own a scorched-fur scent of T'Worlie dismay came from the bat-headed, butterfly-winged being named Nammie.

"What the devil!" he cried. The screens were black for only a second; then they glowed with the green computer symbols that spelled out the same message in half a hundred languages:

"REGRET INTERRUPTION. INTERFERENCE DISTORTING INCOMING SIGNALS. ORIGIN OF INTERFERENCE NOT KNOWN."

Venus whispered, "But we've never had any interference before . . ."

Pertin had no answer. Suddenly he felt very lonely. The tachyonic channels were their only bridge of thought and communication across that gulf of space that was too vast for anything material to cross. With the bridge broken, the thirty thousand light-years between all of them and all of their diverse homes became terribly real.

The T'Worlie beside him was fluttering on frantic wings above its console position, stabbing at the keys and whistling at its mike. After a moment it rose from the keyboard and turned its five-eyed face to him.

"Mode emergency!" it shrilled. "Query implications of signal distortion."

"I wish I knew," Pertin said, shaking his head.

"Propose conjecture! Assume sentient masters of Cuckoo. Query: Have they discovered us? Are they initiating contact? Query probable intentions."

"I don't know, Nammie. What about DFing? Do we know where the source comes from?"

The T'Worlie spun and punched a combination; and all the myriad screens lighted up:

"SOURCE UNKNOWN. DF PROGRAM INITIATED."

And then abruptly the green symbols shimmered off the screen. Patterns of color flashed and vanished in the deep tanks that were their three-D vision screens. A new message appeared:

"INTERFERENCE FADING. STAND BY. SIGNAL RECEPTION RESUMING."

The Sun One sign burned itself onto the screens: a red disk inside a thin green ellipse—the artificial satellite called Sun One, inside the Galaxy itself. Before it appeared the tall, glowing cone of a Sheliak official, back at Sun One. He was speaking, apparently oblivious to the interruption, while his translator turned his soft hooting into Earth English on Ben Linc's screen. Green symbols overrode the image for a moment:

"INTERFERENCE HAS CEASED. SOURCE NOT TRACKED."

Venus and Ben Linc looked at each other.

"What was that all about?" he demanded.

Slowly she shook her silvery head. "At any rate, it's over." All around the dome, beings were resuming their interrupted chores. "One moment, Ben Linc," she added gravely; and then, "Yes, we have concurrence. We authorize you to transmit a call for additional survey forces."

Ben Linc Pertin nodded and cued in the tachyon transmitter. Carefully he began to phrase the report that the supervelocity tachyons would flash toward the distant Galaxy, to the artificial planet called Sun One—where all the races of the Galaxy maintained the headquarters that had launched this survey party—and from there on to the home planets of scores of kinds of beings. His own words might sooner or later reach his own world, Earth.

Ben Linc wondered if somehow, back on Earth, that original Ben Pertin who had volunteered for tachyon transmission long before might hear the voice of his double, and if so what he might think.

But that was not profitable wondering. Behind it lay too much pain, too much loss, too many regrets for what could never be undone. Behind it lay the memory of the girl he had married on Sun One. Zara had not lost her husband; but Ben, her husband, in this copy at least, had lost his wife forever. And it hurt.

THREE

Although the boy named Fifteenth was strong, launching himself from the ground was very hard work, only for emergencies. When at last he began to run out of strength on his first long flight across the plain toward Knife-in-the-Sky he was careful to choose a spot where hillocks gave him a small height advantage for the next launch. A tall tree would have been better, but here there were only fire-trees and bee-trees, and neither was any good for climbing. When you climbed fire-trees no matter how careful you were some of the fire clung to your skin and, although it did not seem to do immediate harm, after a time you sickened and died. And bee-trees, of course, were guarded by their bees. These were not really bees in any sense, but they shared with Earthly bees a disposition to assault invaders en masse, so the boy avoided them.

He did not sleep on his first landing, only ate from the stocks he carried, rested drowsily for a thousand breaths, and then launched himself again. It was unsatisfying flying over the marshes that he soon encountered. There were few updrafts, and only weak ones, to climb in. Nearer home, generations of wingmen had located reliable springs of rising air in many places—where the lowest slopes of the mountain shaped the wind, or where for some reason the ground was always warm. But he was at the edge of the known world already, as far as his people were concerned. He could recognize some helpful signs. Nearly always fire-trees meant rising air, not because the trees themselves were warm but because they only grew in warm soil. But the stands of fire-trees here in the marshes were spindly and infrequent. Better than nothing. Not very good.

So he climbed mostly with the power of his lean, long arms and chest muscles, and flying was steady work. Better than walking. Still, not good.

It did not matter. The boy's purpose held, and after every rest or meal or sleep he launched himself again and drove on toward Knife-in-the-Sky.

He had known that mountain all his life, but he hadn't known how far it was. He slept twenty-three times crossing the alternating marsh and flatlands past the edge of the grass, and eighteen times more crossing what was pure marsh, where he could rest only on hillocks and the steamy mist that rose around him while he slept was malodorous and cloying. Each time he knotted the count into the cord around his throat when he woke, and looked toward Knife-in-the-Sky; and still it seemed no larger.

Beyond the marshes he crossed an endless carpet of thick, bright moss that had a queerly sharp smell which he associated with the electrical storms that rolled around the upper reaches of his mountain —but he had no name for "ozone." Something in the air above the mossland made him sneeze. The moss bore no fruit and it gave him no game. He counted twenty-eight sleeps on his way across it, and came out giddy with hunger and thirst.

He came down, with the last of his strength, on the bank of a shallow river that rimmed the moss world. Flying off again would be hard work, but it couldn't be helped. He knelt and drank the black water until he began to feel ill, and then looked for food in the forest on the far bank. Its plants were club-shaped and leafless, shining with their own cold light like dwarfed, warped fire-trees. Shining daggers of thorns guarded the hard red nuts they bore. He picked a few doubtfully, and looked farther. But there was none of the game he knew from the grasslands near his home, none of the fleet four-legged herd animals, or the horned, two-legged hoppers. His arrows killed a small weakly flying thing that fed on the nuts, but its flesh was tasteless and dry. He roasted some of the nuts, and felt sicker after eating them than he had before.

He summoned the strength to pitch his wings together to make a tent, pegged against one of the club-shaped trees. He rolled inside, curled up in a ball, and tried to sleep. It was not easy. The boy had never known what insomnia was, but he had heard old people speak of it sometimes and now he understood what they meant. He was drained and aching. For the first time he began to wonder if he were not as crazy as his brother had said. His brains truly felt as if they were bound to the ground. His thoughts could not rise and fly over him; they were limited to fear and misery and depression.

After a time he decided that he must eat, no matter what, and rose again.

Here in the marshes the sky was darker than on the slopes of his mountain; there were fewer fire-trees, and the light from the steely bright moss on the far side of the river was of little help. The boy had never heard of concepts like "day" or "night." He had never seen a sun in his sky, or for that matter a moon or stars. There were none to be seen, except for the occasional rare coils of silvery haze that, he had no way of knowing, were distant galaxies. One time was as good as another to sleep, or to eat, or to hunt. But he was not used to being hungry or ill.

It made him feel dizzy and faint, and when he crawled out of his wing-tent and saw the bright cube that whirled away out of sight he thought at first it was the imagining of sickness.

Sick as he was, his brain cleared almost at once. Once or twice before, in the long flights over grass and marsh and moss, he had thought he had glimpsed something small and bright and far behind. But it had always hung just at the threshold of visibility. He knew that the Watchers traveled in huge things that were bright and shiny. But this did not seem very large, nor did it ever come closer. He had heard of the small new Watchers that his brother had told him about. Was this one of them? He could not say.

All he could be sure of was that it had not harmed him so far, at least, and certainly there would never be a better chance to do him harm than while he lay shaking and weak in the wing-tent.

It gave him much to think about, but he could think without fear, for somehow he did not believe that this small Watcher intended to hurt him.

Curiously, the effort of thinking, perhaps also the sense that some sort of creature was not far away, even if hiding, seemed to sharpen his mind and his will. He stood up, drank again from the river, and began to search for the sprays of flame-bright red bloom he had seen from the air. These marked a thick-rooted plant. When he found them he dug out roots, and found among them nests of blood-red worms that, he thought, he had heard the older wingmen of his people describe as edible in bad times.

The roots were sweet and white and good, the worms less good. They were gritty and revolting raw, but he made a fire and soon learned to clean them of their digestive sacs before broiling them. He made his first satiating meal in many sleeps, rolled back into the wing-tent, and slept soundly and well. He stayed by the river bank for three more sleeps, and then felt strong enough to pack himself with roots and smoked worms and go on again.

He flew steadily and low, saving his wasted energy, careful with the now-worn bands of his harness. He strained his neck with watching, ceaselessly scanning the sky all around for orgs, or Watchers, or for another sight of the small Watcher that had fled from him by the river —all the time searching the forest for food, studying the horizon for signs of updrafts that might help him.

The dully glowing forests sloped sharply upward now. He slept seven times in a belt of fog and rain. With Knife-in-the-Sky now lost in the lowering sky his target was gone. He set his course as much as he could by following the upward slopes. When those signs failed, or were doubtful, he drew from his harness the one gift his mother had given him that had been her father's.

The crystal-cased object that glittered like the small Watcher was the size of the boy's thumb. Inside it a needle spun about, but ever seemed to quiver toward a single direction with the end that was brighter than the other. His mother had not known much about it, except that the wingmen of her people used the devices to mark the direction of flight when landmarks failed.

The air grew cooler as he climbed. When he camped for one sleep on a moss-grown rock he woke shivering and chilled. He crept stiffly from beneath his tented wings and found the low clouds gone.

He looked up and caught his breath.

Knife-in-the-Sky filled all the world ahead. The forests lifted toward it forever, rising piles of pale brown and gray and ivory, splashed with vast black masses of fallen stone.

So high he had to stretch his neck to look, the mountain itself rose out of those broken boulders. Walls of dead rock marched up and at the top of that unclimbable wall, higher than he could imagine, the jagged summit slashed across the rippling colors of the sky.

He studied that summit for a long time, looking for orgs while the damp wind that blew down the slopes of the mountain numbed him with unexpected cold. He knew they were there. They were always there, when they were not sweeping down to the lower slopes and the marsh and the grasslands and forests, seeking their prey. Perhaps those distant black spots, so hard to distinguish from the motes of dust that one sees on the surface of one's own eye, were orgs; he could not tell. Whatever, they were still a long way off. He stepped back to see more clearly over that giddy wall, felt a sudden gust as he was caught off stride; and the ground slid away under him. He grabbed wildly for the anchor rope that secured his tented wings, but his chilled fingers slid off it. The wind spun him off the rock; he flailed his arms, trying to get his balance; the moss was slippery, the cold had made him clumsy and he went sprawling over the edge.

The fall was only twenty times his own height—say, a hundred and fifty feet by Earth measures—so there was no real danger. Even without wings he could glide to some extent, as Earthly sky divers used to direct their fall before allowing their chutes to open. He picked out a landing spot where a bank of crimson moss promised some cushion, stretched out his arms, writhed with his body, spun around like a cat dropped from a table, and landed not too badly, considering the sluggishness of his muscles from the cold. A pink cloud of spores rose around his plowing feet and half blinded him. He sprawled, sneezing and choking, and then stood up and looked around.

The clouds below had shifted, and he could see across the great bowl of marsh and plain almost to the slopes of his own mountain. Past the brown and yellow slopes beneath him, the moss world made an endless sea; past it, the marshes, overhung with cloud, traced with thin black lines of rivers. In the hollows white fog lay.

He had not realized home was so far, but he could spare no thought for it. He turned and looked up the rock to where his tented wings and supplies were. Without wings he could not fly, but he could still climb; unfortunately, the rock was very steep and he could not trust his stiffened fingers to seek out holds in its crevices. He would have to climb the long way around.

The boy had no lack of practice in climbing, but as a wingman he disliked it very much. Without wings it could be dangerous. The combination of low gravity and dense atmosphere that his world possessed made the lifting of mass easy, but unbalanced the equation of wind versus inertia; caught by a gust on a vertical face, it was quite possible he could be flung so far out that even the slow acceleration of his world would crush him when he struck ground again. So he sought an easy way and sprang carefully from point to point, and was concentrating so hard on his task that he almost did not see the small Watcher as it swooped past his head and then spun away upward toward the place where his gear waited for him.

The boy shrank back into a crevice in the moss and waited for attack.

The attack did not come. Actually, he had not thought it would; this small Watcher for some reason did not seem menacing to him. And yet what could it be doing with his gear? He could hear nothing. He could see nothing—then, in a flash, he saw something startling: a bright flare of golden light that washed the side of the mountain and disappeared in a moment.

Cautiously the boy eased his way out of the little fold in the terrain and stretched himself to peer upward. He listened; he looked; he smelled; he reached out with all of his senses toward the top of the rock, but there was nothing.

He knelt on folded legs for a hundred breaths, considering. Strictly speaking, there was nothing on the rock that he could not do without. Food, spear, bow, wings, harness—he could not make them as well as the specialists among his people, but he could make them well enough to get by. The wings and harness would be the most difficult, but he had seen enough of his brother's work to know that replacing them would not be impossible.

Still . . . the thing was, the gear on the top of the rock was his gear, and he wanted it back.

If the small Watchers were the same as the big ones there would be no question. His only option would be to flee, and that would almost certainly be useless, if his brother's stories were halfway true. But he did not think there was any hostility stored in the glittering little cube he had seen.

So with great daring, very slowly and cautiously at first but then more quickly and openly, the boy made his way around a boss on the mountainside, up and over it, and emerged higher than the rock where he had slept, looking down on it, an easy spring from it.

He had not known what to expect, but he had not expected what he saw.

The cube was no longer just a cube. It hung in air a yard above the moss, not far from his wing-tent, steady as if it were nailed there, not dipping or even trembling in the winds. But it was growing something. From one face of it a glowing, filmy bubble of something was spreading to form a sphere almost the height of the boy—then taller, while he watched.

The sphere stopped growing. The boy looked and pondered, wondering whether to approach. For dozens of breaths nothing happened, unless a shadowy sort of movement inside the sphere was real, and was something happening.

The boy could see his gear, waiting for him. He could detect no harm in the cube or in the bubble.

He did not come to a conscious decision; but in a moment he discovered that his legs were gathering under him and he sprang toward the top of the rock. He turned in air to bring his feet under him, landed well, spun around to face the small Watcher.

And then something did happen. There was another flash of that intense golden explosion of silent light, and for a moment he was blinded. And when he could see again at all he saw that the bubble was burst open, sliced from within, like an org's egg with the hatchling just coming out; and out of it was stepping—what? A man? Short, fat, squat, dark, curiously clothed—but yes, a man!

FOUR

The figure that came out of the bubble was twice as broad as the boy, and nearly a head shorter. To the boy it looked like one of his own people, but somehow squashed down and wearing strange bright clothing such as he had never seen before.

The wingmen and their women wore no more than they had to: the harness to hold their wallets and fasten to their wings, a few square inches of cloth or shaved leather for ornament, a few more for modesty.

By the boy's standards, the man was fearsomely overdressed. His clothing covered nearly all of him. From waist to feet he wore a sort of bright yellow leotard, ending under bright-colored soft boots. From waist to shoulders he wore a sleeveless tunic. His wrists were ornamented with broad, bright-colored bands that looked as if they had the feel of leather, but were colored in blues and greens and mauves; they held little pouches and bright shiny things that glittered and seemed to move. Even the man's head was covered, with a soft cap which (the boy did not know) could come down to protect his eyes against dust or glare, or if need be could shield the entire upper part of him against rain or cold. And that was a bright orange color; taken all in all, the man was queerly and fearsomely garbed, the boy marveled. With such apparel he could never hope to avoid being seen by org or Watcher or game!

His costume and his queer proportions were not all that was queer about him. Even his face was strange. He was surely much older than the boy, two or three thousand sleeps at least. But his face did not show it. It was not weathered or lined from wind or storm. His teeth were bright and even, as perfect as the boy's own, and far more so than, say, those of the boy's older brother, who had used them to nip off ends of leather for the five thousand sleeps of his adult life.

All this the boy saw in the same photographic glance in which he observed that the man carried no weapon. None at all; neither bow nor knife. Not even a club. Even so, the boy judged, he might not be without danger. His squat frame had the look of strength.

The man took a step toward the boy. It was not menacing. It was comic. The boy had never seen anything like it; the man's step was grotesquely energetic, it propelled him unmeaning into the air. He came down, stumbled, caught himself, fell again in overreaction, and sprawled to the ground. The expression on his broad face was funnier than his ungainly tumbling act itself. The boy could not help laughing. From the ground the man laughed, too.

Then the man stood up, quite carefully, with a wink and exaggerated caution. He spread his hands as if to show he had no weapons. The boy knew that already; he made no move.

The man, slowly and carefully, as if to show that he meant no harm, grasped one wrist with the fingers of the other hand and did something to the shiny baubles on it. Then he spoke to the boy.

When he did, his voice came from two places at once. It came from his mouth in the normal way. Another voice, harsher and more metallic than his own, came stumbling from the bauble on his wrist. The sounds from the thing on his wrist were not the same as the sounds from his mouth, but the boy could understand neither of them. He bent his head in the gesture of negation.

The man looked as if he were irritated with his toy. He touched it again, and spoke once more.

This time the boy thought he caught the suggestion of a word. Strangely, it came from the man's wrist, not his mouth. It sounded rather like the word the boy's people used for "what?" But there was more to it, and the rest was gibberish.

The man shrugged and let his arm fall to his side. Then he grinned, touched his chest, and said a single word. The sound of it was "Ben." The man waited inquiringly, as if expecting a response.

The boy was not sure what was expected of him, other than that the man seemed to want him to speak. The man gestured, pointed to his wrist, and made several other sounds. One sounded like "Pmal," pronounced very slowly and carefully, but what it meant the boy had no idea.

He said slowly, "I don't know what you want me to do."

The man applauded, grinned, motioned for more.

"Well," the boy said, "I am Fifteenth of the men in my people." He paused, a little suspiciously, but the man urged him on. It seemed foolish, but there did not seem to be anything dangerous in it. Hesitantly he went on: "But I am far from my people and no longer one of them," he soliloquized. "So perhaps I can have only a word-name, like an outlaw or a woman. Are you an outlaw? But I am going to get an org's egg. I will hatch it and tame the org. Perhaps I will call myself Org Rider!" he finished, and fell silent, listening to the pleasing sound of the name in his mind's ear.

Excited, the man touched his wrist and spoke again. This time the words from his wrist made sense; they were poorly pronounced, but clearly enough they said: "I am Ben. You are Org Rider!"

From the boy's expression the man saw that communication had begun. His own face reflected joy. He spoke again, and the thing on his wrist stuttered, emitted a few nonsense syllables, and then, very clearly, said: "My people far."

He gestured for the boy to speak on.

But the boy had heard another sound. Frowning, he turned to search the sky.

It was a strangely ominous sound, like the hum of a bee-tree. The boy's first thought was *Org!* Yet the sound was wrong, not the harsh scream his mother had described, but even more fearsome.

Then he saw it: a faint gray glint against the polychrome sky, diving toward them, very fast.

Watcher!

It was like a spearpoint arrowing toward them in the sky; it had no wings, but it moved so fast the boy could hardly realize what was happening. The man heard it, too. Astonishment spread across his broad face. He turned, bounced toward the silently hovering small Watcher, fell clumsily but righted himself and touched it with quick, skillful hands.

At once one face of the small Watcher flared with a bright golden flame, and a bubble began to grow out of it.

The boy did not stand watching this performance. He ran for his weapons. He did not know what good they would be against a Watcher, but he had no other options open to him than to use them.

A bright flash of light from above gave him a split second's warning, then something crashed nearby. Queer sudden yellow flowers bloomed on the black rock, and faded into pale smoke. A sharp reek of burning choked him.

The bubble from the side of the small Watcher had grown tall as the boy now; abruptly it flared brightly gold. Unfortunately for the boy he was staring directly at it when it happened. For a moment he was blinded. Bright lights were out of his experience entirely, except for lightning and the smoky glow of a campfire; the eyes of his people did not have quick recovery mechanisms, since they had no sun in their sky to contend with and no need. He clawed at his eyes in acute pain. He could not distinguish just what was happening.

The man named Ben was clawing at the bubble, trying to drag out of it some glittering object that had appeared inside. The boy could not recognize it; he could barely see the outlines, could barely see when again there was that sudden crash, and a flash of light behind and above him, and yellow flame and smoke exploded on Ben himself. The boy heard a terrible scream, felt splinters of rock as they tore at his flesh, smelled a queerly hot choking odor that took his breath.

Then blackness drowned him. His bow was in his hand, but he had not had time to raise it, or even see what it was that had killed Ben and was almost killing himself.

Consciousness returned, out of a crazy pain-filled fantasy that was not a dream but a memory. He lay face down on hard, wet gravel. He was shivering to a cold, slow rain.

His first thought was astonishment at being alive, his second to get his wings to wrap around him, covering his nakedness against the rain.

When he tried to move something wrapped around his neck, so tight that he could hardly breathe, tugged him back.

Panic shook him. He tugged at the coil around his neck; it would not loosen. His hand flashed to his knife, but it was gone. He was tied by the neck, like a food-beast awaiting slaughter.

Sitting up more carefully, he saw that he was tied to a great machine, spearhead-shaped, that lay on the gravel. It was mottled in brown and yellow, but under it was the glint of silvery metal.

Ten paces away lay the squat butchered corpse of Ben. A faint pathetic mechanical squeal came from the silvery cube of the small Watcher that had brought him; it would bring no one ever again, for the explosion that had killed Ben had blasted it as well, and it lay sparking feebly, cracked and broken, on the gravel.

"Good to see you awake, boy!"

The booming voice caught Org Rider by surprise. He moved suddenly and was jerked back by the choking coil around his neck. When he caught his balance he saw a man, taller than himself, red-bearded, green-eyed, half grinning, rocking on his feet by the small pile of the boy's weapons and wings.

"Who are you?" the boy demanded.

"Why," the man said, "you can call me Redlaw. You're a long way from home, Fifteenth."

The boy kept off his face the sinking astonishment that this man knew his name. "I am not Fifteenth anymore," he said stubbornly. "My name is Org Rider."

The man's laugh boomed out. "An Org Rider without an org? Your brother was right, boy, you're a fool." Then he said, not unkindly, "Oh, don't be surprised. The Watchers don't only watch. They listen as well. We've been listening to you for a long time."

"How?" the boy cried. "I never saw you before!" The man only shrugged and smiled. "I've never seen any Watcher," the boy said. "And you have never been on our mountain I am certain."

"You're making a wrong assumption," the man said. "I'm not a Watcher. I work for them. As butcher in their galleys"—he gestured at the bloodstained apron he wore—"and sometimes as translator, when they want to know what people like you are saying. But I know you are truthful when you say you've never seen a Watcher, because they don't look a bit like you or me."

"Then where are the Watchers?" Org Rider cried.

"You'll see them soon enough." The man stirred the boy's weapons with a foot, and peered at the boy out of shrewd green eyes. "It's not you they care about, you know," he said suddenly. "It's your dead friend here. What do you know about him?"

"Nothing," Org Rider said proudly, fighting back the pain and dizziness that were tearing at him. Dried blood on his arms and in his hair showed where he had been struck. No one had troubled to do anything about it while he was unconscious. "He appeared from nowhere. I do not know how. I had never seen him before. This is true."

"Oh," Redlaw said, "I believe you. Whether the Watchers will or not is something else. But you'll find out—one way or another—because here they come now."

A section out of the middle of the ship dropped flat, to make a wide door and a ramp. Five creatures came flapping out and dropped to the rock around Redlaw, staring from a distance at the boy.

Though they waddled on two legs when they were not flying, they did not look human. They were squat and powerful-looking, like the man who had died so quickly and uselessly. Even more so; they were hardly half the height of Org Rider or Redlaw. But the ways in which they differed from human were extreme.

They wore slick bright armor that looked as if it grew on them, black on their humped backs and red on their bellies; an Earthling would have thought of an insect's chitin, but there were no true insects for comparison in the boy's world. Their armored arms looked thick and muscular, and their wings were yellow-streaked leather—it looked frighteningly like tanned human skin to the boy—that stretched from their arms to their stubby legs. Their faces were beaked. They had no necks. Wide black flexible ears spread out from each side of their beaks. Their multiple eyes were greenish bulges, set on each side of the head, protruding out, behind the ears.

Their hands horrified the boy when he looked at them more closely. For fingers they had short, boneless bundles of what looked like squirming pink food-worms. These twisting worms were palping every seam of his tented wings, every strap of his flying gear.

They emitted a foul odor that struck him in a suffocating wave. It took his breath and stung his eyes, with a sour scent like death-weeds burning. Even Redlaw, who clearly had had opportunity to get used to it, was wrinkling his nose and showing distaste.

The creatures squeaked to each other and then paused, with big ears spread, as if expecting an answer. One of them was holding the needled guide that had been his mother's gift, the direction-showing trinket. The boy shouted: "That's mine! You have no right to rob me!"

"Easy, boy," Redlaw said tightly. "You're very close to being dead right now. Don't push it."

The Watchers squeaked to each other, then once again went through the routine of palping his wings, his garments, his waterskin, his firepot, knife, coils of rope, empty pots. Then they moved, like stumps rocking across the graveled rock, to where the dead man lay.

They did not touch him, perhaps from fear. But they squeaked again, this time peremptorily.

Redlaw scowled uneasily, and puckered his lips to whistle some sort of message. It was not much like the squeaks of the Watchers but it was as close as a human could come, Org Rider thought; and the Watchers seemed to understand it. They replied.

Redlaw nodded and turned to the boy. "I've told them what you say. Two of them think you are lying. One thinks you are too stupid to lie. The other two have not yet made up their minds."

The boy was silent, letting that information soak through his brain.

"You see," Redlaw said, "this strange-looking fellow here is very disconcerting to them." He squinted thoughtfully at the racked body that lay staring sightlessly at nothing. "In a way they know that what you say is true. In another way, they are not sure. Why did he come to you, boy? By accident? They'll never believe that."

"I know nothing more than what I've told you," said Org Rider stubbornly. "If I die for it."

"You just might," Redlaw observed mildly, then flinched as a blast of whistling came from the Watchers.

In quite a different tone he demanded: "Why don't you carry the Watchman's eye?"

"What is it?"

"The talisman of their service!" Redlaw touched a sort of medallion he wore around his own neck. "Like this, boy! To show you are their friend and servant, like me!"

"My people are not servants," the boy declared.

"Maybe that used to be true," Redlaw acknowledged. "Your people lived almost out of range. But times are changing. This fellow here is making them change. I think you will go away from here wearing an eye if you go away at all, Org Rider."

A burst of peremptory whistling, and two of the Watchers waddled toward the boy. The yellow coil around his neck tightened, half-strangling him, forcing him to his knees. The man warned: "Don't resist them, boy! It's your life."

The bitter reek set him sneezing even while he gasped for breath. A leather wing slapped him into silence, knocked him down. A hot, hard-armored body fell on him, and those pink, writhing fingers searched his body, prying into mouth and nostrils, anus and ears. The weight, the pain, the indignity, the lack of air all combined to fill the boy with a helpless fury. He could not cope with it, he could only rage inside himself, in pain and fear, until at last the weight came off him and the Watchers took their foul reek away, whistling disagreeably among themselves.

What they were doing was at that moment of no interest to the boy. He was preoccupied inside himself. He had never been so treated. He had never been so helpless, not even when the girl he was interested in had whispered to him that she had pledged to marry his brother, not even when he was tiny and his mother died. Not ever.

In pain and anger, Org Rider was conscious of one certainty. Whatever happened, he would see the Watchers paid for this.

At length Redlaw's voice boomed: "You can stand up, boy. I've made a deal for you."

He whistled sharply, and the yellow rope fell away from the boy's neck.

"You're to wear the Watchman's eye," Redlaw ordered. "It will show them everything you see. If you have any further contact with these funny-looking fellows, they want to know about it."

"What if I refuse?" the boy blazed.

Redlaw scowled. "I don't care what you do!" he shouted. "It's your life." He tapped the square-bladed knife at his waist. "Maybe I didn't tell you that they have a taste for human flesh."

The boy said staunchly, more staunchly than he felt, "I'll throw it away the minute you leave me."

"Tie it to a bubble-seed if you want," Redlaw grumbled. "If they know you do it they'll kill you. If they don't—it's your gamble, not mine."

He paused, looking toward the ship. From the gaping hatch a sixth, and larger, Watcher flapped down. It was darker than the others as well as bigger, its stubby wings almost black. It flew directly to Org Rider and caught him in a reeking hug, clasping something around his neck. "Careful now!" Redlaw shouted, but the boy had already taught himself not to resist. It lasted only a moment, then the large Watcher fell away.

The object was a heavy black globe, twice the size of the ball of Org Rider's thumb. A slick black cord of some sort of leather held it around his neck.

"Our captain asked me to tell you," Redlaw said, "that if you take it off he will do you the honor to eat you himself." He glanced over his shoulder. The captain of the Watchers had already returned to the ship; the others were flapping slowly after him, no longer appearing interested in the boy or in the body.

"Good-bye, Org Rider," the man said, almost reluctantly, as if he had more he wanted to say.

If he had, he did not say it. He turned away and entered the ship. The hatch closed. At once, a small curved shell tipped down outside the longer shell of the ship. Something whined. A gust of warm wind sent the boy rocking away across the gravel, sliding onto the moss.

The ship rose and slid whining away through the sky. Org Rider watched it until he was sure it was not coming back.

Then he set about gathering his lost gear. None of it was gone, or badly damaged, though it was scattered all over the rock and all of it stank of the death-weed reek of the Watchers.

As soon as he had it, he strapped his harness on, loaded himself with what he had to carry. His torn body was sending messages of pain from the crusted wounds in scalp and arms, and his stomach fought against the clinging reek of the Watchers. He put them out of his mind. He did not even look again at the dead creature who had appeared out of the bubble, or the glittering, broken toy that had brought him.

He turned his back on the campsite that had become so hateful to him, launched himself into the air, turned, and with great, painful strokes continued toward the distant peak of Knife-in-the-Sky. He did not look back.

FIVE

More than a hundred million miles away, far beyond the great broad curve of the horizon, the spinning wheel of the orbiter marched through its endless sweep.

On it Ben Pertin turned away from the monitor screen. The image it showed was as cracked and shattered as the small cube of the monitor itself. All it showed was a ghastly view of Ben's own dead, staring eye, peering emptily forever up into the gaudily clouded sky of Cuckoo.

Ben looked guiltily at the silvery girl he called Venus. He did not think even an alien like her would fail to see the emotions on his face, and he was not proud of those emotions. It was an unsettling thing to see oneself die. The Ben Pertin who had just had his skull smashed and his body blasted on the distant surface of Cuckoo was as much himself as this other body he was inhabiting here, in the orbiting wheel of the survey satellite.

"I'm sorry, Venus," he said.

"Sorry?" she fluted.

He said, "I guess that was a bust. Well, we've learned something from it. First and most important, next time we send somebody down we'd better arm him for bear. No more waiting till he asks for weapons, and trying to get them to him in a hurry."

"Concurred," said Venus. "Also editing appears necessary due to the gravity differential."

"Right. That one-percent gravity is tricky. I—*he* was sprawling all over the place." Ben Linc Pertin managed a smile. "I've never been transmitted in an edited form before," he said. "I don't know how well I like the idea."

"It does not hurt, Ben Linc."

"Of course not."

The silvery girl curled one wing and moved closer to him, studying him carefully. "It is established," she said in her chiming voice, "that my people and Scorpian robots, for example, experience less ego displacement in transmission than do you or, for example, the T'Worlie. Suggestion. One of us can go on the next transmission to the surface of Cuckoo."

"That's an idea. We'll keep it in mind," Ben Linc said. In his heart he knew he didn't want to do it that way. When the next transmission went, he would make it. There were two reasons, one practical, the other not. The practical reason was that, confusing and inexplicable though it was, Earthmen *looked* like the people who roamed this portion of the surface of Cuckoo. With editing, to stretch them out and reduce their musculature, they would look even more so; and the first job of communication with them, building up the store of language that the Pmal translators needed to work, was difficult enough even so. Asking one of these primitives to talk to a robot, or to a T'Worlie, or to a creature like the silvery girl was out of the question.

The other reason was the important one. Ben Linc Pertin had thought it over carefully and, all in all, he had no particular reason to want to go on living.

Ben Pertin was not the first human being in the history of the race to reach that conclusion. It happened often enough, for reasons far more trivial than his own. The thing that graveled Ben Pertin, almost more than the real pains and troubles that infested his head, was that his options were curiously circumscribed. With tachyon transmission, you could die and die and die . . . and still be alive. However many times Ben Pertin let the tachyon scanners memorize his body structure and translate an exact duplicate to the surface of Cuckoo, and however many times that duplicate met a gory death, he would still be alive in orbit. And he would still be hurting.

Other men in his position could fling their lives away in a reckless gamble against death, and find oblivion. He could not. The only gamble he could take was in a fixed game that he could not lose. It made a mockery of courage . . .

"I said," the silvery girl repeated tonelessly, "the T'Worlie Nammie is speaking to you."

"Oh, sorry." Ben Linc shook himself into attention and attempted a smile to the butterfly-winged being that hung in the air beside him. "Hi, Nammie. What's new?"

"Theory," the T'Worlie whistled. "FARLINK proposes explication of tachyon interference."

"Really?" Ben Linc was diverted from his internal pain. "What's that?"

"FARLINK identifies source of interference as exogenous to Cuckoo. Originates elsewhere. Trace-scanning, locates source as tight-beam signal generated in our own Galaxy. Vector closely equivalent to that of human sun, called Sol."

Pertin frowned blankly at the little bat-winged creature.

"I don't know about that," he muttered blankly. "It doesn't seem reasonable. After all, there is only one tachyon station on Earth capable of this distance and that's locked in to Sun One. Certainly it couldn't interfere with reception here—"

"FARLINK adds," shrilled the T'Worlie, fluttering up and down on its bright butterfly wings, "interfering signal can be identified as mating call of female of human species, beamed from your home world, called Earth, to self, here."

"Ridiculous!" Ben Linc exploded. "Nammie, that's insane! Why—"

He paused as a strong ammonia scent made him sneeze. "Wait a minute," he said. "What does that smell mean?"

"Query: *Smell*, Ben Linc?"

"The gaseous emission, which registers in my chemical-stimuli-detecting nerve sensors. I know you T'Worlie express emotions chemically."

"It is laughter," the T'Worlie shrilled triumphantly.

"Ah," said Ben Linc, satisfied at last. "Then that was a joke."

"Confirmation," the T'Worlie cried. "Successful one, query?"

"Pretty good. Sorry. You caught me off guard, or I would have laughed, too."

A whiff of etherlike sweetness expressed the T'Worlie analog of hurt. "Regret joke unsuccessful," Nammie piped sadly. "Not all of communication falsified for purposes of humor. True that FARLINK locates source as near Earth in vector, distance not confirmed. Extreme attenuation of signal renders distance estimate undependable."

"Strange," the silvery girl chimed. "Perhaps we should instruct FARLINK to assemble conjectural explanations of this phenomenon."

"You two go ahead," Ben Linc said. "I have to get some sleep."

"We will carry on while you are unconscious," the T'Worlie whistled. Neither he nor Venus slept themselves, and they were critical of human slumber. "Personal conjecture: Whatever explanations, they will complicate our mission."

And indeed they would, thought Ben Linc Pertin as he headed toward his living quarters, out at the higher-gravity shell of the satellite. There should be no random tachyonic transmissions coming in, especially from the Galaxy itself, where all known tachyon sources had been long since identified, located, and compensated for. It was one more irritation in a life that had become increasingly overweighted on the downbeat side.

"What I need," Ben Linc murmured to himself, "is a meal, a bath, and bed. In that order."

There would not be much pleasure there either, to be sure. The meal would be out of a dry-pack and into a microwave oven, and it would taste like it. With only three human beings on the wheel, and a dozen other races with different diets also aboard, there was not much space to waste on epicurean cookery. The bath would be not much better. The wheel was in free-fall, so the only way to bathe was through a sort of hosedown from jets inside a thing like a huge bottle, and it was all business, even after you learned how to get clean without inhaling several gallons of water. And the bed, of course, would be solitary.

Ben Pertin hurled himself out of the communications room, in a savage mood. He was the first human being to reach this point in space, tens of thousands of light-years outside the galactic spiral.

He was a conqueror, by any standards the history books could measure.

What he felt like was a victim.

Pertin's "bed" was a cocoon. It felt like a prison. Fed and bathed, he floated in it but could not sleep.

There was a sore place in his mind to which his consciousness always returned, like something caught in a tooth that the tongue cannot resist probing.

That something was himself. Another self: the Ben Pertin from which he had been copied. That Ben Pertin was forty thousand light-years away, in the artificial satellite that hung in the Orion gas cloud and was called Sun One. To Ben Linc Pertin, he seemed both farther, in the sense of being something unattainable, and closer than his own skin.

That other Ben Pertin—Ben Charles—would be enjoying the domestic pleasures of marriage, as well as an interesting and productive career with all the amenities Sun One offered its citizens. Lucky man, thought Ben Linc, hating him.

Yet that man too was himself. Only a couple of months earlier they had been not only identical but coincident. That was before Ben Linc had come here. He remembered perfectly well what had happened. He had got up that morning out of the arms of his new bride, kissed her good-bye, but only as any suburban commuter kisses his wife good-bye at the station, and entered into the tachyon-transmission chamber on Sun One.

There the tachyon beams had scanned his body, built up a pattern of atoms and molecules and transmitted that pattern on the super-speed waves of the tachyons, the particles whose *lower* limiting velocity is the speed of light. And that pattern had been received here, on the orbiting wheel that spun around the strange astronomical object called Cuckoo, forty thousand light-years away. And here it had been reconstructed, atom for atom and link for link.

So on Sun One, one Ben Pertin had walked out of the chamber, in no way different than he had gone in. He had done whatever he had had to do in the balance of that working day, and at the end of it returned again to Zara, his/their wife.

But on the wheel, another Ben Pertin had floated out of the receiving chamber and had felt the instant shock of knowing that he had lost the gamble. He was the one on the wheel, which he looked at with some curiosity but not much pleasure.

If you had put the two Ben Pertins side by side, no clue could have told you which was "original" and which "copy." Both were originals. Neither was a copy—except in some abstract, irrelevant sense that meant nothing when it was considered that each had a complete store of everything Ben Pertin had ever had, from DNA linkage to the last, most evanescent, half-gone memory of infancy.

There was only one real difference: one was *there*, the other was *here*. One was living a normal life on Sun One. The other was doing a necessary job, without joy, on the orbiter, which he would never leave.

That was the paradox of tachyon transmission: since it was only a pattern that was transmitted, the object being transmitted remained unchanged. No matter how often you left, you always stayed behind.

Ben Linc Pertin tossed angrily against the restraining web of his cocoon. That was the damned unfair part of it! his mind cried. Why couldn't Zara join him?

It would cost her nothing! Like him, one of her would walk out of the tachyon chamber on Sun One, the other would be here. They would be together. He would be no longer alone . . .

He groaned resentfully, angrily, petulantly.

The worst part of his resentment was that, in the end, it was directed against himself. It was his own fault that Zara was not here now. It was he who had persuaded her not to come with him at first, not until the orbiter had been made more comfortable. She had wanted to come. But she had listened to him, finally agreed, promised to come later.

Lying deceitful promise! Now she not only had not come, she would not even answer his tachyon messages. Not for weeks! First he had suggested she might come—then asked outright—finally pleaded. No answer.

When Ben Linc Pertin finally fell asleep, his dreams were harsh and punitive.

He woke in time for an all-hands review of the material gathered on Cuckoo.

In all, there were forty-one beings living on the orbiter at that moment, counting collective entities as a single creature. They fit nicely into a cylindrical chamber not much more than fifteen feet across, partly because most of them were rather smaller than human beings, mostly because in free-fall, placement was volumetric rather than planar. The sole T'Worlie acted as sort of general chairman for the meeting. Out of the bat's head perched on his butterflylike body he squeaked a short sentence, and all around the room the Pmal translators of the various beings rendered it into their own languages:

"I will display the information gathered so far on Cuckoo."

In the center of the chamber a stereostage display quickened into life. It showed a deep red sphere, floating in nothingness. There was no hint of size, because there was nothing nearby to compare it with; but the voice accompaniment to the display began to give the values for its physical characteristics, and all the Pmal translators faithfully relayed the information to their owners. Radius, slightly under one A.U. Mass, about equal to Sol. Density, very low—less than what in some Earthly laboratories was considered a hard vacuum. And yet the thing had a solid surface.

This was a familiar wonder to Ben Linc and the other beings, but they listened anyway. So much about Cuckoo was still unbelievable, even now. Not only did it have a surface, but on that surface creatures lived. The sphere grew and broke off a section, which expanded, turning slowly to present itself to each of the creatures in the room. It grew larger, and they were looking down on a landscape between two enormous mountains, and there was the strangest thing of all. Not only did creatures live there; they were creatures biologically close to some races of the Galaxy itself.

That was impossible.

Cuckoo had never been part of the Galaxy. Its present course was aimed arrow-straight at the Orion arm of the Galaxy. It had clearly been on that course for a very long time, and it had originated somewhere else, from some starcloud other than our own.

Ben Linc Pertin, listening and watching, realized something was touching him. He turned, and it was the woman of the Purchased People who was there as proxy for some water-breathing race from a star on the far side of the Galaxy, always invisible to Earth and never named by it. She said tonelessly, "While you were sleeping, Ben Linc Pertin, this came addressed to you with the last lot of supplies."

He nodded thanks—not to her, heaven knows; the imprisoned personality inside the skull neither expected thanks nor would know what to do with it; but to the distant mollusklike creature that owned her and operated through her body.

He was about to turn back to the hologram, when he realized what the woman had given him. It was a message cassette. There was no reason for anyone to send him a sealed cassette unless it was private; there was only one person who would want to send him a private message.

That person was Zara.

Suddenly Ben Linc wanted nothing so much as he wanted that meeting to end so that he could put that cassette in his private stereo-stage. But it wouldn't end, and he could not leave, now that the topic had turned to one of his own specialties, the meteorology of Cuckoo.

Long since the orbiter had dropped automatic weather stations all along its trail, and they had begun to show tentative patterns for the climatology and air-mass movements of the enormous sphere. It was only a beginning. In that immense ocean of air, the seeded stations sketched out only a line, but still Ben Linc had to summarize what was known.

As he finished, the FARLINK screens lit up with an overriding message:

"ATTENTION. PROGRESS REPORTED ON TACHYONIC INTERFERENCE. FOLLOWING SAMPLE ANALYZED."

The computer blanked out, then displayed shaped waves glowing on the screens, followed by endless strings of binary numbers, while bird chirps sounded in the speakers. "Conjecture," whispered the T'Worlie that hung beside him, a vinegary scent of excitement showing that its equivalent of adrenalin was flowing. "Analysis shows message!"

But Nammie's conjecture was wrong. The curved screens flashed again with the all-stations call indicating urgency, then lit up with the message in half a hundred scripts:

"LINGUISTIC ANALYSIS OF THIS SAMPLE NEGATIVE. TECHNICAL STUDIES, HOWEVER, IDENTIFY SIGNAL AS COMMUNICATION OF TUNING DATA FOR TACHYONIC REPLICATION TRANSMISSION. PRESUMPTION: SOME MATTER IS TO BE REPLICATED FROM CUCKOO TO SOURCE."

"Ben Linc," the silvery girl chimed in sudden comprehension, "do you understand what that means? It means we can replicate our own matter at the source of this transmission. We can send a copy of one of us! We can see where this signal comes from, by sending someone there who can report back, in a language we can understand!"

"If he lives long enough," Pertin grunted. He understood the importance of what was being said, but in his personal scale of values there was nothing quite so important as the cassette he had been clutching all this long while in his hand.

And at last he was able to excuse himself, hurl himself through the passages of the orbiter to his private cocoon, squirm in, seal, and then slip the cassette into the stereostage.

A silvery glitter of cloud sprang up before him and condensed into the face and form of Zara, his wife, looking meltingly beautiful and overpoweringly sad.

She gazed at him silently for a moment, as if unsure of what to say. And then—

"Dear Ben," she said, "I don't know how to tell you this. I'm sorry to answer you this way. The truth is, I just can't face you."

She paused, biting her lip.

"You see," she said, "I'm not going to come to join you. I know how disappointed you will feel—disappointed in me, because I promised. But I can't.

"I'm pregnant, dear," she said. She hesitated, and added, "You know that Ben and I—I mean, *you* and I wanted to have a child. We got permission before—before you left. Well, now we're going to, in about five months.

"So you see I can't come now. It would be one thing for you and me to live on the orbiter and to know that we'll die there. Being together would make all that worthwhile. But not our baby, Ben! I just can't do that.

"Of course, after the baby is born . . . if you still want me—

"Well, we'll talk about it then. I promise you, Ben, dear, I want to be with you. All of me wants to be with all of you! There must be a way!

"But for now I can't see what it is. I—" She hesitated, then said in a rush, "I'm going to stop now, Ben, because I'm going to have to cry. I do love you! Oh, God . . ."

And the image faded and was gone, leaving Ben Linc Pertin more alone than he had ever been.

SIX

Org Rider washed his torn garments in a rain pool and spread them on a rock to dry, but the death-weed stench of the Watchers was still in his nostrils. He was out of the storm area now, the rock where the stranger had been killed and where the Watchers had treated him with such contempt far out of sight in the rain clouds. He was cold, and his aches and pains were enormous; but he was alive and free. It was more than he expected.

He fished bare-handed in the pool for horny brown scuttling creatures and kindled a small fire to broil them. They were quite like pond-dwellers he knew from his own mountain, and when they were cooked they tasted as good. He was overpoweringly weary, but he forced himself to catch more of the scuttlers and prop them over the fire to smoke for his pack.

Then he wrapped himself in his wings, and was immediately asleep.

When he awoke the first thing he felt was the black weight of the Watchman's eye against his throat.

His fingers closed around it, and he was close to ripping it off and throwing it in the pool. But it could not harm him while he was wearing it, he thought, and he had not forgotten the warning about what would happen to him if he took it off.

He put it out of his mind. Warm and dry, he filled his waterskin, caught and broiled one more meal of scuttlers, then strapped on his gear and dove out from the hillside to catch the wind.

He was more cautious than ever now, turning unexpectedly to search the sky behind him to see what might be following. Nothing was, neither small Watcher nor ship carrying the repellent creatures who had marked him with the thing around his neck. He was not so far from the rocky, desolate upper reaches of Knife-in-the-Sky that orgs would be unexpected. But he saw nothing like an org . . .

Until it was almost too late.

The far thin scream drew his eyes aloft. A pale brown fleck was dropping out of that high gray haze, sliding down across the long blade of the summit.

It grew as it came toward him, taking shape and color. A slim, winged fish-form of bronze and silver: the body bronze, tapering to a narrow waist behind the stubby wings; the tail and wingtips shining silver. It was beautiful and terrible.

And it was coming toward him.

Org Rider woke out of the trance that held him and realized his danger. This was not a dream, it was a creature that could kill him in a single careless rake of claw or tooth. And he was exposed in the open air, where its speed and skill were far greater than his own.

He dived, flapping desperately, staring over his shoulder to watch it come. It grew so close that he could see the shape of the individual lapped triangular scales, bronze and silver. Its powerful legs unfolded, spreading cruel black talons that stretched toward him. He closed his own wings and arrowed toward a black crevice below, where two great boulders had tumbled together. Even in that moment the beauty of the org choked his throat. To own that power! It was worth the risk of his life . . .

But it seemed his life was already forfeit; his fall was slower than the org's dive. His weapons were useless; the bow hanging from his harness, the spear impotent in this free-fall. Even the knife would only annoy the org, it could not hope to prevail against that wide red mouth spiked with shining fangs.

On impulse, without thought, he snatched the cold hard sphere of the Watchman's eye from his throat. He did not even feel the bite of the thong as it broke free. He flung it into the org's great mouth.

Confused, the creature broke away, lost momentum, soared past and away. It went by with a roar of wind and a strange falling note in its scream. It recovered almost at once, wheeled and returned . . .

But by then Org Rider was deep in the crevice between the boulders.

For many hundreds of breaths the org stayed near the crevice, moaning to itself in anger and frustration, scrabbling at the rock with its claws. Its intelligence was too high to let it come in after him; in the cramped quarters, his spear was a more deadly weapon than its claws. And yet it did not leave.

Its nest had to be nearby. Org Rider knew that nothing else would keep the creature there so long. There was prey in plenty easier to find. Mere hunger did not account for its tenacity.

The thought was like a sniff of dream-fungus, intoxicating, dizzying, a little frightening. Where there was a nest there were eggs. Where there were eggs was one to steal.

Methodically Org Rider unstrapped his wings and lightened his pack. He dared not fly so close to the org's nest. He would have to move fast, and could carry nothing that he did not urgently need. His only way to reach the nest was to thread the maze of spaces between the boulders, where the org might not see him and would hesitate to attack. He wondered briefly what had become of the Watchman's eye. Had the org swallowed it? Was it broken, so that the Watchers might come angry and avenging at any time? He could not tell.

Leaving everything behind except for knife, compass, and a coil of rope, he breathed heavily to charge his muscles, rocked to test his footing, crouched and jumped. He was only in the open for a moment, in a long surge from shelter to shelter. The org was out of sight. He could hear its baffled screaming, but did not see it and assumed it therefore did not see him.

The journey to the top of the boulder pile was long and hard, and beyond it a naked cliff rose above the highest crevice, a dozen times his height.

Org Rider could leap that far; any of his people could. Yet it tested his strength, and he would be exposed while leaping, off balance and vulnerable when he landed. He peered out, saw no org, and leaped without allowing himself time to be afraid.

He soared upward, caught the slippery rock at the rim of the cliff and pulled himself up onto it.

Before him lay a level mile of flat, black rock. In the middle of it rose a rough pink cone.

The org's nest.

Although it was in view, no more than half a dozen long leaps away, it was not yet in reach. A great org hovered over it, scales gleaming in the high blue light of the peak. It had not seen him, but if he approached it would be a matter of moments only. It would never let him reach the nest.

He needed to think. He could not remain in the open for that purpose; he spotted a narrow crevice and scuttled across the flat rock, hugging the ground as inconspicuously as he could.

He drowsed and thought for a long time, and at the end of it the solution to the problem seemed as far away as when he began. It was maddening to have come so far and to fail now. Yet where was the choice? He could stay there for a long time hoping that the guardian org would wander away. That hope was foolish. Far more likely the other org would give up its fruitless sentry duty at the crevice between the boulders or below, and come up to join its mate; and then he would have two to avoid. With two adult orgs nearby it was no longer a question of being able to steal an egg, but of survival. Sooner or later they would find him. And that would be his death.

But as he crouched and drowsed his problem was being solved for him. He did not know it at first. He heard the raucous shrieks of the org, realized tardily that there were two orgs now crying out their rage and resentment, and heard with his mind what his subconscious had been listening to for long moments: a dull, distant *slam, slam, slam* unlike any other sound he had ever heard.

Cautiously Org Rider poked his head out of the crevice and was just in time to see a brilliant flare of golden light.

Dazzled and half-blinded by afterimages, he knew at once that again one of the small Watchers was nearby. Squinting to see what was happening, he saw a naked machine in the air, quartering away from him, emitting the slamming sounds and puffs of smoke. It was curiously ugly, like a stick figure of an org or a person; it had wings, but they did not move, were rigidly extended. And the two orgs were attacking it, screaming in fierce rage. Pieces were falling from it, broken bits that scattered down across the face of the mountain. One seemed to have the shape of a man, and it was from it that the yellow flare had come. But if it was a man he had forgotten his wings and did not know how to hand-soar to guide his landing; he tumbled end over end, disappearing from sight. The machine itself slammed crazily on.

There would never be a better chance.

Blind and caught unawares, Org Rider knew he had to act. He did not stop to think. He was out of the crevice and leaping for the pink cone in less than a breath.

Now was when he needed wings! But he did not have them, and so could only leap, guide himself with his hands, come down with his legs already under him, and leap again. He could hear the distant *slam-slam* of the machine, and the scream of the orgs, but he dared not leap high enough to see what they were doing, lest the orgs see what *he* was doing. At least the sounds were still distant—and he was already tumbling over the rim of the nest.

Built of stones plastered with org manure, it had a good, clean, dry odor, a little like the smell of parching grain. The shallow pink cup held a single egg.

Even in his mad haste, Org Rider took time to look at it, and to feel his heart catch at the sight. Smooth ball, mottled bronze and blue, it was too large for his arms to close around it. The surface felt warm and elastic, yielding slightly when he touched it. It had a friendly feel.

But the yells of the distant parents were not friendly. Gasping with his haste, Org Rider wound and knotted his rope to make a sling for the egg. Its weight was almost nothing, not much greater than his own. He slung it over his shoulder, scrambled to the rim of the nest, and leaped away.

A breeze had freshened, sliding down the mountain; it was at his back, and it made each leap half again as long as before. At the second leap he craned his neck around. Neither orgs nor the queer slamming machine were in sight. He could hear the distant angry baying, but it seemed less furious now. That was not advantageous; it meant the adult orgs were calming down, presumably having destroyed the machine. It would not be long before their fierce parental pugnacity drove them back to the guarding of the nest—and when they found it empty their rage would become incandescent, and all directed at him.

If they could find him.

His life depended wholly on making sure that they did not. He came to the edge of the tableland and leaped straight out, not even looking back.

It took all his skill to guide his descent into the best hiding place he could see. The bulk of the egg was a sail that unbalanced and tumbled him; the one free hand he had for air-swimming was not enough to make much difference. But in the slow, gentle gravity of his home falling could seldom be dangerous, although he was concerned about the safety of the egg. He hit hard when he hit. At the last moment he had thrown himself around to cushion the egg with his own body.

He was—for the moment, at least—safe.

And the egg was his!

He had landed in a vale of boulders, half buried in banks of gray, mossy stuff. A mountain stream purled and cascaded languidly down the slope. Org Rider had chosen the spot for that reason; as soon as he could regain the breath that had been smashed out of him and move he scratched and leaped his way to where a thin, bright ribbon of water leaped out from a sill of rock, and slid and scattered behind it.

What he had hoped for was there—a dry place behind the waterfall. It would do. The sound would drown out any noise he made, even from the keen hearing of the orgs. The spray would carry scent away. The curtain of lazily falling water would screen them from the vision of the parent orgs . . .

"Them."

With a start, Org Rider realized he was already thinking of the egg as if it were grown and mature. He let himself grin with wolfish joy; the worst part was done, that dream would yet come true!

But now he had work to do. Cautiously he ventured out and, one eye on the sky and both ears alert, tore armloads of moss out of the hidden sides of the boulders and carried them back to make a nest for his egg. When at last it lay safe, he took time to rock back on his haunches and inspect it.

It was there, real and true, and truly his. He studied every inch of its blue, bronze-speckled surface, so smooth and warm. It had no crack or flaw. It had not been harmed by the abduction; and, best of all, from its warmth and certain mysterious sounds of movement inside it, it showed every indication of being very near to its hatch time.

His heart filled to bursting with joy and pride, Org Rider sat back and rested for a long moment, planning what next to do.

As near as he could tell, he had come down somewhere near where the cartwheeling figure from the slamming machine had fallen, but a long, long way from where he had left his weapons and supplies. He was in a sort of great natural chimney, with steep rock on all sides. He drank his fill of water from the falls, and it was cold and sweet. He found nuts with queer paperlike shells growing nearby, and though they tasted faintly unripe and he did not want to eat very many of them, they stilled his hunger.

His first step was to try to get his cache.

He crept to the edge of the falls and looked up.

As soon as he was away from the gabble of the falling water, he heard the distant agonized screams of the orgs. They had learned of their loss now, it was clear. The long moaning bellows sounded of rage and the promise of revenge.

But they were far away, perhaps as far as the other edge of the tableland where they had built their nest.

There was a cluster of bee-trees nearby. Org Rider regretted that; the creatures who hived in the trees were dreadful enemies when aroused, and it was known that they had some chemical loathing of orgs. This would perhaps make the adult orgs approach only reluctantly, which was good. But what if they should smell out and attack his egg?

He could not guard against every contingency, he decided with a pang of worry and regret; it was the first time in his life that he had felt like a parent.

Reluctantly (but he had no choice!) he turned his back on the egg, and started out to hunt for better food, his cache, and a good way out of the giant chimney in which they lay.

The boy was gone a long time, longer than he planned, for at one point in his search the adult orgs came wheeling and shrieking overhead and he had to hastily bury himself in the undergrowth beneath a stand of flame-trees. Small creatures like red insects shared his hiding place with him and, although they did not sting, their crawling over his flesh was maddening; but he dared not leave. He lay motionless, half drowsing, for a long, long time, not even able to lift his head to see what was happening when the bellowing screams of the orgs were so close that it seemed certain they had spied him. They had not; of this he was sure, because he was still alive. When they were more distant he dozed again, and he dreamed a frightful dream in which his cherished egg hatched and turned into a black-winged Watcher that stank of death-weed and came at him with a throttling-noose that bore a Watchman's eye . . .

He woke trembling, and found the orgs were gone.

He had not located his cache or a way out, but there was food of a sort, succulent stalks from a purple bush that tasted sweet and meaty, some torpid red watersnakes that were dull enough to allow themselves to be caught. He returned to his waterfall feeling cheered and expectant, looking forward to seeing his egg, touching it, listening for its tiny slow heartbeat and the stirring sounds inside it.

With a wary eye out for the orgs he ducked under the lazy waterfall, and shouted with astonishment and anger.

The egg was there, luminously blue in the half-light under the falls. But a creature was crouching over it—a squat man-shape, black-haired and nearly naked, smashing at the egg with a red-smeared rock. The man looked up in fear and astonishment at Org Rider's yell.

And then, for almost the first time in his life, Org Rider felt the creeping terror of superstitious fear. He knew that man; it was the stranger from the small Watcher. He had seen him dead.

SEVEN

Some tens of thousands of light-years away from Cuckoo, on the inner curve of one of the spiral arms of the Galaxy toward which Cuckoo was hurtling, there was a G0-type star of no great intrinsic interest that had in orbit around it the planet Earth.

Earth and its dominant race, humans, were new among the galactic races. They were fully accepted as equal members. The streets of cities like Chicago and Peking were already used to the sight of darting Sheliaks, glittering Scorpian robots, and a hundred other races. Every major city had its own tachyon-transmission center, through which flowed the traffic of many worlds. All the buildings were alike in that they were huge, new, towering over the structures around them, filled with the enormous mass of hardware that met the power requirements of tachyon transmission. Each wore proudly the gauzy spiral that was the emblem of the Galaxy.

Across the tiled flooring of the great concourse of the tachyon center in Old Boston a young woman named Zara Gentry walked with grace and assurance. She had been there before. She had been almost everywhere, for Zara Gentry was a famous stereostage personality, known everywhere for her on-the-spot reportage of the Earth's doings to the Earth's people. She had been everywhere and tried almost everything. She had in fact been herself a volunteer for tachyon transport, several years before. One copy of her lived on Sun One. Another worked and lived in an orbiting station around the planet inhabited by the Boaty-Bits, in the constellation Boötes. Those two she knew of, for they were direct copies sent from Earth. There could well be more. The tachyon duplicates could themselves have been duplicated; there could be a hundred Zaras, or a thousand.

It was strange, Zara reflected, how little she knew about those other selves. They were so much herself, and yet so different; so close to her, and so impossibly far away.

The whole process of tachyon transport was loaded with trauma. She well remembered the quirky fears that had beset her when first she volunteered to be scanned, mapped, blueprinted, and recreated thousands of light-years away. It had been unbelievably scary; she had signed up and called to cancel her signature; signed again and with-drawn again. At the end it was only her conscience that made her go through with it, because by then there had been such an investment of time and training that she could not let it be wasted.

So she had walked into the tachyon-transmission chamber—

And, moments later, walked out again. And it seemed that nothing had happened at all.

She knew with one part of her mind that every atom in her body had been identified and placed in its exact coordinates, and that the blueprint that carried her minutest specifications was even then rac-ing, tachyon-borne, through the Galaxy toward Sun One.

The other part of her mind was wholly occupied with wondering where her date would take her that night for dinner; and that dichot-omy had been as frightening as the process itself.

It was frightening and unsettling to think that somewhere someone who was exactly, identically *you* was doing things you did not know about, might be terrified or joyous, angry or ill; might even be dead, and you would never know, except as you might hear of what had happened to some former acquaintance. It was frightening and unset-tling, but you could not go on being frightened and unsettled forever. So you put it out of your mind. You told yourself that you would keep in touch with your other selves. For a while you did. The two Zaras had exchanged tachyon communications for weeks and months, and then, less frequently, for a year or so. They had even spoken "face to face"—at least, in tachyon-borne stereostage communication.

But all that was now years in the past. When she had sent the second copy of herself to the Boötian planet she had tried to keep in touch with her, also, but that too had trailed off.

And now she was about to expose herself to the trauma for the third time.

Zara grinned to herself, dodging a Purchased Person who carried a hive of Boaty-Bits as she made her way to the elevators. I never learn, she thought good-humoredly.

But it was exciting, you had to admit. Especially this time! This copy of herself was going clear out of the Galaxy entirely, to the strange object identified as Lambda One and more familiarly called Cuckoo. With less fear than anticipation, she rose to the hundred and eighteenth floor and reported for her checkup interview.

The man in charge of her transport was old, tanned, lean, good-looking; he had bushy white eyebrows and a great sweep of white hair like high surf breaking over his forehead. He maintained dignified objectivity in what he said, but they had become friends over the last weeks. "Zara! It's nice to see you again. Well. Tomorrow you make the great leap forward. How do you feel about it?"

On her program Zara would have answered, *"That's a dumb question—look at the psych test profile in my folder. You know how I feel better than I do."* But she wasn't on her stereostage program; she said, "Well, a little scared. Otherwise fine." And she smiled.

"That's natural enough," he agreed absently, leafing through her folder. "Mmm. Yes." Something in the folder seemed to attract his interest; he stared at it thoughtfully for a long time. Then he raised his head and said again, "Mmm. Yes. Have you seen the legal officer?"

"Not yet," she confessed.

"Oh, but that's very important!" He was upset. "Please don't put it off any longer, Zara. The documents must be signed. You know that the copy of you will be, to all legal intents and purposes, yourself. It can sign your name as well as you can—no," he said, correcting himself ruefully, "not 'it.' 'She.' She is the same as you, Zara. She has an equal right to all your property and is equally obligated with you on the fulfillment of contracts, unless you state clearly *in advance* which of you shall have which property and responsibilities. You must file your statement of settlement at once!"

"I will," she promised. "I have done this before, you know."

"Yes, of course, but each time you create a copy you create the same problem." Then he relented, smiling. "To be sure," he said, "when you come right down to it, the problem is more legal than real. There isn't much chance you'll ever see your copy again, is there? And a half-interest in a condominium in Buzzard's Bay isn't going to mean much to the copy of you that's on Cuckoo. But there is always the chance some question could arise, and so you have to file that statement. Otherwise they won't accept you for transmission."

"Don't make that too tempting," said Zara, not wholly joking.

"Mmm," he said thoughtfully, and made a checkmark on her personality-profile card.

"I really do want to go," she said quickly. "Or at least, I'm going to."

He nodded. It was not an unfamiliar reaction; if the tachyon boards rejected applicants who were doubtful they would never send anyone at all. "I see you've been issued all the cassettes."

"*And* listened to them," she said.

"So you're about as well briefed on Cuckoo as you can get, I imagine. Do you have any questions?"

She said, "Well, those briefings are more distinguished for the questions they raise than the answers they give, aren't they? I mean, nobody seems to know exactly why the object's as funny as it is. The size is all wrong for the mass, and nobody seems to understand how come there are creatures so much like humans and Sheliaks and Boaty-Bits on it."

He grinned. "If we knew things like that, we wouldn't have to send people like you to find them out for you. That's why you're going." He hesitated, looking thoughtfully at her papers. "That in general, of course. But there seems to be some particular reason for you. Do you happen to know why you were requested by name?"

"No, I don't," she said. "And I've wondered. The request came from Sun One, I understand. I have a copy there. I suppose *she's* behind it. But we haven't been in touch lately, so I don't know any more than you do."

"We could send her a message, if you like. You could ask for yourself."

"Oh," Zara said, "actually I'm rather intrigued by the mystery. I'm not fearful about it. That other Zara can't have changed all that much in a couple of years. If she thinks it's a good idea for me to go to Cuckoo, then it probably is. I mean, after all, she is me." She hesitated, then said, "The only thing that does puzzle me is why she doesn't send a copy of herself."

The man said with visible pleasure, "You don't know how glad I am that you asked that. I can answer it. It puzzles me too, so I got her records. The other Zara, you'll be pleased to know, married a man named Ben Pertin. He's a copy too, of course; his identification is Ben Charles Pertin. And she expects to bear their first child in a couple of months. My impression is that she was anxious enough to go, but not with an unborn baby going along."

"Ah!" said Zara, vastly relieved. "I'm glad for her. What a nice thing to hear about yourself!"

"And you yourself, Mrs. Gentry? I see you're married. Are you planning a family?"

"Why, very likely," she said, "but I'm not pregnant now."

He nodded and closed her folder. "I think that takes care of all the loose ends," he said. "See the legal officer; get a few more shots. Then you'll be all ready to go."

"I'm ready now," Zara Gentry said.

When she was through with the legal officer—an episode which left her with the feeling she had signed a part of herself into slavery—she took the express elevator that dropped her into the physical-training rooms below ground. The *splat* of firearms told her the weapons class was in session. She tarried at the door, looking in at the range. The cassettes had been quite candid about the possibility of physical danger on Cuckoo. Several transportees had already experienced close calls, and two were dead. Besides the known predators—winged creatures like flying seals, armed savages, creatures like Sheliaks gone mad, and others—there were countless trillions of square miles of surface that had been only sketchily photomapped from orbit. What dangers they held no one could tell.

The other thing that troubled Zara in the conscious part of her mind was that the Zara who went to Cuckoo would not be, quite, the Zara Gentry who filled the stereostage receivers on Earth. Cuckoo's surface gravity was so preposterously slight that the first transportees had nearly destroyed themselves leaping about like jumping beans. Her physical attributes would therefore be slightly modified. They had promised that her appearance would not be changed, but she would be a little weaker, a little slower in reaction time. Even so, they said, she would have to watch herself; but it was thought that a little extra strength and speed might be helpful, against the known and unknown dangers of Cuckoo.

The class was ending, and one of the men caught sight of her, grinned, waved, checked his gun with the instructor, and came toward her. "Three bull's-eyes and twelve in the first circle," he said proudly, running a hand through his tousled mop of red hair. He was no taller than Zara, but weighed more than she did, and had muscles like steel and a great barrel chest. He would need a great deal of editing, she thought, leaning forward to be kissed. "I'm all set, dear," she said. "We're due for shots in half an hour, and that's the last."

"Great," her husband said, putting an arm around her. "Cuckoo, here come the Gentrys!"

EIGHT

Org Rider's knife was at the stranger's throat before he could check himself; but the man was so helpless, so battered, that even the white-hot rage that the threat to the egg brought boiling up in him wavered.

The man was both desperate and startled. He brought his arm up, less in a gesture of defense than as pure reflex. He was tremendously strong. His gesture brushed Org Rider's hand and knife away as if they belonged to a child. The violence of his own movement set him lurching against the sheet rock wall behind the waterfall; his head met rock, and he slumped to the ground, stunned.

Org Rider dropped to his knees and embraced the egg fearfully. Its bright curve showed no damage. He pressed an ear against its warm, pliant shell, and heard the even, faint throb of the young org's heart, along with a random skittering noise that, Org Rider knew, meant the creature was close to hatching.

Then he turned to the intruder.

The crawling sensation at his back was still there. There was no doubt of it, the man who lay before him was the man the Watchers had killed. Yet here he was, alive! Cut, scratched, battered—all of those things. But he was not dead, although he had been.

The boy studied him carefully. His clothing was not quite the same as before; the colors were different, and the puff-sleeved tunic he wore was torn and filthy. The bright metallic things on his arms seemed different, but they were the same class of things as he had worn before.

No doubt about it, it was the same man!

It dawned on the boy that this man was the figure he had seen falling from the slamming machine. Perhaps in that there was some sort of explanation; perhaps the machine laid eggs that hatched into identical creatures like this one. He had never heard of such a thing, but he had never heard of a dead man being alive again, either.

Remembering that the man in his previous life had spoken a few intelligible words, Org Rider said carefully, "Are you hungry?"

The man opened his eyes warily. There was no comprehension in them. He stroked the metallic clutter on his wrist with his other hand as if the effort were too much for him, and motioned the boy to speak again.

"Are you hungry?" Org Rider repeated. "I have some food."

The stranger shook his head, but his eyes fell on the pouch of food Org Rider had dropped. He stretched out his hand toward it.

"You are hungry, then," Org Rider said. Quickly he cut a slice of flesh from a watersnake and tried it. The taste was sweetish and good. He put a thin strip of it against the stranger's bearded lips. The man whimpered and sucked at it eagerly.

"It will be better cooked," the boy said, and offered some of the tender purple stalks. The stranger chewed at them while Org Rider whittled a drill, twirled it to light a fire, and set some of the snake meat to roast. It did not take long, and the fragrant scent of roasting meat was as tantalizing to Org Rider as to his guest; they shared the first half-cooked strips contentedly while the rest were cooking.

Then Org Rider forgot the stranger, because the egg made a sound like ripping cloth.

In the nest, the egg was rocking from the thrusts of some internal eruption. A dark split opened, and spread across the luminous, bronze-flecked blue shell.

Org Rider squatted next to the nest, watching in fascination, urgently needing to help but not knowing how. Inside the egg dull thumping sounds accompanied thrusts against the thick internal membrane. It ripped, and ripped again.

And through the rips the boy could see the dark, wet head of the baby org glistening.

The stranger limped over to watch him, then shrugged and went to the waterfall. He drank thirstily out of the shell of a seed cone, his eyes fixed on the boy and the hatching egg.

The org's head burst through the slit, slick and black. Almost at once it began to dry, changing to a pale, tawny color. The huge eyes opened, the pupils wide and black and mysterious, rimmed with luminous blue. It fixed its gaze at once on the boy.

Fascinated, Org Rider stared back. It seemed to be resting, and he thought its gaze was pleading with him. For what? He could not guess, until he saw that the infant org was laboring for breath and realized that the effort to tear through the membrane was exhausting for it. Org Rider seized the edge of the glistening membrane and hacked at it with his knife.

The rest of the great head came free. The short trunk uncoiled, opened, waved. The hatchling made a faint, strangled, mewing cry, and the odor of its breath came up around the boy, a warm, sharp scent like the nest it had come from, a little like the odor of parching grain. Org Rider leaned forward and wiped from the tip of the infant's trunk a thick brown clot. It was breathing more freely now.

Satisfied, the boy relaxed his attention and realized for the first time that, over the clash of the waterfall, the stranger was shouting at him. Org Rider turned, and saw the man, face savage with fear, pointing toward the sky.

The boy ran out from under the waterfall, and peered upward. Was it the org's parents, still hunting their offspring?

As soon as he was out from under the falls the sound he heard told him it was not: a roaring, familiar whine.

It was the mottled ship of the Watchers, or one so much like it that he could not tell the difference. It was flying low over the pool below the waterfall, its sound magnified by the black walls surrounding him to a shout of distant thunder.

In sudden dread the boy realized he had been seen.

He turned in indecision, peering back into the cave behind the torrent. Would they take the tiny org away from him? Worse—he remembered the warning about the Watchman's eye; and he had thrown it away. Would they punish him?

The gaunt stranger babbled fresh gibberish and pointed again at the sky, and the boy saw that a gray fleck had separated from the ship. The ship flew on, up over the rim of the canyon and away; the fleck dropped toward the pool and in a moment spread great wings and circled gently down toward where they were standing.

Org Rider pushed the stranger back inside the cave, and ran to his org. Its jaws free, it had ripped the luminous membrane off, except for a few rags that still clung stickily. Its tail unfolded, wet and delicate. Its whole body burst out in a rich cloud of that parched-grain fragrance.

It was twice the boy's length, now that its full dimensions had unfolded out of the egg, but it was still an infant, and drained of strength by the struggle to hatch. Its short trunk lifted to sniff him, then it slumped to the damp rock floor of the cave.

The boy began to rub it down with his wadded shirt, drying it and warming it, crooning to it a song he had learned from his mother. Sleepily the org arched its thin body to meet the strokes of his hand, and its voice seemed to echo the song.

It was out of the question to leave the org, and impossible to move it. It would be an hour or more before it could fly, and he could not carry it and his food, and still manage the tricky rocks around the falls. He stared desperately at the stranger, wondering how to get him to help.

And then beyond the stranger, in the luminous arch under the edge of the waterfall, another figure appeared.

It was not a Watcher; it was human, tall, with a fire-red beard and keen green eyes.

"Redlaw!" the boy gasped.

"Young Org Rider," acknowledged the giant, grinning through the flowing beard. "I see you've got your org after all!"

The giant reached out for the boy's hand. Org Rider drew back instinctively, fingers leaping toward his knife, before he decided the gesture was friendly and allowed Redlaw to shake hands with him. "I followed you here," the giant boomed. "Saw two adult orgs looking more frantic than usual, and wondered if you were what they were worrying about. I see you were!"

The boy grinned, then said, "Followed me? But how? I got rid of the Watchman's eye—"

The giant's laughter boomed. "Clever about it, too, weren't you? We located it—inside an org! And the Watchers aren't going to like it if they see you again, so I recommend you don't let them. So you'll have to get rid of that!" And his finger shot out to point at the compass on the boy's wrist.

"But that was my grandfather's!"

"No doubt. But where he got it, or someone before him, was from the Watchers. It's trade goods, and they can trace you by it as easily as by a Watchman's eye. Made for that purpose."

"But—but," the boy said, "but if that's so, why didn't they come down and kill me?"

"Thank me, boy!" the giant boomed. "I convinced them you'd been eaten by that org. When it came to explaining how one telltale was inside the org and the other here, I really rose to the occasion! Said it had been excreted. But you'll have to take it off before you leave this place, or they'll know you're still alive; org excrement doesn't move from place to place by itself." He peered wonderingly at the stranger, then at the egg. "What's all this?" he demanded.

"My org!" the boy said proudly. "Look, he's hungry!" And ignoring Redlaw for the moment, he ran to slice strips from the watersnake remnants and offer them to the hatchling. It devoured them delightedly, great eyes fixed on the boy. It had preened itself and its external surface was now nearly dry. Most of its body became a pale gold, shading into white along the tips of its tail and its wings. Not yet scaled like the adult orgs, it was covered with a fine velvet that felt like fur but was in fact soft fleshy protuberances that would turn into chitin.

Org Rider fetched water in a seed-cone cup and doled it out to the infant, which slobbered its gratitude and demanded more of the watersnake.

While the boy was tending his org, Redlaw had discovered the stranger. Org Rider paid no attention until the giant called his name.

"We've got to move on, boy," he said. "Take off that compass. Don't break it; they'll know it if you do that. Just leave it here."

"Move on where?" Org Rider asked. "My org shouldn't travel yet—"

"No choice, boy," Redlaw boomed. "This fellow you've got here, he's what the Watchers are looking for. Says his name's Ben Yale Pertin"—he pronounced the alien syllables carefully—"whatever that means. And he's from outside the sky."

"That's insane," Org Rider said seriously. "There's no such place."

Redlaw nodded somberly. "Time was I'd have agreed with you, but the Watchers think there is. They spotted him somehow. It's not you they're looking for right now; it's him. And if we want to keep him alive we've got to get him where they won't look."

"Where's that?" the boy demanded bitterly, slipping the compass off his wrist and gazing at it. "They know where this is. They must know you are here—"

"Not necessarily," the giant boomed, but his voice was thoughtful. "I crawled out through a disposal hatch when they weren't looking.

—But you're right about the telltale. When they miss me, they might come zeroing in on it. And I don't know, boy, if the three of us can travel fast enough to get out of range."

"*Four* of us!" The boy turned to look at the org, now sleeping. It stirred and crooned in its sleep, the pliant trunk lifting to sniff toward him. "There's Babe," he said. "I won't leave him."

"Is that his name, Babe?"

"It is now. And he can't travel yet."

"You mean he might travel right away from you, don't you?" The boy held his ground. "I'm not taking that chance!" he said.

"I don't know, boy," Redlaw said at last. "Our friend here probably can't travel very fast anyway. But we can't just stay here. They won't just kill us, boy, they'll eat us right up, you and me and your org. This other fellow might not be that lucky; they'll want him to talk."

"Talk about what?"

"Where he came from. Weapons. What he's up to, him and his friends that pop up all over." Redlaw looked ill at ease, then suddenly he grinned. "I know! We'll use their own telltale to confuse them! I can move fast enough by myself; I'll take it a good long way down Knife-in-the-Sky and drop it off a cliff somewhere. Let them hunt it there! They won't have any reason to come back here then, and this is as cozy a spot as we'll find." He was already standing, beginning to strap his wings on again. "Keep our friend fed, boy," he said. "Stay out of sight! I'll be back in a thousand breaths or so—if I'm lucky!"

It was more than a thousand breaths. It became fifteen hundred, then two thousand.

Org Rider could have stayed in the cave forever, delighted with watching his hatchling grow stronger every breath; but the growth required food, and he had at last to steal out from under the waterfall and forage. Redlaw had left his cleaver; the boy took it and bounded along the river course to the forest, where huge fat golden moths trailed gray wakes of sickly bittersweet fragrance. The boy despaired of catching one of them without exposing himself, but the trees themselves were sources of food; he leaped to hack off huge seed-cones with the cleaver, split them open and found them full of edible seeds as well as wriggling blind horned grubs, probably those of the moths.

When he came back to the cave behind the waterfall the stranger called Ben Yale Pertin was sleeping again. The boy regarded him with suspicion tinged with fear. He had not forgotten that he had seen this man die once; he did not understand how it was he was alive again, but something about it made the bristles at the back of his neck crawl.

But for the moment Babe was more important. The young org was awake and eager; he drained the water Org Rider brought him, then whimpered and crooned for more food. The grubs went into his capacious maw so fast that before the boy knew it they were gone, and he and his sleeping guest—or captive?—were still unfed. No matter. The humans could go hungry. A new-hatched org had to eat or die.

The stranger woke briefly, just long enough to drink some water, look around for food, find a few scraps, and return to sleep. Org Rider sat with his hatchling, singing softly to it as his mother had taught him. It pleased him immensely as it responded; but it woke again to be fed, and the scraps that were left were meager. Another thousand breaths later the boy decided he had to forage once more. At the waterfall's edge he paused uncertainly, then dived for the shelter of the vegetation.

At once he realized he was in danger. The sound of the waterfall had drowned the sound that came from the sky, the shrieks of the angry adult orgs.

He burrowed under a thick cluster of tough gray-green vines, inedible and useless to him but not, he discovered, to some tiny biting creatures that disputed possession with him. It was many hundreds of breaths before he dared venture out.

He stood beside the vines, listening. The shrieks of the orgs were far away again. But there was something else; a clattering sound, more like the sound of the stranger's slamming machine than anything else the boy could remember hearing, but not much like that, either.

Something appeared over the lip of the canyon and dropped toward him. As it hit the pebbly fringe of the pool it made the clattering racket, was followed by something else like it, and then by the huge form of Redlaw, dropping easily down toward the boy.

"Hurry!" the giant cried. "There are orgs up the slope, and a Watcher ship cruising around. Get this stuff inside!"

"But I've got to find food," the boy protested.

"You won't have a mouth to eat it with if we don't get under cover," the giant promised grimly. Org Rider could not argue with that clear wisdom. The clattering things turned out to be collections of queer metal shapes, held together by vines. He took one batch, Redlaw the other, and they managed to get them inside the cave.

Then, panting hard, the giant said proudly: "I found it, boy! I found his slamming machine! Couldn't carry the whole thing, it was banged up so bad. But I took all the loose pieces and brought them back."

From the floor the stranger who called himself Ben Yale Pertin propped himself on an elbow, staring at the collection of bits and pieces. He said something in his unintelligible speech and creakingly got to his feet. Dried blood was black on his nearly naked, half-starved body. Org Rider felt compassion for him, mingled with the dread and the anger. Not much of the anger was left, since Babe had not been harmed by the man's attempt to crack the egg and eat it, but there was still a vestigial core of dread.

The man shuffled over in his curious stumbling gait and thumbed through the hardware excitedly. He fumbled out a flat black oblong with a handle and touched it in some way that Org Rider did not understand; it sprang open, revealing queer-shaped shining things that looked like tools. With them the stranger began to assault the bangles he wore on his wrist. Org Rider involuntarily stepped back, remembering how those bangles the other stranger had seemed to speak to him with a voice of their own.

"Go to it, Ben Yale Pertin," Redlaw boomed lustily. "Fix up your gadgets for us! That's what I want you to do!"

"*What* is?" Org Rider demanded.

"Why, I want him to repair those trinkets of his. They're powerful things, boy! Weapons. Machines. I don't understand them, but I know they're something that's never been seen in the world before, and I want them."

"For what?"

"Ah," Redlaw boomed in delight, "for the big job that's ahead of us, son! This funny-looking fellow is our chance to deal with the Watchers. Nothing in the flatworld has a chance to break their power, certainly not your people. Not even me, and I know a good deal more than anyone else you've ever met about weapons and how to use them. But this lad has weapons I mean to have."

Org Rider stared at the scarecrow figure disbelievingly. "He's only a man," he said. "Not much of a man at that. Our potter was bigger than he is, and I beat the potter in fair fight."

"You won't beat this one, boy. He's stronger than you think."

"Stronger than the Watchers?"

"His weapons are! And he'll give them to us, I promise. Or—"

"Or what?" the boy asked, as Redlaw came to a halt.

After a moment the giant finished his thought somberly. "Or we'll kill him and take the weapons away from him," he said.

NINE

When they stepped out of the tachyon-transport chamber, Jon and Zara Gentry were greeted by a female creature, human in shape, but with great angel wings.

"Welcome to Ground Station One," she chimed in a voice like sweet bells. "My name is Valkyrie, and I am pleased to see the first representatives of Planet Earth arrive on the surface of Cuckoo."

Zara looked doubtfully at her husband, then reached out a hand, which Valkyrie took politely. Clearly she had been with human beings in some other environment before coming to Cuckoo; the custom of the handshake did not disturb her at all.

Beyond the silver girl floated a glittering cloud of Boaty-Bits that changed shape like a swarm of diamond bees. Over them, partly obscured by their dazzle, a T'Worlie swam gently in the air. From it came a shrill whistle that Zara's Pmal rendered into, "I identify you, Zara Doy."

Zara looked doubtfully at her husband, who shrugged. "I am Zara *Doy,*" she said. "Or was. This is my husband. In our custom I have taken his name and so I am called Zara Gentry now."

The T'Worlie did not respond. In the languid gravity of Cuckoo it did not need to exert itself to fly, it was enough for it to ripple its wings slowly. From it there came a sharp but not unpleasant odor like the pickle jar in a warm pantry.

Neither of the Gentrys had ever seen individual Boaty-Bits or T'Worlie in the flesh before—if "flesh" was the right word for the Boötians, whose chemistry was not very like organic. They had no difficulty in recognizing them from stereostage pictures, but nothing in the stereoviews had prepared them for the sense of whirling power in the Boaty-Bits, or the acrid odor of the T'Worlie. "My identity," it rapped metallically through the Pmal translator—how quickly, Zara thought, they became accustomed to listening to that rather than the shrill pipings of the T'Worlie itself—"can be described as one Nommie. We did have mutual identification on Sun One, but I perceive you are a different version."

"And I knew you, too," sang the silver girl sweetly. "Will you look around your new home?"

It was a confusing new home. From the inside it was hard to make out a plan, but Zara Gentry had seen stereostage images of it: spherical shells blown out of some transparent golden-hued material, linked together and outfitted to meet the needs of its inhabitants.

They had arrived in the largest of the bubbles, which was elevated above the others. From it Zara and her husband could look out to see a distant flat plain rimmed by mountains. They were themselves on a mountain, for she could see, just outside the bubble, rocky slopes that fell away endlessly. Turning to look out the other side, she saw a shelf of woodland, and then the rest of the mountain rising incredibly toward the sky. Its top was not in sight. Once, as they approached a Sheliak, the shapeless bun exuded a stalk that formed lips and made a sound their Pmal translators rendered as: "It gives joy to encounter you once more."

It was disconcerting to be recognized by creatures she had never seen. Flushing faintly, Zara repeated her apologies for being a different version; it was soon apparent to her that nearly all the beings here were direct copies from individuals on the artificial planetoid called Sun One, where all the races of the Galaxy had representatives to mediate and interpret their differing interests and goals.

After so long a voyage—tens of thousands of light-years—Zara felt she should rest and freshen up. But of course tachyon transport was not tiring. The patterns of their bodies, carried by faster-than-light-tachyon particles, had not "really" moved anywhere. When they were in transit they were only concepts, so to speak; they were patterns, and had no more sensation or thought than a schematic diagram. Nevertheless she was fatigued. It was culture shock, she thought: the impact of so much change in so short a time. She pleaded fatigue in any case and without demurrer—no two races of the Galaxy *really* understood each other's foibles—Valkyrie showed them their own quarters.

In the "morning" Zara woke to her first "day" on Cuckoo and incautiously got out of her cocoon as if she were still on Earth. Even edited, her muscles were disproportionate to Cuckoo's needs. She flew off the airbed as if it had exploded, catching her balance at the very last second necessary to keep from crashing into the wall.

The noise roused her husband, in the bunk over her own. He opened his eyes and said, "I dreamed we were on Cuckoo." He looked around and added, "I never had a dream turn out to be true before."

Zara was listening only politely; she had gone at once to their stereostage, to refresh her memory of the place to which they had exiled themselves for the rest of their lives.

Cuckoo was an enormous ball that hung in empty space, forty thousand light-years outside the fringing arms of the Galaxy.

It had been a puzzle for all the Galaxy's scientists since the cruising robot scoutships of the bat-winged T'Worlie first detected it. It was a perfect monad of polar opposites: huge and hard-crusted, yet with an average density not much above that of a total vacuum. Alone in space in the emptiness between galaxies, heading toward the Milky Way at a velocity that was a substantial fraction of c.

There was no such thing as day or night on the surface of Cuckoo. There was no external object bright enough to light it up. What light there was to see by came from bright phosphorescing clouds that hung in its thick air.

It was as big as a solar system, nearly two A.U. in diameter. Did it rotate? Yes, in a manner of speaking—to Zara the question was confusing, coming down to rotation relative to what? Relative to the nearest globular cluster of the Milky Way Galaxy, Cuckoo turned on its axis once every eight hundred-odd Earth days. To natives of Cuckoo the rotation would have been difficult to understand and of no importance at all; there was hardly ever anything to see from the flatlands where they lived, and even from the high mountains it was only occasionally that one might catch a glimpse of the Milky Way. It would take many generations to realize that that tipped spiral puddle of light rose on one horizon and, over the course of an Earthly year and more, slowly climbed to its zenith and disappeared below the western sky. The Milky Way was not the only thing that could be seen in the sky—M-31 in Andromeda was quite visible from the mountains, with a little luck, as were the Magellanic Clouds. But the Milky Way was by far the biggest and brightest object, occupying nearly half the sky when fully risen.

None of these were of any use in telling time. Ground Station One was on galactic arbitrary standard time, a metrication that cycled at some thirty Earth hours. Zara found out quickly that it was close enough to a terrestrial day to be recognizable, different enough to be disconcerting. It made their first "day" very long.

Even so, there was hardly time enough to do all they had to do. The briefings on Earth had been intriguing and even useful; but here in the face of the massive reality of Cuckoo, swelling all around them, both of the Gentrys had everything to learn. It was exhausting. They spent hours just in learning to deal with the flimsy gravity of Cuckoo. Even in their down-muscled edited forms, every step sent them flying at first. ("I know I've been trying to lose a few pounds," Jon grinned, "but this is ridiculous.") They had to learn to deal with the representatives of the nine other races in Ground Station One. T'Worlie, Sheliaks, Scorpians, and all, each had its own purposes and needs, and all had as much right to be there as Zara and Jon. More, thought Zara fairly; the galactic culture exchange had been going on for thousands of years before humanity had become aware of it.

And above all they had to learn what was on Cuckoo itself.

There existed, in the central workroom, a three-dimensional stereostage program which, on command, conjured up a slowly spinning image of the body itself. Much of it was blank even yet; the tachyar mapping, scanning the surface of Cuckoo from the orbiting space station, had not completed even one full revolution, and some ninety percent of the surface of Cuckoo had been mapped only at extremely long range or not at all. This did not at first appear. The basic sphere was wholly featureless to the naked eye, except for some blurry discolorations. The program could on command magnify any desired portion. Where the scan was complete, such portions showed seas, mountain ranges, forests, deserts—a thousand different kinds of locales. This one little area that they were now exploring Zara saw with dismay, was only an insignificant point on the globe—yet it stretched half the diameter of Europe! There was simply too much to map. Less detail showed on their globe than the maps of the Elizabethan admirals had showed of the interior of Africa.

Valkyrie was a patient teacher and even-tempered friend. Zara found herself relating to the silvery, winged creature as if she were another human. It was a shock to remind herself that this shape was probably nothing like Val's "real" body, in whatever hellishly inhospitable environment she had lived in on her home world. It had been edited into a more viable form, but Zara knew very well that the shape they saw was not her own.

Fortunately for mankind, most of the races of the Galaxy were close enough to oxygen-breathing, water-based mammals that the consensual common environment, when races met, was usually in an atmosphere human beings could endure. Even races like the Scorpians and the Sheliaks could tolerate it; it was not what they were used to, but it did not matter, since one was robot and the other so protean that it could survive anywhere. For those races to whom oxygen and water were poison, there were two alternatives. They could borrow the bodies of oxygen-tolerating species—humans were very popular for this—by inserting tachyon-coupled transponders into their brains. The bodies were then wholly controlled by the creatures who had taken them over. Zara had seen enough of such men and women, incurable criminals called Purchased People; they were common enough on Earth. The other alternative was to edit the "pattern" transported by the tachyons into some form that could stand air, water, and the temperature limits of the consensual environment. Val's people had chosen that way to go.

To be sure, editing was not uncommon for all races. Zara and Jon themselves were edited. Their physical strength was an actual handicap on Cuckoo, so their new bodies were altered in the physics and chemistry of the musculature to a sort of compromise between what was appropriate to Earth, and what was desirable on Cuckoo, where each of them weighed only a few pounds. At the same time their proportions had been altered, making them taller and thinner, and thus less strange for the natives of Cuckoo.

They were impatient to start to explore the surface of Cuckoo; it was what they were there for. Val apologized, in that voice like the tinkling of sweet bells: their equipment was not yet ready; their flying-belts had to be made to measure, and their new measurements had not been available. They would come soon, she promised. Meanwhile—

Jon halted her. "What I don't know," he said, "is what happened to the other parties that have gone out. I understand they didn't come back. I don't know why."

"They died," Val chimed sweetly.

Zara said, conscious of an unease in her body, "Well, we know that much. We don't know what happened, though." There was something working inside her that she could not quite analyze: a feeling that she should be more terrified—it was death they were talking about—and an opposite, intellectual understanding that said that this life they now had was only an appendage to a "real" life back on Earth, and its death would be only an episode that they "really" might not even ever know. It was fundamentally disturbing, a thought she could not quite deal with and could not wholly suppress.

But Val was answering their questions: "We have dispatched eight individuals to the surface direct from the orbiter, prior to the establishment of this station," she chimed. "All eight have terminated contact with the orbiter. Five are known to be dead. The other three are probably also dead. Six of them were human beings and two Sheliaks—actually," she corrected herself, "one was a human being and one a Sheliak, replicated respectively six and two times."

"Persistent human being," Jon commented grimly. "What killed him?—them?"

"It is not known in all cases," Val said brightly. "Please come." And she spread her great silvery wings and arrowed out of the smaller chamber where they had been talking, into the great central bubble. A Sirian eye was hovering just before a stereostage, patiently studying the scene it portrayed; it did not look around as they came in, but there was a strong sting of ozone in the air. Jon and Zara saw that there was a whole bank of stages beneath the transparent belt that gave them their view out onto the surface of Cuckoo, each with a different scene. Val touched the controls of an unused stage and it filled with a shining silver mist that swirled and hardened into an image of a mountain peak.

"This is the top of the mountain we are on," Val explained. "Observe the bare rocks. Look closely." She waved, and the peak shot nearer so that they could see details. Something that glowed with a faint, unpleasant bluish sheen was clinging to the rock. "That slime," she said, "appears to be a part of a growth process in the mountain. It is violently corrosive—whether through chemical or radioactive reactions we are not sure. The second Sheliak came in contact with it, and literally rotted to death while still in communication."

Zara shuddered. Jon said, "It sounds unpleasant."

Val turned her harshly beautiful stare on him. "It is probably quite undesirable for organic creatures," she agreed. "As you know, Sheliaks do not experience pain in the same way as most sentients. This one was able to describe what was happening until its central nervous system failed entirely. It was not attractive," she finished thoughtfully. Zara wonderingly thought that, whatever the metallic form Val wore as a convenience, in her native state she might well be as frail and delicate, even, as a human.

"There may have been other deaths due to the slime," Val went on. "The three of which we have certain knowledge, however—the other Sheliak and two of the men—were due to flying creatures." She manipulated the controls and displayed an org. "Also," she said, "there are intelligent machine-using creatures of which little is yet known. They may be involved. And, of course, there are analogs of many galactic races. There is no shortage of dangers on Cuckoo. We simply do not yet know what they all are."

Zara Gentry turned slowly, studying the bank of stages. The ones that were in use were panning slowly across a vista of woods, plains, and lakes. These were only monitors, through which the sentients present in Ground Station One could see what was being transmitted to the orbiter and on by tachyon transmission to receivers all through the Galaxy itself, where the images were being recorded and studied. As they watched, one of the stages emitted a harsh electronic squeal for attention. It stopped panning and locked onto something large and winged.

"Found something," Val chimed. "That is one of the flying creatures. The stage is programmed to follow it for a period of time, in case we wish to study it. If not, it will resume scanning shortly. And over there"—she pointed to the stage in front of the Sirian eye—"is what is perhaps the most severe real danger."

The stage revealed a vehicle. Zara asked in astonishment, "The machine users?"

"Yes," the silvery girl agreed. "Those creatures have no analog in the Galaxy. They apparently are evolved autochthons, and may be eligible for participation in the galactic councils. But much of the other life is not native."

She touched the controls again, and displayed a tree that seemed to be emitting a sort of shimmering fog.

Zara looked closer, and gasped in surprise: "Are they bees? No, wait—I think they're Boaty-Bits!"

"Yes," Val chimed. "Boötians. And here is a recording of Sheliaks." She displayed another image, then another and another. "Antarans. Canopan semilizards. Some of these are not to be found in this vicinity, but do exist in other areas of the surface of Cuckoo. Altogether twelve of the sentient races of the Galaxy have been logged on Cuckoo, including—"

And she touched the controls again, and showed the figure of a tall, spare woman in a breechclout, grinding grain.

"Human beings!" Zara Gentry cried. "How did they get here?"

"How did any of them get here?" the silvery girl chimed. "That is a primary mission for us, to find out how that happened. It is definitely established that, however it happened, it was a long time ago: there have been marked evolutionary changes. You can see some physical differences in your own race, no doubt. And some of the species— Canopans and Antarans in particular—have regressed to nonsentient forms, or at least to nonculture forms. The Boötians may retain hive intelligence, we're not sure because we have not been able to communicate and, as you know, they do not under normal circumstances employ artifacts. The only ones we are sure are nonregressed are your own race, and a small colony of Sheliaks, very far from here."

"It's crazy," Jon Gentry said wonderingly.

The silvery girl laughed like sleighbells. "Of course! Isn't that why the object has its name? It was one of your own people, I think, who originally called it 'Cuckoo.' "

Their tailored flying equipment arrived, designed and built on Sun One and transmitted via tachyon transport to them here. The Gentrys strapped it on awkwardly. None of the other sentients in Ground Station One could be of much help. Val had no need of the flying suits, having wings; as had the Sirian eye, the Scorpian robot, and the T'Worlie. In any case the anatomies were so different that the Sirian, for instance, simply could not understand the concept of a belt.

The first items they put on were wings. Zara stroked them between her fingers doubtfully; they were ridiculously tiny, proportionately smaller than the membranes that supported a flying squirrel. "They are only for directional control," Val chimed. "And perhaps for a gentle landing, if for any reason your drive should fail."

Zara was still doubtful. But her husband seemed to accept it, and she looked further. The drive unit itself strapped to their backs. It was simple pulse-jet. It was designed to require only water as "fuel"—not really fuel, but a working medium that would have to be replaced as it was discharged. The actual energy source was a compact star of radioisotopes, which released heat on command. The heat flash-boiled the water. The exploding gas for the jet was only steam. The water was carried in two kidney-shaped flasks of soft plastic strapped around their waists.

"They look very small," Zara said doubtfully.

"The first exploring parties had larger drive equipment," Val chimed. "Some had actual vessels, and they rode inside. It did not keep them alive."

Jon glanced at his wife, and said quickly: "Let's try them out!"

They worked beautifully. The hammering sound of the jet was unpleasantly close to the base of their skulls, but as they gained speed the sound seemed to dwindle behind them.

They returned to the bubble complex rather regretfully; it was a joyous thing to be able to swoop and circle around in the thick air of Cuckoo!

The rest of their equipment was simple enough. Personal necessities: soap, toothbrushes, toilet paper, changes of clothing. Food—not much of it, just iron rations, heavy on protein and vitamins but by no means tempting to the palate or calculated to satisfy a large appetite. "I'm not too crazy about living on that stuff for a week," Jon grunted.

"You need not," Val sang. "You eaters can subsist off the native flora and fauna well enough. You have eaten meals prepared from it already."

"That steak last night?" Zara exclaimed.

"Yes. And the salad. And the beverage. Of course, for myself I need only energy, and I get that from the power packs. But I understand there is as much of the biota here that is edible as there is on your own planet."

That left only one item. With some dismay, Zara hefted a gun that had been custom-built for her hand. "The lower trigger is a projectile," Valkyrie said. "The upper, a laser beam. Lower for food, upper to kill instantly."

"What about you?" Jon demanded.

Valkyrie tolled somberly, "I have my own weapons built in, Jon Gentry. We may need them to defend ourselves. Remember the first eight explorers!" She hung in the air, slowly fanning her wings, regarding them with her bright, silver eyes. "You will need to sleep again," she said. "And when you wake we will begin."

Zara's breath caught in her throat. "So soon?"

"So soon," Val echoed.

When her husband was already in his upper bunk, face turned away from the light and the gentle sounds of his breathing becoming deeper with sleep, Zara Gentry lingered in front of the tiny mirror, stroking her face with cream. She was not looking at herself; she was staring into space and had forgotten what she was doing.

What had made her forget was something she had remembered: that tens of thousands of light-years away, another Zara Gentry was, at that very hour, perhaps making her way through the crowded flyways of New York toward the stereostage studios for her regular nightly appearance. What would she be talking about, this other Zara? Her emotions when she volunteered for tachyon transport to Cuckoo? Her immense relief when she stepped out of the chamber and found she was still on Earth?

Zara absently wiped the cream from her face and rested her chin on her hands, framing the sentences in her mind that that other Zara Gentry would be using to open the broadcast: "Well, friends, I walked out of the chamber and back to Earth"—cut to long shot of the tachyon-transport building, pan of the chamber itself with Zara coming out of it—"and it was queer. Queasy. I don't know how to describe it. I knew that here *I* was. And yet at the same time I was somewhere else: out on the surface of Cuckoo, so far away that I can't even see it with the biggest telescope on Earth, *I* was entering a whole new existence."

She caught herself reaching for the stereostage recorder, to make a note for the opening of her next broadcast.

There would be no need for that. Not here, not ever here. Whatever else happened, this Zara Gentry was forever doomed to stay on Cuckoo. Oh, perhaps she could physically be carried to the orbiting station in a rocket, if she swung sufficient weight. But that was most unlikely, and that she would ever leave in any other way was impossible.

But after a moment she did reach for the stereostage recorder, and said into it: "For transmission to Zara Doy Gentry on Earth. Zara, dear—dear me!—myself, dear . . . I don't know how to address me! But I am here and well. Jon is also well, and in a few hours we are going to begin to explore the surface of Cuckoo. In my edited form I am tall and thin, just as I always wanted to be. And—dear distant self —I can tell you one other thing about me: I am afraid. Not panicky. Not crippled by it. But *scared.*"

Scared or not, she went on to give a bright, entertaining ten minute account of what had happened since arriving on Cuckoo.

It was the least a girl could do for herself, she reflected, settling gently into her cocoon. And it was oddly comforting, to know that she would in fact be on the stereostage worldwide one more time—herself, not just that other Zara Gentry. As she drifted toward sleep she thought that a girl in her position could use all the comfort she could get.

A hundred and twenty degrees of arc around the circumference of Cuckoo swung the orbiter called Cuckoo Station. It was a strange-looking thing, about the size of a three-story house in its main dimensions, but with extensions that shot spindly towers half a mile into space and trailed filmy sheets of laminated metal and plastic for more than three miles around it. It did not look as if it could survive the faintest summer breeze. This was correct. It could not. It never needed to, for Cuckoo Station had never known an atmosphere around it; it had been created in orbit, out of the tachyon-transport cell dropped by the doomship that had brought the Galaxy's eyes and ears to Cuckoo and then gone on with its dead or dying crew.

The sentients who inhabited Cuckoo Station were quite similar to those on Ground Station One. This was not surprising. Most of those on Ground Station One were duplicated copies from the orbiter itself. One individual who was not duplicated in the station on the surface of Cuckoo was the human being named Ben Linc Pertin. Partly this was because he had already been duplicated enough times on the surface of Cuckoo; he had watched himself die three ways so far, and suspected three others. Partly it was because, for the past few galactic days, he had reported himself sick.

He had felt sick. Sick and despairing. When he reported himself back for duty it was not because he really wanted to get back to his work on the orbiter, it was only because it, or anything, was better than lying in his cocoon and watching stale repeated dramas on the stereostage. He relieved his predecessor on the monitoring detail, a T'Worlie named Nlem, and sucking a bubble of coffee to wake himself up began to reel disinterestedly through the transmissions of the last few days to see if anything had happened.

Something had.

Pertin sat up so abruptly that his motion jerked the bulb of coffee out of his hand. Tfling, the Sirian eye who was conducting some incomprehensible research of its own in the monitor chamber, emitted a staccato ripping sound of electrical energy as it flung itself desperately away from the sprinkling drops of liquid. Pertin's Pmal rang with the harsh, angry accusation: "Danger! Water deleterious! Destructive! Hostile action perceived!"

"Sorry, sorry!" cried Pertin, trying to backtrack the stereo image and at the same time activate the emergency air-purification systems. He managed, but not without further anger from the Sirian—reasonably enough, Pertin knew, but he was not in a mood to be reasonable.

As soon as possible, he spun back to the beginning of the message he had sampled. It had been aimed at Earth, and of course intercepted routinely by the orbiter for information purposes. It was a personal message, and the face of the girl sending it was what had startled him.

It was Zara!

He listened to the whole message, then turned off the stereostage, sick again and dazed.

Zara *Gentry.*

And here on Cuckoo—only light-minutes away!—but with *Jon* Gentry. Her *husband.*

Automatically his hand reached out for the transmission switch: he keyed it to the ground station and croaked: "Orbiter calling, personal communication, please respond."

The station was on its toes—or on whatever passed for toes in a T'Worlie. The creature who responded almost instantly stared out at Ben Linc Pertin and said through its Pmal translator, "Greeting, Ben Linc. I have joy that you are well again."

"Thanks, Nlem," Pertin said. "I want to—"

"It is now Nloom," the T'Worlie said. "Nlem is the version still aboard the orbiter with you. Nleem is the other version transported here."

"Nloom, then, dammit! Please. I have to get a message through right away."

"For whom is your message?"

"For my w—" Ben Linc stopped and swallowed. "For Mrs. Zara Doy Gentry," he croaked. "May I please speak to her at once?"

The T'Worlie, who had known Ben Linc well enough in their time together on the orbiter, stared at him thoughtfully out of its five eyes. Finally the Pmal chirped, "It was my conjecture you would have a message for her."

"Sure I would. Can I speak to her?"

"Negative. She has left with a survey expedition. Their circuits are fully occupied with telemetry and necessary administrative communications at this time. There will however be a direct channel opening in"—the T'Worlie spun in the air to look at something out of Ben Linc's field of view, then spun back to look at him—"in about two and one-half hours. I can then relay a message if you wish."

"I'd rather talk to her direct, Nloom," Pertin pleaded. "Can you patch through then?"

"Affirmative," the T'Worlie chirped, "although that is of course contingent on Zara Doy Gentry's desire to use available time for that purpose." Nloom hung there silently for a moment, and added: "Friend Ben Linc, it is a different version here. She does not know you, I think. What shall I tell her of your desire to speak with her?"

Ben Linc hesitated.

Of course the T'Worlie was right. This Zara had come direct from Earth. If she had heard of his existence at all, it was only casually— someone her Sun One duplicate had met there and married. She did not know him; worse, she herself was married to another man.

What could he say to her?

To that question he had no answer at all.

"I don't know, Nloom," he said dismally. "I guess—I think you'd better forget I called. I have to think this over."

He flipped the switch that dissolved the compassionate stare of the T'Worlie into a silvery mist as the stereostage went blank. He sat there, staring into the empty tank of the stage, seeing nothing, feeling nothing but a wretched, suffocating, overwhelming ache of loss.

TEN

That other Ben Pertin, who distinguished himself with the middle name "Yale," sat, filthy, bruised, and exhausted, ravenously tearing with his teeth at the flesh of a kind of watersnake, watching the skinny boy croon at the monster called an org.

He was delighted that the other human—or near-human, the one called Redlaw—had found his equipment and brought it to him. But it was badly damaged. He had managed to repair the Pmal translator enough to get across a few words to the man and the boy; but it was not functioning well. All he had been able to understand was that they wanted to use him to fight some enemies—no doubt the ones they called "Watchers." Why, he did not know. He also did not know if he had any freedom of choice about fighting. Was he an ally or a draftee?

But at least he was alive, and he had not expected that much when the boy caught him trying to break open the egg. The first thing Ben Yale tried to get across through his Pmal translator was an apology for that. He hadn't known it was a pct. He had only been hungry. Whether the boy had understood or not, he could not tell. That lean, sharp Indian face was hard to read. The boy's words through the spottily functioning Pmal had hardly been reassuring: "Mine . . . not kill . . . punish!"

Now the org was perched on a rock, swaying uncertainly as it regarded the watersnake in Ben Yale's hands. Pertin half-turned, watching the creature over his shoulder. It was still learning to keep its balance. Wings not yet unfolded, it looked ridiculous, like a trunk-faced, big-eyed fish with bird legs.

The exploring trunk reached out toward him, and Ben Yale swore under his breath, tore off a shred of the watersnake and threw it to the org. The boy cried something, which the Pmal clucked over without producing a single intelligible word. From the curtain of spray that concealed the cave, the man named Redlaw said: "He says: 'Meat not spoiled? Not make org sick?' "

Ben Yale shook his head. "It doesn't taste very good, but it doesn't seem to be harming me any," he said. The giant muttered something to the boy, who stared appraisingly at Pertin then, reluctantly, bobbed his head.

"Can give more," the giant said generously through the Pmal.

"I think I'd rather have a drink," said Pertin, not caring whether the translator dealt with it or not. He pushed past the giant, under the shrouding waterfall and out toward the lake.

The boy followed him, carefully scanning the sky. Pertin was not flattered. He knew the boy's concern was not for his own safety, but for fear he might attract the attention of some predator or enemy to the rest of them. Particularly to the org.

Pertin knelt on the gravel beach and leaned forward on his spread hands to drink. The water was cold and good, but it gave him little pleasure.

His position, when he thought it over carefully, was not very happy. The giant, Redlaw, seemed to want to talk only about weapons, and he had none; they had not been in the junk the giant had carried from the wreckage of his ship. To the younger man, Org Rider, he appeared to be only an inconvenience, possibly useful to taste doubtful meat for the org but otherwise a net liability. Neither of them seemed in the least interested in Pertin's reason for being on their world. What he had tried to tell them of the great universe outside had been received by the giant without comment, and by Org Rider, apparently, without understanding; the Pmal translator, in its damaged condition, seemed to function sporadically with Redlaw and almost not at all with the boy.

Ben Yale Pertin stood up and looked around him. He did not even notice the beauty of the scene: the deep, rock-walled valley in which he stood, the lazy waterfall behind him, the cold little lake with water so deep it looked black, the strange, colorful vegetation. Back on the orbiter the prospect of exploring these jungles had seemed interesting, to the extent that anything could interest him more than his own misery and loss without his wife and future. Back on Sun One, when he and Zara had been together, it would have seemed enchanting, a marvelous holiday surrounded by beauty. And farther back still, on

Earth, before he had ever submitted to tachyon transmission, when there was still only one of him and that one knew nothing but cities and crowding, this whole scene would have seemed a total fantasy.

Now his eyes did not even register its color or its strangeness. It meant no more to him than a cell.

By the side of the lake Redlaw and the boy were building a fire, roasting nuts they had gathered, muttering to each other, too far away for the Pmal to pick up what they were saying and try to render it into English.

The giant stood up and walked easily toward Pertin. His green eyes were cold and judging. He put his fists on his hips as he stood before Pertin, towering over him nearly two feet, and spoke in his liquid tongue, rapidly and at length.

The Pmal, stammering to keep up, produced bursts of words: "Orgs gone. Watchers gone. Safe to travel. Can now find other slamming machine, other man like you. Can find killing things!"

Ben Yale Pertin kicked a pebble aimlessly into the water. "Travel?" he repeated. "You want me to come with you somewhere, to find another ship with weapons?"

Redlaw nodded vigorously, the bright beard bobbing. "Go soon now, two hundred breaths," the Pmal rattled. "Travel long, hard. You become ready."

Get ready? Pertin looked around him, almost smiling. What was there to do to get ready? What to pack, what to miss? He was ready to go anywhere anytime . . .

But for Ben Yale Pertin where was there to go?

They did not dare fly, and Org Rider's muscles began to ache very soon with the unaccustomed strain of trying to move at ground level, under the cover of the trees. The young org—he called it "Babe," lovingly—wanted desperately to fly, and so Org Rider's task was twice as hard, for sometimes he carried the fledgling, and sometimes kept up a running stream of talk with it, encouraging it to keep hopping along on its wobbly legs, cajoling it back when it attempted to fly. That was what his mother had taught him to do: talk to the infant org, let it know always that you were there. She swore that the orgs could even understand words after a while, like human children. And indeed Babe had already seemed to know what words like "fish" and "water" and "meat" meant.

That was more than the dumpy stranger knew. Org Rider did not like him. He had gotten over the superstitious fear he had felt when he first saw him bending over Babe's unhatched egg; he could not understand how this man could be alive when a dozen sleeps before he had seen him dead. But the puzzle had receded into the back of his mind and lost its power to instill fear. He wanted desperately to ask the man about it, but the clacking machine the stranger talked through did not seem to work well with him, and Redlaw only shrugged and reported that he could not understand what the man had said to him. "The words are clear enough," Redlaw rumbled. "He says it was *another* him. How can there be another? He could not say."

When they had eaten four times they decided to sleep. They were a good distance from the last place they had seen either orgs or Watchers, and so they risked building another fire and roasting more of the green nuts that hung all about them. The stranger moved a little way apart from them and flung himself on the ground; in a moment he began to snore.

Org Rider stroked Babe softly along the gently squirming length of its trunk and listened to what Redlaw was saying about the stranger: "He says he comes from another world. He knows arts the Watchers don't—arts that I think are strange and frightening to them. But he only speaks of these things, he does not have the weapons to prove them." Redlaw scowled at the fire.

"What is 'another world'?" Org Rider asked.

Redlaw shrugged morosely. "What he says about his world is not to be believed. He says it is not flat."

"Not flat? You mean mountainous?"

"No, not mountainous. Round. A little ball, so tiny that men have gone all the way around it."

"That is unlikely," Org Rider agreed.

"What is even more unlikely," continued Redlaw, glowering across the fire at the sleeping stranger, "is that he says our world is also curved like a ball. This is clearly false, but he holds to it. He says that in his place everything is very heavy. A man can't jump much above his own height. And he says, let me see—oh, yes. He says that although there are trees and plants and clouds on his world, they do not glow of their own light. None of them."

"How strange! It must be a gloomy place. How does one see?"

"There is one cloud," Redlaw said. "He does not call it a cloud, but it is in the sky, so what else could it be? It is so bright that its light hurts your eyes, and so high that it looks quite small."

"I have never seen such a thing," Org Rider declared. He peered around, squinting through the leaves at the great flank of Knife-in-the-Sky rising above them. "Where is the way to such a place? Over the mountain?"

"Farther! He says you climb beyond the rain clouds and beyond the flying rocks. He says you come up into a darkness where there is nothing at all. The darkness is bigger than you can imagine—so big that, when you begin to cross it, our flatworld shrinks to a point you can't even see, like an org flying out of sight toward the top of the mountain."

"It is all too strange for me," Org Rider said uneasily, stroking Babe. "If his world is so far away, how is it that he is just a man?"

"He does not know, he says," Redlaw growled. "He says he and his friends came here for learning, and that is one of the things they wish to learn: how it is that he is so like a human person, though from so far away."

"I wish him luck," Org Rider said dubiously. "I saw the machine he came in. It made a great noise in the sky, like slam-bang-bang, slam-bang-bang. But in spite of all the noise, it was slower than the orgs. They ripped the wings off it and tore it apart in the sky. And when the Watchers caught him, he died." Org Rider added thoughtfully, "I do not understand how that can be, either. But I have seen it, so it is so."

Redlaw rumbled impatiently, "It was another like him, he says. Part of that is nonsense, for he says it is him and says it isn't him, both.

"What is not nonsense," he added somberly, "is that he has something the Watchers fear. I must have that from him, or he must die."

They traveled fast and far, and the strain began to tell on all of them. Even Redlaw grew short-tempered and gaunt-faced. In some ways his was the most difficult job of all. Ben Yale Pertin was ill and injured; Org Rider had Babe to care for and often to carry; so it fell to Redlaw to keep alert for Watchers or for wild orgs, and there was never a moment while they were moving when he could relax. When they rested over the campfire they no longer talked amiably, they bickered. It troubled Org Rider that Redlaw seemed sometimes to believe in the stranger's insane stories, and other times to hate and mistrust him. He could not hear the stranger directly; whatever the machine was that Ben Yale Pertin had worn on his armbands, it seemed to respond only to the squeals and whistles of the language of the Watchers, not to normal human speech. So Org Rider could only communicate with him through Redlaw's imperfect understanding, and he was not sure how much was getting across.

Conscience made him try to correct some of the stranger's errors. "I have thought," he told Redlaw gravely, "and Ben Yale Pertin is wrong about our flatworld. It is not round; my mother has told me this. And also I understand how he looks so like us."

Redlaw scowled at him, then guffawed. When he was done laughing he chirped for a moment in the language of the Watchers, and then turned to Org Rider. "Ben Yale wishes to be enlightened, young one," he said, his tone half laughing but not pleasantly. "So do I. Please tell us what your mother has to contribute."

The boy said stubbornly, "It is truth, all people in my tribe agreed to that. The flatworld was made by the makers." He peered into the fire, trying to remember exactly. "My mother used to say they were terrible beings, taller than people, shining with light of their own. They sang death songs, and the songs themselves killed those who displeased them."

He waited for Redlaw to finish translating, chuckling, then went on: "My people came from seven eggs the makers had made, in a cave down under the bottom of the world. The eggs were guarded by seven keepers, but still they were stolen by the Watchers. The evil creatures first blinded the keepers with death-weed dust, and then stole the eggs for a feast. As our guest would have done with my org," he added carefully.

Redlaw choked, but managed to translate and receive a reply. "He apologizes again for that," he reported. "He says he was hungry and did not know better."

Org Rider nodded and went on: "The feast was to be at the top of the Watchman's tower, where the blinded keepers couldn't climb. But the makers were angry, when they found the keepers blinded and the eggs gone. They did not sing their death song, but they sang a special song for the wild orgs. And the orgs heard it as they flew over Knife-in-the-Sky.

"Seven wild orgs dived on the feast, and carried the seven eggs in different directions, all around Knife-in-the-Sky. The orgs hovered over the eggs, keeping them warm. When each egg hatched, it produced a boy and a girl, and two of every creature that is useful to a man.

"But the Watchers spied where the orgs had gone, all but one. One by one, they found the eggs just as they hatched, and devoured the hatchling creatures, and killed the orgs that guarded them.

"But the seventh org they did not kill. It flew out into the shadowworld, where Knife-in-the-Sky hides the flatworld from the Watchman's tower. Here the hatchlings escaped. Green grass sprouted from the droppings of the creatures. The boy baby and the girl baby were nursed by the wild org that had saved them. They grew to be man and woman, and the parents of all our people.

"And what has come to me," Org Rider ended gravely, "is that one of the other eggs did in fact get safely away, and its hatchlings were the parents of Ben Yale Pertin!"

The giant was laughing boisterously. Org Rider paused. "What's the matter?" he demanded.

"What rot, boy!" Redlaw boomed. "Ignorant superstition!"

Org Rider leaped to his feet. "It is as my mother told it to me, Redlaw."

"It is nonsense," Redlaw insisted. "You should spend a few sleeps with the Watchers some time! You'll learn the difference between savage myths and scientific truths. I do not know whose superstitions are worse, yours or Ben Yale Pertin's."

"And what then is truth, all-knowing Redlaw?" the boy demanded stiffly.

"Ah, that I don't know," the giant confessed. "Some of the things Ben Yale Pertin says may have truth in them somewhere. He says our world may be hollow—"

"Hollow!" Org Rider cried scornfully.

"Yes. Does that seem unlikely? It does to me, too, and yet I know there are levels below. The tower of the Watchman guards one of the gates to those levels. I have been there while a captive of the Watchers, and I know. And there is some truth in what your mother told you, too, I think. There are such things as keepers and Watchers, and that is where they live. But—"

He was silent for a time, staring across the fire at the sleeping stranger. Then he stood up.

"It is time to sleep," he said, his voice hardening. "We are wasting time."

Fast and low, they kept going. They were halfway around the thrust of Knife-in-the-Sky's largest bastion, carried by Redlaw's driving purpose. For Org Rider that purpose seemed strange and remote; he could understand Redlaw's burning hatred of the Watchers, who had enslaved him and threatened his life; but now that they were free of the Watchers it seemed pointless to seek revenge. The boy himself was most occupied with his young org, who seemed to grow in size and intelligence and maturity with every breath. When Org Rider woke, the infant org was hopping unsteadily toward him, seeking not food— he was capable of finding his own well enough by then—but affection, the ritual rubdown of his golden fur with a handful of moss. Org Rider did not neglect the duties his mother had described to him. In particular he talked to the org, crooningly, repetitiously, and was rewarded by having Babe repeat some of the words to him. It was not rote replaying, like an earthly parrot's; it was almost like the first experimental use of language of a human child. The org's delicate highpitched voice could repeat words like "food" when it was hungry, "sleep" when tired, and a dozen others. If it mangled some of the syllables, it nevertheless made itself clear.

Babe's stubby wings began to unfold as the boy groomed them. Tapered triangular fins, they had been molded invisibly into his sleek flanks. They looked almost too thick and too narrow to be useful in flight, but the boy's caressing fingers could feel their muscular power.

When they were fully spread, the boy determined to show Babe how they were used. He climbed a rock, the org hopping after him, spread his arms, and leaped toward another rock, flapping his arms.

To his surprise, Babe understood at once—so quickly that before Org Rider had reached his goal, Babe came sailing over him on quivering wings.

"Oh, good for you, Babe!" the boy shouted in delight. But the delight faded and congealed into panic, as the org kept going, past him and up, up over the sheltering leaves of the forest screen. He wheeled in a climbing spiral and screamed with a sound the boy had never heard him make.

Fear took the boy's breath. Was Babe calling to the wild orgs above the cliffs? He looked back to his companions for help; they were no help—Redlaw sound asleep under a mossy rock, Ben Yale Pertin watching apathetically. Without thinking, Org Rider crouched on the rock and kicked himself into the air, using every bit of strength in his legs and body, leaping a dozen times his own height, straight at the wheeling org.

Babe saw him and joyously dove to meet him. His young clumsiness made them collide, spinning the boy off balance, knocking the breath out of his body. But the org was up to the needs of the moment. Org Rider felt the velvet trunk coil around him protectingly. Strong and supple, it held him, then lifted him to the org's sleek-furred back, just above the rippling wings.

The boy lifted his voice in a shout of breathless triumph. "Now I am truly Org Rider!" he crowed. "Faster, Babe! Faster and higher!" And the org echoed in its piping voice:

"Faster, Babe! Faster, faster!"

Org Rider clung with his knees, fists locked in the golden fur, leaning against the wind of their flight. The throb of wings became a purr as Babe dived across the treetops, climbed again, then wheeled toward a clearing, so close above the yellow-bladed shrubs that the boy saw the giant moths fluttering about in terror. The boy's first alarm became a wild elation. His own wings had never lifted him with such speed or strength. He clapped the org's golden flank and called into the wind. "Good, Babe! Good!"

And the org piped happily, "Good Babe!" as it circled and dived again.

At last the boy found that Babe would respond to voice and tug of fists and kick of heels. Thoughtfully he drove the org back toward the clearing where the giant moths fluttered and cried, "Food, Babe! Eat! Get it!"

"Food Babe!" the org echoed, and showed its understanding by diving at one of the moths to catch it in spread talons. "Home Babe?" it piped questioningly, and Org Rider cried:

"Yes, Babe, home. We'll cook it and eat it. You've earned your food this time!"

They flew high, while the boy searched the flank of the mountain for the place where they had left Redlaw and Ben Yale Pertin. All the trees looked alike to him, all the clearings much the same. He caught a glimpse of something metallic, high above them on an outcropping, but it was not small enough to be Redlaw's cleaver or the stranger's peculiar instruments. He began to feel dismay . . . and then realized that Babe knew better than he; while he was searching the treetops for a clue, the org had already zeroed in on their campsite and was beating toward it powerfully.

When they landed, the boy got off his org's back and said solemnly, "Now I am truly Org Rider, and no longer a boy!"

Redlaw was staring at him with anger, and a touch of wry admiration. "No longer a boy, yes," he rumbled. "But a fool anyway! Listen, Org Rider who is no longer a boy. What do you hear?"

The boy, perplexed, stood still, ears tuned to—what? That distant shrill whistle?

"Do you hear it? Do you see it?" Redlaw demanded. "Over there— beyond the bee-tree. High in the sky!"

The boy looked. He had not heard it, because of the whistle of wind in his own ears, but now he heard it clearly and saw it, too, falling like a thick, blunt spear toward the slope of the mountain. A ship of the Watchers!

"If they saw you," Redlaw muttered, "then, man who is no longer a boy, you will not live to be a man very long."

The sputtering Pmal translator on Ben Yale Pertin's wrist caught only a few words, but they were enough to warn him. The Watchers were nearby.

Pertin did not need to hear more; he had encountered the Watchers. They were the ones who had shot his ship out of the sky of Cuckoo. In any other world they would have killed him, for he had fallen more than a mile to earth; but in Cuckoo's gentle surface gravitation he had survived with only cuts and bruises—and would have missed those if he had been less panicked and in better shape, he knew.

That kind of knowledge was no comfort. Pertin feared the Watchers. He feared dying, even when he welcomed it; there was no kind of future that looked good to him, unless by some miracle Zara should appear and offer a new life here. That was fantasy. Reality was that he would die here, and he would hate it.

The boy, ignoring the danger from the sky, was splitting and skinning the body of the golden-furred creature like a moth, spitting it over the fire. The yellow dust from the creature's fur gave Pertin a fit of sneezing, but soon the aroma of its roasting meat reconciled him to the dust. When it was done, Pertin humbly waited his turn. The best bits went to the org. Redlaw had second choice, then the boy; then last came Pertin. But there was still plenty left, and it was delicious.

By the time they had finished it had begun to rain, great fat slow drops that touched the fire and extinguished it. Gray clouds came dropping in to the tops of the trees.

The red haired giant bounded chuckling and happy over to him, and whistled something that the Pmal translator rendered as: "Rain clouds hide us from Watchers. Now we go! Youth has seen your ship, we find it, get weapons to kill Watchers!"

"But you have been to the wreckage of my ship," Pertin objected, perplexed. "I had no weapons—"

"Not *your* ship, *like-your* ship!" the Pmal crackled in response to the giant's squeals. Pertin gave up the struggle to understand; it did not matter. What mattered was that they were to move again. This time the boy did not need to worry about his org, who flew on above them, so he and the giant, unfettered, made very fast time. It was all Pertin could do to keep up with them. They kept on, and kept on. They did not stop even to eat, only paused long enough to pass Pertin a handful of hard roasted moss nuts, now cold and almost tasteless; he munched them as best he could while they went. Three times they ate, pausing once to drink at a vine-covered stream and to relieve their bowels and bladders, each time hurrying on.

Then Redlaw and the boy stopped and waited for Pertin to struggle up next to him.

"There!" the giant crowed. "Look! Beyond the gray moss, between the boulders. See! What do you see?"

Dizzy with weariness, Pertin tried to focus his eyes. See? Yes, there was something there, something bright that caught his eye.

The glint of light was metal. He glanced at the others, then joined them in a stumbling, hopping run up the gentle slope, and there, half-hidden by purple-flowered moss, was the wreck of a machine.

It was not his ship. It was smaller, and it clearly had been there for a long time. The moss had overgrown it completely, except for a few lengths of metal . . .

Metal? Yes, clearly it was metal. But there was something strange about it. The color was not clean silver, but stained with a watery bluish radiance that looked unfamiliar, but vaguely ominous.

He scurried toward it. It must have been a man-carrying machine. Perhaps the machine one of his predecessors had used? He could not say. It was so torn and broken that he could not be sure. He tore at the moss, peering inside through a dark opening rimmed with shattered crystal. A sharp scent stung his nostrils; it did not seem to be coming from the moss, but from the bluish coating on the metal itself. Now that he touched it, it felt slick, slippery, moist—quite repellent . . .

A shrill squeal came from behind him, and his Pmal rapped out: "Do not touch! Not! Not!"

Confused, he stood up. Redlaw and Org Rider were coming toward him, anger and concern on their faces. "What's the matter?"

They looked at him—curiously, they were looking mostly at his hands, it seemed—then at each other. They did not speak for a moment, then Redlaw spoke, his voice oddly gentle. "Clean hands," the Pmal translator rapped. "Wipe on moss. No! No! Do not touch metal!"

He shrugged, not understanding. He seemed to have got some of the blue slime on his fingers. Obediently, he bent and rubbed his hands on the soft gray moss—

What he was rubbing against, he suddenly realized with a heart-stopping sensation of nausea, had the shape and texture of a human skull.

He clawed at the moss. It was a skull! A whole skeleton, in fact, the flesh rotted away, but the bones still queerly dressed, under the moss, in the imperishable plastics of an explorer's jungle garb, red top, orange-and-yellow pants, great white gauntlets, and on the shrunken forearm bones the coils of translator, recorder, direction-finder, time-keeper, and all the other instruments one wore.

The giant spoke, and the Pmal chattered: "Danger! Do not touch stranger bones. Serious! Be warned!"

Pertin looked up at them, aware of the bluish radiance that clung to the bones, aware that it still befouled his fingers, in spite of his efforts to rub them clean.

"Danger?" he repeated dully. "Yes, I suppose so, if you say so. But you're wrong about one thing. They're not a stranger's bones. I know those bones very well, and I know the clothes they wear, too. I ought to. They're mine."

ELEVEN

Far away, around the great bulk of Cuckoo, the orbiter was preparing to transmit its observer along the tachyonic path FARLINK had charted to the source of the interfering transmission in the Galaxy. They still didn't know how far it was, exactly. Roughly in the direction of Earth, yes; but at extragalactic distances, that could mean anywhere from Rigel to Canopus, and farther than that in the line of flight from Cuckoo.

And that was only one of the things they didn't know. Would the transmitted duplicate find breathable air and bearable temperatures when he stepped out of the receiving box?—or sphere, or inflatable bag, or whatever sort of enclosure might contain an uninvited guest; it was only a convenience that made all the inter-communicating galactic races use essentially the same sort of equipment. This wild card might take any form.

"I'm glad I'm not going," Ben Linc Pertin announced gloomily. He didn't sound very glad, even to himself. He found precious little to be glad about these days, and could look forward to not much better.

Venus chimed softly, "I'm glad for you too, Ben Linc. It is less hazardous for an edited form like myself."

Ben Linc Pertin in quick confusion said, "Oh, I'm sorry. I was just thinking—"

"That it was dangerous and unsure, yes. But less so for me. In any event," she continued melodiously, "FARLINK has chosen me and I have consented."

He said miserably, "I am sorry, Venus. I've been into my own troubles and not thinking about yours. I know how it tears you up to send a self away to suffer or die somewhere; I've done it often enough."

The silvery girl looked at him curiously, "That is so, Ben Linc. But

—forgive me—in this form it is less painful. If I were in my own true form I would feel there was more to lose."

"Wait!" the sentient ape named Doc Chimp II said, holding up a hand that contained a banana. "There's a message—"

It was FARLINK. In the recreation room where they were awaiting Venus' time for the tachyon transmitter there were no screens, but the wall speakers sang out with the computer's electronic voice. "Stand by," it signaled, the Pmal of each being translating the words automatically into its own language.

"Wonder what that is," Doc Chimp mused. "Well, cheers!" And he held up his banana in a sort of toast. Pertin responded with his tumbler of Scotch and water, while the silvery girl sniffed at cloudlets of luminescent mist she sprayed out of an atomizer.

"Orders!" FARLINK's voice rapped out of the speakers. "The transmission of Replicate 4182, known as Venus, is canceled. A newly detected singularity in the incoming signals has altered the estimate of requirements. Stand by for assignment of replacement."

"Congratulations, Venus," Doc Chimp cried. "That's a last-minute reprieve, if I ever heard one. Wonder who they'll send instead? A Scorpian robot, maybe? A Sheliak. Or—"

"Orders," the wall speaker rasped. "The substitute for transmission is required to proceed at once to the tachyon station for replication. He is Replicate 5153, known as Ben Linc Pertin."

"Oh, no," Doc Chimp cried.

"Communication of regret," shrilled the T'Worlie, Nammie.

"I'm sorry, Ben Linc," the silvery girl whispered.

Pertin stood numb. He had not expected it; he did not know how to respond.

"Replicate 5153," FARLINK growled from the wall speakers. "There is the time pressure. Proceed at once for replication!"

"Come on, Ben Linc," Doc Chimp said as gently as he knew how, taking one arm. He gestured to Venus, who took the other; and the two of them walked the unresisting Ben Linc Pertin along the corridors to the radial shaft that led to the tachyon transmitter. He let them. He felt nothing . . .

Nothing while he was on his way to the transmitter.

Nothing (except the sudden surprising hard metal lips of Venus against his own, just before he went inside) as he entered the transmitter and stood through its silent omniscient scan.

Nothing when he looked around, and realized *he* was that *he* who had remained behind.

Nothing, even, while the chimp and the silvery girl escorted him back to the rec room, the T'Worlie fluttering behind. They chattered doubtfully among themselves, then pooled their small quotas of open-choice mass to buy him two more Scotches, doubles. He gulped them down, hardly tasting them. He was still *here,* as if nothing had happened. But he was also *there.*

And he could never come back.

Later, he was not sure how much later, there was a final message of progress from FARLINK. "The transmission," the speakers rasped, "has been successful. First acknowledgment of arrival has been received, along with samples for environmental analysis. Unfortunately they are not life-sustaining beyond a fairly short period."

There was a small silence before Doc Chimp said, "Well, anyway, Ben Linc, congratulations. You arrived."

"I arrived," Ben Linc agreed. "And I'm dead."

Down inside the atmosphere of Cuckoo, nearly two hundred million miles away from the orbiter on Cuckoo's far side, the exploring team was practicing its flying skills.

The expedition, so far, was going well. From their altitude, miles above Ground Station One, miles out from the slope of the enormous mountain, even Cuckoo looked almost small—not the great sweep of its surface, to be sure, but the detail on it: tiny trees, winking bright puddle of lake, silvery thread of river. In the air itself were the curious bright clouds that sailed around, each seeking its own level, seeming to drop spores of some bright seedlings; living glowing things that gave Cuckoo almost the only light it had, bar the glow of plants and animals on the surface itself.

They did not know these glowing clouds to be dangerous, but they gave them a wide berth. Anyway, there was plenty of room in the sky. Not only to travel to a destination, but for pleasure too: Valkyrie and Zara and the T'Worlie took joy in doing loops and barrel rolls, soaring far off from the little procession of Scorpian robot, Sirian eye, and husband, as they chugged sedately along, and returning. Zara found herself laughing from sheer physical joy. She weighed so little in

Cuckoo's air that it was almost irrelevant whether she was flying head up or down. She followed the piping, frolicking T'Worlie up in a loop. Below her the great sloping flank of the mountain seemed to subside into a plain; then the plain tipped and became a slope that rose in the other direction, then passed out of sight completely as she topped out her loop and began to come down.

In her earplug communicator her husband's voice, faintly amused and faintly annoyed, said, "If you three will please stop playing, we'd better stay close together. This is dangerous territory, you know."

Rebuked, Zara flopped over and flailed her wings to get her bearing. The T'Worlie, used to flight, darted back and hung before her, exuding an odor that she would come to recognize as an expression of rueful embarrassment, like a child caught in the cookie jar.

Zara burst out laughing. She caught sight of the silver girl, far overhead, soaring down toward them with great, strong strokes of her wings. Zara cried: "Come on, Val, Nleem! Race you back to the others!" And she let them signal agreement and start their powerful, effortless flight back toward the sober, sedate members of the party. Then she aimed herself headfirst toward the three distant dots, folded her wings except for a tiny web from wrists to hips for control, and activated her pulse-jet. *Thrump, thrump, thrump, thrump* . . . The radioisotopes poured heat into measured slugs of water, flashed them into steam, expanded them into the pulse-jet, and she arrowed toward the others at a hundred miles an hour, easily passing the gallant but small T'Worlie, catching up with Valkyrie and leaving her behind a thousand meters from the steady three. Stopping was the problem; she shut off the jet and tried to lose speed by zooming sharply up; but in Cuckoo's wan grip the loss to gravity was so small she found herself looping the loop again, involuntarily, before, laughing and dizzy, she was properly back in line with the rest of the party.

Her husband, in line ahead of her, turned to look disapprovingly at her over his shoulder. "About time you got here," he grumbled.

Zara, who was concentrating on an even, rippling flow of her wings, gave him a docile, absentminded smile. What a butterball he was, she thought dispassionately; even in the stretched-out edited version for Cuckoo, his round body and pipestem legs made him look like a stork. "The Scorpian's getting a strong signal from one of the transponders,"

Jon added. "That means we are getting near one of our objectives—probably a downed exploring ship."

"How nice," said Zara, winking at the silver girl. Valkyrie did not wink back; her copy of Earthly human anatomy was not close enough for that. But Zara could hear her chuckle.

Three places ahead of her in line, the Sirian eye raised itself out of the file on its crackling spread of electric forces, and turned to confront her. It had no expression, but she felt reproof in its stare. The tiny sphincter mouth, surrounded by the forty crablike little legs, worked convulsively. Zara could hear no sound from it; Sirians used sound for communication, but the frequencies were far higher than Man's; twenty thousand Hertz was a low basso-profundo note for them. But the Pmal caught it, and rapped reprovingly in her ear: "Estimate: Your use of jet propulsion has increased our risk. Assumption: Such sounds in past have attracted predators. Validation: Air-palping reveals several unidentified traces moving toward us at three hundred and seventeen degrees right ascension, minus six degrees declination."

"Confirmed," the Scorpian robot stated without passion. It did not speak aloud at all. Its talk circuits used radio waves, but the Pmals picked up and faithfully translated the messages.

Zara pressed her elbows into her sides and felt herself begin to drop. It was not what she had intended, but it was better than floundering around while she tried to adjust her telescopic visor. She caught a glimpse of something at the indicated position, realized she was falling farther behind and below the others than she wanted, flapped herself back into position and at last got a clear look at what the Sirian had reported.

There were three of them, all right. But of what? A body gleaming like metallic copper; stubby wings that shone silver at the tips; great claws that were coming out of concealment from under the creature's body, in anticipation of combat.

For a moment she knew terror; then she heard her husband's voice, triumphant and challenging. "Tallyho!" he shouted. "I've got 'em!"

And without waiting for comment from the others, he aimed himself and fired his jet.

From directly behind, Zara got the full roar of the pulse jet as it *thrumped* giant smoke rings of steam, thrusting him like an arrow toward the onrushing orgs. There was a confusion of argument that the Pmals were unable to handle, too many beings shouting at once. What they were saying was clear enough, but Jon Gentry was paying no attention. He had the taste of blood on his lips, and he was on the hunt.

The orgs were wise in warfare. They split up to come at this lone attacker from three directions at once. Against any of the beings that were their natural prey the strategy was winning. Against galactic weapons, it was hopeless.

Gentry's hours on the practice range on Earth had not been wasted. The first spark-hiss that marked the firing of his laser was a miss, but the second found a target. Three times then the cobalt-blue streak of his laser reached out to touch an org. Three times the creature hit screamed, the pain bellow of a tortured beast, and each time the scream was cut off as the blue ray burned through the scales and flesh in a split second. Each org flamed briefly, and then tumbled, slowly and ungracefully, toward the mountain flank far below.

Gentry stopped his pulse-jet, and returned to them by wing power alone. As he came close, Zara could hear that he was singing. He swooped past her, touching her with what might have been meant for a caress of affection, but sent her spinning. "Got 'em!" he shouted. "That was worth the whole trip, Zara!"

The silver girl chimed, "It is true that you killed those creatures. I do not think it was wise to attack single-handed, however."

And the Scorpian robot muttered through its Pmal, "Confirm statement as to organic creatures. Propose consequential probability. Premise: Organic creatures are not principal adversaries. Second premise: Use of laser weapons may be counterproductive at this time."

"Ah," Gentry grumbled, "you're just scared—" Illogically, Zara thought with resentment; all the Galaxy knew that Scorpians could not be frightened, since they were not only very nearly physically indestructible but had little emotional attachment to life.

Val chimed: "I suggest we proceed to our objective. I have a strong transponder trace from a point on the mountainside fifteen kilometers away, nearly in direction of flight. The characteristics are compatible with one of the previous exploration ships."

"Propose we go there now," the T'Worlie twittered through the translator.

"Why not?" Jon Gentry said with careless courage. "I think we've seen we can deal with any problems that come up."

Zara dropped back a few meters, looking at her husband curiously. This—what was that old word? machismo?—this kind of behavior was a side of her husband she had not known very well. Of course, on placid Earth there was little occasion for physical conflict, but even so she could hardly reconcile this fire-eyed warrior with the gentle, sedentary, rather dull man she had been married to for three years on Earth. She had never questioned his courage. It had simply never occurred to her to consider it. If she had been aware of it at all, she might have considered it as a sort of mildly disturbing anachronism, like an excess of body hair or a desire for raw meat.

She was jolted out of her reverie by a sudden gabble in the Pmals. Once again several members of the party were speaking at once. The first clear transmission was from Val, who cried: "I think we are in trouble!" And it was confirmed by the Sirian's little sphincter mouth, which squeaked its inaudible message that the Pmal translated as:

"Air palping now registers three new high-speed traces vectoring toward us. Correction. Four traces. Correction. Five, six, six-plus traces. Points of origin widely separated. Suggest indications are that technological intervention is now occurring."

T'Worlie and humans, plus Val, tried desperately to see what the Sirian and the Scorpian had detected. Even for Val, however, they were still out of sight, but Val confirmed the locating: "I have the trace," she agreed.

"Recommend seeking cover," chattered the Pmal, responding to the Scorpian's signal.

Jon Gentry snorted, "What, run away? Not me! We've got weapons, let's use them."

Val pealed, "That is countersurvival, Jon Gentry. I have an alternative proposal. You organics seek cover. The Scorpian and I will intercept the opponents."

"Concurring," the Scorpian chattered through the Pmal translator at once.

"No bloody chance!" Jon Gentry blazed. "I guess you don't know much about Earthmen! Fighting's nothing strange to us. We came here to carry an equal share of the load, and that includes fighting. We're not going to hide behind a bunch of aliens!"

"He *means,*" Zara cried quickly, "that we feel an obligation to help. And honestly, Val—don't you think we can take care of ourselves?"

The silvery girl swept her great wings up to a point over her head, thus dropping and turning toward Zara. "Doubt it very much," she pealed. "Please study the approaching objects at thirty-four degrees right ascension, eighteen degrees plus declination." She paused while Zara struggled with her telescopic visor.

"Oh," Zara said at last. "They are—formidable looking, aren't they?"

They were that. Blunt spearpoints, mottled in colors of bronze and gray that glinted with underlying metal, they were arrowing toward the galactic party at easily supersonic speeds. And those were only two. How many had the Scorpian reported? More than six—

These were not animals or primitives, these were complex and powerful technological devices, and, Zara thought with a sinking heart, no doubt armed accordingly.

"I accept offer," the T'Worlie chirped. "Come!" And Nleem stood on his head in the air, and swam his deceptively filmy wings to drive himself straight downward at the forest cover beneath them. There was a spatter of electrical fields, and he was followed by the Sirian eye.

Zara wailed nervously, "Please, Jon! Let's do what Val says." She tried to catch her husband's eye, but he was already higher than she, peering toward the approaching Watcher ships eagerly. "Please?" she coaxed.

"Not a chance!" he snapped. "You go ahead. I'm going to fight this out!"

"Then I'd better stay, too—"

"No way! Damned if you will, Zara! Now get out of the way—there's going to be a fight, and I don't want to have to worry about you getting hurt!"

Angry, and in a way she could not define, afraid—it was not physical fear, it was a deadly feeling that something was changing irrevocably in her life—Zara turned herself over in the air, aimed herself at the rapidly diminishing forms of the T'Worlie and the Sirian, and activated the pulse jet. *Thrump, thrump, thrump*—the acceleration was terrific. She was catching up on the Sirian and the T'Worlie very rapidly.

Her previous experience had made her cautious. She did not want to overshoot this time; that would mean driving herself into the ground below. She judged the distance as well as she could, allowed the jet to build up speed for a moment, then, when she gauged she had plenty of margin left, cut the pulse and arrowed down on inertia for a few seconds. Then she rotated herself and applied maximum counterthrust with the jet to slow her fall.

Zara had thought she had left herself a large margin on the side of caution. In fact, she had started the counterthrust far too late. It slowed her headlong drop—feebly, tardily; just enough so that when she struck the treetops she was traveling at something like thirty miles an hour.

She hit hard, broke off sprigs and branches, went flying through a tangle of vines that ripped at her skin and bruised her brutally. Every snag hurt her, but every snag slowed her a fraction, so that when she hit the soggy, mossy marsh under the trees she knocked herself unconscious, but lived.

When she came to, she was alone.

She could see very little of the sky, but in it were neither husband nor allies, nor even the enemy ships that had been attacking them; and of the T'Worlie and the Sirian eye that she had been trying to join there was no trace at all.

TWELVE

Org Rider involuntarily started to move forward to help Ben Yale Pertin, but Redlaw caught his arm.

"Don't touch him!" the giant rumbled. Then, looking past Org Rider to the stranger, he lowered his voice, adding, "There's nothing you can do for him now. That slime doesn't thrive on vegetation. But it eats flesh. He's done for."

"But—but it's only some kind of sap, or something like that. We can take him to the river, wash it off—"

"You're not hearing me, boy. There's no chance for him at all. If he's lucky, he'll be dead in five sleeps. If he's not, he'll linger on for a dozen. But there's no way to clean him now, and he's death to touch."

Pertin was staring at them, aware they were talking about him, suspicious of what they were saying. He asked a question that Org Rider could not understand, but Redlaw chirped some sort of answer in the whistling screech of the Watchers. Under his breath he said to the boy, "He said those bones were his. What can he mean by that?"

Org Rider said, with the uneasy fascination of horror, "It is as it was before, Redlaw. Remember? He died already, and was alive again. Can it be that he dies many times, and always lives again?"

"If he lives again after that blue slime gets through with him I'll be astonished," the giant rumbled. "Ah, well. We can't help him, but we can feed him. I'll get some food. You build a fire."

"What about the slamming machine?" the boy cried.

The giant nodded somberly. "There it is," he agreed. "We'll ask Ben Yale Pertin if there are weapons there. But if they've got that blue slime on them, it will be ticklish work to find a way to use them."

"Can't we clean them?"

"Ah, yes, clean them. But it's being sure they're clean that's the hard part. And one single drop of the blue murder, so tiny you might not even see it, is enough for death. If you see it anywhere on you, boy, on toe or finger, wherever, don't wait. If it's on a toe, lop off the foot! It's miserable work to do, but it's your life if you don't!"

Numbly, the boy nodded and turned to his org. "Don't go near him, Babe," he ordered. The soft trunk squirmed out to touch him reassuringly.

"What I think," ruminated Redlaw, staring at Ben Yale Pertin, who was scrabbling feverishly in the wreckage of the ship, "is that this slamming machine is not his but another's. Identical ships. Maybe identical people. I think it landed on the living peak of Knife-in-the-Sky, touched the slime, and then it came down here. Its occupant, perhaps another Ben Pertin, came out and touched the slime. When he did that, it was too late for him."

The boy nodded somberly. "Stay with this one, Redlaw," he said. "Perhaps you can help him. I will get food." But he felt as he left the org with a cautioning word and turned into the forest that there was no way for Redlaw to help Pertin, and that his real reason for going after food was that he could not bear to see him doomed thus to die. To die a third time! It was heavy enough to die once. What courage these people must have, to die again and again!

He was fortunate almost at once, scouring the wet black gravel along a sluggish stream, when something like a buried log humped itself and sprang free of the black muck. The boy caught his knife and waited; in a moment he was rewarded, as the "log" ripped suddenly down the back.

A wild-flower sweetness exploded into the air, and a delicate pink shape thrust and thrust, struggling to escape from its black prison. Org Rider paused, entranced. It was almost too beautiful to kill for food! But he thought of the dying Ben Yale Pertin, and of his org; he had no choice. He waited only until the lacelike wings of black-veined rose unfolded, and the new-hatched creature gripped the sides of the canoelike shell and slowly pulled itself free. Huge luminous eyes, glowing with the rosy red of live coals, gazed blankly at him and were just beginning to focus when he was upon it with his knife, stabbing the new life out of it.

When they had the skinned and gutted body of the butterfly-creature broiling over the low fire Redlaw had made, the giant took him aside. "Here is what I have secured," he said with satisfaction. "Look!" And he offered a handful of gleaming objects to the boy.

Org Rider recoiled. "They're from the slamming machine!" he cried.

"Yes," Redlaw agreed. "But I have taken them out myself, from the interior, where the blue slime did not penetrate. Ben Yale is angry at me because I would not let him touch them. I made him understand that the blue slime is very deadly to us—though I did not say that it was also deadly to him," he added in an undertone.

"What do they do?"

"This," Redlaw said proudly, "is a weapon." He held up a thing shaped like a short seed-cone, with a slim cylinder perched at an angle across its tip. "It is not what I had hoped for," he admitted. "It is only a laser. The Watchers, too, have lasers. Still, it is better than anything we have had so far!

"And this"—he held up a thing like tiny windows, set in an elastic band—"is for far-seeing. Look through it, Org Rider! You will see as far as you can travel in a dozen sleeps!"

The boy took it gingerly. The elastic part clasped his skull gently but firmly as he put it on; the transparent part hung just over his eyebrows. Squinting upward, he caught strange, bent glimpses of the treetops and clouds, like watersnakes seen through the turbulence of a rapid. He shook his head, and the visor popped into place in front of his eyes.

Suddenly the great broad yellow leaves of the tree over his head rushed in on him, and the bright golden clouds beyond swooped down almost within arm's length. Involuntarily he ducked and yelped.

Redlaw guffawed. "Startles you, doesn't it?" he rumbled. "But you'll see Watchers coming at you through that a hundred breaths before your bare eyes will see them, boy. And this thing—Ben Yale Pertin calls it an 'audio log,' whatever that is—listen!" And he touched a switch on it, and a voice—Ben's voice, the boy realized—began to speak from inside the box somewhere. Org Rider could not understand what it said, to be sure; it was in that strange gibberish tongue the stranger used. But it was his voice, beyond doubt.

Redlaw's mood changed. He dropped the audio log to the ground and stared at it angrily. "But there's not what I wanted," he muttered. "Not a weapon that the Watchers don't already have. Not anything that will let us destroy them!"

"Perhaps Ben Pertin does not have any such weapons," Org Rider offered.

"He has them! Or his people do. I'd kill him, if it would make him get them for me! But how can you kill a man who's dying already?" He stared at the squat man, then glanced past him at the woods. "Boy, what's the matter with your org?"

Tardily Org Rider realized that Babe had wandered away from his side, was on the hillside above the wrecked slamming machine. He leaped to his feet, tensely afraid that the org might somehow brush against the blue death. But it was not near the machine and showed no interest in it; something else was engaging its attention. It stood upthrust on its great talons, huge eyes staring frozen into the sky, soft pink trunk squirming upward as if to feel what the eyes were looking at.

"What is it?" Org Rider demanded sharply. The org did not even look at him. Then, reflected in the org's eye, he saw a peculiar flash of bright cobalt blue; startled, he looked upward through the leaf canopy and saw, lancing through the sky, a line of cobalt fire that winked, flashed again in a different place, and again. The light was so intense it almost blinded him, who had seen few bright sources of light in his life, but he was almost sure he saw several small dots around the bright blue beams. A distant rushing sound, as of cloth tearing, came to him from where those bright beams flashed, and was repeated again and again. "Lasers!" Redlaw bellowed.

Remembering what he wore, Org Rider jerked the far-seeing visor into place, and after a moment of frantic search, found the magnified images of what was going on above him. A man! A man wearing a queer tree-trunklike thing strapped to his back, pointing something like the weapon Redlaw had showed him; and around and below the man, falling like dead leaves through the sky, two, no three orgs. Dead. Slain by those bright blue bolts.

The boy peered under the glasses, trying to make sense of what he saw, and became aware that there were other dots in the sky. It took him time to find them through the visor, but there they were—four or five creatures, and what strange creatures they were! Something that looked like a winged woman made of silvery metal! A tiny creature with frail wings and a hideous five-eyed head! A thing that looked like an enormous eye, unsupported in the air! A machine, a—what? he could not say for sure, but something that looked like a single great cube of metal with metal attachments hanging from it—also floating unsupported in the air. And with them—

Org Rider caught his breath, steadied the glasses, and looked again. A woman. A girl. Dressed like Ben Yale Pertin, or the man who had beamed down the orgs; but a girl whose pale face and bright eyes were like no other woman he had ever seen.

He was jolted out of his reverie by Redlaw. "Give me that far-seer," the giant growled, snatching it off Org Rider's head. He bounded over to a clearing, jamming the visor onto his own head, upward. "Blood and death!" he muttered. "What are those things?" He lifted the lenses away from his eyes and stared blankly at the boy. "Did you see them?" he demanded. "Queer machine things! Animals like nothing I've ever seen!"

Org Rider nodded soberly. He heard the distant screams of orgs, wondered if they were the three he had seen killed, the sound reaching them so late because of distance; then realized it would not be that. These screams were nearer.

And suddenly the strange sights he had seen in the sky were driven from his mind, as he heard those wild screams repeated—less raucously, but closer at hand. He turned and shouted, "Babe! What are you doing?"

The young org turned the great eyes on him. The trunk was quivering and snaking out, now toward Org Rider, now toward the sky. The boy bounded over to the org, caught it around the neck. "Don't listen, Babe!" he begged, and the org mimicked, in his own voice:

"Listen . . . listen . . . listen!"

"Stay, Babe," he coaxed, stroking the org's quivering head. He could feel a roughness beneath the velvet, along the ridges over the great staring eyes, and knew that the hard bronze scales of maturity were beginning to form there. The shrieks of the wild orgs sounded again, nearer. "Please, Babe," he begged.

The org's trembling stopped. It froze, staring into the sky, and the boy saw what its huge eyes had discovered. Black and narrow and swift against the gray sky, two orgs were scudding over the treetops, up-mountain, away from where their fellows had just been slain. And the cries they were shrilling were of fear and warning.

The drives of his genes and chromosomes were too strong to resist.

Babe answered with a hoarse, hooting cry, and launched himself into the air.

The first stroke of his powerful wing struck Org Rider, sent him tumbling across the mossy rock. As the boy picked himself up, Babe paused for an instant high above him. "Please," it screamed, hoarsely mimicking the boy's own voice. "Please . . . please . . ."

And it spun in air and climbed into the bright sky to follow its wild kin.

Alone and desolate, Org Rider stood watching until Babe and the others were out of sight.

THIRTEEN

Ben Yale Pertin had not been fooled by the red-haired giant's pitiful attempts to dissemble. He had caught enough of the giant's meaning through the translator to know that, from Redlaw's point of view at least, the blue slime was very bad medicine indeed. Pertin was not unconcerned about that; he was very much concerned indeed, but he also was sure that these barbarians did not know much about medicine. His first concern was to find the medicpac in the wrecked exploration ship. He did not trouble to clean the slime off; not after the first trial at swabbing it from his skin had taught him something new about pain. But he swabbed it with anesthetizing and antiseptic creams from the pac, covered it with self-sealing bandages, and sterilized the whole area with a cleansing spray. The bone-deep itching began to fade away at once, and the pain went with it. Pertin then fished out the bottles of vitamin supplements and swallowed a week's ration at once, before he went looking for proper food. A self-heating can of beef stew, another self-heating can that produced instant black coffee, a can of peaches in thick syrup—he stopped eating at last not because he was no longer hungry, but because he began to think he would burst.

Then he turned his attention to less immediate problems, such as the two barbarians he was with. They seemed much taken with the laser gun, the telescopic visor, and the audio log; well, let the giant play. It did not matter. The log was only a spare. The weapon was more serious, in a way, but he had been at their mercy for—what? a week? a month? How could one tell in this place where there was never anything like day or night—and they had not killed him as yet. Giving them a weapon did not much change anything. Of course, if he had kept the weapon it would have put the odds in his favor, he mused. But he still had the bazooka—and his own superiority over these savages . . .

He watched incuriously while Org Rider stroked his hatchling and the giant puzzled over the hardware, idly stroking the bandages on arms and legs. They were beginning to tingle again, he realized. That was odd, but there was no real pain. The only necessary thing was to get himself in contact with civilization again, whereupon full medical treatment would of course be available.

Unfortunately, this exploring ship was of a different model from the one he himself had been shot down in, and although there was a radio he could not make it work. Batteries run down? That seemed unlikely; most electrical systems were powered by radioisotopes and *they* didn't run down. Broken in the crash? It didn't seem to be. He came to the conclusion that it was working, after all, but that the frequency on which it was operating was simply not monitored any longer. He explored further around the craft, and came across the prime audio log.

Maybe that would give him a clue, he reasoned, and thumbed it back to the beginning of the record, then turned it to PLAY.

"Ben Tom Pertin," it whispered in his earplug, "reporting on landing on surface of Cuckoo."

Hearing his own voice in his ears gave him a thrill of unexpected unease; that voice came from vocal cords that had once lodged in that blue-smeared skeleton before him. But the voice was going on:

"First entry into atmosphere accomplished without difficulty; initial target, anomalous formations on top of mountain. I landed without exiting vehicle because of low air pressure at this altitude. The top of the mountain was bare rock, which seemed to be covered by a blue lichen or greasy substance of some sort, which glowed quite brightly. I observed the anomalous formations and have photographed them for transmission. I do not understand them. There appears to be a sort of crater on top of this mountain, although it is clearly not volcanic; there is nothing resembling a lava flow, outgassing, or anything else indicating activity of that sort. On the lips of the crater are some truncated cones which have the appearance of artifacts . . ." There was a click, and then the voice resumed: "At this point the viewports of the vehicle began to cloud over and vision began to be impaired. I do not know the cause of this. Perhaps the temperature differential caused the ports to fog up. As I cannot leave the vehicle I am breaking off this section of the survey to attempt a landing at a lower altitude."

There was another click, and then the voice resumed—but a different, fearful, worried voice now: "Report two: Vision did not improve. I was forced to fly and land by radar, and landed with some difficulty. I do not know if the vehicle is damaged. The blue material appears to be covering the viewports. I will reconnoiter outside and return for further report." *Click* . . .

And then nothing, nothing but the faint distant hiss of the recorder coil unwinding under the scanner heads.

Ben Yale let it run through, hoping against hope for more word, but there was none. He had felt there would not be. He could write the rest of the story himself. He stood at the port of the vehicle, looking out at the great yellow-tipped trees, the marshland and moss, the distant river; and he could imagine that other he standing in that place and looking at that same view, and venturing out to explore this strange new world . . . and never noticing the blue slime that clung to him as he swabbed experimentally at the viewports, or steadied himself against the landing skids. And then, later, trying to get back to the vehicle and medicpacs, and not quite making it—as the skeleton outside attested . . .

Ben Yale scowled, rubbing absently at his bandages, refusing to entertain the unwanted thought that kept popping into his head: suppose this other Ben Pertin *had* used the medicpacs . . . and suppose modern galactic medicine had not been enough to stop the inroads of the blue slime?

Belatedly he became aware of the excitement outside. What were they rattling on about?

He activated the Pmal translator on his arm, and managed to catch a few words of what the giant was shouting. Something about aliens in the sky?

At once Ben Yale was all attention. Now he remembered hearing the *zzzzt* of laser weapons, and the screams of those creatures like the one the boy appeared to keep for a pet. Something was surely going on, but what?

He leaped to the top of the vehicle, staring toward the sky. Yes, there was something there, tantalizingly at the very limit of visibility, something that looked like tiny dots proceeding in file across the broad dome of Cuckoo's heaven. They were terribly near some of the bright clouds in Pertin's line of vision, which made the identification of them even harder; but surely that one creature that glinted so brilliantly had to be one of the winged girls?

And that other—was it human?

He stood benumbed until he heard the screams of wild orgs passing overhead, and remembered to scramble out of sight just in time; he did not want them dining off him! He saw the boy's org join them without any particular interest, and then realized something was going on overhead.

The straight line of beings had broken up. Several were dropping away, the others changing course. He heard the scream of high-speed transport, and caught the distant glint of some sort of air vehicles moving in toward the dissolving party of creatures.

Ben Yale pawed at his forehead, and realized the visors were gone; the red-haired giant had picked them up, now seemed to be playing with them. Pertin bounded over and grabbed for them.

To his surprise, the giant fled from him as if he were carrying the plague. "Give me my glasses!" Pertin roared, pursuing. The giant ripped off a series of words, which the Pmal struggled over and produced:

"Don't touch! Stay away! I'll kill!"

"They're mine!" Pertin said stubbornly, and, hesitantly, Redlaw glanced at the boy, shrugged, and slowly drew them off his head. He did not hand them directly to Ben Yale but dropped them on the ground and stepped quickly back.

Ben Yale didn't care; he snatched them up and put them on, staring blindly at the sky.

It was so hard to find anything at this extreme distance! Twice he caught a corner of one of the bright clouds, and the magnified light dazzled him. Then he found something, lost it, zeroed in on it again: It was a vessel, like the ones the giant had called "Watcher ships." It looked ugly and dangerous, and it was heading purposefully, at high speed, toward where the party had been sailing along. He sought the party again, without success until he heard the *thrump-thrump-thrump* of a steam rocket. Peering under the glasses, he saw the string of steam puffs the jet left behind, and managed to get the person who was using it in quick focus just a moment before it dropped out of sight.

Before *she* dropped out of sight.

Ben Yale stood transfixed, heedless of the shouts of the boy and the giant, staring emptily into the now empty sky where he had just seen, diving at breakneck speed for the jungle, the girl he had left behind him on Sun One and had thought never to see again in this life, Zara Doy.

FOURTEEN

When Zara realized that she was alone on this strange planet, she was not so much afraid as deeply resentful. She had not had the practice of much physical fear. There was little occasion for it on tamed, human-filled Earth. The sorts of fear she had learned to experience were fear of the unknown, as when she had volunteered for this assignment—and that was more excitement, really—and, from time to time, the fear, or the angry suspicion to be more exact, that some rival was going to damage her standing with the stereo audiences, or that she might fail to perform well in a broadcast.

It was only as time passed, and the only nearby sounds she heard were of stirrings and whisperings in the forest around her, that she began to understand that that quivering in her shoulders, that jumpy need to look around all 360 degrees at once, were the beginnings of terror.

She was not quite alone. She had her communications equipment. She could be in touch with the ground station in any moment. She might even hear, through the Pmal links, some message from her partners, if they happened to come close enough to her. But nothing came from the Pmal, and she drew her hand back a dozen times from the switch that would activate the long-range communicator. Something had drawn those enemy ships toward them—homing on their transmissions? She did not know, but until she felt more sure she was reluctant to risk bringing them back.

And she could hear them, could even catch glimpses from time to time that had to be them, circling low over the treetops, searching. Searching, she felt quite sure, for such of their quarry as had evaded them—like herself.

What had become of the others?

Of only one thing was she sure: in the fight, her side had not triumphed, because there the stranger ships were, roaming boldly around. Val and the Scorpian had lost that battle, and if they survived they too were in hiding.

She thought of her husband and wondered if he had taken part in that fight, or if, at the last moment, he had sheared off and followed after her. There were two conclusions from that thought. If he had followed her, he should be nearby. If he had not, he was probably dead.

At that moment she realized the drone of the enemy ships was no longer distant.

She crept to the edge of a fern-bordered lake, and peered cautiously upward. The drone grew louder, a ceaseless, crushing, killing sound, and something appeared over the trees.

It was long and tapered, with finlike wings at the end and mottled markings that were no doubt a form of camouflage. It poked into the little circle of sky over the lake like a thick, blunt spear.

Zara Gentry cautiously pulled back, away from the black water of the lake, into the doubtful shelter of the trees. The Watcher ship floated out over the lake, supporting itself easily with the thrust of its propulsive jets against the light gravity of Cuckoo. A thin golden snake was trailing below it, slipping around the treetops, dropping into the black water. A snooper device, Zara guessed, and tried to be perfectly still.

The mottled vessel slowed still more, the golden snake growing slack in the water, seeming to writhe around as it sought for something to strike at. Inch by inch Zara crept backward, until she was wholly covered by a patch of great vines with bright blue flowers. She was not alone in her hiding place. Insectlike beings were there too, and welcomed her presence enthusiastically as a source of nourishment.

The mottled ship dropped gently toward the beach and came to rest, not more than fifty yards away. A wide door fell open in its side, and became a gangplank.

Zara could not help gasping at what came out. T'Worlie, Sheliaks, Sirians, and all had not prepared her for the hideousness of the creatures in the ship. An armored, black-beaked, hunchbacked creature waddled out across the lowered platform, and flapped down to the beach on stubby yellow wings.

Zara wriggled uncomfortably, trying to dislodge the small blood-sucking insects, at the same time uneasily conscious of a bad smell of some sort. She could not identify it. Then it hit her hard, and she realized it came from the creature on the beach, a foul odor of carrion and decay, even at this distance strong enough almost to turn her stomach.

The creature flapped awkwardly into the air and flew around the perimeter of the lake. As it came near, Zara willed herself to look down without moving a muscle. The reek was overpowering as the creature flapped overhead.

After a moment she dared to look up, and saw that the Watcher had returned to the beach. It shrilled some sort of message at the unseen crew of the brown-mottled ship, and slowly other creatures like it began to come out of that dark doorway. One by one they vaulted across the flat platform and glided into a ragged line before the first Watcher.

All of them engaged in a colloquy of whistles and screeches, until another appeared from the ship and hopped and flew down to them with what looked like a bundle of white staves or lances, which he passed out to the others. The squat Watcher squealed something, and all of them rose hooting into the air.

Zara realized she was in desperate trouble. This was a search party, no doubt of it, and more likely than not she was the quarry. Perhaps they had seen her dive into the forests here, or perhaps she had given herself away in some other manner. No matter; they were intent on a trail, and at the end of it would be Zara Doy Gentry.

She whimpered in fear, trying to decide what to do. But her choices were so few! She could use the laser weapon at her belt, hoping to kill a few of the creatures before the others killed her. She could try to flee— but where? And with what hope of success? Or she could continue to cower in her bower of vines, being eaten by the tiny biting insects, until the creatures found her. None of those was very attractive . . .

And the time when she would be found did not seem very far away. One of the Watchers was circling near her. She heard it shriek, almost overhead, saw the bright-spotted blackness of its slick hard body, saw the flash of its bright yellow wings. She couldn't tell which way its huge, bulging greenish eyes were looking, but for a moment she thought it had seen her.

But then its great, pliant ears cupped toward something ahead.

Squealing, it flapped out of sight, brandishing the long white staff. She caught a gasp of relief—tainted with the creature's evil reek.

She lay quiet, while the hoots and squeals of the searchers kept up an insane dialogue all around her, until finally they seemed to concentrate and grow farther away.

She dared to peer out, and saw that, one by one, they were landing near their vessel again.

Had they given up the search? Were they about to get back in their ship and go away?

She crawled out of the tangle of vines to see. They were in a confused, bickering huddle around the ship. The golden snake that had hung into the water was wriggling insensately about, touching them and recoiling, darting into the underbrush and rushing blindly back. They ignored it. They seemed to reach a conclusion, then, and two of them leaped ponderously back onto the platform and disappeared into the ship.

In a moment they reappeared, bearing great platters of what looked like raw meat. They dropped in their ungainly way to the beach and began to parcel out bits of meat among their fellows.

It was lunchtime, Zara realized. Their table manners—pretending they chose to use a table, which they did not—were atrocious. They bickered and fought over the choicer pieces, throwing the bones and offal carelessly into the woods. The squealing noises did not stop while they ate; they clearly had no compunction about talking with their mouths full, if indeed so gross a species had compunctions about anything.

At that point it occurred to Zara that she had been thinking of them as animals.

But they were not animals. They used advanced technology. They communicated among themselves.

And if she could get a little closer to them, her Pmal translator might be able to pick up enough of their squeals and screeches to give her some idea of what those communications were.

With agonizing care she slipped along the margin of the lake, eyes firmly on the feeding Watchers, until she was less than a dozen yards from the sandy beach where they had landed. She activated the Pmal and held it to her ear. It would take time for it to store up enough speech to be able to deduce meanings, but it should only be a few minutes before it could at least identify and translate a few words . . .

Time was growing short. They were close to finished with their meal. A few of them had evidently been detailed to the task of cleaning up, and were picking up left-over pieces from the platform of the ship. One flapped and waddled toward her.

She became conscious of her exposed position, but the Watcher did not seem interested in exploring the undergrowth; it was only looking for a place to dump its tray of slop. It did so, and turned away.

For just a moment Zara felt a quick thrill of relief.

Then she saw what the slop consisted of.

"Dear God!" she moaned aloud, unable to prevent it.

The hooting and squealing rose like a barnyard chorus as the Watchers caught the sound. Hopping and flapping their great yellow wings, they came at her, and the golden snake that had hung from their ship writhed faster than any of them. Before she could move it had slipped across the beach with the sine-wave wriggle of a side-winder, touched her gently, then locked on her.

She was held so tightly she could hardly breathe, much less run.

But she hadn't been able to run before that, either—not run, and not even stand up. Not since she looked at the trash and offal the creature was throwing away, and saw one rounded bit of waste, melon-sized and bloody, roll languorously toward her and stop . . .

She knew then what these creatures had been feeding on, when she realized that she was looking at the severed head of her husband.

What followed was for Zara a desert of half-understood misery. The choking coils of the golden rope seemed to have intelligence of their own. They wrapped themselves around her, bearable when she was still, tightening cruelly with every move she made to work them off. She was tumbled face-down on the talc-white beach, with the hideous squeals and hoots of the Watchers piping querulously or menacingly all around her, their foul reek choking her nostrils. All that was merely painful. What was unbearable was the memory of the empty, staring eyes of her husband, fixed on eternity. If Zara had been asked to describe her marriage, back on Earth, she would have defended it as a convenient thing that cost little to maintain and, if it gave little in return, was no burden to her. His death had killed no part of herself. But it was pain nevertheless, pain to see this close person destroyed so

callously, used so demeaningly, to stuff the maws of these filthy creatures.

It was only then that Zara began to realize that she might share that
same fate herself.

She struggled to turn over, free her mouth from the choking sand.
The golden coils punished her, but gasping and panting she managed
to flop onto her side. "Please!" she begged. "I mean you no harm! Give
me the metal thing there—it will let us talk to each other." And she
tried, at terrible cost of agony as the golden coils remorselessly fought
her movements, to point to the Pmal translator, whispering away to
itself on the sand.

The hideous mask-faces thrust themselves at her, hooting and
whistling. She knew what they said was a language of a sort, and it was
frustration to know that a few yards away the Pmal was surely translating faithfully every word—but inaudibly, because she had set the
sound so low lest they hear her. "Please!" she screamed as one came
near her with a great curved cleaver. It paused, seeming to enjoy her
fear. The gabbling whistles and honks burst like laughter around her.

She closed her eyes, and tried to remember her brief training. What
were her options? Talking was useless, with the Pmal gone. Her laser
weapon was long since taken away. They had left her only the other
instruments strapped to her arms—medicpac, chronometer, communicator . . .

Communicator!

She took a deep breath, and forced herself to relax. She lay still as
stone for long seconds, remembering where the transmit switch was
on the communicator, feeling with her body-image senses where her
hands were, where the switch was. There would not be much freedom
of action.

Then she flung herself onto her back, forcing her hands together,
clawing with the fingers of her right hand for the forearm of her left.

The golden coils responded at once by tightening so violently that
she thought she felt bones snap; but she had touched the switch!
"Help!" she screamed. "This is Zara Doy Gentry calling! Help! Please!
Help me!"

A hundred-odd degrees of arc around the great bulk of Cuckoo,
Ben Linc Pertin was talking to himself.

On his watch duty, desolately killing time while trying to solve the insoluble problem of what to do about the wife that was not his, he had observed a curiosity. The comm frequency that had been abandoned because no transmissions had been received and its owner, that other avatar of himself named Ben Tom Pertin, was presumed dead had suddenly come back to life.

When he first beheld himself he was aghast. This devastated face, harried, sick, and in pain, was himself! "Ben Tom!" he cried. "What's the matter?"

The face in the stereostage reflected annoyance. "I'm not Ben Tom," it snapped. "And I don't know what you mean. What's the matter with you people? I've been trying to call for—I don't know, days!"

"Sorry," Ben Linc Pertin said. "But what do you mean, you're not Ben Tom?"

The ravaged face split in an unpleasant smile. "Glad I'm not," he said. "Ben Tom's dead. I'm Ben Yale. Remember? When you—we—volunteered for the sixth time? Well, that's me. I lost my ship, nearly lost my life. I've been through hell, Ben Linc! But at that I'm better off than Ben Tom, because his bones are twenty feet away from me. This is his ship I've found; my own was destroyed, communications and all."

"You look as if you've been through hell," Ben Linc agreed fervently. "What are those bandages?"

The walking skeleton looked incuriously at his arms and legs. "Oh, some sort of fungus, I think," he said. "It itches. It hurts, too, but I've blocked it with stuff from the medicpac. But I imagine I'll need treatment."

"Well," cried Ben Linc, finding something to be cheerful about for the first time in some days, "I think I've got good news for you, Ben Yale. We've just been transmitting a new model exploring ship to the ground station. This one's armed and armored, ready for anything, and it's got full ground-to-space capability! We can get it over to you and have you up here in orbit in jig time—as soon as it's ready."

"Fine," Ben Yale said—strangely, thought his duplicate; why wasn't he more excited? But he was looking narrowly at Ben Linc. He said at last tangentially, "Have you heard anything from Zara?"

Ben Linc shook his head. Then he corrected himself. "Yes, as a matter of fact I did," he said. "I don't remember—did you split off before I got her message about not coming because she was pregnant?"

"Pregnant?" Ben Yale demanded. "I don't believe it!"

"Well, it's true. That is—it's true of our Zara. But there's another copy of her—" He stopped. He was not sure how much he wanted to say.

"On Cuckoo, right?" Ben Yale cried. "I knew it! I saw her, Ben Linc! She's in trouble. Not more than five thousand yards from here!"

"Trouble? No, I don't think so . . ." Ben Linc started.

"Don't be a fool, Ben Linc!" his avatar cried. "I tell you, I saw her!"

Ben Linc Pertin hesitated, filled with confusion and a painful mixture of hope and fear. Another Zara, so close? But in danger?

"Stand by," he said. "I'll scan that vector." And his fingers danced over his console to FARLINK, ordering a search for transmissions from a point five thousand yards at twenty-seven degrees from Ben Yale's signal.

From her perch across the console from him, Venus sat quietly regarding Ben Linc Pertin. "What is the matter?" she asked, spraying a tiny violet cloudlet from her atomizer.

He shook his head as the rich menthol scent reached him. "It's Zara," he said. "Something I don't understand. And one of my replicates down there, looking—well, I don't know what's keeping him alive."

"I ache with your pains," Venus said softly. Though her stare had always seemed blankly opaque, he felt her compassion through it. "So difficult for you, to see yourself. I have at least been spared that. I have no contact with my replicates, save one or two—and then, for one of us to die in this edited form would not be bad."

Distracted, Ben Linc scowled at the console. There was no response to the search, although he could see that the program was functioning. Lately he had found it more and more difficult to distinguish sleep from waking. His sleep was filled with troubled dreams, and his waking life was a nightmare.

The dreams lingered with him, even when he was awake. He shivered, remembering one dream—

"SCAN UNSUCCESSFUL," FARLINK's screen reported. "NO UNIDENTIFIED TRANSMISSIONS FROM AREA."

"Continue," snapped Ben Linc, reinforcing the verbal order with his keyboard.

And he stared into space, remembering that one dream. In it he had been a child again. On Earth. Not the Earth he had left—so many replications before!—but the Earth he imagined, as it had been before the first contact with the Galactic civilizations. He had been sitting at a child's desk, in an upstairs room with an open window, looking out over a sunny yard, reading a book, when something had come in from outside. It had fluttered through the window, lit on the page in front of him. When he raised his hand to slap it it had leaped away, and he saw it was no common fly but a tiny five-eyed bat shape with bright butterfly wings. When he heard it squeaking, and caught its faint vinegar scent, he knew it was a T'Worlie—incongruously there in that pregalactic age, but somehow Earth's first visitor from deep space.

He seized a flyswatter to kill it. Its shrill scream of protest hurt his ears, and its fear was a carrion reek. Wings whirring, it rose to fly away, but he smashed it on the open page.

For a moment he felt secure in that dream . . .

And then he heard a droning roar from outside. The sun darkened. Shadows filled the window. When he looked out he saw that the sky had turned black with alien beings descending—T'Worlie and She-liaks, Boaty-Bits and Scorpians, endless processions of a thousand shapes and sizes all arrowing down upon him . . .

He had wakened then briefly, tossed and turned, and drifted off again . . .

To even worse horror.

Now he dreamed that he was his other self, Replicate 5160, at the strange tachyonic station to which he had been transmitted. But his form was no longer human. He had been edited, transformed into a thick metal block, unable to move. He understood at last—attempting to shudder, and failing—the silvery girl's abhorrence of the form into which her own body had been recast to survive in an oxygen atmosphere. His case was worse. He was a chess piece in a three-sided match; he stood on a queer triangular game board, a hapless piece in a game that FARLINK played against two terrible opponents.

One opponent was a bright thing of lambent white flame, writhing and twisting and flickering, without any ordered shape. The other was equally shapeless; but black instead of bright. They reached across the board with curling tongues of bright fire and terrible empty blackness, as if to move their pieces; but Ben Linc could not see their pieces, only the ones on his own side. One was the pseudogirl Venus, her silver body frozen rigid. Another was Zara Doy, alive and moving but imprisoned under a bell jar, pale and gasping, agonized for air. A third was Doc Chimp, a lifeless figure in brightly painted metal like a cheap child's toy, holding out a tin cup. The pieces moved, or the board itself moved them, responding to FARLINK's rapped electronic orders; but FARLINK was losing the game. Most of its triangular spaces were already empty. The last move had isolated Ben Linc, far from his companions. A fluttering tentacle of icy blackness stretched out toward him, and he knew that it was going to remove him from the board and then the game would be ultimately, irretrievably lost . . .

"Ben Linc," chimed the voice of the silvery girl, "where are you?"

He came back to the reality of the orbiter and the screen. "Sorry, Venus," he muttered. "I was thinking about . . ." His voice died out, but hers picked up the thought from him:

"About that other Ben Pertin? About Replicate 5160? About all those others of you, Ben Linc?"

He nodded. There had been no other signal from the copy of himself sent back along the tachyon trace to whatever that galactic source of interference had been: one more dead Pertin, he thought; the Universe is getting seriously polluted with my corpses . . .

He sat up abruptly and realized FARLINK was still methodically scanning the surface of Cuckoo for a signal that did not seem to be coming. He sighed and reached from the console to terminate the program—

And at that moment the screen lit up:

"STAND BY! FREQUENCY DETECTED! NO COMMUNICATION AS YET!"

And while his fingers were still poised over the console he heard it. There was no doubt.

On the emergency frequency.

Zara's voice.

And the words:

"Help! This is Zara Doy Gentry calling! Help! Please! Help me!"

In the wrecked survey vessel on the surface, Ben Yale Pertin heard Zara's voice repeated from the orbiter. That voice had traveled nearly half a billion miles, round trip, to get to him, but on the instant flash of tachyon transmission it had taken less time than was measurable. The time the message had taken to travel from the speaker on the satellite to the microphone three yards away that had picked it up was longer than the time for the message to fly on the backs of tachyons through space.

He burst out of the vehicle, limping and rubbing at his bandages, but traveling as fast as ever he had moved in his life. He was not in pain now. He had been steadily doping himself with pills and salves from the medicpac; he was no longer quite sober or sane. Although the pain of the ulcers under the bandages was blocked, the effects of the blocks were shaking the stability of his mind. All things seemed possible. The entire Universe seemed ready to meet his commands. He scrambled through the undergrowth toward Redlaw and Org Rider, shouting, "My wife! She's in danger! We've got to help her!"

FIFTEEN

Org Rider was too full of mourning for the loss of Babe to feel any great concern about the dying stranger's excitement—until Redlaw translated some of what he said.

"I do not understand all," Redlaw said, "but it is a woman of his people and she is a captive of the Watchers. I expect they will eat her," he added, moodily stroking his cleaver. "He wishes us to save her. And he says, too, that if we do this a great ship of his people will come to battle the Watchers for us."

Redlaw paused, uncertain. "I do not know if he is telling the truth," he said. "He is a dying man. Perhaps he has the madness of the dying?"

Org Rider shrugged, but he was thinking about what Redlaw had said. With Babe gone, he was not happy enough to care much about danger. And the woman the stranger spoke about. If she was the one he had seen so briefly as she dashed herself into the treetops—but was that possible? could she have survived that nightmare plunge?—no matter; if it was she, there had been something about her that had appealed powerfully to him.

He said mournfully, "What does it matter if he lies? Let us do as he asks. Where is this woman?"

Redlaw scowled and gestured down the slope of Knife-in-the-Sky. "He says he knows precisely and will show us. But how can he travel? I have seen men before, eaten alive by that blue slime. They do not travel through the jungle! But he is doing it. It is something in those cloths he puts on his ulcers, perhaps, or in those small things he eats and drinks from the metal box. I wish I knew—" Redlaw gazed doubtfully at Ben Yale Pertin, still shouting and gesticulating at them to hurry. "And there is so much more he says that I cannot understand."

"No matter," Org Rider said. "Let us save the woman. For him," he added politely, as an afterthought.

Even so, they were far too slow for Ben Yale's liking; and then the trek through the jungle was longer and harder than they had expected, more than two thousand breaths, because Ben Yale insisted that they wait for him. He chose to carry some great metal thing from the ship that he called "bazooka." It was a wonder he could move at all, even without that weight. Beneath the stained bandages—though he had replaced them just before they left—the blue slime oozed out, always spreading, always etching new ulcers into his flesh. And it was a constant peril to be near him in his clumsy lunging through the trees. A single accidental touch of the blue slime might have meant death for either of them.

But the two thousand breaths were over, and in time they reached a point where they could see the distant black gleam of the tiny lake. There on the far shore loomed the mottled hulk of the Watcher vessel.

Org Rider wished for the far-seeing glasses, but of course they were no longer safe to use: Ben Yale had touched them. He squinted across the lake. With mounting excitement he saw: yes—there she was! The very girl he had seen. Wrapped like the prey of a cord spinner in the golden coils of the Watchers' device, lying helpless on the blinding white sands of the little beach.

Even so, even at that distance, she was beautiful. Disordered as her hair was, it had the reddish glint of far lightning. Something about her made him think of his brother's wife. Yet this girl was more beautiful by far, in spite of the drained pale cast of her face and the terror in her expression.

He glanced at Redlaw, and started to move toward the lake.

The giant stopped him.

"Wait!" he rumbled. "Ben Yale says he has a plan. He says that this 'bazooka' is a weapon. He wishes us to go around the lake, to be ready to attack the Watchers from the forest. He says from here, with this weapon that he has carried, he will destroy the Watcher ship. When he has done that, we are to kill those who survive with his weapon and"—he patted his cleaver—"this one!"

"What weapon does he have that will destroy the ship?" Org Rider demanded suspiciously. "You told me he had no such weapon."

"He lied," the giant growled moodily. "I knew he lied. And perhaps he is lying now, how can I tell? I can understand so little of what he says!"

"What does it matter?" repeated Org Rider, quelling the rising surge of feeling in himself. "Let us do as he asks."

They left Ben Yale just inside the undergrowth, lying on the scarlet moss, peering over the sights of his tree-trunklike weapon, chuckling and muttering to himself in his strange language. And they moved like ghosts through the vegetation, circling around.

They paused fifty yards from the beach. The foul deathweed stench of the Watchers reeked in their nostrils as Org Rider whispered savagely, "How do we know when he will destroy the ship? We should have arranged a signal."

"Should have, should have," Redlaw rumbled. "But we didn't, boy." He scowled toward the beach. "If only I were sure of him. I hate like poison to get closer! Those golden ropes of theirs can smell a man, and they never sleep. Still—" He sighed. "I'll try to get them with this thing"—he patted the laser weapon—"and you go after them with your bow. With any luck they'll be disorganized . . ."

He broke off. There was a sharp, flat crack from across the lake and a puff of grayish smoke. Out of the smoke emerged a needlelike metal object lancing across the lake toward the Watcher vessel. It struck, and opened into a bright flower of flame.

Blam.

The sound of the explosion was far louder than they had expected. The mottled vessel of the Watchers seemed to lift off the sand, and fall slowly. Bright flame spouted from the hole that the stranger's weapon had made in its side.

"Curse him," Redlaw howled, "we should have been closer! Do the best you can, boy!" And he loped toward the Watchers, firing with the laser weapon. Sounds like the tearing of paper came from it, and Watchers fell before it.

Org Rider ran to the side of the lake, dropped to one knee, and began launching arrows toward the Watchers. While one was still in the air he was notching and aiming the next. He did not wait to see how successful he was, but out of the corner of one eye he saw one Watcher leap high over the vessel with a startled squeal, an arrow protruding clear through him. Another, squalling and hooting, lay on the ground, tugging at a shaft through his throat, while his drumming feet revolved him in a complete circle around his shoulders.

"They've broken!" Redlaw exulted over his shoulder. "Come on, boy! Let's go in and finish them off!" As he spoke his laser weapon sliced through the golden coils, and another blast from it burned a crisply sizzling hole through a Watcher skull. Now the giant flung the laser to the winds and, screaming as he leaped, bowled in on the Watchers, hacking at them with his cleaver. Org Rider was just behind. The two of them drove the Watchers back like avenging angels. With every stroke of Redlaw's cleaver and the boy's knife a Watcher squealed and fell from their paths.

Zzzzzzat!

The noise was louder than anything Org Rider had ever heard, and for a moment he did not understand what it was.

Then he saw that the Watcher vessel was not, after all, quite dead.

From a round bulge on its top something flashed like lightning, and the great ripping sound lashed at his ears again. The Watcher ship was firing its main armament. Not at them, Org Rider realized—not that there was any question about that; if the laser cannon had been aimed at them they would never have known what hit them—but probing across the lake for the bazooka. *Zzzzzzat!*, and a bee-tree went up in smoke, smitten by a lightning bolt. *Zzzzzat!*, and a sudden corridor opened up in a stand of deathweed.

"Grab the girl!" Redlaw bawled. "Let's get out of here before they finish with Pertin and start on us!"

There were still Watchers alive and Org Rider yearned to catch and kill every one; but he knew Redlaw was right. He bounded to the side of the girl. She was just beginning to sit up. The blood had been squeezed out of her limbs for so long she was numbed and tottering.

Org Rider felt almost as dizzy as she was. All this was so terribly new and confusing! The needle-bright light of the laser, the harsh explosions and lightning-bolt sizzling of the long-range battle across the lake were entirely out of his experience, in a life lived in the perpetual pink-gray dawn of Cuckoo. He was not afraid; but he was disoriented.

Still he had to act. He grabbed the girl's arm and pulled her away. She did not resist, except to break free for a moment and pick up a piece of metallic equipment. Then she was with him, bounding as fast as they could into the shelter of the woods, Redlaw close behind. The last Watcher on his feet outside the ship challenged Redlaw, but lost his head and half his trunk to the keen-edged cleaver. Then the giant was beside them, shouting, "Hurry! We've got to get out of sight!" The girl could not have understood his words; but she didn't have to, the need was clear.

At last there was another bazooka shot from across the lake, and this one was clean and true on the bulge at the top of the Watcher ship. It blew up in a gout of flame.

All three of them cheered.

"We did it, boy!" the giant bellowed. "Beat the Watchers in fair fight! It's the first time it ever happened in all the time of the world!"

Org Rider crowed in pleasure, pummeling the girl's back as though she were another man. Exultant, laughing, as delighted as he, she clapped him on the shoulder with a force that sent him spinning.

He picked himself off the ground and looked at her with new respect. She was no timid, frail maiden! She was as strong as he. And yet—she seemed more feminine than any woman he had ever seen. More so even than the girl who had married his brother. A glow of color began to light her death-pale face, and he found himself staring into her widening eyes. They were a bright-flecked brown, like the wild flowers that colored the grassworld after the rain. Even with the hated reek of the Watchers still fouling his nostrils he could smell the faint scent that came from her, a clean sweetness that swept away the Watchers' fetor and left him with the fragrance of the rain itself, after the flatworld had been brown and dry.

"Stop mooning, boy!" Redlaw ordered, laughing as he said it. "We've beaten one shipload of Watchers, but they're not through yet. There'll be more. When this ship doesn't report in, they'll send another to look for it. If they managed to send off a distress report, that ship is on its way now!"

Org Rider tore his eyes off the girl. "All right. Which way?"

The giant gazed about. "We'll have to go back around the lake," he decided. "First place, we'd best try to find Ben Yale, if he's still alive. Second, I don't think we can get out this way. That's bare rock up there. We'd be easy targets on it—and I see blue on those rocks, boy; I think it's the slime. We don't want to go near that."

Org Rider nodded and turned to the girl. Speaking as clearly as he could, gesturing to make his meaning plain, he said: "Come. We leave here. Now."

She laughed. She touched the metallic thing she had picked up and spoke, and from the thing came a flat, dead voice that said: "I understand. I agree. And"—to Org Rider even the lifeless metallic tone of the translator could not keep all feeling out of the words—"with all my heart I thank you both."

The boy was enraptured. He recognized the speaking machine; it was the same as Ben Yale's, but whole and working properly. In Ben Yale's conversations with Redlaw he had become accustomed to being excluded; it had not occurred to him that an undamaged machine would make it possible for him to be in one-to-one contact with this wondrous person.

He caught the girl's hand, and they followed Redlaw back toward the lake margin—

And stopped.

From behind the wrecked Watcher vessel a lance of green fire spat out at them.

Redlaw shrieked in agony and spun away, clutching his arm. "Run!" he bawled, setting them an example. They blundered after them, and at every leap Org Rider expected that green fire to burn through their backs.

They stopped almost up against the bare rock wall that cupped that edge of the lake. "There was one still alive," Redlaw gasped, holding the place on his upper arm that had blossomed into a blood-red blister of pain. "It's lucky he fired when he did! If he'd waited he'd have had me clean, and you two as well." He scowled up at the mountain. "We can't go up that way," he muttered. "And we can't go back to the lake, because he's waiting there."

Org Rider risked raising himself to peer around the multiple boles of a flame-tree. He could see the Watcher, broad yellow wings slowly stirring. One was damaged, and dragged; the Watcher had been hurt, too. But he held the thing that looked like a black stick, and spat green flame, without faltering.

"If we can't go forward," Org Rider said, "and can't go back—and can't stay here, because there'll be another Watcher ship before long—then what do we do?"

They waited and watched, but the creature remained steadfastly alert.

"We have no choice," Redlaw groaned at last. "We have to kill him. His gun outranges our weapons, and his bug eyes can see us in every direction. It won't be easy."

Redlaw scowled at his cleaver.

"The only way I see to take him is to rush from all sides. He may kill us all, but I don't think so. One of us will get him. But the other two—"

He hesitated, then he finished: "At least one of the other two will be dead."

"No!" the boy shouted. "Not her. She has suffered enough from the Watchers. You and I can do it, Redlaw!"

The girl, listening, shook her head. She spoke in that pretty, singing voice, and the metal voice from her arm echoed, "I can perform my share. I thank you for your good heart."

Org Rider stared at her and said, "Please don't. I don't know your name—"

She said in her own voice, not through the translator, "Zara." It sounded like music to him as he rehearsed it several times, tasting its flavor.

"Zara. Please, Zara, don't do this. You are not a warrior. Redlaw and I can handle the Watcher."

The giant thundered, "Idiot boy, we can't! Our only hope is three attacks at once. *That* is a faint enough hope—two is suicide!"

The girl spoke, and the Pmal rattled flatly, "It is decided, Org Rider. I again thank you, but now let us act. Tell me what I must do."

The giant rasped, "Come in from behind the ship. Get close to him. The beast has a hard shell, but there are soft joints. One is where his neck would be, if he had a neck. There's a pale stripe above his black hump. Stab him deep in the middle of that, if you can."

Org Rider watched the girl go on her longer, roundabout trip with his breath caught in his throat. She would not die! He would see to it. The first one to display himself to the Watcher would surely be the first one fired on; the other two would have a chance at least minutely better. Org Rider determined to be that first one.

But it would be foolish, would even endanger them, for his break to come much before their own. It would simply mean that the Watcher would pick him off quickly, and then have only two foes to confront. So he squirmed to his place and waited, watching the faint ripples in the underbrush that marked the movements of Redlaw and the girl. Could the Watcher see and understand those same ripples? He did not know. He could only hope.

Something was tugging at the back of his mind. What was it?

Then he recognized the growing sound from the sky, and looked up. Down at him dived a great org.

Org Rider froze. It was his death he saw coming. With only the knife left—the bow was long since cast away—he could not prevail against talon and fang. All he could do was stare at its savage splendor. He crouched numbly, waiting for the hooked black talons to strike.

Even in that moment he saw the blue beauty of its huge, hooded eyes, the bright flow of its form, the even sheen of bronze scales shading into the silver flash of its narrowed wings. Wonder at its clean, sleek power made his throat ache. Orgs were better and greater than men! Surely they were more beautiful. It was his death . . . but if he had to perish, here on Knife-in-the-Sky, it was better to be killed by this mighty org than by the waiting Watcher.

But dying that way would not serve Zara . . .

Org Rider leaped to his feet, yelling and bounding toward the Watcher ship.

As he had expected, the Watcher was staring up with his great blind eyes, distracted by the org. Perhaps after the org finished with him it would go for the Watcher next! Org Rider glanced toward the Watcher, husbanding his charges as he nervously waited under the shelter of the ship, then back toward the org.

It screamed again.

The bright wings opened a little, flaring it toward him out of the bottom of the dive, and he saw the scars that marred its lean perfection. A long, dark wound, not fully healed, where the scales had been ripped from its flank. A break in the brightness of one wide wing.

The screaming changed . . . and queerly, became words.

"Babe!" blared the mighty voice of the org, repeating his own voice like a tape under maximum gain. "Babe come back!"

The boy heard his own voice thunder down at him from the sky and could hardly understand. But what the words did not explain the actions did. The org dipped down over him. Its golden-scaled trunk snatched him up into the air, squeezed him almost too hard, flexed to set him on its back above the widened wings.

Then recognition hit him.

It *was* Babe! Changed—older—hurt, but Babe! Scales had replaced the infant fur. The healing scars told of combat. But it was he!

A laser scream spat past his ear and brought him out of his dreaming. He kicked the org strongly and shouted, "Fast, Babe! Over the trees!"

The beast responded instantly, putting the loom of the ship between them and the Watcher. And Org Rider sobbed, "Babe! I'm so glad!" He stroked the bronze scales. Yards below he could see the top of the trees and caught a glimpse of Zara's terrified pale face, staring up at them. What could she be thinking? Had she ever seen an org before? Did she understand that Org Rider was master, not prey?

But looking at her brought him back to the needs of that moment. He wheeled Babe around, low over the treetops, and shouted down: "Now! Let's get him!"

And as he saw the mighty form of Redlaw leap free and begin to run toward the Watcher, he gouged his heels into Babe's scaled side and commanded, "Kill, Babe! The Watcher! Kill him!"

The chaos of the next moments was indescribable. Org Rider heard the shouts of Redlaw and the shriller, fainter cry of the girl. He saw the cleaver glinting in the hands of the giant.

Then he was around the ship and beating back in toward the Watcher.

The black stick crackled. Bright light blasted Org Rider's eyes; a sudden electrical stench choked him. But it had been a miss; he was still alive!

And then they were on top of the Watcher. Babe bellowed as his striking talons ripped the Watcher out from under the hull. They all tumbled in a slow-motion heap, boy, org, and Watcher together. The reek of the squealing Watcher stung his throat as he stabbed and stabbed with his knife to find the death place.

In the end it was Babe that took the last of the life from the Watcher, the great claws simply wrenching the hideous head free of its body. The shrilling scream stuttered and stopped abruptly, and the ugly carcass toppled slowly forward in death.

"We did it!" Org Rider called. "Babe, you're a hero! Babe—"

But the org did not respond.

Shaken, Org Rider lifted his head free and stared. The delicate pink trunk was trembling violently. The huge eyes were dulled. As Org Rider reached out to touch him, Babe screamed in pain.

The Watcher's laser had found its mark after all.

As Redlaw and the girl came running up, Babe fumbled out to touch the boy with his shuddering trunk. The voice that mimicked Org Rider's own said, "Babe go. Babe go . . ."

The light went out of the great eyes, and the org was dead.

Org Rider sat mourning with the great head in his lap, Redlaw and the girl standing helplessly by, until at last Redlaw rumbled, "Sorry, boy, but we've got to get out of here. The Watchers'll be after us any time now."

Org Rider looked up and nodded somberly. "I know." He got up, reaching a hand to the girl. "Are you all right?" She smiled, in both reassurance and compassion; he needed no translator to understand that, or the look of sympathy in her eyes.

There was a sudden scream of high speed from the sky, and all three of them looked upward in instant reawakened fear.

"Too late!" Redlaw raged. "Fiends of hell! There's the Watcher ship on us, while we're standing around like fools! We can't get away now. We'll have to fight—and we've nothing to fight with but the Watcher's own lance!" He dove to the side of the decapitated beast, choking in fury as much as the evil cloud of its deathweed stink.

The girl stopped him.

Her clear voice, repeated through the translator on her arm, said: "It's all right. It's not a Watcher ship. Look."

Unbelieving, Redlaw and the boy craned their necks to stare upward.

The vehicle that was settling down on them was far larger than any Watcher ship either had ever seen. Even the colors were different: bright silver, crisp black, a flare of yellow-white gas from its underjets.

"They've come to rescue us," Zara said. "We're safe now. All of us."

SIXTEEN

In the orbiter Ben Linc Pertin watched in a fever of excitement as the survey ship picked up Zara and her two companions. He stared at her image in pain and wonder. So tall and thin she was, in her edited version! So worn and pale, with the stresses of her battle with the Watchers! He wanted desperately to talk to her, to say words of love and welcome; but although he was hard pressed with grief and loneliness he was not mad, and he understood that their relationship would have to mature in its own way. To him she was his loved and missed wife. To her, coming from an earlier Zara Doy, he was a stranger.

And then there was the solved puzzle of why she called herself "Zara Doy Gentry." She had married someone else! He had scarcely felt that shock when he learned that that husband was dead, fodder for the maws of the Watchers. Shock again! This time a different kind of shock, a reprieve, even if purchased at the cost of a man's life—who could not have been a bad man, Ben Linc told himself with one reasoning part of his mind, for Zara to meet and marry him. But another part of his mind was bursting with joy. How strange for his wife to be a widow and a wooable stranger, all at once!

And suddenly he was exhausted. He had stayed by the communicator for twenty-two hours, past the time of his regular duty, through the new Zara's cry for help, up to the moment of rescue and for some time beyond. Now he had to sleep. He decided against attempting even to leave a message for this to-be-won Zara, and headed for his cocoon. There would be time. It was a long voyage up from Cuckoo and around to where the orbiter swung, nearly half a billion miles now. It seemed even longer in the urgency of his anticipation.

Yet there was no way to shorten it. Even with nuclear rockets, the acceleration of the survey ship was limited to what its rescued passengers could stand. That was not much. Redlaw and Org Rider had lived all their lives in the gentle pull of Cuckoo, and even Zara and Ben Yale Pertin, in their edited versions, could hardly stand a single gravity of acceleration. For Ben Yale even that much was dangerous; he had been swept from the jungle into full medical cocooning, instantly.

Ben Linc fell asleep, thinking of Ben Yale coming up from Cuckoo, battered and foul with the ulcers of the blue slime . . . and of that other Ben Pertin, Replicate 5160, lost somewhere at the transmitter of the tachyon interference, at a point unknown inside the Galaxy . . . and, above all, of the sweet and smiling face of Zara Doy, now Zara Gentry, who might sometime soon be Zara Pertin again . . .

He woke to Doc Chimp screaming in his ear:

"Ben! Ben Linc! Wake up! You've been found, you're still alive. Oh, wake up, Ben Linc Pertin, there's a signal from you coming in!"

Heavy with sleep, Ben Linc Pertin stumbled after Doc Chimp to the terminal dome. His mind was fuzzed with visions of himself in all his myriad guises. Sometimes he was not sure which he was: the innocent back on Earth who had never left, the one on Sun One who was still happily married to Zara Doy and happy father of her child, any of the dead ones . . . all of them . . .

But one dead one was not dead!

In the dome, the huge image of a haggard human face was repeated on half a hundred screens, all around the curve. Half of the face was haggard with dirt and grime, the other half caked with dark blood; a ragged wound on the scalp still oozed, untended.

It took Ben Pertin a moment to recognize himself: Replicate 5160.

"See!" Doc Chimp chirped in his ear. "It's you, Ben! Not dead! The message started coming in a few minutes ago. But it's awful bad, Ben Linc; you can't understand a word of it, without the Pmal translators."

Ben Linc was still stupid with sleep. "You mean I'm—he's speaking some other language?"

"Not that, Ben Linc," the chimpanzee said gently. "Look at him! He can hardly talk in any language. The Pmal has to put it into words we can understand. Even then—well, it's in symbol-script, not sounds. He must have had some bad times, Ben Linc."

And it was so: the soiled and battered mouth was moving, but no audible sound came through the wall speakers. Instead bright computer symbols were dancing under each screen:

". . . INCOMPLETELY EXPLORED. IN SHAPE, THIS OBJECT I FOUND MYSELF ON IS A LARGE, FLAT DISK, ROTATING SLOWLY. MAYBE A THOUSAND FEET ACROSS. IT'S SOME SORT OF SPACECRAFT, BUT IT DOES NOT APPEAR TO BE UNDER POWER NOW—MAYBE NOT FOR A VERY LONG TIME.

"THE LEVELS TOWARD THE RIM ARE SEALED AND COLD. VERY COLD. I BELIEVE THE CREW IS HIBERNATING THERE TO WAIT FOR THE NEXT PLANET. ONE PLACE LOOKS LIKE A CONTROL FORM. SPHERICAL. STARS IMAGED ON ITS INSIDE SURFACE, AND A POD HUNG IN THE CENTER FOR THE PILOTS—BUT THERE ARE NO PILOTS THERE. HIBERNATING, I GUESS. I COULD NOT IDENTIFY THE STAR IMAGES, BUT I DID SEE WHAT LOOKED LIKE A REPRESENTATION OF CUCKOO. ONLY IT WAS STRANGE. IT WAS ALL MADE OF METAL. NO SOIL, ROCKS, SEAS, MOUNTAINS—JUST A GREAT SPHERE OF METAL.

"I THINK—"

The bloodied head turned suddenly and vanished from the screen.

For an instant the screens were dark; then shapeless blotches of color flickered over them. FARLINK interposed its own message, in all the tongues of the viewers:

"TRANSMISSION INTERRUPTED. STAND BY."

There was a sudden rush of squeal, cry, shout, and roar from the beings in the terminal room, as each one chattered to its neighbor about the message. Ben Linc, sick at the sight of his destroyed self, muttered, "I don't understand. What is it?"

Venus floated over toward him and filled him in quickly. "Your replicate reported in a few minutes ago, Ben Linc. He was in a ship, but some sort of mechanical device—a robot, but not a fully sentient one, I'm sure—attacked him as he came out of the receiver, and it is only now that he has been able to report."

"Ship?" Ben Linc shook his head, trying to clear it. The source of the distant unidentified tachyon transmission that they had actually intercepted en route to Cuckoo—a ship? There were no ships equipped with tachyon facilities that could possibly have a link with Cuckoo, not anywhere in the known Universe . . .

Of course, there was always the *unknown* Universe, he thought, the muscles of his back crawling.

"And there were representations of many beings there, Ben Linc," the silvery girl went on excitedly. "Your people! Boaty-Bits. Sheliaks.

Your replicate thinks that the ship is a sort of advance guard for Cuckoo, sampling inhabited planets, sending specimens back. That would account for— Wait, here it is again!"

The ravaged head shook itself together into view on the screens. It was more horrid than ever; Pertin's replicate had been in another fight. Fresh blood was dribbling down the beard-spiked chin, and the lower front teeth were gone. The hollowed eyes were darting frantically from side to side, as the ruined mouth tried to form soundless words.

"IT'S LOCATED ME AGAIN," the bright words flashed. "UGLY THING. THICK OVAL SLAB, BELTED WITH SENSORS, CRAWLING AND JUMPING ON A FRINGE OF TENTACLES. IT DOESN'T COMMUNICATE, BUT IT HAS JUST ABOUT KILLED ME. WE'VE BEEN PLAYING HIDE AND SEEK. NOW *I* THINK IT HAS WON THE GAME, AS SOON AS IT FINISHES BREAKING THE DOOR DOWN . . .

"ANYWAY, THAT'S MY REPORT. KISS ZARA FOR ME—IF YOU CAN, BEN LINC. THAT'S ALL FOR—"

And there was no more. The image exploded and died, and FAR-LINK underlined it after a moment with:

"TRANSMISSION TERMINATED. NO FURTHER PULSE FROM SOURCE."

The belt of screens blazed and went blank.

A stir of strain ran around the terminal chamber, and muted hootings and clangings and shrillings of communication began.

Ben Linc Pertin shook his head slowly, trying to take it all in. There was so much, all happening so fast. Another death of a double. A real flesh-and-blood Zara on her way. And on the larger scale, the fantastic mystery of a scout ship from Cuckoo, sampling inhabited planets.

He tried to tell Nammie and Venus how he felt. He caught a burnt-fur scent from the T'Worlie that surprised him, until he recognized it.

Fear.

The T'Worlie was afraid of what the message meant.

For a moment Ben Linc allowed himself to share that fear of the terrible unknown, of the race that must have built that ship; but thoughts came flooding back, and his fear melted into anticipation; and that was how it was with Ben Linc Pertin on the orbiter.

With Ben Yale Pertin on the survey ship, spiraling around toward the orbiter, things were somewhat different.

They were better than they had been in a long time, he told himself. The survey ship's medical facilities were dealing nicely with the blue slime. He spent three days in the cocoon, while his skin was gently soaked away and a new one grown on. Then, swathed like a mummy in circulating-field bandages, he was allowed into the common room where the others were gathered, his humanoid nurse, a Purchased Person, following after him. "I'm all recovered," he announced.

Somewhat warily, his three companions from the battle against the Watchers welcomed him. They had received medication too, and looked fine—especially Zara, Ben Yale thought greedily, devouring her with his eyes. Redlaw and Org Rider gravely shook his hand, a skill they had just learned. Zara came over and patted his head. She drew back and looked at him. "Not really, I think," she said. "Not *all* recovered. But far better than the last time I saw you."

They and the ship crew had been talking excitedly over the strange message from the orbiter, which had been relayed to them. While the Purchased Person made him comfortable in an open-end hammock, Ben Yale listened. "—explains so much," said the Pmal, speaking for a horse-headed Canopan, the ship's pilot. "Explains why some of you races are duplicated on Cuckoo. That scout ship must have been twenty thousand years sailing through the Galaxy, picking up specimens and sending them back. And of course some got loose and multiplied. They wouldn't know they weren't indigenous."

Org Rider rapped indignantly, "That is our home! Our people have lived there forever—"

The Canopan snickered a whinnying laugh. "No offense," its Pmal said good-naturedly. "But what puzzles me," he went on, "is that picture of Cuckoo the replicate found. All made of metal! But it isn't like that, it's a world. A funny one, but still—"

"Wait," Org Rider cried through his own translator. "Perhaps I know something here! For there is a part of our world that is metal. A desert, that lies far beyond our grassworld, beyond the shadow of Knife-in-the-Sky. My mother heard about it from a chief who owned an org. He tried to cross that metal desert once, looking for another grassworld beyond the reach of the Watchers. He nearly died there."

The other beings looked at Org Rider, who returned their various kinds of gaze steadfastly. "It's true," he said. "It is all bare metal, harder than any axe or knife. There's nothing alive on it. No light except the dim glow of the clouds. The chief flew until his org grew so weak he had to give it all the food they carried for both of them. And then on the way back, trying to return to save their lives, he grew weak too, so weak that it had to carry him in its trunk. And," he cried, remembering more as he spoke, "that is of course how our world began. Everyone knows this! It was a hard bare shell, the first org's egg. Before the makers made their great fire to hatch all things from it."

He paused, puzzled. The beings were making a great variety of sounds, but the Pmals were not translating them into language. They could not; the sounds were laughter.

"But it is true," he insisted.

Zara smiled and gently put her hand in his. "It is puzzling," she said.

Ben Yale Pertin cleared his throat.

"Zara," he called.

It pleased him to see that she released the boy's hand to turn to him. "Yes, Ben Yale?"

He hesitated. How to tell her that she and he had once been married?—*were* married, and having children, on Sun One. He could not think of the right words, and as it was so important to him, and he wanted to be able to touch her, to kiss her, to hold her in his arms when he talked of these things, he temporized and turned what he said a different way. "I'm sorry about—about your loss." He could not bring himself to say, "about your husband's death."

"Thank you," she said. "It was a shock. But I've had a little time to get used to it."

The Purchased Person suddenly spoke, the voice human enough but the thought behind it coming from heaven knew who, heaven knew where. "Had you considered you could have him again?" it demanded, in a voice oddly, harshly male.

Zara looked surprised, and Redlaw rumbled, "She said that before once, when you weren't here. Have your husband make another copy and send it to you—whatever that means," he added, knotting his brows and staring about. Redlaw had never heard the expression "culture shock," but he was well on his way to drowning in it. Org Rider seemed to accept everything with grave interest and comfortable admiration; but he was younger, of course. For Redlaw this sudden exposure to such strangeness was difficult.

Zara said thoughtfully, "Why, that never occurred to me."

From his cocoon Ben Yale uttered a muffled groan. Damn that savage! he cursed furiously. Giving her that idea—

She was speaking again: "He might very well volunteer for replicating again, at that. He was—*is* a kind person, Jon is. But—"

She looked around and suddenly shook her head, smiling. "I'm sorry to be bothering you with my personal problems," she said.

"No, no," called Ben Yale, suffering. "We want to hear. What were you going to say?"

"Well, just that I wouldn't like to ask him to. I know it doesn't mean anything to be transmitted, in real terms. You're not any less for having a copy made. But in psychological terms it does, and you are. Especially for Jon. It was hard enough for him to volunteer the first time. I wouldn't want to put him through it again."

Ben Yale exulted in the cocoon. So Zara would stay free! Of course, he mused, that did not mean she would marry *him*. Not *necessarily*. There was always that other Ben Pertin, Ben Linc, waiting hot-handed on the orbiter for them to arrive. Ben Yale knew with what impatience his double would be waiting, and what his intentions would be; he could not mistake them, because he shared them wholly and exactly. And besides, he thought, he had time. The survey vessel still had two days to go before it reached the orbiter. It had been three days already—days wasted, he complained to himself; but there had been no way to help it, he had simply been physically unable to court Zara. But now—now things would be different. He closed his eyes, dreaming of how they would come to the orbiter. By then he would be out of his bandages, and rid of this pestilential Purchased Person nurse. He would take her to dinner—no, he thought regretfully, scratch that; there was no place on the orbiter for anything like that. But he would take her aside. In the rec room, at a time when not many others would be around.

She would be grateful to him, he estimated complacently; had he not saved her life? Or at least helped to do so? And she would have the interest women always felt for a hero in him. And he would tell her, very gently and simply, about his love for herself, Zara Doy; and how they had been married, and how much they had loved each other . . .

He scowled. The thought of Ben Linc Pertin intruded. Ben Linc would have almost the same advantages as himself, bar, of course, the couple of days before they got there. But a couple of days might not be enough to awaken her romantic interest.

He nodded to himself, sealed up the end of the cocoon with a quick motion—startling the Purchased Person who stood wide-eyed beside him—and flipped on the stereostage, putting through a call to Ben Linc Pertin on the orbiter.

When he saw himself, or the Ben Linc version of himself, he was startled. So haggard! So sad! For a moment he almost thought it was a replay of that terribly depressing version of himself from the unidentified ship; but then Ben Linc spoke. "Oh, it's you," he muttered. "What do you want?"

Ben Yale said carefully, "I think you know, Ben Linc. It's about Zara."

Ben Linc nodded lifelessly. "Yes. I suppose I should have expected you to call. I'm sorry, but—well. What can I do? I'll just go on being lonely. I've had plenty of practice—as you know."

Startled, Ben Yale stared at his duplicate. Elation and a nagging, suspicious fear fought with each other in his mind; he struggled to keep his voice level, even as he was wondering what had made Ben Linc give up so easily. "I admire you for taking it so well," he managed to say.

"You do?" Ben Linc looked surprised. Then, slowly, "Well, I kind of admire you, too. I mean, you actually look content, and God knows I can't; I don't feel it. Well, it's too bad we both had to be losers, but maybe it would be even harder if we weren't." And without another word he broke the connection.

Losers?

Ben Yale shook his swathed head, unbelievingly. *Both* of them losers?

And then a sudden fear chilled him, and he opened the end of the cocoon once more and peered out at Zara—

At Zara and Org Rider, sitting quietly, whispering at each other, the boy's hand caught in the girl's two, their shoulders touching.

Losers.

A couple of days had been time enough to awaken her romantic interest, after all.

But not for him.

On Earth astronomers were studying their tachyon transmissions of the object called Cuckoo. Almost invisible in the flood of light from the bright stars Benetnasch and Cor Caroli it swam in toward the center of the Galaxy.

Its course would take it very near the volume of space occupied by Sun and Earth. It was very, very far away. It would not get there for many thousands of years . . .

But it was coming.

WALL AROUND A STAR

PROLOGUE

Something is coming.

Something very large is spanning the immense emptiness on the way to something inconceivably larger still . . .

And in it I sleep.

I sleep as I speed through the great nothingness, the width of a planet in every second, with nothing for thousands of years' time behind me, and nothing for thousands of years before. I dream as I sleep. I dream of vast worlds and the unseen threads of purpose that join them; of ships like worlds, and of worlds erupting in ion bursts as they die. I have been sleeping for a time so long that there is no language to describe it. Then, for a moment, I wake.

Is it time?

I reach out to the distant starcloud before me. The stretch is immense, and it weakens me. I catch at a star and taste its planets. I savor some of its living things, and bring them closer for HIM.

HE does not stir.

It is not yet time.

I waken some of my sleeping puppets and hurl them ahead to survey and to learn. And then I return to sleep, while the great cloud turns majestically before me, and we draw ever nearer. Now and then the least of my slaves and senses whisper to me. Strangers have appeared. They touch the farthest outreach of my person. They come, they scramble about; they die.

They are not important. I do not trouble to wake fully for them, because the time is not yet.

But it is coming. It is coming soon.

ONE

Jen Babylon was physically exhausted, but he was too angry to go to sleep. He dropped his briefcase of tapes and transcripts, too precious to trust to a bellboy, in his hut and stamped back along the beach toward the only lights visible, the tethered schooner that served as a bar and late-night snack shop. For a miracle it was not raining, but the mosquitoes were out. In five weeks in Western Polynesia he should have had time to get used to them. But that hadn't happened. He hadn't gotten used to the hostility of the Free Polynesians, either, and if the desk clerk hadn't been one of them he was certainly a sympathizer.

He stopped, his train of thought interrupted. Somebody was walking up out of the lagoon.

For a moment he had been startled; few of the guests swam after sundown, when some people thought the sharks came in from the open sea. But swimming, after all, was one of the things people came here for, and there was no northern-hemisphere insistence on lifeguards or regular hours here. So it was not surprising there was a swimmer. It was not even surprising that the swimmer was female, and apparently entirely nude. Here there was no northern-hemisphere hangup about skin, either. What was a little surprising was that she was walking straight up to the beach, not sidestepping the little patches of sea growth, not even staying on the paths raked free of shells and broken coral. She reached the high-water mark, and stopped, looking around in what appeared to be some uncertainty.

Babylon stopped a meter or two short of where she stood. She was a striking woman. Not beautiful, perhaps. Too slim to be classically beautiful, and her coloring was—strange. It almost did not exist. Even in the weak light from the Moon and from the rigging of the distant schooner he could see that her hair was so pale as to be almost transparent, like spun lucite, and her eyes were almost colorless behind colorless lashes.

He realized he was staring, and stammered, "Excuse me." There was a little pile of clothing tucked between the roots of a banyan. He said helpfully, "Is that yours?"

She looked at him in a strange way. Not as one person usually looks at another, making contact eye to eye, but as one looks at a statue, or a machine. It was not in any way hostile, but Babylon could find no other way to interpret it. He felt himself on the defensive. "Excuse me," he said again. "I'm going to have a nightcap." Just at the pier he turned. She was standing there, with the clothing in her hand, looking thoughtfully at one of the chambermaids going from cabin to cabin to turn down the bedspreads.

He ordered a brandy and ginger ale. His anger had begun to simmer down, but a certain amount of irritation remained to mix with the fatigue. His grant had been for eight weeks in the islands, traveling from one tiny atoll to another to find the oldest surviving Polynesians and get them to speak what they remembered of the native tongue into his bubble-recorder. Of course, there was no such thing as a pure Polynesian tongue anymore. The grandfathers' grandfathers of the old people he talked to had already begun to incorporate words of French and English and Russian into their everyday speech; the consonants had shifted to match the white man's way of writing them down, rather than retaining the original, not quite reproducible sounds of the untouched islands. But that was his specialty. Jen Babylon's first doctorate was in evolutionary linguistics, his second in semantic analysis. He was the world's outstanding expert in the history and development of tongues. "Babylon's Algorithms" were taught in every university in the world, as a procedure for mapping loan words from a known contaminating tongue against current dialects and reconstructing the lost original of the dialects. Not just in this world. Babylon's contributions to linguistic theory were among the very few specimens of human scientific thought that any of the other races of the Galaxy considered worth the trouble of knowing about. That knowledge gave Babylon a good deal of pleasure. It was a source of pride for him. Sources of pride were welcome. Babylon had spent his youth as a college grind, subsisting on scholarships, seldom finding time enough to go out and raise hell with his peers, seldom finding anyone who wanted to share hell-raising with him when he did. He was not the sort of man who attracted women. He was too short, a little too plump, a good deal too soft ever to look heroic or macho, and although he could speak easily in fifteen languages and get by with some difficulty in half a dozen others, he had never learned the words to talk to a girl.

So when the woman from the beach entered the bar he glanced at her only briefly, and then turned away.

She was dressed now—at least, she had wrapped a pareu around her, though she was still barefoot and her glassy-soft hair was wet. To his surprise she came up to the bar next to him. She inspected the stool beside his, sat on it, and said, in a voice almost as colorless as her eyes, "I'm going to have a nightcap."

Well, there were times when you didn't really need the right words. "Would you like to join me? Yes? I'm having brandy and ginger ale."

She looked at the drink as he held it up. "Yes," she said. "Brandy and ginger ale."

But even after he had bought her a drink the woman did not seem to want to talk. She was willing to listen, apparently, as she tasted her drink and stared about the little bar. "I'm going back to Boston in the morning," he offered, without getting a response. She seemed interested in the rope festoons and seashells that were the principal decorations. There was almost no one else in the bar; February was not the tourist season on Mooréa, and the hotel's complex of thatched-roof cottages was almost deserted. He tried again. "I've been out in the smaller islands. I'm in linguistics."

The woman did not respond, but the bartender looked up from his American newspaper crossword puzzle. "Were there a lot of those *Polynésie-libre* types out there?"

"Quite a few," Babylon admitted. "I think I would have had more cooperation from some of the old people if it hadn't been for them. But they didn't make any real trouble for me."

"Bet they didn't," the bartender said. "They caught one of the ringleaders, you know. That Te'ehala Tupaia. A mad bomber! Worst of the lot. Between them and the Kooks, this place is going to hell."

Babylon was startled. "No! I didn't know you had Kooks out here."

The bartender shrugged moodily. "Not right here, but over yonder"—he waved toward the distant lights of Papeete, climbing the mountain on the other side of the strait—"there's plenty of them all over Tahiti. I never go there anymore. Would've stayed in Cleveland if I'd wanted to see a bunch of nuts dressing up like freaks and acting like the world was coming to an end. Maybe it is. When I was a boy—"

Jen Babylon didn't want to hear about how things had been when the bartender was a boy. "Are there Kooks where you come from?" he asked the woman.

She glanced briefly at him through her pale eyes, then away. "No."

"There are plenty in Boston," he told her. "It's a new religion. They said that object that was discovered a few years ago—Cuckoo, most people call it—anyway, they think that when it reaches our Galaxy we will all be destroyed. Or reborn, as something bigger than human. Or something . . ." She wasn't paying attention. At least, she wasn't looking at him, although there was something about her that made him sure she was hearing every word. He was receiving mixed signals from her, and it was both irritating and in some way provocative.

More irritating than provocative, on balance; he was still not over the anger left from his unsatisfactory conversation with the desk clerk. Were there any messages for M'sieur Jen Babylon? Perhaps yes. Perhaps no. One had so many messages—but it was obvious the hotel was nearly empty, and there were hardly any signal lights glowing over the room indicators. But couldn't he just look? With great regret, m'sieur, not at this moment, since the press of duties was so formidable. And m'sieur's bags could not be brought just now, but surely within the hour, perhaps. Babylon had stalked out, jangling the key to his cottage. He was certain that there must be messages, if only one from the university to explain why he had been called back so urgently from his field trip.

"Do you want another drink?" the bartender asked. "Looks like you'll be here awhile."

Babylon realized that the staccato drumming that had been nagging at his consciousness was rain, beating down on the moored old copra schooner with the sudden violence of any tropical storm.

"Might as well. How about you?" he added to the girl.

She stood up. "No." She moved toward the door without looking at either of them.

"Miss, where are you going? It's pouring out there," the bartender cried.

She paused in the doorway. "I'm going to Boston in the morning," she said. Babylon and the bartender glanced at each other, then turned together to stare out of the porthole. She strode steadily down the pier, ignoring the downpour, looking neither to left nor right until the rain swallowed her.

It was five drinks later before Babylon was willing to follow her. The rain had diminished, but not stopped. By the time he reached his hut he was soaked and more irritable than ever. The desk clerk did not even answer his call; the vision cube glowed orange and empty, with a taped voice saying brightly in four languages that the guest's call would be returned as soon as possible. Babylon understood them all, and none of them made him happier. He was more certain than ever that the clerk was a Free Polynesia fanatic, with the cold rage toward all Europeans that he had experienced on the outer islands. But knowing that did not suggest anything to do about it. He slept.

He did not sleep well—too many drinks, too much fatigue, too much irritation. At first he was dreaming of his speech laboratory in Old Cambridge, and the dean was snapping at him as he tried to puzzle out an obscure unknown language. His best Pmal translators could offer no clue; his computer rejected all programs as nulls or errata; and he was aware that more than his job, or even his life, depended on the outcome. He woke abruptly, in a sweat of fear, fumbling for his glasses.

It was still raining. He had slept less than an hour, but a cold wet wind was coming in through the slatted blinds. He closed them and climbed back into bed, reassuring himself that it was only a dream.

This time his dreams were more pleasant. A beautiful woman who seemed transparent as glass was leading him through a marvelous drusy cave. All about them were faceted diamonds and opals and rubies set into the rock walls. Not rock; even the walls glimmered and glowed, like a precious metal. The woman did not speak, but he was content to be with her in silence. And then he looked away, and turned back to her, and she was gone. In her place was a cluster of great bright flowers that hung in air, while giant butterflies swam among them. It was hard to tell blossom from butterfly. Both seemed to be speaking to him, too low to understand, in tones like the chiming of a golden bell . . .

He woke up.

There was a chiming, and it came from his stereo cube. The bright

orange number 4 danced under a legend that read MESSAGES WAIT-
ING.

He sat up on the edge of the narrow bed, rubbing his eyes as he
peered nearsightedly at the stereo. Jen Babylon was one of the very
few human beings who wore glasses, rejecting both contacts and
surgery, preferring to accept the amused stares of his colleagues and of
strangers. And of course the confounded things were never there
when he wanted them. He could see, behind the glow of the messages-
waiting legend, what looked very much like the fluttery figure of his
dream, but its outlines were fuzzed and unreal as the dream itself.

His search for his glasses was not in the least helped by the fact that
his head was feeling the drinks he had had the night before, or that it
was only five in the morning, more than an hour before he had
planned to get up. When at last he found the glasses, next to the bed
where they always were, the image snapped into clarity.

It was a butterfly! Or not quite, but something with filmy wings and
more eyes than seemed necessary, dancing back and forth in the
limited loop of the stored image.

It was a T'Worlie!

Babylon's jaw dropped. There were only a handful of T'Worlie on
Earth. One of the oldest and proudest races of the Galaxy, they spent
little time on the new member of the Galactic Confederation, the
Earth, or its semicivilized peoples. And this one, he saw at once, was
not on Earth. The T'Worlie came from a light-gravity planet, far out
in the Orion arm. One of the reasons they disliked Earth was that its
heavy pull crushed them to the ground; a T'Worlie on Earth had to
creep around the surface like a wounded moth, prisoner of a tenfold
weight increase that its filmy wings could not support. But this one
was flying free.

Bemused, he stared at it for several minutes before it occurred to
him that the message itself might answer his questions. "Release
message," he ordered the stereo, and at once the repeating loop
opened out and the butterfly creature drew itself up and spoke to him,
dancing and whispering. It was speaking in its native language, Babylon knew, but the whispery-chirpy T'Worlie speech was not one of the
galactic tongues he understood at all. "Translation mode," he commanded, and obediently the stereo interrupted the audio portion of
the message to recirculate the message through its built-in Pmal cir-

cuits. Out here in the islands one could not expect really sophisticated machinery, but the artificial voice-over was clear enough:

"Communication for Dr. Babylon Jen," it rattled. "Mode urgent. Concur requisition to study unidentified spacecraft. Urge immediate compliance." And the image faded.

Babylon got up and made himself a cup of coffee from the autobar. It was strongly laced with chicory or some other substance, not at all what he was used to in Old Cambridge, but it contained caffeine enough to shock his nervous system awake.

He stood frowning at the lightening sky across the strait. What requisition? What was he being urged to comply with immediately? Above all, what "unidentified spacecraft"? And how much of his uncertainty was due to the inadequacy of the stereo's primitive translation circuits, and how much to the peremptory nature of the T'Worlie?

The stage chimed gently to remind him that there were other messages. He sighed and said, "Release next message."

As he turned back to the stereo an ugly image was forming. It was not flesh and blood at all. It was a queer, box-like shape that hung in space within the three-dimensional stage, so lifelike that he could almost smell the acrid reek of the faint wisps of steam that issued from its edges. It was a robot, probably Scorpian—and again, since it hung easily in air, almost certainly not originating from Earth.

The creature spoke, and the Pmal rattled out its translation:

"Jen Babylon," it rapped, "you are not under any circumstances to accept transmission to Cuckoo. The consequences will be extremely grave. You have been notified."

Babylon swore softly to himself; it was a morning for confusing messages. "Release next message," he commanded; might as well get all the confusion at once.

This one at least was human—even a human being he knew! It was the dean of his department, Margaret Kooseman, seated at her desk and beaming pleasantly at the transmitter. "I'm terribly sorry to interrupt your trip, Jen, dear," she said, "but this is a very great honor! Not only for you. The whole school will benefit." Her leathery old face was flushed with pleasure. "By now," she went on, "you will have received your travel itinerary, and I suppose this message will catch up with you somewhere before you get to Boston. Please come to see me as soon as convenient. I want to take you over to the public-relations people so we can get a little publicity out of this appointment for you. I can't tell you how much I envy you!"

And the stage went to orange fuzz again.

Babylon did not try to interpret. He snapped, "Release last message."

But all it was, was a telephone code and instructions to call someone named Ben Pertin at it; and, when Babylon tried the number, it did not answer.

That was a puzzle of a whole other kind. Ben Pertin! He knew the name. It was an old school chum whom he had not seen in a good many years. Why would Pertin be calling him here? For that matter, how had Pertin tracked him down? He had not himself known he would be staying at this hotel until the peremptory recall order and travel instructions caught him between atolls, the day before . . . And something else nagged at him about Ben Pertin, although he could not think just what.

It was all very puzzling. Babylon, sitting on the tiny porch of his shack, with the rising sun making ripples of blood on the gentle lagoon, could understand only that he was being asked to do something, which someone else didn't want him to do, but which the powerful dean of his department could see a solid advantage in for herself.

He shook his head and got up for more coffee from the autobar. One alien creature told him to do something. Another ordered him not to. His dean was all smiles and sweetness without saying what she was being sweet about; and he had a call from someone he hadn't seen in years; and why was it all happening? What had suddenly made a respected, but really rather obscure, professor of quantum-dynamic linguistics suddenly so interesting that people sought him out?

There was no answer. He lifted the cup to his lips—then caught sight of the stereo box. The time! He should have been packed and out of there! That *Polynésie-libre* desk clerk had failed to call him; and now he had about ten minutes to get to the island's hoverport!

Jen Babylon's specialty was the deep structure of language. The fact that it was technically called "quantum-dynamic linguistics" offered clues as to what it was all about, but hardly one human being in a thousand could have explained what the name meant, and fewer than one in a million had any real grasp of its principles.

Linguistics had come a long way since the early studies of Chomsky and Babbage and Korzybski and Claude Shannon. As the pure study of the structure of language, it dated from Chomsky's discovery that sentences which seemed identical in structure were, in fact, essentially and wholly different from each other, and that, even more puzzling, every English-speaking person knew this without knowing that he did. The sentences were not complicated: "John is easy to please." "John is eager to please." Everyone understands both those sentences, and generations of grammar-school teachers have shown their ten-year-olds how to parse them, as if they were identical. Then Chomsky came along. He pointed out that they could not be the same since if you translated them from the active to the passive voice they could not follow the same rules. "It is easy to please John" is good English. "It is eager to please John" was instantly recognized as a false sentence by everyone who spoke the language, even the ten-year-olds. From clues like this Chomsky developed his theory of deep structures and of an underlying rule of law that pertained to all languages—every language that had ever existed on Earth, and even every language that ever could exist, anywhere. Sometimes his rules were called transformational grammar, and that was the beginning.

At about that same remotely historical time, Korzybski began that search for meaning he called semantics, Shannon developed the notion of the unit-quantity of information that he called a bit, and many workers, building on the pioneering Babbage and others, developed rules of expression that permitted them to draw diagrams and equations to test statements for truth or falsity. Boolean algebra and Venn diagrams played a part in what Jen Babylon did, but they, too, were only a beginning. The science was known as quantum linguistics when he came to it. The "dynamic" part was his contribution. For with Babylon's Algorithms, it was easy to write computer programs that could penetrate the deep structure of even a totally unfamiliar language, given almost any contextual clues at all.

Jen Babylon, however unprepossessing he might seem at first contact, had revolutionized his science, and now, still young, he was receiving the rewards and paying the penalties. Sometimes they were the same thing. Travel was one of the perquisites, but it also kept him from any permanent relationships. He needed the freedom to go where his work took him, sometimes at a moment's notice: to Indonesia to work on the symbolism of predawn man's first few scratched symbols (were they true writing? the most exhaustive studies had yet to be sure); to Baffin Island, to tape a few dying words from the suddenly discovered last survivor of a vanished Eskimo tribe; here to Western Polynesia. Even to the Extra-Solar Studies Commission in Beirut, when a thorny problem came up in designing translators for the languages of the other galactic races. So he spent a great deal of his time in aircraft. When he missed his shuttle to the supersonic field on Tahiti, he had experience and resource enough to find another hovercraft from the other side of Mooréa; he battled through customs, carried his bag in his hand, and leaped onto the hydrogen-fueled 3000-class jet just before the doors closed and the loading ramp pulled away.

He was used to having people stare at him as he made one of these last-minute rushes. This time, though, the heads were turned in a different direction, and to Babylon's surprise he saw the woman from the hotel beach standing in a distant aisle, looking as remote as ever while an Air France stewardess expostulated with her. At least this time she was dressed! But she seemed to be wearing the same pareu, no more carefully tied than before. Whatever the problem was, it was submerged in the seat-belt sign's urgency; Babylon strapped himself into his reclining couch. The big hydrogen jet streaked off the long over-the-water runway from Faaa-Faaa Airport and pointed its narrow nose toward the distant North American shore. As it climbed at its steady 3,000 kilometers an hour Babylon pressed the sleeper button, and his chair elevated and extended itself to become an upper berth. He had cultivated the ability to sleep when he could; and he began to drift off easily . . .

And then came abruptly awake.

Ben Pertin! The man who had called him, the man he had not seen for years—suddenly Babylon remembered why that was so. They had lost touch, true, but there was a stronger reason than that.

It had been just a few years after graduation, in an accident while spearfishing in Long Island Lake. Pertin was always a restless, ever-moving sort of person, always looking for a new experience.

He found one there, at the bottom of Long Island Lake. His oxygen regulator failed, and he drowned.

TWO

The stewardess woke him up in plenty of time for him to drink a cup of coffee, splash water on his face, and be ready to disembark, but the Kooks had other plans. They interfered. The main landing strips at Logan-over-the-Sea were blocked by a Kook demonstration. The plane had to circle nearly an hour, at a prodigious waste of hydrogen fuel, while the airport police struggled to get the religious procession off the runways. By the time the plane got to its dock, and Babylon had completed the customs formalities and reclaimed his bag, it was full morning, and he decided against going back to his apartment. It was time to find out what this was all about.

He had difficulty getting to a phone because the remnants of the Kook mob were still being rounded up in the main lounge. They were disagreeable-looking people. It was an article of faith with the Criers of Cuckoo to renounce everything of this world; they wore clothing till it fell off them, they ate barely enough to sustain life, they preached the imminent coming of Cuckoo the Savior and Destroyer at every hour of each day. All of this left them little time for any of the normal preoccupations of humanity—such as earning a living. Their fasting had the additional effect of making them terribly, scarecrow lean— very much like the only race of indigenous humans that had been found on the strange, extragalactic object itself.

That, and their other habits, had one more effect. They smelled bad. Babylon averted his face, and tried to avert his nose, as he called the university's code on the stereophone. "This is Jen Babylon," he told the message-taker. "Please enter an appointment with Dean Kooseman for me in, let me see, half an hour."

The empty golden glow inside the stage stirred silently, and then a sweet mechanical voice said, "Thank you, Dr. Babylon. Your appointment is confirmed."

He tagged his suitcase for delivery directly to his apartment and hurried toward the Cambridge subtrain.

He stopped short, staring at a knot of the Kooks being herded toward the limits of the airport.

Because of Babylon's specialty, he had some familiarity with the languages, and thus with the appearance and life-styles, of a dozen or more of the major races of the Galaxy. And because the application of his algorithms required contextual clues, he had spent a good deal of time studying the collective societies of the creatures from Boötes, and the methane worlds that swung around the core stars, and the plant-like beings who swam in the seas of a planet in the Orion gas cloud. Like everyone who lived in a major city, he sometimes caught a glimpse of, sometimes even met, some T'Worlie or Arcturan as they limped around the hostile Earth streets.

But—here? For among the ragged human Kooks there were three who were not human at all, two doughy, soft Sheliaks and a creature who looked like a purple sea anemone. That was hard to understand! As recently as the few weeks ago when he left for his field trip, the Kooks were scarce, unimportant, and, of course, always human. Barely human; they came from the cast-offs of society. But if they were now attracting the great old races of the Galaxy there had been some significant change . . .

Dean Margaret Kooseman, at whatever age she was past eighty, should have been retired decades ago to make room for younger people. But she was kept on, year to year, because of her immense prestige in the field. It did not matter to the academic decision-makers that most of that prestige was borrowed from the discoveries and innovations of her underlings, whose papers were always coauthored by M. Kooseman, Ph.D., D.H.L., Sc.D. She got the credit, because she was the boss. "Jen, dear!" she cried, getting up to brush her leathery lips across his cheek. "Isn't it exciting? Did those crustaceans bother you on Mooréa?"

At eighty-plus, she was still a surprising woman. "What crustaceans?"

"Why, giant crabs of some sort. It was on the news this morning. They swarmed ashore out of the sea."

"I don't know anything about giant crabs, Margaret." He sat down on the edge of the very soft, very deep armchair she kept so that she could put her visitors at the disadvantage of being trapped in it. "I was laid over in Greater Los Angeles for almost ten hours, so it's been some time since I left Mooréa, and that must have happened after I left. Anyway, that's not what I want to talk about."

"Of course not, Jen dear! You'll do the school great credit. When the call came in from Tachyon Transmission Base requesting your services I was simply *thrilled.*"

Tachyon transmission! But he was not surprised; the summons, and the warning, had certainly come from off Earth, and there was no other real way to travel in space. All physical objects were bound by Einstein's immutable speed law; it was only when coded as tachyon bursts that one could travel a light-year in less than one year. "What I don't know," he said, "outside of why I'm supposed to do this in the first place, is where I am supposed to go."

"Why, Cuckoo, dear. I thought I told you. Didn't you get my message?"

"I got your message and you didn't tell me. For God's sake, Margaret, why am I supposed to go to Cuckoo?"

"Because you are the world's greatest expert in quantum-dynamic linguistics, of course."

"But *why?*"

"Oh, well, Jen," she said vaguely, "they didn't exactly state, but of course it doesn't matter. It's not just your own career that's at stake, or even the school's honor. It's quite a feather in the cap of the human race! There's not a lot of respect for humanity in most of the Galaxy, you know. To have those stuck-up creatures send for a human being to solve a problem that they can't handle is—well, it makes me proud! And there's no use asking me what the task is because I don't know, but of course it doesn't make any difference." She was looking faintly annoyed. "It will only take a minute of your time," she pointed out.

He scowled at her. "That's not true."

"Yes, it is, Jen dear. Oh, not for the you that goes to Cuckoo, no. That might take days, I don't know, perhaps even weeks. But the you that's here in this chair will be right back in it this afternoon. You just walk into a box, and then a minute later you walk out of it again, and that's all there is to it. The scanners read out the total data on every atom of your body, and then they transmit your blueprints over the faster-than-light tachyon beam to—wherever. Wherever in the Universe you want to go. In this case, Cuckoo. And when the blueprints get there, they're read and used to form high-energy plasma into an instant, exact, living duplicate of yourself. He is you in a sense, Jen, that's true. But the other you—the real you that's sitting in my chair right now—*that* you will be sitting there again when the other one's a zillion light-years away."

"But—Cuckoo! Why, that's clear out of the Galaxy! And besides, I've heard of foul-ups. Transmissions that got garbled. People coming out of the other end in the form of messes that you wouldn't believe."

"No, Jen, not anymore. The signals are self-regenerating now, and that just doesn't happen—well, not often, anyway. Unless they've decided to edit the transmitted person in some way, to make it possible for him to survive in the new environment—but why are we talking about this, Jen? It's all the other you, isn't it?"

"I don't want to go to Cuckoo!"

The dean leaned back and looked at him thoughtfully.

"Jen, dear," she began, sweetly enough, "I've always said my department is about as loyal to the university as any faculty we have. Of course," she added meditatively, "I certainly would not want to put any pressure on you. You know that. It's not the way I do things. Never fear, if you chicken out there'll be plenty of other volunteers! So, in a sense, it doesn't matter. But on the other hand—"

Here it comes, Jen thought, as she reached across the desk to pat his hand. "On the other hand," she said, "there's your own future to consider. I'm not getting any younger." She smiled the shark's smile that had been in the dreams of generations of students and junior faculty members. You never knew when Margaret Kooseman was going to open those jaws and eat you up. "When I retire, Jen, I'll of course nominate a successor, but the final decision is up to the faculty senate. And then this would look *very* good on your record. I mean, if you had any interest in becoming dean yourself."

"Margaret! That's blackmail!"

"No, Jen, just the facts of life. You're due over at the Tachyon Transmission Base in three hours."

"Three hours! I can't be ready that fast."

"There's nothing to get ready, Jen. I've had two of your graduate students pack up your Pmals and your microfiche library already. It'll be there when you are."

"But— But—clothes! Personal possessions!"

"You won't have any need for personal possessions on Cuckoo, Jen. They'll give you everything you need. So that's settled." She beamed at him fondly. "And listen, Jen. If you and that pretty graduate student of yours are free tonight, two of the trustees are coming to my place for dinner. I'd be honored to have you come and be introduced, as the university's first volunteer for Cuckoo!"

For all of his life Jen Babylon, like most of the human race since the beginning of time, had been one, single person, with a single past and a single future and no complications about which "he" was "him." There was something terribly troubling about facing up to the knowledge that in just a few hours he was going to be split in two. Two of him! Two Jen Babylons! One here, living the cherished familiar life; the other in some unimaginably distant place, doing heaven knew what. It was not even comprehensible, in an intellectual sense. But there was something heavy and quivering at the pit of his stomach that comprehended it fully, and was in shock.

The mechanical voice of his cab sang sweetly, "You have arrived at your destination, sir. Please insert your credit tab under the flashing orange light and then exit on the curb side of the taxi."

He was at his home. "Oh," he said. "All right." In spite of having slept three separate times in no more than thirty-six hours, he felt no more than half awake as he stumbled into the lift shaft and up to his small fiftieth-floor apartment. It wasn't until he had tried the electrokey three times without getting the door open that he realized it was locked from inside.

Someone was in his apartment. He knocked, frowning. Perhaps it was Sheryl, the graduate student who had supplied as close as he came to a relationship. But it was not like her to be in his apartment when he wasn't there, especially since she probably had no idea he was nearer than Bora-Bora or New Guinea.

When the door opened it wasn't Sheryl. "Good God!" Babylon said, startled. It was his mysterious caller of the night before, Ben Pertin.

But it was not the Ben Pertin he had known in the undergraduate days. This one looked far older and more worn than the dozen years between could explain. "Jen! It's good to see you," Pertin exclaimed, and then responded to the expression on Jen Babylon's face. "Sorry about the way I look," he said wryly. "Things are pretty rugged on Cuckoo."

Babylon shook his hand absently and then, realizing that it was after all his own threshold that he was standing at, entered his tiny apartment. Pertin had been there for some time, it appeared, and had made free use of it. Glasses were stacked at the utilitarian kitchen area, and the neck of an empty bottle protruded from a trash basket. The sleeping couch was in its daytime mode, but the dangling edges of bedclothes showed that it had been used. "Your friend Sheryl let me in," Pertin explained apologetically. "I meant to clean up before you got home, but—"

"It doesn't matter," Babylon said automatically, and then realized it was true. In comparison with Pertin's presence here—from Cuckoo! —it mattered not at all.

"I'm sorry if I've been rude," he said, "but you're quite a surprise! The thing is, I've just been told I'm going to Cuckoo myself."

"You are! God, Jen, that's marvelous! I hardly dared hope you'd do it."

"Actually," Babylon said, "I don't seem to have much choice."

Pertin's face fell. "Well, I'm sorry about that," he said, with embarrassment. "But we really need you! You see, we just—"

"Wait a minute, Ben. What do you mean 'we'?"

"I mean us, all of us on Cuckoo—all the people, and the other races, too. That's why I came here to get you—and, of course, I'm still there, too," he added, in a tone that seemed packed with both pain and rage.

"Because you were tachyon-transmitted here?"

Pertin nodded, and sat down in one of Jen's chairs, reaching for a half-finished drink. "The Sheliaks'll be furious," he said. "They forbade me to do it, but you're needed, Jen. A few weeks ago we sent out a probe and it found something. A ship. Or perhaps a fleet of ships; or a city—it's hard to tell where one leaves off and the other begins. It's immense, and it's terribly old. And we can't get close to it." He finished his drink moodily, started to get up to make another, and then, remembering, looked guilt-stricken. "I hope you don't mind my helping myself, Jen? Would you like one?"

"Go ahead, fix your drink. What about this ship?"

"It transmitted a message—aural, received by the external microphones on the probe, and visual, received on a dozen instruments at once. We can't understand it. I'm convinced that it's the key to entering the ship, but without it—well, it repeated the message three times. And then the lander probe stopped sending. It was destroyed."

"You must have Pmal translators—"

"Oh, hell, Jen, of course we do. They don't work. The language of the message is so different from anything in the Galaxy, anything else we've encountered even on Cuckoo, that there were no analogs to work from. So we need the best linguistics person there is—and that's you, Jen. So I came here, and pulled a few strings with the tachyon-transit people, and they pulled a few at the university . . ."

"Thanks," Babylon said, with an edge to his voice.

Ben Pertin seemed to shrivel suddenly, as if expecting a blow. And then he laughed. "Oh, I don't blame you, Jen. Cuckoo's the garbage heap of the Galaxy, and all of us on it are stepchildren. They transmitted us out there, and most of us die, and no one cares about that. And the ones that are left are trying to do a job—or some of them are, anyway—and no one cares about that, either. Cuckoo is *big*, Jen! You'd think all the races would get together to study it! But we can't even get supplies. And most of the time it seems that half the beings there are principally concerned with trying to keep the other half from getting the job done. It's rotten, Jen." He grinned without humor. "And so you say, how do I have the nerve to make you come out there? Well, I do have the nerve, Jen. You're needed. That's all."

He finished his latest drink and stood up. He frowned abruptly and caught at the arm of the chair for support. "Sorry," he said. "I've been celebrating being home. Now I'll just run along—"

"You might as well stay and have dinner," said Babylon grudgingly.

Pertin thought that was funny. "What dinner?" he giggled. "I've been staying right here waiting for you—and, of course, I had to eat. There's not much left, I'm afraid."

Babylon said, "You leave a lot to be desired as a guest, Ben, but—" He shrugged. Obviously his old school friend had been under more pressure than he could handle. "We can go out and eat, you know."

"Not tonight. There are a couple of people I need to see. One's a girl I've been thinking of for a long time. The other's . . . myself."

"Yourself? But Ben—" Babylon clamped his lips shut on what he had been about to say; it was far better for Pertin to look for that other self and not find it than to be told, just now, why it could not be found. "I understand," he finished. "Good luck."

"I do want to see you, Jen," said Pertin, already halfway out the door. "Tell you what. I'll come back tomorrow and take you out for a drink, all right?"

"All right," said Jen Babylon. But as the door closed he was wondering which Jen Babylon would keep the date.

THREE

What is the etiquette when you are going to go away forever, but also stay behind untouched? Who do you say good-bye to? How seriously?

Forget the etiquette, Jen Babylon told himself. Who do you want to see again, if you are never to see her again?

The only reasonable answer was Sheryl, but Sheryl did not answer either her home line or her forwarding page. Babylon kept trying until the last minute before he had to leave his apartment, and as a consequence was late for his appointment at the Base. His jitney started off toward the great plaza along the banks of the Charles briskly enough; but at each intersection it hesitated, seeming confused. Its limited vocabulary did not allow it to explain its problem to its passenger, but as they approached the Base itself Babylon could see the answer. Six gray hovervans with bars on the windows bobbed gently at the approach to the Base, while furious militiamen struggled to clear a way. All the other approaches were blocked off hopelessly, and this one nearly so, by the largest mob Babylon had ever seen assembled in one place—and every one of them a Kook.

Babylon paid off the jitney and made his way on foot, marveling at the carpet of humanity that spread across the great lawn, the walkways, and even the roadstead. How strange they looked! Some were strange because they could not help it, being aliens from planets that circled stars thousands of light-years away: Babylon spotted several creatures that were in no way human, a doughy flying thing like a saffron amoeba, a T'Worlie like the one who had addressed him so strangely, a couple he did not recognize at all. Of the humans, all looked strange because they cared so little for the way they dressed— or cared so much about demonstrating their difference that they wore the shabbiest and filthiest of garments. Others, the women in particular, looked strange because they had made themselves so. Odd fashions had spread from the other galactic races to Earth. Customs from all over the skies had become a part of Earth's culture, and some of these women wore psychedelic scents, diamond-spangled body paint; and all—all—were starved lean in mimicry of that one known "human" race of Cuckoo. Babylon stepped across prone bodies, lying on the grass and yearning toward the great white block of the Base. A militiaman hailed him: "You! Get out of there. We've got to get these vans through."

"But I've got an appointment for transmission—"

The militiaman shook his head. "The plaza's blocked off till we get this mess cleared up. The Kooks aren't so bad, we can fly the vans right over them as they stay on the ground, but you'd get creamed. Unless, of course, you want to lie down, too?"

Babylon grinned and turned away. There had to be twenty thousand people on the lawn. He marveled that this mad movement had grown so huge so quickly; there had been only a few isolated individuals as recently as a month or two ago. Off toward the river bank a militia platoon had kept a lane cleared, and he managed to get through. At the entrance to the Base he was stopped again, this time by an animated debate between a couple of civilians and a militia officer. "Are they Kooks, too?" Babylon asked a militiawoman with stripes on her arm.

She pushed her helmet back and frowned thoughtfully. "Wouldn't say so exactly," she said. "Least, they're not the same as the dreary bunch on the ground. What they are is lawyers."

"Lawyers? For what?"

"Something about the convicts in the vans," she explained. "Go on inside. You'll see the whole thing in there, then you can come back and tell me."

In the stately, echoing foyer to the transmission facilities there were fewer people but a greater stir. Stereostage cameras were set up at one end of the lobby, and a very pretty woman was talking animatedly to a group of young, angry men and women. They weren't Kooks. What Babylon could hear of their conversation made it clear that they, too, were lawyers—apparently from the ACLU—trying to prevent something about the prison vans outside. "What they want to do," one of the lawyers was declaiming, "amounts to an unconstitutional prolongation of their sentences."

The young woman frowned thoughtfully. "But I don't see how. These are all lifers, aren't they?"

"That's the exact point! They're sentenced to serve their natural lives in prison! But what the Tachyon Base people propose is to send them off to this place, Cuckoo, as recorded patterns, capable of being animated at any time at all—even a hundred years from now. So they may well be dead, and their sentences therefore completed, and yet they will still be subject to involuntary servitude thousands of light-years away!"

Babylon started to move closer, but his way was blocked by another militiaperson, this one a young woman with the crossed batons of a first lieutenant. "Whom do you want to see?" she demanded.

Babylon identified himself. "I'm due for transmission to Cuckoo right now."

"They're behind schedule—of course," she said, and pointed. "Wait over there. There's priority stuff to go before you do." And she was gone before Babylon could question her. He reluctantly sat down on the bench indicated, where a small boy, perhaps ten years old, perhaps less—perhaps anything at all, Babylon conceded to himself, because he was no judge of such things—sat kicking the toes of his shoes together. He was hunched up in the attitude of patient obedience to the whims of grown-ups, but he looked up at Jen Babylon. "Hello," he said.

Babylon nodded, and sat down at the other end of the bench. There was increasing noise from outside the Base, the shouts of militiamen, the whine of hovervans, and a rumble from the crowd of Kooks. He wondered if the militia had carried out their plan to drive the hovervans right over the worshiping Kooks. If so, it hadn't gone well —there was a sudden crescendo of shouts, and then the drone of the fans muted to idle. Babylon wondered what the Kooks would think if he joined them. Or if they knew that he, or at least a copy of himself, would be on Cuckoo within the hour.

"My name is David Gentry," the boy said.

Babylon nodded.

"That's my mother over there," the boy persisted. "Her name is Zara Gentry. She's famous." He kicked a foot toward the stereostage cameras to show the woman he meant, his hands thrust down in his pockets.

"That's nice," Babylon said, only half listening. At the desk before the transmission chamber itself a worried-looking man in a red suede jumpsuit was fumbling irritably through some papers. Babylon leaned toward him and caught his eye. "I'm supposed to be transmitted now," he called.

The man scowled and read a name off one of the papers. "John Babylon?"

"Actually it's Jen. Jen Babylon."

"Whatever it is." The man shuffled that paper to the bottom of the stack. "You'll have to wait."

"But I'm scheduled for Cuckoo—"

"Of course you are! You and fifty-seven others. We'll call you when we're ready, don't worry." And he was off, moving faster than Babylon would have believed likely.

"They're all mixed up here, Mr. Babylon," the boy said. He was a nice-looking kid, with startling green eyes under the long lashes of childhood. "Are you scared?"

"What?" Babylon's full attention was caught at last. He frowned at the boy, then shrugged. "You know," he said, "I think I am, a little. You see, I'm going to be transmitted by tachyon beam to another planet—"

"I know," the boy said scornfully. "Who doesn't know all that? *I* wouldn't be scared."

"You wouldn't?"

"You bet I wouldn't! Boy! Going off to another planet, way outside the Galaxy, meeting all those great alien races and all—boy!"

"You make it sound pretty nice," Babylon said wryly. And, the way the boy described it, it really did. The part that was far from nice was that, for at least one of him, it would be a one-way trip.

"I hope David isn't bothering you too much?"

Babylon looked up, startled. The voice had been attractively, huskily feminine. The face matched it, and it had the same arresting green eyes and long lashes as the boy. "This is my mom," the boy introduced them importantly. "Not only is she a newscaster, she's been tachyon-transported herself. Twice!"

Babylon fished the name from his memory. "Zara Gentry. Of

course! I've seen you many times on the stereo. Your son isn't bothering me at all, honestly."

"I only talk to him when he isn't doing anything else," the boy explained to his mother. "Can I go get a drink of water?"

Zara Gentry looked around the great hall, now relatively quiet. "All right, but don't get in anybody's way." She watched him trot away and then turned to Jen Babylon. "Aren't you the one who's going to Cuckoo to investigate something mysterious?"

"I guess so. I don't know how mysterious it is—except that it's mysterious to me, anyway. My specialty is linguistics. They seem to think I can help them."

"Mmm." She looked at him speculatively, and Jen Babylon realized she was trying to assess whether interviewing him would be a waste of tape. Evidently she decided it would, because she relaxed and said, "Isn't this awful? I've covered Base events a hundred times before, and they usually just go like clockwork."

"Do you know what's holding things up?"

"The Civil Liberties lawyers have asked for an injunction—they want to keep the Purchased Persons from being transmitted—and they're waiting to hear. Of course, that mob of Kooks out there means that the messenger from the judge's office probably can't get through anyway, so we may be here for some time."

Babylon laughed. "Hurry up and wait. They dragged me back from Polynesia at top priority for this—and now I just sit here."

"Polynesia?" The woman looked at him as if she were reassessing. "Were you there when those crustaceans came ashore?"

He shook his head. "After I left, I guess. I just heard some rumors, nothing more."

"Pity," she said, losing interest again. "It's quite a story. They're not the same sort of crabs that are local there. Something special. Quite large, and— Oh! Excuse me! Time to get back to work."

And she was up and away, toward the great central doors of the foyer. Metal heeltips clicking against the terrazzo floor, the militia squad paraded into the Base and formed a double file across the foyer. Between them, the ragged line of convicts shambled haltingly toward the transmission chamber. The noise outside showed that the Kooks were still there, but evidently the militiamen had managed to get through. And, judging from the fact that the ACLU lawyers were standing silently to watch the procession, the request for an injunction had been denied. Babylon saw Zara Gentry excitedly directing her cameramen to cover the scene, and himself moved closer for a better look.

They did not seem as if they needed a squad of militiamen to keep them in order. They had the blank faces and preoccupied stare of all Purchased People, the convicts whose bodies were sold to whatever bidder chose to make use of them. They came in all shapes and sizes, as various as the gaping onlookers or any other random ordinary clutch of human beings. There was a young girl with flowing blond hair between two immense, squat, dark-skinned men, a stout grandmotherly woman of at least sixty following a scar-faced boy surely still in his teens. The militia squad did not seem to be earning their pay. Society did not appear to need much protection from the stumbling, slack-jawed convicts. Not a spark of volition was visible in any of them.

They came quite close to Jen Babylon as they lined up for their transmission. How many of them were there? Fifty-seven, someone had said, with fifty-seven individual life sentences at least among them, for no fewer than fifty-seven separate terrible crimes. Babylon wondered what the crimes might have been. Only doers of victim crimes or unforgivable crimes against the state—murder, rape, kidnaping, terrorism, and the like—were sentenced to be sold as some other creature's puppets. And then only if the convicted criminal refused psychiatric help or was a multiple recidivist.

It struck Babylon that he was looking at people who would be his neighbors in a very short time, for they were destined for Cuckoo.

But that was wrong. Whatever made these fifty-seven creatures individual would be blanked out by the power of the creatures who purchased them. They would be no more than containers for alien personalities. Babylon wondered uneasily what their new owners might be like. They could be almost anything. With all the races of the Galaxy exchanging representatives, there were a great many who could not survive in such appalling stews as the damp, oxygen-rich air of human birthright. The opposite was equally true, to be sure, but humans were not made welcome on some of the more advanced planets, whereas nearly every race had sent at least a few observers to see quaint, primitive Earth. Some came in edited forms, rebuilt to adapt to terrestrial conditions. Others bought convicts like these from the penal authorities, and impressed their own wills on the human bodies.

So whatever these fifty-seven might have been in their own persons, when he met them again on Cuckoo they would be Other. They would *become* alien in their drives and motivations, whatever their physical forms might have preferred, and every act and thought and sensory impression would be relayed to their distant owners, on whatever chlorine-aired or stormy liquid world they inhabited. There was a superstition that long-term Purchased People came to resemble their owners—whether primate or lizardlike, energy beings or dissociated swarms. This was nonsense, Babylon thought. *Probably* it was nonsense . . .

But he was glad, all the same, that he was not one of the fifty-seven.

"Hey, you—hold it!" It was a militiaman's voice, but there was more laughter in it than threat. The knot of Purchased People clotted to a stop, and a small figure darted through them and past the laughing militiamen. It catapulted into Jen Babylon and stopped.

"Excuse me, Mr. Babylon," it said. "Mr. Babylon? Have you seen my mom?"

It was the kid, David Gentry. Babylon turned him around by the shoulders and steered him toward his mother, vivaciously speaking into her microphone while her cameramen were shooting the Purchased People, and as he watched the boy scurry toward her a hand fell on his shoulder. It was the man in the red jumpsuit.

"Mr. Barnaby?"

"That's 'Babylon.' "

"Yes. Come with me for briefing, and don't get mixed up with that lot. You transmit right after them."

"And about time," said Jen Babylon.

The official stiffened. "Do you think I don't know that? Shocking how these people interfere! The traffic that's piling up—the schedules that have to be rerouted—shameful! I've always said it's a mistake to coddle these jailbirds," he said, glaring at the Purchased People as he led Jen past them. "Scan 'em and file 'em, use 'em when you need 'em —what's the use of letting them walk around when they're not being used for anything? I tell you, Mr. Barabbas, criminals ought to be treated like criminals and not like regular full-fare paying passengers like yourself! No wonder the country's going to the aliens!"

It all happened so quickly there was hardly time to wonder if it would hurt. It didn't. There wasn't any pain at all. They inventoried his clothing and the contents of his pockets, gave him a claim check for the baggage that had been transmitted on ahead, and pointed to a door. He went through it, expecting a waiting room. It wasn't a waiting room. It was a tiny chamber, close as a coffin, and the door slid terminally shut behind him. A sweet electronic voice urged him simply to stand still. He closed his eyes on the studded walls and then, even through closed lids, saw a brilliant flash of searing blue light. His skin tingled. He heard one sharp crack, like a jumping spark. A bittersweet sensation washed through his mouth, and he caught a stinging whiff of something acrid and strange—ammonia? Something worse?

And then it was over.

Something shifted all his senses. The sensory illusions were gone. The electronic voice announced that the transmission cycle was complete. A door opened, not the same one, and Jen Babylon pushed through into the foyer of the Base.

He caught the stout man's scarlet sleeve. "Is that— I mean, is it all—"

The man looked at him pityingly. "Your first time? Yes. It's over. Go about your business."

Babylon let go, taking a deep breath of the air of the world he had been about to leave—the world that *one* of him had already and irretrievably left. It tasted very sweet.

He gazed around the foyer with pleasure. The last of the prisoners was just being conducted out through the double doors, and Zara Gentry and her son were gone. The voice of the man in the scarlet suede suddenly erupted from behind, lashing at an assistant: "Can't you keep count? There were fifty-seven of them, it says so right here!"

"Fifty-eight," the assistant said doggedly, waving at a luminous-number counter on the wall.

"Fifty-eight including *him,*" snarled the stout man, jerking his head toward Babylon.

"No. Fifty-nine including him. See for yourself, chief."

"Ah, what's the use?" demanded the man. "How can they expect us to do a good job when the traffic piles up like this? That whole party for Sun One is due for transmission right now, and we're not re-aligned! If we could just get this crowd cleared out . . ."

He was staring nastily at Babylon, who took the hint and strode briskly across the foyer and out the double doors.

There it was! Earth! He was still there! The grass-fringed bank of the Charles had never looked more beautiful, and even the last of the convicts, now being herded back into the hovervans, looked merely pathetic. Or most of them did. Strangely, one of them was looking directly at Jen Babylon. It was one of the big, dark-skinned men, easily two meters tall and muscled in proportion. Babylon could not make out the expression on the man's face. But there was an expression, and there should have been none.

FOUR

A sweet electronic voice urged Jen Babylon to stand still. He closed his eyes on the studded walls and then, even through closed lids, saw a brilliant flash of searing blue light. His skin tingled. He heard one sharp crack, like a jumping spark. There was a moment of strain and vertigo, and then a door opened and he pushed through into the—

Into a place where he had never been!

No time had transpired for him. He felt no sense of change. The thought in his mind was, Ah, well, that's done, now I can call Sheryl about that dinner with the dean—

And then he saw where he was; the thought perished, and something trapped in terror inside his mind screamed, Dear loving God, what have You done? This is *me!* A harsh flood of light stung his eyes. He tasted a dry, sour tang at the back of his throat. He was floating! There was nothing under his feet, nothing but air. He felt a terrifying sense of falling. As any organism will when first deprived of the comforting anchor of its home gravity, his body spasmed in panic. He flailed wildly. His glasses went flying. One hand struck something light and fragile, and a sharp reek of vinegar struck his nostrils. He bounced against some sort of machine, caught an edge of it, and stared around. A creature with filmy wings and the tiny, hideous face of a bat was twittering shrilly at him. The creature was too tiny to be frightening, no larger than a crow, but it was furious. "Did I hit you? Sorry," he said. It stared angrily at him out of an excessive number of eyes and flew out of sight.

He caught his breath. The truth was all beginning to penetrate. Good-bye Sheryl. Good-bye comfortable little apartment, good-bye hopes of becoming dean. All those things now belonged to the life of someone named Jen Babylon; but he was not *that* Jen Babylon. He never would be again.

He shifted position, lost his grip, and floated, tumbling, out into the room again. It was disorienting, but his mind was too full of sudden rage to care. It was a fraud! He had been cheated! It was not some disposable duplicate that was condemned to live out the sorry tatters of a useless life on Cuckoo—

It was himself!

From just outside his range of vision a voice spoke:

"Ah, welcome, dear fellow Earthman! Allow me to assist you."

Long, dry, leathery fingers gripped his shoulder and stopped his tumble, and Babylon saw his rescuer. At first he thought it was an organ-grinder's monkey, escaped from some antiquarian zoo: red vest, hat with a bright green feather, bright shoe-button eyes. A chimpanzee!

But the creature lacked the broad, protruding lips of the circus animal, and it spoke in easy English. "You did, I'm afraid, upset the T'Worlie," it chattered, "and we're both a little bit in the way here. Allow me to assist you. Your first experience in free-fall, no doubt? Yes, I remember the feeling. But we don't bother much with gravity here. Not here," it chattered, courteously tugging Babylon toward a corridor lined with handholds, "and not anywhere around here. Not even on that great clumsy ball out the window— Oh, of course; there's no window in the tachyon chamber, is there? But not to worry. You'll see all you want of Cuckoo, I promise. And more."

He clapped a skinny black hand to his unsimian high forehead. "My manners! I'm Napoleon Chimsky, Dr. Babylon. You can call me Doc Chimp. Now we'd better move along. Have you got everything?"

"I didn't bring anything," Babylon said bitterly. "Some stuff was sent on ahead—and, oh, yes!" He clapped his hand to the bridge of his nose. "My glasses. They came off when I came out of that machine—"

He stopped, suddenly aware that, for the first time in a score of years, he was seeing clearly without them. The chimpanzee chuckled. "You've noticed, eh?"

"I can see!" Babylon cried.

The chimpanzee bobbed his high-domed head. "A little service of the management," he said largely. "As long as you were being coded for transmission it was easy enough to make some, ah, minor improvements. It's called editing. Things like eye readjustments, minor circulatory problems, even malignancies—they can all be edited out automatically. I think you'll find there's not a plaque of cholesterol anywhere in your system, Dr. Babylon." His stare became thoughtful. "It's little enough to do for us, everything considered," he said obscurely, and then, "But please come along! It's really not a good idea to stay here."

With one hand dexterously catching at handholds, the other tugged Babylon gently down a corridor. Babylon involuntarily shrank back at the entrance. There was neither up nor down, and the corridor looked like an endless deep well dropping away beneath him. "Disconcerting? But you'll get used to it!"

The T'Worlie flew past them, chattering angrily. "Mimmie's a bit annoyed with you, I'm afraid," Doc Chimp chuckled. "We're all at sixes and sevens here, right now, because of the large shipment coming in and all the complications."

"You mean those prisoners who were being sent?"

The chimpanzee nodded disdainfully. "The Purchased People, yes. And the legal problems. They should have been out of the tachyon-transporter long ago, but we've had orders to keep their codes stored for a while . . . And, of course, there's worse than that." He sighed, then brightened. "Well, just go through that door, Dr. Babylon. There's somebody waiting for you. I'll go back and soothe Mimmie a bit." And he turned and was gone, launching himself back down the corridor with an amazing thrust of his skinny arms.

Babylon pulled himself carefully through the doorway, and looked around.

"Jen! Jen Babylon! Is it really you?" And Ben Pertin came off the wall toward him, arm outstretched.

Babylon hardly heard what Pertin was saying to him, hardly knew what he was responding. This person was not the Ben Pertin he had gone to school with, wasn't even the copy who had visited him in his apartment only days earlier. The pleasant face was lined and bloated; the grip was flabby, the breath a clear sign of heavy and recent drinking. Pertin was not only unkempt, he was hardly even clean. His hair had not been cut in many months, and had not even been washed in a good long time. It swung behind him in two snarled tails as he moved. When the copy arrived on Earth, it had no doubt taken time to wash and dress and get a haircut before Babylon saw it; but this was the real Ben Pertin.

But the flabby face was split in a grin of incredulous joy. "You made it! I didn't really hope you'd be in time. Did anyone see you?"

"In time for what?" Babylon demanded.

"Going down to the surface! It's all fixed. There's a robot ship going to pick up mass for the tachyon plasma tanks, and we'll be on it—but what about it? Were you seen?"

"A T'Worlie, I guess," Babylon said.

"Old Mimmie! That's all right. He's on our side . . . or I think he is," Pertin mused. "It's the Sheliaks you have to worry about, and Valeria, and the damn Sirians—and worst of all the Scorpians. Well! I'll be ready in an hour, and the ship boosts ten minutes after that. So all we have to do is hide you until then."

"What am I hiding from?" Babylon demanded. "Look, Pertin— what have you got me into?"

The smile faded, and the worn, bloated face sagged into lines of misery. "I guess I played a pretty shabby trick on you, Jen," Pertin admitted. "But it's important. Look, let me show you." He dived back to the console where he had been loosely lashed to the wall, and struck a series of buttons. The blank wall—or floor, or ceiling—toward Babylon's left hand dissolved in a silvery mist, shrinking abruptly into the sharp image of a steel-colored ball hanging in emptiness. "That's it, Jen," said Pertin. "That's Cuckoo. Wait while I wipe off the cloud cover—there." The silvery shine disappeared from the globe as Pertin made adjustments. "That's it, Jen. The whole big damn balloon. Bigger than a billion Earths. Oceans. Continents. Jen, there are *rivers* that are a thousand kilometers wide!"

"I don't see any rivers," Babylon objected.

"Because they're too small to show at this magnification. Look closely. Do you see those little dots, here and there—that one in the lower-right-hand quadrant? Those are the parts we've explored. The biggest of them is about the size of Australia—and all together, we've mapped less than a millionth of the surface. It's as if we'd explored the Boston Common, and that was all we knew of Earth."

"And you've been doing this how long?"

Pertin shrugged morosely. "Ten years and a bit," he said. He shook his head angrily. "Not much progress, right? But it's not our fault! If we had the support— If we could get our requisitions filled for high-velocity scanners— If we could launch ten thousand satellites, with all the instrumentation we need— If anybody just *cared!* But we get nothing. Not even from Earth. Not even replacements. We're all worn out here, Jen. The ones of us who still care are tired. We've all died a dozen times—and there're plenty of beings here who don't believe we ought to do even as much as we're doing!"

"Hey, slow down!" Babylon said, rubbing his head. "You're giving me more than I can handle. What do you mean about dying a dozen times?"

"Oh, you know. Transmitter copies." Pertin was staring angrily at the great sphere. "There's dead Ben Pertins there"—he flashed a red arrow at one of the dots—"and there, and there. And a couple that aren't dead, quite, but might as well be for all the purpose their lives have—if we don't solve this thing." He made some adjustments and all the red arrows winked out but one. "Anyway," he said, continuing to stare at the wall, "Doc Chimp's going to come back for you in a minute, so we can hide you until the ship's ready. I'll explain all the rest of it as we go."

"No, wait," Babylon objected. "Where are we going—and why?"

"To check out that abandoned spaceship, naturally," Pertin said impatiently. "Why do you think I got you here—so you could make a chess partner? You're here because I think you're the only one who can help out." He glanced sharply at the door, as there was a distant sound of chatter. "That's Doc now," he said.

"You didn't tell me where!"

"Oh, that part's easy enough," said Ben Pertin, pointing to the globe on the wall. "That red arrow there, where one of the dead Ben Pertins is. That's where we're going."

The place where Jen Babylon found himself was an enormous hollow polyhedron, orbiting around the great bubble that was called Cuckoo. Doc Chimp whispered to him as they skulked through the corridors, stopping in sudden fright at every noise, and Babylon gleaned that each face of the figure was designed for beings of a different race. "There's hundreds of them here, Dr. Babylon," he hissed, towing Babylon with one long, skinny arm as he guided them through the passages with the other. "And most of 'em crazy! But I guess Ben Linc's told you all about that."

"Ben who?"

"Sssh! Not so loud. Oh, that's your old friend Ben Pertin. *This* Ben

Pertin, that is. He gives himself a different middle name each time he replicates—me, I'm just old Doc Chimp, no matter how many of me there are. And there're plenty now, believe me. Here we are!"

The enormous strength in those skinny limbs stopped them without a jar, and he hurled Babylon into a small chamber. "Got here without being spotted!" the chimpanzee crowed as he followed. "Hope this place is all right," he added anxiously. "It's only a little hole in the wall. Used to belong to the T'Worlies, they used it mostly for nesting, I think. Smells like it, too. But it's not so bad, and anyway it'll only be for a little while. Let me close the door," he added nervously, pushing himself back to the entrance. "There. Now, let's see if you've got the names straight. That's Ben Lincoln Pertin you just saw. There's another one around somewhere, Ben Yale, but I don't get along with him so well. Neither does Ben Linc."

"It must be pretty confusing."

"Oh," the chimp said, considering, "not really. You can always tell Ben Linc by—" The bright monkey eyes narrowed evasively.

"By what?"

"Oh, well, Dr. Babylon, I guess it's no secret. He drinks."

Babylon burst out in laughter. "No, that's no secret."

Doc Chimp looked aggrieved. "He's my friend, Dr. Babylon. He's got a lot on his mind, and I'm really glad you're here, for his sake."

"Well," said Babylon, considering, "I'm glad to be here—I think."

"That," giggled the chimpanzee, "I doubt. I'd be a liar if I said that myself. I've been here eleven years, two months, and a week, and that's a bunch of days and nights, Dr. Babylon, especially as I've never been able to get them to tachtran a pretty little girl chimp out here for company."

Babylon said, "I didn't think—I mean, it never occurred to me—"

"You didn't think I was interested in that? Or capable of it, maybe? Really, Dr. Babylon! I guess you've never been at Yerkes or the Max-Planck Institute. There's whole colonies of us back on Earth. They made us, you know. Loosened up the skull so the brain could grow, changed around our face structure and throat musculature so we could make words—I make them pretty well, don't I? They used to think we'd come in handy for getting into small places where human beings couldn't go. And we did. We came in even handier in free-fall, though. So," he said wistfully, "where I wound up was Sun One. Or one of me did. Heaven knows how many of me there are, scattered around the Galaxy—and not a girl chimp among the lot of us. Now," he said, stealing a glance at the tiny watch face almost hidden in the fur of his wrist, "I'd best go out and scout the territory. You just make yourself comfortable, Dr. Babylon. I won't be long—and then we're off!"

The lander was shaped something like an earthly garbage truck, square and equipped with hatches and endless-belt buckets to load up with whatever was at hand. It didn't matter what. All the tachyon receiver's plasma tanks needed was nuclear particles to engineer and shape into whatever elements were needed to reform the objects transmitted. The best substance was the densest, which was why the lander descended clear to the surface for solid matter instead of scooping up gases anywhere in Cuckoo's atmosphere.

But the lander was a great deal bigger than any earthly garbage truck. Jen Babylon saw it through a port as they crept furtively through the empty corridors, and he decided it had to be a hundred meters in length, more than half of that in its other dimensions. They did not enter the main cargo section; there was a small built-in control section at one end, like the cab on a truck, and that was their destination.

Ben Pertin was waiting for them as they arrived, and sprang forward to grasp Babylon's hand. "You know," he confessed, "I was beginning to think that I'd dreamed you being here—wishful thinking, you know! I've had so much of it these years—but it's true, you're here. And just in time!"

"In time for what?"

Pertin looked surprised. He pulled at one of his greasy pigtails in exasperation. "Why, to go and get some language samples, of course, and bring them back for processing."

"Processing how? With what? In Boston I had a ten-million-dollar lab—what do I do here?"

Pertin said irritably, "Oh, hell, Jen, we have equipment! Pmals and integrators—we've got the FARLINK computer that taps into almost anything in the Galaxy, although I admit it's hard to get time on it. Anyway, you can always tachtran data back to yourself in Boston, you know!"

"But—"

"Now, that's enough 'but,' Jen!" Pertin snarled. "We don't have time to argue. This thing's going to take off in about five minutes. It's under robot control, but Doc's tinkered with the programing. It will bring us right down to where the other party was lost—"

"Hey," said Babylon. " 'Lost'? What do you mean, lost?"

"Oh, that's all right," Pertin said reassuringly. "We didn't know what we were up against that time. Now we're warned. We'll be okay, Jen."

"You're sure of that?" Babylon demanded.

Pertin hesitated, then grinned weakly. "How can you be really sure of anything?" he asked. "We've got a real good chance, though, and of course if worse comes to worst we all just hop in the tachyon transmitter and we're right back here in the orbiter. Now, look, there isn't much time. This is a robot lander, and it uses more G-forces than most of them, so you'll have to strap yourself in. Doc? Help him out, will you?" He was fastening straps around himself as he spoke. "Next time you go down," he said, crisscrossing webbing across his chest, "you'll go de luxe. We've got landers that'll let you down easy as a nesting dove—have to, you know, so we can fly the autochthones around. They're built so flimsily that a good sneeze will wreck them. Not much gravity on the surface of Cuckoo, you know."

He rambled on, while the chimpanzee secured Babylon's harness and sprang into a niche of his own. Doc Chimp didn't bother to fasten himself; evidently he had enough confidence in those simian arms to dispense with assistance. And then they waited.

Pertin said, with a note of alarm, "Hey, we should have left before this. Doc? Did you screw the program up?"

"Not a chance, Ben Linc! You know me better than that!" the ape protested.

"Then what the devil's holding us up? I'd better take a look myself." And, aggrieved, Pertin began to unsnap his harness.

Before he got out, Doc Chimp flung himself across the room to the door. "Wait," he snapped, his monkey face contorted in worry. "Somebody's coming!"

Somebody was. Now even Jen Babylon could hear the sound from outside, faint, staccato hissing like malfunctioning air brakes.

"It's a damn Scorpian," Pertin whispered, his face woebegone. "We've had it!"

A discolored metal cube sailed in through the door and halted itself in midair with a rush of steam. Metallic optics tilted themselves toward Jen Babylon, and a drumroll of sound struck his ears. Babylon recognized it as language, but it was not one of the galactic tongues he knew. Doc Chimp came to the rescue. "Here, take my Pmal," he said. "Didn't think you'd need one for this, but—" He shrugged.

The robot rattled peremptorily again, and the Pmal translator echoed in Babylon's ear: "Jen Babylon. You were notified. You were not to come to Cuckoo. The consequences are grave."

The words had an eerie familiarity for Babylon: of course, it was the same message he had received on Earth. Perhaps even the same robot. "What are you going to do?" he asked apprehensively.

"I am going to take action," the robot thundered. "Since you would not remain on your foul damp planet, events must take their course. I propose to join you in this expedition to discover for myself the nature of this wrecked spaceship. Then we will see."

"We'll see that you're going to blow Cuckoo up!" Pertin flared defiantly.

"That is one of the available options," the robot acknowledged. "It is strange and worrisome. It presents a threat to our orderly existence, and that cannot be permitted. But that decision has not yet been reached."

"I suppose you're going to try to prevent us from going there now," Pertin said. "Well, you won't get away with it!"

"I have no such intention," the robot declared. "I have merely revised the programing to allow a short delay. I suggest you frail organics restrain yourselves; this lander will boost within fifty-five seconds!"

FIVE

As the robot lander made its occasional course corrections, it spun lazily sometimes this way, sometimes that. The port by Jen Babylon's head sometimes showed the great sweep of black, oppressive nothingness that was the external sky, broken only by the distant spiral glitter of the Galaxy that contained his home. Then there was a shudder and a slow swing, and he was looking directly down on the vast bulk of Cuckoo. It did not grow as they approached. It had seemed endless even in the first minutes; but as they descended the scale enlarged. Mottled blurs resolved themselves into mountain ranges and seas. Pale-hued splotches became clouds—cloud banks hundreds of thousands of kilometers across, many of them, with tints in every frequency of the spectrum of visible light. From where he clung behind Babylon's neck, Doc Chimp chattered: "Impressive, isn't it? A world with air and seas and land—twenty thousand times the diameter of Earth! Half a billion times the area!"

"Give it a rest, Doc," Ben Pertin begged, staring at the instrument panel. "We're about to enter the atmosphere—anyway, Jen's head is bulged out with facts and figures by now. We don't want it blowing up."

"Thanks," Babylon muttered; because the joke was almost true. For many hours—he had lost count of how many—Pertin and the chimp had been talking endlessly, often both at once. In one ear Doc Chimp whispering fearfully of strange cabals among the alien creatures on the orbiter; in the other Ben Linc Pertin, alternately sobbing about his loneliness and his lost love, and boasting of how much they would accomplish now that Jen Babylon was here. Both kept a wary eye on the Scorpian, but if the robot paid any attention it was hard to detect. It hovered in the middle of the control cabin when the thrusters were off, occasionally darting to the instrument panel or to the ports with jets of hot-oil-smelling steam.

It was all too much to take in, but the central facts were certain. Fact one: Something strange was going on in the orbiter. Fact two: Something stranger still waited for them on the ground, a wrecked spaceship of unimaginable age, still capable of defending itself against intruders. And fact three: This was the end of the road for Jen Babylon. Whatever else happened, Jen Babylon—or some Jen Babylon—would live out his life on and around that peculiar body called Cuckoo; and from that verdict there was no appeal.

"Let's hear what's happening," Pertin muttered, and moved a switch. At once the sweet electronic voice of the pilot program spoke to them from the instrument panel:

"Approaching entry point. Prepare for deceleration, increasing to twenty-eight meters per second squared, plus or minus three. Warning! Ten seconds. Five. Two. One—"

The safety rack squirmed behind Babylon's body, dragging him with it. Outside, the black sky turned gray, then blazed into a sudden flare of orange as the thrusters hurled forth their vapor. He felt crushing pressure for a moment—three full gravities!—then slightly less.

"Sorry about that," Doc Chimp giggled in his ear. "Ben Linc warned you this lander was a rough one."

Babylon didn't answer. He was staring at the spectacle outside the port. There they were, the layered clouds of Cuckoo: steel dust in the highest reaches, from crystals of frozen oxygen; lower down, luminous seas of rose, gold, green.

These were not the ragged, diffuse clouds of Earth. Their edges were sharp as knives. They were swarms of tiny airborne creatures, collective beings like the aliens from a world in the constellation Boötes, called Boaty-Bits. Each was a separate entity, but together they made a superindividual, a flock or school or herd that moved together through the air. Lower still were real clouds . . . and below that, sinister and dark, the rough surface of Cuckoo itself.

"Prepare for landing," trilled the sweet voice of the pilot program.

Another sudden surge of thrust; a twisting moment of vertigo; and they were stopped. Actually, the landing was surprisingly gentle. The surface gravity of Cuckoo was so insignificant that landing was only a matter of slowing the speed at the proper time. There was no clutch of gravity to cause a real crash, only the possibility of flying into the unyielding surface.

As Babylon struggled with the straps of his restraining cocoon there was a sudden stillness. Only a moment; felt more in the brain than perceived in any sensory organ. And then an immense sharp crash, like a pistol shot beside the ear. Babylon shouted in surprise and sudden shock. To his wonderment his fellow travelers seemed to take it as a matter of course. Even Ben Linc Pertin only nodded, and offered a weak laugh.

"Worse than ever," he crowed. "Why, they missed us by several minutes!"

"What in God's name was it?" Babylon demanded.

Pertin sobered. "I told you the ship tried to repel invaders," he said, busying himself with his own harness. "But it's very old, Jen, and its reflexes are slow. And getting slower. Why, the first time I landed here it only missed us by a fraction of a second! Of course," he added soberly, "its aim's bound to get better as we get closer in."

"Pertin," blazed Jen Babylon, "I've had a bellyful of you! This is the last time I let you get me into something I can't get out of!"

Pertin shrugged morosely. "Better get your gear on," he suggested, strapping a slim cylinder to his own shoulders. "You want me to apologize? The hell I will. I didn't ask for this job, either—and you might as well know there's a good chance that this will be the last time for anything at all, for either of us!"

There was not much gear to put on, but none of it was familiar to Babylon. The Pmal translator was the easiest part, and the least strange: it was a simple language processor, but good enough for most galactic tongues, and Babylon had worked with far more complex versions of it back in the linguistics labs. A thruster was strapped between his shoulders—"Walking's much too slow here," Doc Chimp chattered as he helped Babylon on with it. "Believe me, you've got to move briskly if you want to make it past the defenses!" And there were a dozen tools and implements and weapons, none of which Babylon had ever seen before: getting into the ship was evidently not going to be easy!

The lander lay in a small declivity, with only the mottled sky of Cuckoo overheard. There was not much light; only what the distant clouds gave, no more than starlight on Earth. Babylon had hoped that on Cuckoo he would weigh some normal amount again, but the soap-bubble object was so tenuous that he seemed to weigh no more than a kilogram. Underfoot was a waste of sand, velvet-black, trackless, untroubled by any wind. But it was not featureless. Blue sparks of light flashed from random points within it, like the glow of a tropic surf with its luminescent organisms. Babylon could see the outline of his feet against the diamond sparkles of the sand more clearly than he could see the rest of him, or the others.

"Better get started," said Pertin, his voice queerly strained as he peered over the gentle rise toward their objective. "Go easy with your thruster, Jen. Take time to practice; stay behind the rest of us, you can catch up later."

Doc Chimp showed him the little lever that turned on the gentle steam jet, all the energy needed to move about in the insignificant gravity of Cuckoo. But even that was a lot! At first thrust he soared into the ebony sky, suddenly meters up in the air.

Doc Chimp, giggling, jetted after and caught him. "That way, Dr. Babylon," he said, pointing. "No sense trying to get back to the orbiter this way—you'd never make it." Then he sobered as they leveled off. "Question is," he muttered, "will we make it at all?"

They were in the heart of an immense dark plain, and throughout it were scattered vast dark shapes. They looked like buildings, though Babylon knew that they were not. But they were not natural, surely? He could not see the tops, could not even guess how high they stood. But far up he could see a section of a distant, pale cloud, cut off where a corner of one of the structures intersected it. It was at least two hundred meters over his head. "Doc, what *are* these things?" he demanded, staring about. "It looks like a city!"

"Heaven knows, Dr. Babylon. The T'Worlie say they're natural—maybe living organisms. But, oh, don't they look like a good old Earthly city skyline? Not as nice, though." The chimpanzee was staring about worriedly. "We'd best move along—look, Ben Linc and the Scorpian are halfway there."

"Where's 'there'?" Babylon demanded.

"Right where those structures are thickest," sighed the chimp. "You'll see. Oh, never fear. You'll see." He twisted his spidery body in midair, activated his thruster, and soared away, Babylon following clumsily. The gentle Cuckoo gravity was forgiving and in a few moments he was able to control the direction of thrust well enough to keep a course. Below and behind him the lander had started its automatic scoops, shoveling the diamond-sparkly dust into hoppers for transport back to the orbiter, to be turned into plasma mass for the tachyon receiver. Directly under him was a cluster of jet-black prisms, then a tetrahedron of dull copper, then to one side half a dozen tall tapering cones that glowed pale gold. There were cubes like blocks of blue ice, glassy cylinders, spidery shapes that could not have existed on a denser world—they stretched for endless kilometers across the sparkling sand, and ahead of them, past the forms of Ben Linc Pertin and the robot, they seemed to cluster around a darker and less regular shape.

"That's it," Doc Chimp called over his shoulder, pointing as he flew through the sultry air. Real fear was in his voice as he added, "We'd better get there fast—looks like they're waking up again."

Babylon realized that something had changed. The structures which had been only hazy outlines in the gloom were sharper and clearer now. His eyes had not become dark-adapted; the shapes really were brighter, with a glow from inside. As the chimp and Babylon caught up with the others, the Scorpian robot rattled peremptorily, and Babylon's Pmal translated: "Caution! I sense a powerful electrostatic potential building up!"

"Get down!" Pertin yelled, gesturing toward the ragged shape at the center of the structures. The robot spurted steam and arrowed toward the ground, Doc Chimp and Pertin following quickly. Swearing, Babylon struggled to direct his thruster and join them. He made it —barely. As he touched ground and was caught by the skinny arms of the chimpanzee the brightest flash he had ever seen crackled through the air above them, followed by the grandfather of all thunderclaps.

In the blinding blackness that followed, Babylon lay sprawled on the cold, dry sand, his ears ringing. He felt a tingle over his head and arms, and the air had a biting tang of ozone.

"Close," Ben Linc grunted, pushing himself erect. "Thank God they're slow. It'll be four or five minutes before the next one." He peered at the great irregular black shape before them, then gestured off to the side. "See that gouge?"

The diamond sand was plowed into a furrow so huge that Babylon had not seen it at first. It stretched as far as the eye could see, and in it structures like the ones all around them had grown. "That's what this ship dug out when it crashed," Pertin said, "and that's the way we came last time. There's not as much shelter there; maybe that's why Doc and I got aced." He said it so easily! Babylon thought. But he was talking about the death of his own self—or one of his selves—a self as real and aware as the one that was speaking. "There wasn't any entrance on that side," he continued, "and that's probably why we got it. But tachyar surveillance shows one over here somewhere." He was peering around the bleak, shattered face of the huge object before them. "Wish I could see it," he grumbled.

The Scorpian robot, hovering just above them on the lazy wisps of its steam jets, rattled out: "Possible entrance structure detected. Ferronickel alloy. Surface oxidized as if from great heat and long exposure. Structure intact." A lance of red laser light sprang from one of the faces of the cube to indicate the spot.

Cautiously Babylon activated his jet, rising a bit to get a better look. "I think we can get in there," he decided. "We'll probably have to cut—"

"Get back down here, man!" cried Doc Chimp, clawing at his ankle; and the Scorpian reinforced him:

"Electrostatic potential building again," it rapped out. "Nearing maximum—"

Flash and thundercrack struck at the same instant, well over their heads, and at once Ben Linc Pertin leaped up. "Now!" he cried. "Let's see if we can get inside before the next one!" And he was already arrowing toward the spot the Scorpian had pointed out, with the robot close behind. Doc Chimp grasped Babylon by the nape of the neck, activated his own thruster, and dragged him through the air.

"Sorry to be rude," he panted. "But I don't want to be airborne when that goes off again—"

"But there was plenty of time between shots before," Babylon choked out.

"Oh, Dr. Babylon, never think that," cried the ape. "They speed up, you see. That's how we got killed before. Now!" And he dragged Babylon down to the shelter of the huge, ancient artifact.

A third bolt raged through the air they had just left. Babylon felt an electric sting in his teeth; it was that close.

Amazingly, Ben Linc Pertin was jubilant. "Made it this far," he cried, "and I never thought we would! Now all we have to do is get inside!"

Something, very long ago, had plunged through the shallow gravity well of Cuckoo to wind up in this strange, black place. According to the tachyar observations, it was irregularly shaped metal with a gross mass in the tens of millions of tons—very similar to the orbiting objects they had detected high above the body, but had never been able to reach to study. Pertin's conjecture was that one of the orbiters, ages ago, had crashed there. The reason was anyone's guess; but the fact was their hope. Every other installation on Cuckoo or around it had defenses of such might that it was impossible to get close. But this one was a wreck. Its defenses still existed, all these unimaginable ages after its crash, but they had been weakened, had become less sure and deadly.

"Deadly" was an appropriate word, Babylon thought, peering up at the irregular wall of metal that was the shell of the spacecraft. Black, rugged, shrouded in mystery, it seemed to emanate an aura of menace and immense age. Doc Chimp, peering up along with Babylon, whimpered faintly and shook his furry head. "Oh, Dr. Babylon," he mourned, "what are us civilized primates doing here? That thing doesn't want us!"

"Grab your tools and shut up," Ben Pertin ordered. "We're safe here for a little while—I think. But I don't want to be hanging around out here if this thing gets the range and decides to blow us into atoms!"

"What can I do?" Babylon asked, as Pertin and the chimpanzee began pulling tools out of their backpacks.

"Stay out of the way," Ben Linc panted. "When we get inside you'll have plenty to do, but this is specialist work. I got a Watcher to show me how the seals on their fortresses work—I think this is the same plan."

"Keep an eye on that robot for us, won't you?" asked Doc Chimp, extending a metal construction like a pair of dividers.

Babylon nodded, and turned away. The Scorpian, ignoring what the humans were doing, was thrusting away along the bottom of the derelict. So close, Babylon was able to get an idea of the object's real size. It bulged out over their heads, roughly a globe a thousand meters through, but misshapen by design and by chance. Great wedges and crevasses had been torn out of it as it plunged through the air and along the ground; others seemed to have been designed into it by its builders—whoever they might have been. Or whatever. It had piled up a scarp of debris and soil at one end as it struck, so that one side was buried under dozens of meters, while the other, the one they were on, lay nearly bare. Twisted and fused stumps of mysterious instruments jutted from it.

"Babylon!" Ben Pertin panted. "Now give us a hand!"

He and Doc Chimp had deployed the most complex of their tools, an affair of suction cups mounted on long pipestems. One set was affixed to a dimly outlined circular area that they had decided was an entrance port, the other to the scarred old hull itself. There was a crank that was meant to turn the inner circle; but in the fragile gravity of Cuckoo there was nothing for either man or chimp to brace himself against. Babylon grabbed the handle, overlapping the grips of the other two; but all three combined had not enough weight to move it.

As they struggled a drumroll from behind told them that the Scorpian had returned. "Desist!" their Pmal translators barked. "I will move that!" Panting, they backed away as the robot moved in. Metal grapples on its fore end locked around the handle of the crank. It positioned itself carefully, and then erupted a shrieking blast of steam. The crank quivered and began to turn, and slowly the inset disk shuddered free. "Get back," the chimpanzee chattered, as the Scorpian began to revolve with the crank. It looked like a hissing, white-plumed pinwheel as it spun faster and faster around the narrow circumference of the crank arm; and then it stopped, and the disk slid free.

An explosion of light came from inside. "Good heavens," Doc Chimp cried. "It's still got power, after all this awful time!" And so it did, not only for its weaponry but for a host of automatic machines, all activated by the opening of the port. A vast hooting clamor reverberated through the chamber. As the sound died, Babylon heard a beeping trouble signal from his Pmal.

"It's language," he cried. "The ship's talking to us!" He checked the machine translator and found what he had expected: its input circuits had diagnosed the presence of language, but it lacked any sort of translation match to deal with it.

"I think I know how to translate it," Doc Chimp muttered hoarsely. "It's telling us to get out!"

The Scorpian rattled: "Dr. Babylon! Are you recording all this?"

Before Babylon could speak, Doc Chimp interposed: "I'm doing it for him. Don't worry, sound, vision, even smells and vibrations—it's all in here!" He patted the bubble-recorder strapped under his arm.

"Then let us proceed," the robot declaimed. "This cavity is an airlock. The ship itself lies beyond that second valve."

Again the three terrestrials struggled to attach the gears and suction cups, and again the robot disdainfully ordered them away. The loud hooting continued, and the flood of light waned and waxed in varying hues and intensity. Babylon, leaping back to give the robot access to the crank, recognized the barest outlines of pattern in the sounds and lights, confirming the Pmal's diagnosis. But none of it resembled any language family in his experience, and he took time to check Doc Chimp's recorder to make sure it was all being preserved.

"What's the matter, Scorpian? Getting tired?" Doc Chimp called. The shriek of steam was perceptibly weaker, and the flashing pinwheel slower as the robot toiled at the crank.

"Acknowledge datum," the robot rapped. "Reaction mass significantly depleted. Project inability to repeat process more than one more time."

"We won't need more than this one," Ben Linc Pertin cried as the disk fell away. "We're inside!"

And they pushed through the circular hole into silent gloom.

Whatever energies the ship had stored seemed all concentrated in the external defenses and the lock itself. The interior was dark and still. Ben Pertin produced a search lamp, and the Scorpian suddenly did something that caused the end of one of its tentacles to flare into light. In the uncertain illumination they stared around.

If this were really a ship, Babylon thought, its crew must have been beings far larger than men. The passageways were tall and wide, and every outrageously unfamiliar structure was immense. They slid across wide planes of massive metal lace—perhaps decks? perhaps perforated for lightness? or for ventilation? The decks were at a crazy angle, and only the easy motion possible on Cuckoo's surface allowed the party to move across them. They scuttled around immense rectangular structures, some pale green, others eye-straining deep metallic blue, and stared with awe at a thick column of blackness. Too light-absorbent to be anything material, it rose through one opening in the deck and vanished through another opening above.

Ben Pertin halted, flashing his light about in silence for a moment. "My God," he said at last.

The Scorpian robot, sailing across the empty space, brought up sharply near his head. "Reference not understood," it rapped severely. "Request clarification."

Pertin shook his head wearily. "I can't explain it to you. It's just that—ah, Jen, what did I bring you out here for? I thought all we had to do was get inside and then it would all be clear. And now that we're here, in this ship that's heaven knows how many million years old—I don't know what to do next!"

A furious drumroll came from the robot. "Clarification understood. Problem not significant. I will lead the expedition from this point."

"You!" Pertin said contemptuously. "How would you know? You weren't even supposed to come along!"

Another drumroll from the robot, and the Pmal translator rattled into Jen Babylon's ear: "Objection irrelevant. Follow!" And the silvery cube steamed away. The white-hot spark of light at the end of its tentacle shrank with distance, outlining vast regular shapes that glinted with metal or soaked up the light like carbon black.

"Ben Linc," the chimpanzee quavered, "I don't like this place, and most of all I don't like following that tin can! If we primates don't know what to do, how would he?"

Pertin scowled and rubbed his chin. "For that matter, how did he know we were coming here?" he asked. "There're things going on I don't understand! But what choice do we have? Have either of you got a better idea?" He paused for a second, then nodded. "I thought not, so let's tag along. At least he's moving slower now—too much reaction mass gone, I guess!"

Babylon tagged after the other two, his thoughts as bleak as the choking darkness they moved through. Doc Chimp, taking Babylon's skill as now established, had left him to struggle with the delicate balance and aim of his thruster by himself; and in the black, with no reference points to guide him, his skills were barely up to it. The distant spark of the robot was almost out of sight; the search beam Pertin carried was rapidly receding before Babylon could get squared away.

As his arms flailed, his wrist passed before his eyes and he caught a glimpse of his watch. He looked again, then swore in disbelief. Less than ten hours had passed since he had emerged from the tachyon transporter! Less than a week, really—never mind whatever time he spent as a stream of coded pulses between Earth and the orbiter—less than a week since he had been quietly taping Old Polynesian in the Southwest Pacific, with no worry greater than whether there would be fresh pineapple again at lunch. It was incredible. There had simply been no warning, no hint anywhere in the world he could see that he was about to be thrust into this mad adventure, played for stakes he did not understand, against opponents he did not know.

And meanwhile he sailed down immense black corridors on the trail of the winking flare of the Scorpian robot.

When he caught up with the party they were clustered around a narrow doorway that led into a vast black room. Pertin was expostulating with the Scorpian, to no avail. The robot rapped a contemptuous dismissal, and sailed into the blackness. The hot blue arc on its tentacle flooded the room with harsh light and the three terrestrials peered inside.

What they saw was a hollow globe, with a bridge across it. At the center of the sphere the bridge widened to form a disk rimmed with structures, faced with dials and knobs and buttons, patterned with strange symbols. Doc Chimp chattered nervously, "Are we going in there, Ben Linc? It looks awfully strange to me!"

Pertin shrugged. "I think he's found the right place," he admitted grudgingly. "God knows how. That Scorpian knows more than he ought to! When we get back to the orbiter I'm going to have a lot of questions—questions about how this thing came to be and how it was destroyed. If it was an orbital fort, brought down by military action, was it maybe manned by mutineers against whatever rules Cuckoo? What sort of beings were involved? And what was their quarrel?"

"Mighty big questions." Doc Chimp jumped and clutched a metal bar three meters above the bridge. A railing, maybe, if giants had walked it. He clung there, squinting uneasily into the dark ahead. "Don't ask them too fast. I think the answers could kill us again."

Babylon pulled his shoulder pack forward and started his own set of omnirecording instruments. Doc Chimp's might be adequate, but he chose to take no chances. There was no knowing what this race had used for communication—sound, modulated light, radio, perhaps even gamma-ray signals; the recorder would sample everything.

The rap of the Scorpian robot interrupted him. "Desist!" his Pmal rattled. "I have not instructed you to record."

Babylon looked up at the shining hulk of the robot, which had flashed back toward him and hovered ominously overhead. "I'm doing my job," he said.

"Correction! Language specimens of second priority! First priority assigned to technological data, emphasis weapons systems!"

Babylon felt a sudden rush of fury. "You idiot," he snapped, "language is why I'm here! I know nothing about weapons!" He stopped as Ben Pertin touched his arm.

"Let me handle this, Jen," the other man said, and confronted the robot. "Buzz off," he ordered. "We have an assigned mission and you're only a hitchhiker. We're looking for records of some sort, not weapons."

The robot hovered silently, its thoughts unguessable; then, without responding, it flashed away. "Oh, how I loathe that thing!" Doc Chimp chattered. "Come on, Dr. Babylon. Do what you have to do, so we can get out of here!"

How far all this was from the orderly acquisition of knowledge in some library or among some distant tribe! Jen Babylon could not believe that he was here, in this ancient vessel, on this incredible world. Yet his reflexes worked as well as in Cambridge or on Mooréa. He found himself involved in the puzzle of what, for these long-dead people, had constituted a language. The more personal puzzle of what was going to happen to him next remained outside his focus of thought. They sailed through immense black corridors, dived into pits of black mystery, emerged along the bridge that widened to form a disk. All this Jen recorded on his instruments and fed into the emerging pattern in his brain: the language, then, was not wholly unlike human, in that it used graphic representations (the markings on the instruments) and sound modulation (the challenge at the entrance) to convey information. That was pure profit! It could have been much harder.

Somewhere in the shadows they saw the robot's hot blue arc, cutting into something or carving something away; Babylon shuddered at the thought of what forces it might be releasing, but did not hesitate. He reached out and touched the devices before him . . .

They were still alive! A dial glowed. Shadows began to flicker across the dark curve before him. "Oh, Dr. Babylon," whispered the chimp beside him in awe, "we're looking outside! Those are the towers!"

They were; the picture shook and then firmed itself. Babylon could make out the angular outlines of the crystal mountains—or crystal beings—around the wreck, and the vast swath it had cut when it fell. Squinting upward, he caught a pale shimmer of color, clearly the luminous sky of Cuckoo; but beneath them was only darkness shot with brief flares of scarlet and gold. "It's the control room, all right," he said. "The walls are a screen to show everything around—damaged now, I would guess, so that only part of it works. Help me find a readout or tape speaker—some sort of records!"

"I don't know what to look for, Dr. Babylon," the chimp complained.

"Neither do I! Use your brain!" The chimp turned away dolefully; Pertin was already touching, peering at, even smelling every object in sight. It was not even physically easy. Babylon decided that the operators of the ship must have been twice human height, and their hands must have had no human shape; everything was uncomfortable and unfamiliar. From the doorway Doc Chimp chattered:

"Look here, Dr. Babylon! There's stuff missing!" There was a thing that might have been a cabinet, but its shelves were empty. "Somebody else got here ahead of us! Oh, Dr. Babylon, what do we do if they come back?"

"Oh, come off it, Doc," Babylon snapped. "It was probably ten thousand years ago—anyway, what do you suppose these things are?"

It was a rack of slim black hexagonal rods, neatly stacked on spindles on a massive block of something slick and black. Each hexagon was patterned along one face with markings that could be nothing but writing. Babylon gently pulled one off its spike. It was light enough to be plastic, strong enough to be steel, and apart from its markings totally featureless.

It was Doc Chimp who found the answer to the puzzle. "That slot," he chattered. "Wouldn't one of them fit into it?"

They clustered around, peering at the six-sided slot in the corner of the block. They did not have to speak; Babylon knew the same thoughts were in all their minds: tape recorder of sorts? Or weapons-arming system? Or self-destruct commands? Or something wholly unguessable?

There was only one way to find out. Babylon slid one of the hexagons into the slot before either of the others could object.

There was a soft chime, and the block became semitransparent. Swirling plumes of colored light moved within it.

Babylon bent to his instruments, and the Pmal monitor beeped instantly. "Receiving apparent signal," it whirred. "Wave shapes indicate high-order complexity. No apparent match in database."

Babylon pulled the hexagonal rod out of the slot, and the colors died. "I think this is what we came for," he said. "I don't know what it is—ship's log, maybe; maybe porn shows for the crew—who knows? But it's some sort of corpus, in some sort of context. If we can get it back to FARLINK I think I might be able to reconstruct it."

"Get what back?" Pertin demanded. "Those sticks?"

"All of them—and the block, too."

"Jen! That's got to weigh hundreds of kilos!"

"Do you have a better idea?" Babylon demanded.

Pertin stared glumly at the block. At last he sighed. "Guess we'd better get that damned Scorpian back with his torch; that thing's never going to come loose any other way." He tugged at the block experimentally. "Nope. Part of the structure. And how do we know that cutting it free won't ruin it? And even if we did—"

But while Pertin was talking, Doc Chimp was tugging and poking and prying; down at the base of it he was poking his long fingers into unfamiliar recesses, and something clicked. The chimp shoved at it with his skinny arms, and the whole block came ponderously free.

Babylon exhaled a sigh of relief. "Thank God for small favors," he breathed. "Now we just—"

A dull explosion stopped him.

For a moment he thought the recording device had been booby-trapped, but Pertin snarled: "That crazy Scorpian! He must've bit into something that bit back! I'd better find out what he's up to—and then we'd better get the hell out of here!"

The block would have weighed half a metric ton on Earth, but here its weight was only a few kilograms. Nevertheless, it had its half-ton of mass. When Babylon and the chimp pulled it out of place, it moved slowly at first, like a half-ton ice floe afloat in still water; but then it kept coming with inertia that would not be denied. They managed to get it moving back in the direction from which they had come, just as Pertin returned with the Scorpian's bright light visible far behind. "He found his damn weapons!" Pertin yelled, half sobbing and half laughing, "and much good it did him! The idiot blew himself up. He's going to be damn little use getting back with this stuff!"

Babylon cut his thruster, panting, as the massy block for a moment seemed willing to go in the right direction. "He can't help us?" he asked in dismay.

"He can barely help himself—and he's got a thousand kilos of bits and pieces that he's pulling along. Come on! Let's get this thing back to the ship if we can—the Scorpian'll have to take care of himself!"

If we can . . . The outcome was in doubt. The three of them attacked the block like pilot fish nudging a shark, and slowly, slowly they made their way back through the ship, back out the entrance port, with the distant howling of the crippled Scorpian always behind; and then the trouble had only begun. Moving the mass was easier out in the gloomy canyons walled with those broken pillars of pale and shifting light, but the towers were not wholly quiescent now. They woke more quickly, fired their Jovian bolts more accurately. A dozen times before they were clear of the towers the lightnings struck close enough to leave them gasping and tingling.

With the line of flight reasonably clear, Doc Chimp, complaining vigorously, was sent back to help the Scorpian. The two parties arrived at the ebony plain almost together, the chimp gibbering frantically, "Ben Linc! Dr. Babylon! Please, wait for me! Don't leave this old monkey in this spooky place!"

In the faint light from the luminous, distant sky, Babylon could see that the robot had been sorely stricken. There were great gashes in its shiny surface, and the steam jets puffed only weakly and at strange angles; but it would not relinquish the net of objects it was bringing home. The chimpanzee had a net of its own, larger than Doc Chimp himself.

And then Ben Linc Pertin cried out in dismay: "The lander! It's been hit!"

Clearly the towers had not suspended their attack while the party was in the ship. The lander's scoops lay bent, scorched, half-retracted on the ebony velvet sand. There were great rents in its hull; the pilot window was shattered; fuel had leaked and burned out of split tanks.

They would never get back to the orbiter in that.

A wartime sailor of centuries before, seeing his torpedoed ship go down in the middle of a shark-filled, stormy sea, must have felt as Babylon did at that moment. It was their link with the real, gentle world outside; and it was gone. "Jen!" Pertin roared in his ear. "Don't daydream—get inside!"

"For what?" Babylon managed; but Pertin did not answer, and then his hands were full. Pertin was already dragging himself in through the shattered hatchway, tugging at the unwieldy block from the ship. Babylon guided it, flailing desperately out of the way as one corner of it threatened to crush his foot between its own bulk and the fabric of the lander, and then they were inside. To what point, Babylon could not imagine. The thing would never fly! Its shattered hull might protect them for a brief time, but when the lightnings found them again it would be all over for it—and them.

And one struck almost at once. Babylon's muscles convulsed in a tetany of shock. Not more than a millionth of the energy of the discharge flowed through the hull and into him, but it was the worst pain he had ever felt. Dizzy and shaken, he felt himself thrust out of the way by the skinny arms of Doc Chimp, crowding in behind him. "Oh, Dr. Babylon," the chimp chattered, "what a terrible place this is! And now what?"

Pertin snapped brutally, "Shut up and help me with this stuff! You too, Jen! Come on!"

"What's the use?" Babylon demanded, but no one took the time to answer. Pertin was opening a gate in a locker behind the control couches, now smoldering faintly, and the chimp was thrusting the great block toward him. Cryptic lights raced and flashed in patterns over the gate, and Pertin exhaled a sigh of relief. "Get the damn Scorpian, Doc!" he ordered, tugging at the block from the ship. "Give a hand, Jen!"

Another bolt smote the ship, stunning Babylon. Doc Chimp rolled back into the lander on the heels of it, shoe-button eyes rolling in terror, chattering with fear. "Here he is, that clanking mass of confusion," he gasped, as the Scorpian limped slowly after him, "but what we need him for I'll never know."

"Just shut up and bear a hand!" Pertin was opening the gate again—

For a moment Babylon's heart had leaped with hope—he recognized the box at last, a tachyon transmitter, their one remaining hope of escape. But when the gate opened and he saw what was inside, the hopeless anguish closed in again. The block was still there! Unchanged! The machine obviously had been too damaged to work, and they were doomed!

Queerly, Pertin and the chimp were pulling the block out and shoving the robot's bag of tricks in its place—glinting crystal rods and disks, ebon artifacts of geometrically strange shape, hexagons like the ones Babylon himself had brought. "But—but it's not working!" Babylon objected feebly.

The chimp stared at him, incredulously. Pertin did not answer: the lights flashed, the door opened again, the two wrestled the net sack out and turned to Babylon. "You next!" Pertin ordered.

"But—for what—"

"Dr. Babylon," the chimp chattered pleadingly, "will you get *in?*"

Unwillingly, Babylon bent himself double and allowed himself to be squeezed into the chamber—helped, at the last, by Pertin's firmly shoved boot. He felt the door slammed upon him.

For a timeless moment he was crushed into an unbearable position, in a chamber without light or air—

And then the door opened again.

He was dragged out by a creature that looked like a figure poked out of dough, sprouting tentacles that gripped him and pulled him free. The gloom of the wrecked lander was gone; he was in a harshly bright metal chamber, and as the Sheliak released him he flew across it and slammed into a wall.

He was alive. He was on the orbiter. Somehow he had been saved. That was the greatest wonder. He was alive.

Dazed, Jen Babylon caught a cable and hung against the wall as a squirming, flailing Doc Chimp sailed at him, collided, scrabbled for a hold. Arms and legs grappling the cables, the chimp panted, "We made it, Dr. Babylon! Oh, this poor old monkey never thought he'd see this place again! Watch out!" Behind him, the smoking hulk of the Scorpian robot soared out of the tachyon chamber and crashed against the wall. It made no attempt to grasp a hold, and its jets steamed at random; it floated slowly out toward the middle of the chamber.

And that was all.

Doc Chimp moaned softly beside him and sprang out toward the chamber. There was a quick exchange with the doughy Sheliak, and then the chimp launched himself back to the wall, his face working with woe.

"Oh, Dr. Babylon," he sobbed, "poor old Ben! That's the last of us. He didn't make it."

Babylon stared at him uncomprehendingly. "I—I don't see how any of us did," he managed.

The chimp's sobs turned into what was almost a giggle. "Tachyon transmission, Dr. Babylon," he said. "That's all. Confuses you, doesn't it?—but I thought you'd know, seeing you just came all that way from Earth."

"But the machine didn't work! I saw Ben take the block out again!"

"The *original* of the block," the chimp corrected. "It's still there, though the duplicate's here—probably slagged to a cinder by now, just like poor Ben. Just like the originals of you and me."

Babylon stared at him with horror. *"Us?"*

"The ones that stayed behind," the chimp explained, and giggled hysterically. "So you're beginning to understand, Dr. Babylon? And now you know how it feels! What it's like knowing you just died, ten thousand kilometers away!"

It was more than ten thousand kilometers.

The lander was a smoking ruin. That other Jen Babylon lay half stunned, with the dead body of the chimp behind him at the shattered door of the transmitter and the wrecked Scorpian robot lodged queerly across his legs, waiting for the final bolt that would end his pain. Had he made it to the orbiter? Did some "he" still live— somehow, somewhere?

His last thought, as the final bolt caught him, was that, even if the answer was yes, it did not ease the terror or the pain.

SIX

Something wakes me . . .

Is it time?

I stretch out in my sleep and taste the troubling emanations from my Watchers and my slaves. A ship has been invaded, an invader wiped out. There is nothing there to justify disturbing my sleep. But it is troubling.

I reach out to the farthest of my Watchers and my slaves. One is floating in the all but liquid air of a giant planet with a ruddy, dark sun; one moves about a queer old city, far from her crustacean slaves; one has died on the surface of a cratered rock in the heat of a blazing star.

There is nothing to trouble me in any of this, or in any of the others. But I am troubled.

I have been troubled before by stupid slaves, by fools forgetful of their origins and their destiny, by craven idiots who rose against me, thinking to destroy even HIM. They were themselves inevitably erased. HIS misguided enemies have forever been erased and forever will be, with no need to disturb HIM. Until HIS time, there will never be trouble. There cannot be, for HIS plan allows no trouble.

HIS time? Is it near?

I reach out to every slaved being and instrument, and I find nothing. It is not yet time for HIM.

But soon.

I return to sleep, and to the waiting of many million years.

SEVEN

"I give you greeting," said a voice in Jen Babylon's dreams. He struggled against waking up, failed, and opened his eyes.

Hanging in the air in front of him was a creature with five oddly placed eyes in a bat's gnarled face, supporting itself on filmy wings. "I am Mimmie, Dr. Babylon," said the creature through the Pmal translator by Babylon's head. "I am familiar with your work on linguistics and wish to associate myself with your efforts."

Still more than half asleep, Babylon said automatically, "Good morning." He pushed the restraining webs of this place he had slept in aside and sat up, catching himself just in time as the muscular effort almost flung him across the sleeping chamber . . . and memory flooded in.

"It is known," the creature went on remorselessly, "that Earth sapients have prolonged start-up periods after power-down status. Query: Are you functional?"

Babylon straightened out, grasping one of the catch-cables and reaching instinctively for his glasses. His ears were still ringing, and he felt a stiffness in his joints that had not been there before coming to this strange place. "If you mean am I awake, yes." Not finding the glasses, he remembered they were no longer necessary.

"Disjunct, Dr. Babylon," the creature said politely. He had already recognized it as a T'Worlie, that oldest of space-going races, the ones who had originally discovered Cuckoo. Perhaps the T'Worlie he had met before. From it a series of pungent, not unpleasant aromas wafted: a vinegary scent of curiosity, burnt-honey of controlled impatience, coppery concern. "You seem perturbed."

Babylon said bitterly, "I guess you could call it that, yes."

"Confirmation," the T'Worlie agreed. "You are concerned over recent happenings on surface."

"Wouldn't you be? One of my oldest friends dead—"

"Reference is assumed to Ben Pertin," the T'Worlie piped. "Understood. Offer ameliorating data: There is no shortage of Ben Pertins in vicinity of Cuckoo. Fourteen-plus known specimens, at least three surviving."

Babylon shook his head, incredulous. How could one relate to these creatures who took life so lightly? Even the humans like Ben—like the *late* Ben—himself? Much less this thing that floated before him.

Still, the situation was interesting. His scholarly mind awoke to curiosity. Babylon had learned some of the T'Worlie scent vocabulary as a part of his graduate studies. But to sniff the stoppers of tubes in the linguistics lab at the university was no real analog to the presence of a creature sending them out in waves of feeling. Babylon shook himself, dismissing the burden of worries and fears as best he could. "Did you say you wanted to help me?"

"Confirmation. Mimmie, deceased, was our race's greatest linguist, Dr. Babylon."

"I see. And you studied with, uh, this Mimmie?"

"Negation, Dr. Babylon. I am identical with this Mimmie. I am Mimmie."

"Oh, I see. You're a tachyon copy," Babylon said, feeling an embarrassment that he could not account for.

Garlicky waves of amusement came from the T'Worlie. "Confirmation. I am tachyon copy of Mimmie. You are tachyon copy of Dr. Jen Babylon."

Babylon was startled, but then he grinned. "Right you are, Mimmie. As you say, Earth sapients have prolonged start-up periods after power-down. I'll be pleased and honored to work with you. Do you want to get started?"

"Disjunct confirmation, Dr. Babylon. Confirm that I want to get started. Potential negative feasibility of doing so. Council meeting has been requested with you in attendance concerning events resulting in loss of lander and damage to Being HG-87, Scorpian robot."

Babylon was startled. "I'm going to be put on trial? When?"

"Negative trial, Dr. Babylon. As to time, twenty hours, error bar two hours plus or minus."

"Great!" Babylon snarled. "I come all the way out here to do a job for somebody who gets himself killed in the process, I nearly get killed myself— Oh, hell," he said, as the T'Worlie exuded a saffron scent of sympathy, "I guess there should be some sort of inquiry, after all. Twenty hours? Well. That's a long way away; do you want to get started on the data I brought back?"

Since Pmal translators were a human invention, though greatly improved by technologies borrowed from other galactic races, the T'Worlie was not entirely familiar with them; but with Jen Babylon working alongside he quickly joined in running through the first tests on the data from the wrecked ship.

Pmal translators operated in three separate modes: synchronic, diachronic, and morphological. For most human languages, the synchronic mode was usually enough. It only meant that the translator stored words and matched them against its library of known words. A sample of a few dozen lexigrams would allow it to recognize that the language was, say, from the Indo-European group rather than the Algonkian or one of the languages of Southeast Asia. Generally it could also instantly detect the rattle of Sirians, the tweeting of T'Worlie or the half-dozen other principal galactic tongues. A few more words would generally cut between, say, the Germanic and the Latin; no more than a couple of sentences would allow it to determine that the language was not French or Portuguese or Romanian, but Italian, and then it was only a matter of discriminating the right dialect. From then on it deployed its database of languages and grammars, and cross-mapping was easy.

Of course, it was not really that simple. Spoken languages do not come in discrete packets of "words." "Words" are a linguists' invention. The analyzed sound trace of any spoken sentence shows breaks and fusions that do not correspond to the conventions of the written language. The Pmal circuits that learned to average out the actual pauses and redivide the sounds into the units of formal analysis were quite sophisticated; they were, basically, what made Dr. Linebarger's translators work.

When the synchronic mode failed, the Pmal had the diachronic resource. It matched root words against its database of known proto-languages, looking for resemblances according to a complex algorithm of vowel and consonant shifts. It was this aspect of linguistics in which Jen Babylon was one of the Galaxy's great experts. But it failed him now. The portable Pmal could not even make a beginning.

Even the programs Jen Babylon had brought from Earth, now stored in the FARLINK memory, could find no analogs in any of the families or phyla or even macrophyla in the store.

Remained morphological mapping. In this mode the portable Pmals were very slow, and even Jen's own programs pored over the possible match between sounds, colors, and rhythms of the data taped from the block, matching them against hypothesized events and phenomena, for hours without result. The T'Worlie fluttered away, and returned with a Sirian eye tugging instruments of its own to Babylon's workplace . . .

And another blank. None of the known languages or dialects of the Galaxy matched in any way to the phonemes, symbols, or structures of the unknown tongue. Or tongues.

Or gibberish.

After eighteen hours of trying to decide which, Jen Babylon was exhausted. When the skinny form of Doc Chimp peered around the doorframe and asked, "All right if I come in, Dr. Babylon?" he suddenly realized how tired he was.

"Certainly, Doc Chimp. But I was just thinking of going to sleep. Maybe a night's rest will give me a clue about this language."

"It hasn't been working out?"

"Not in the least, Doc. There is no great galactic language cognate to it, both Mimmie and I will attest to that."

"What a shame," the chimp said sympathetically. "I suppose, of course, you've also tried matching against the native languages of Cuckoo? Well, certainly—"

"Native languages?" Babylon repeated.

"—certainly you have, you don't need a dumb old monkey to tell you *that!* Please excuse me, Dr. Babylon." The chimp looked embarrassed at his own presumption. "However," he said, "that's not why I'm here. I thought I'd better take you to the hearing myself—this place is so confusing!"

"Hearing?" Babylon realized how fatigued he was; all he could seem to do was repeat what Doc Chimp said. And then he remembered. "The hearing!"

Doc Chimp nodded, his little shoe-button eyes worried. "I wish you'd been able to get a little rest first," he said fretfully. "To make a good impression, you know. Although this isn't anything serious—don't misunderstand me—or at least it shouldn't be. Although the way things are going now, you never know what's going to be serious and what isn't, and that's the truth, Dr. Babylon!"

Babylon took a deep breath, and pulled himself together. The inquiry meeting had escaped his mind entirely, and now that it was at hand it began to seem worrisome indeed. If only Ben Pertin were here to advise him!

But he wasn't, and that was that. "All right," he said. "Just let me speak to Mimmie first."

The T'Worlie was hovering politely a few feet away. "You wish me to proceed with the matches of the Cuckoo tongues in your absence," it trilled, and the Pmal conveyed the English words. "Confirmation, Dr. Babylon. Will do so." And it fluttered away to the instruments, leaving a frying-bacon scent behind that Babylon recognized as laughter.

It was the first real chance Jen Babylon had had to look around the orbiter. The shock of the death of his own duplicate, the rising concern about the council meeting he was about to face, even his fatigue were set aside as he rubbernecked like any tourist. So strange a place! he thought as he launched himself after the chimpanzee from one handhold to another, and: What am I doing here, anyway?

But there was no answer to that.

They shot through corridors, drifted across open common rooms. Babylon had expected to see more beings than were in evidence. They encountered only a few; but what a few! Another of those doughy shape-changing creatures called Sheliaks, a great blue Sirian eye, with little crablike pincers hanging below the orb, passing them with a ripping sound of electrostatic force, a silvery cloud of insectlike creatures that he recognized as Boaty-Bits. Once he saw four or five actual human beings, working over a dismembered copper-colored machine. He almost called to Doc Chimp to pause so that he could speak to them, when he noticed the telltale opacity of expression and incipient locomotor-ataxia gait that told him they were Purchased People. Convicts, who had been bought as proxies by creatures so alien that they could not survive in oxygen-bearing air, supporting a water-based chemistry. He wondered if any of the group who had been transmitted with him were among them, but recognized none.

Doc Chimp was cowering at an intersection, gesturing frantically to him to stop.

Babylon caught a handhold with flailing arms, started to speak, saw the pleading look in the chimp's eyes, and desisted. There was a droning, malevolent sound growing in the next corridor; it peaked, a triangular shape shot swiftly past, and the chimpanzee sighed. "That's a deltaform, Dr. Babylon," he whispered. "They're the worst of the lot. I just didn't want him to see us here."

The little ape's shoe-button eyes were dull, and his fur seemed bedraggled; all the cheerfulness with which he had come to meet Babylon was gone. "Why shouldn't we be here?" he asked the chimp. "I was summoned to the meeting, after all."

The chimp coughed apologetically, lifted his kepi, and scratched the hairy scalp beneath it. "Well, that's what I was just getting around to telling you, Dr. Babylon," he said. "The meeting's not for almost an hour yet. We're going to make a little stop first. We're almost there," he added, pushing himself away and across the broad corridor. Babylon pursued hastily.

"Where's 'there'?" he demanded of the retreating chimp.

"It's Ben Linc's room," the chimpanzee called over his shoulder. "Real nice place, too. Old Ben came here years and years ago, you know, so he got first pick of quarters. Fixed it up to suit himself." He caught a holding strap and hung by the side of the passage, just outside a door, until Babylon caught up with him.

Babylon clung to another strap, looking around. It seemed almost ghoulish to be going to the room of his dead friend. "Why are we doing this?" he panted. "Couldn't it wait till after the meeting?"

"I don't think so," the chimp chattered nervously, looking up and down the hall. "You'd better go inside now, Dr. Babylon. This is the place."

Babylon hesitated. "I really don't see why—"

"Just go in, Dr. Babylon!" said the chimp, doing something with the door. As it slid open he caught Babylon's shoulder in his astonishingly strong hand and gently thrust him inside.

The door closed behind him.

The room Ben Linc Pertin had slept in was dimly lit, but Babylon could make out the shape. It was a good deal more homey than the bare cubicle Babylon had been given: a faceted, polyhedral enclosure, with most of the interior faces covered with flat photographs of scenes from his life. Next to the entrance was an exterior shot of the great orbiter Sun One, where Ben Pertin had first been transmitted from Earth. Over his bed loomed the immense majesty of a mountain that, Babylon knew, had been the grave of several Ben Pertins; it was called "Knife-in-the-Sky" in one of those Cuckoo languages that, Babylon remembered to hope, the T'Worlie was now feeding into the great Pmals. And, in the bed—

In the bed something was moving. A figure sat up and peered at Babylon, and a familiar voice said, "Well, Jen, about time you got here!"

In astonishment, Babylon lost his grip on the handhold. "Ben!" he gasped. "But—but you're *dead.*"

Two of the facets of the cubicle glowed a little more brightly, as Ben Pertin turned up the lights of his room. "Why, I guess I am, a lot of me," he said bitterly. "Grab hold of that strap, for God's sake. Else you'll be bumping all over the place."

Babylon flailed around until he caught the end of the holding strap and pulled himself back to the wall, still unable to take it in. "You're a tachyon copy," he guessed.

"Well, sure—what else? We all are. But if you mean I'm not the Ben Pertin who got blown away with you down by the old ship you're wrong."

"But we left you there!"

"Yes, you did," Pertin agreed moodily. "Oh, I'm not blaming you—after all, I pushed you in ahead of me. But I have to tell you I didn't like it, after you'd all gone and the tachyon transmitter shorted out. Still, that's all water under the bridge now. The important thing's what we do now."

He sat up, and for the first time Babylon realized Pertin was not alone in the bed. A slower stirring on the far side of the coverings produced a female human face, which stared at Jen Babylon without speaking. "Excuse me," Babylon said automatically.

Pertin scowled. "For what? Oh, you're looking at Doris." He laughed. "Don't worry about Doris; she's a Purchased Person. Her owners have this academic interest in human sexual behavior, so sometimes when things aren't busy for them they let me borrow her for a while. And sometimes I need to, believe me. Never more than when I finally got the transmitter fixed and got back here!" He threw the covers off; the movement half buried the woman, who seemed not to mind, perhaps not even to notice. "But that doesn't matter," he said sharply. "Listen, Jen! I told Doc Chimp to bring you here without saying anything, because out of all this trouble we've got a good break!"

"What's that?"

"No one knows I'm here!" he cried triumphantly.

Babylon pulled himself over to a more comfortable position—more comfortable mostly because it hid the bright, empty eyes of the woman named Doris. "I really don't see why that is going to help us translate the language," he said.

"Not help us translate. Help us get this place straightened out!" Pertin snapped. "As long as they don't know I'm here I have freedom of action, don't you see?"

"To do what, exactly?" Babylon demanded.

Pertin hesitated. "Well, that I can't say, exactly," he admitted. "What I know for sure is that some of them are out to wreck this place —even destroy the whole of Cuckoo! And, no, I don't know which ones. Not for sure. The Scorpians, yes, almost certainly. The deltaforms—I wouldn't put anything past those bastards! I don't think the T'Worlie are in it, or the Sheliaks, either, although there's always a chance of an aberrant individual in even a friendly race—"

"Ben," Babylon said patiently, suddenly feeling a rush of sympathy for the worn, harried man who had once been his friend, "are you sure you're not imagining all this?"

Pertin scowled at him. "You're not one of those aberrants yourself, are you?" he demanded. "No, of course not. Sorry. But you just don't know what it's like here. Sometimes I even worry about Doris, although her owners have never, *ever* shown any interest in the politics of what happens here; they're just curious, want to observe without taking part. I even worry about the Doc. No. Don't think I'm crazy, Jen—even if I am. I know I'm not crazy on the subject of some of these creatures wanting Cuckoo destroyed, and you and me with it!"

He flung back the cover, launched himself across the chamber to a cupboard, began pulling out fresh clothes. "While you're in the meeting, I'm going to look around. The worst ones are sure to be at the meeting—they only convened it to embarrass you and Doc Chimp, and any other friends of mine that might still be around. Say! I wonder! Do you suppose they could have arranged it so I'd be left down there to die? —No, I suppose not; but they would have if they could!"

A thought was insistently forming itself in Jen Babylon's mind, and the word that summed it up was paranoia. What did you do with a man who had gone over the edge? Heaven knew Pertin had every reason; but that did not make it easier. He said gently, "You know, Ben Linc, I think you ought to rest a while longer."

"Don't call me that!" Pertin spun to glare at him. "Ben Linc Pertin's dead down there in the lander. The one you're talking to is— is—is Ben Omega Pertin. The last of the Ben Pertins—and maybe one too many, at that!"

The situation was getting to be more than Babylon could handle, exhausted as he was, with his mind full of a hundred other concerns. A scratching at the door rescued him: Doc Chimp, leathery face poking in timorously, warning that it would not do to keep the meeting waiting. Fortunately it was only a short distance, but Babylon found time to say a word to the chimpanzee as they brought up before a larger, more official-looking door than any he had yet passed through. "Hold on a second," he panted. "I'm worried about Ben!"

The chimp poked its muzzle at him in what would have been a pout if he had had lips. "You're worried, Dr. Babylon? What do you think I've been, all this terrible long time?"

"Well—isn't there a medical service here on the orbiter? Some sort of psychotherapy?"

Doc Chimp looked puzzled. "What would Ben want therapy for, Dr. Babylon? Any more than any of the rest of us, I mean? . . . Oh, I see!" The leathery lips split in a grin. "You think he's having delusions about the wickedness of the deltaforms and the Scorpians and all those other beasts and buckets of junk! Wish it were true, Dr. Babylon! I'm afraid he's sane as you and I where that's concerned—maybe a lot saner! Now," he said, reaching for the door, "spruce up your posture and put a smile on your face! Make them think you've got the Galaxy by the tail and you'd just as soon as not swing it out past Andromeda! 'Cause if you let them think for a minute you're weak or scared—then you'll find out just how evil those beings can be!"

The room was huge and irregular, and it seemed to be packed with creatures and—things! Some he recognized, others not. A furry, big-eyed kitten-shape purred on the fat black cushion of its life-support system. A slithering eel-like shape squirmed restlessly in among and behind the other creatures, with tentacled eyes that thrust themselves in all directions. Babylon caught his breath. There was a creature that was the surest shape of a nightmare, clad in armor that glittered slimily like an insect's chitin, black on its back and scarlet on its belly; its eyes were multiple globes of greenish jelly, and it had yellow, leathery wings. It was staring directly at Babylon, and without volition he moved away. And that was only the beginning: a pair of T'Worlie, a silver hive of Boaty-Bits, three Purchased People, a soggy-dough Sheliak—and, yes, there was a Scorpian robot. No, wrong. There were two of them, but one was stripped down, most of its casing removed, the propulsion system dead. It traveled on the back of the other one like a papoose. There is no easy way for a human being to tell one mass-produced Scorpian from another, but Babylon was sure that the one being carried had been his companion down below.

There was a racket of drumroll, squeak, shriek, and yowl as he came in, but the sound stopped. Everyone turned and stared at him, and Jen Babylon halted, gripping a handhold, for the first time aware of just what sort of council he was dealing with.

Doc Chimp, entering behind him, saw his hesitation and moved to ease it. He launched himself toward the center of the room, thrusting one long, skinny paw against Babylon's shoulder and stopping himself with a recoil-less collision against the Sheliak. "Let me introduce you!" he shrilled, hanging lazily in midair with the red flaps of his vest flying like small wings. "Folks and gentle beings, this is Dr. Jensen Babylon, our planet's most distinguished expert in quantum-dynamic linguistics—and not unknown to members of his craft throughout the Galaxy. Even here! He has come to risk his life for us—even to lose it, now and then, as so many of us have. Bid him welcome, beings all!"

The uproar broke out again, dominated by a roar of surprising volume from the kitten-shaped creature on the black hassock. Babylon's Pmal translated: "Terrestrial monkeys behave like monkeys everywhere. Be still, primate, for significant business of this council!"

Doc Chimp licked his lips, but faced the kitten bravely. "True," he chattered, "I am only a humble monkey, and no one cares for me. But no one cares about any of us here. We go to our many deaths without hope of reward. Yet be of good cheer! With terrestrial primate brawn and terrestrial primate courage to help you, you may yet—"

"Be still!" the growl thundered. "Babylon! Why are you here?"

It was not a question Jen Babylon had expected. The only true answers were that he didn't really know, and certainly had never desired it, but Doc Chimp was glancing at him nervously and he saw that the little creature was actually trembling. He temporized. "I thought this meeting was to discuss the wreck of the lander," he said.

Uproar of many queer voices again, with the kitten's basso purr breaking through: "It is to discuss *you,* Dr. Jen Babylon. We have no use here for quantum-dynamic linguistics practiced by primitive races. You are a waste of scarce resources! What makes you think this language can be translated? Suppose the creatures who spoke it do not think of the world the way we do? Suppose their interests are internal? abstract? mathematical? Suppose their mode of communication is telepathic, or evocative, or—"

Suddenly Babylon was fed up. "Suppose you shut up," he snapped. "It's obvious that your race is among the primitive ones in this respect! Look. What do you use language for? To communicate. What do you communicate about? Matters of mutual interest. Without the mutuality there is no communication—not because the language fails to conceptualize the material, but because the material itself is not mutual—"

He paused, because Doc Chimp was shaking his head worriedly. "At any rate," he went on after a moment, "I have confidence that I can untangle the language. FARLINK will help. If necessary I'll send tapes back to my lab—to the laboratories in Boston for analysis by the mainframe equipment there. Trust me, we'll get it solved," he said, aware that he was trying to placate this group of unpleasant personalities.

A rattle sounded from the whole Scorpian, translated by the Pmal as harsh laughter. "Negative trust," it said. "Defer decision on 'solved.' Not relevant in any case. Entire project, also entire function of investigation of 'Cuckoo' object, as well as 'Cuckoo' object itself, of no further importance. Recommend termination."

The meeting went on beyond that, but Babylon understood little of what was happening. The galactic creatures seemed to have had the practice of the disorderly assemblies long enough that they could understand what was going on. Or more likely, didn't really care.

Babylon had not. When all of them were chirping or buzzing or thundering at once, the Pmals were swamped. Only fragmentary phrases came out, in disconnected order.

Yet when they were outside Doc Chimp said moodily, "Well, I think it went well enough, Dr. Babylon—"

"Jen, please."

"—Jen, but you never know with these creatures." He tugged Babylon out of the main corridor into a smaller one, heading back toward their own quarters of the orbiter; a flight of T'Worlie fluttered out of the way, exuding a quick barnyard odor of mild annoyance. "But maybe you'd better do what you said and get your other self back on Earth to help. We may not have very much time."

"All right," Babylon said, gasping with the effort of trying to match the chimpanzee in tug-and-kick along the corridors. "I don't see what the hurry is, though."

The chimp paused, grabbing a handhold with one skinny arm and snatching Babylon in midflight with the other. He glanced up and down the corridor, his face stiff with worry. "You don't?" he whispered softly. "I thought you were listening, inside there. Didn't you wonder what that Scorpian meant by 'termination'?"

EIGHT

He should have taken the subtrain to Cambridge, but he wanted the exercise. Now the weather had turned wet and cold and the wind whipped raindrops up the Charles River. Jen Babylon shivered and tried to walk faster across the bridge.

That was hard to do, because there were knots of people standing about, staring at the water—strange time for rubbernecking! Babylon stepped down off the sidewalk to pass one milling cluster, coming perilously close to the rushing stream of hovertaxis and vans, and an elderly woman stepped out ahead of him, coming toward him. "Careful!" he snapped, rescuing her from the traffic lanes.

"Oh, sorry," she said, putting her hand out to reassure herself by touching him. "Ugly-looking things, aren't they?"

Not knowing what she was talking about, he nodded, slipped past her back onto the sidewalk, and found himself in a clear place. He glanced over the railing at the water, and then he saw.

The river's edge was alive with huge, glass-bodied crabs.

The woman had certainly been right; the ugly things surrounded the water-filtration plant like scuttling crustacean ghosts. Babylon imagined he could hear the clicking and slithering even on the bridge, though it was impossible, of course, with the traffic so close behind him. Filthy creatures! And more and more of them all the time, appearing at shipyards and LH-storage facilities, stopping traffic on main arteries and even threatening the tachyon-transmission center. The authorities first tried to control them, then to destroy—explosives, flamethrowers, clubs, even by running Army tanks and road rollers over them to crush them. But the beings were virtually indestructible. Men with hammers, they had discovered, could blind them by pounding their eyes into rubble, and then the creatures became immobile and could be carted away. But they multiplied faster than one-on-one tactics could destroy them—in what way, no one knew. In the Middle Ages people believed that mice were spontaneously generated in piles of unwashed clothing; now the best opinion anyone could give was that the crabs appeared automatically in shallow water. So much for the steady advance of scientific knowledge!

They were a problem—but not particularly Jen Babylon's problem, and he had plenty of his own. A robot hovertaxi hesitated before him, waiting for a clump of pedestrians to get out of the way, and Babylon gave up the thought of exercise and jumped in. His problems were waiting for him at the university. It was impossible to put them off forever—though, Babylon thought wistfully, what an attractive idea that was! It seemed impossible that only a few weeks ago he had been taping old native dialects on Bora-Bora, with no worry in the world except the hope of promotion and the demands of his work.

As soon as he got to his desk he tried one more time to confront the most personal of his problems by dialing Sheryl's call code on the stereophone.

And, one more time, it was her recorded image that answered him, not herself. "I'm terribly sorry," it said, "that I am not able to be here in person just now. I am occupied in higher work." Higher work! Madness, Babylon thought, as the recorded figure paused. There was a look of exaltation on her gaunt, consecrated face. This was not the offhanded, faintly bored Sheryl who had been his bed companion for so many months. The real Sheryl was drawling and mostly amused, where this person was . . . obsessed; Sheryl was fastidious about her appearance and dress, while this person had thrown on the first garments that presented themselves, and her hair had not been washed, or even brushed, for days. In a sudden burst of rapture the figure whispered, "I Cry the imminent majesty of Cuckoo" . . . and vanished.

Babylon watched the image shatter into golden mist and fade away. He was sorely troubled. It was not as if he had any commitment to Sheryl. They had never talked of any permanent relationship, much less marriage. Yet—they had been lovers for more than a year, had shared more intimacies than merely the bed. Could he let her do this to herself?

Or—more to the point—did he have any way to stop her?

A voice from the doorway brought him face to face with the second of his problems: Dean Margaret Kooseman. "Oh, Jen dear," she whispered, a sad smile of compassion on her weather-beaten face, "how terrible this must be for you. Such a sweet, pretty girl, to get mixed up with those horrid Kooks!"

"Yes, well, thanks, Margaret," Babylon said gruffly, taking off his glasses to see her more directly. It did not pay to let Margaret Kooseman too far inside your private life. "What can I do for you?"

She came in and sat primly down beside his desk, relaxed as she gazed around the room. In one corner the processor was turning pages in an old missionary's dictionary of Hawaiian, inputting dialects to correlate against Babylon's own, more recent data; in another, two different information-handling machines were purring to each other as they matched sounds against sense. "What a nice, orderly person you are, Jen," she said approvingly. "In this very disordered world, you're priceless!"

"You're very kind, Margaret. Is that what you came here to tell me?"

"And so direct and to the point, too," she sighed, favoring him with a smile. "But you have to let me just breathe hard for a moment, Jen. I've just come from a faculty senate meeting and, oh, the noise and argument there! You know what they're like." He didn't, of course; plebes like himself weren't allowed in. "And this time worse than usual. Those crabby things! We were given some samples by the Public Safety Commission to try to figure out what to do about them—and would you believe it, everybody wanted them? The veterinary medicine school said they were animals, Charley Kentwell said they belonged to him because they were silicon-based and therefore inorganic chemistry, the computer people claimed they were machines— we had to give one to each of them to shut them up."

"I wouldn't have thought there was any scarcity of them," Babylon commented.

The dean nodded enthusiastically. "You see what I mean? You're always right to the point! But there's more to it—somebody even suggested you ought to take time out from your very valuable work to study them, because there's a chance that they come from one of the known galactic planets, and may have a language—"

"Margaret!"

"No, of course that was silly. I put my foot right down on *that*.

Especially since I'm afraid you're going to have to postpone all your other work for something else, anyway."

So at last they were coming to the point! Babylon's voice was almost shaking with repressed anger as he demanded, "What are you talking about?"

"Cuckoo, I'm afraid."

"But I've already done what you asked!"

She nodded sadly. "Isn't it terrible? One does so much, and then they always demand just one more thing from you. This time it's a packet of data from Cuckoo." She fished in her dispatch case and brought out a glimmering silver ball. "This is it—ion-coded, because there's so much of it. You'll have to feed it into your databank before you can work with it. It just came from the tachyon station for you."

"Margaret! My work with the ancient Polynesian dialects—"

"Yes, isn't it a pity? But we can't give you any more processor time, so you'll just have to feed all that into slow storage and clear the machines for this. I know I can rely on you. That's why, when I retire—"

"Give me the damn thing," he said sharply, unwilling to hear those vague promises again. What a waste! At least an hour to clear the databanks of the ongoing material—another hour, maybe five or six hours, for the processors to assimilate this unwieldy mass of material from Cuckoo—and then God knew how many more hours and days of puzzling it over before he could get back to his real work.

She smiled and got up, coming around the desk to touch the top of his head with her dry lips. "You're so good, Jen," she sighed, setting the gleaming sphere gently on his desk. "And, oh, yes, there's a message for you on the stereostage concerning this stuff." She giggled. "It's so funny, really—it's from yourself!"

Universities, which are always underfunded in comparison with the projects they would like to undertake, cannot function without copious supplies of slave labor. These are called "graduate students." I suppose I should be grateful, Babylon told himself, that at least Margaret gave me two extra pairs of hands—of course, I had to beg for them.

But the two graduate students were a big help all the same. Marco, the Filipino-Malay-American, had listened quietly to his instructions, nodded and gone off to arrange storage for the Polynesian material;

Althea, the blond young woman from Texas, went to work instantly with a portable processor to read out the index codes from the glittering sphere and plan its storage in the databanks. She was quite a pretty young woman, and having her move about his office, with the faint wisp of perfume that seemed to follow her everywhere, reminded Babylon uncomfortably that it had been a long time since he and Sheryl had released their sexual tensions on each other. He punched out Sheryl's code once more, got the same response, swore to himself . . . and, after a moment's thought, replayed the message from Cuckoo.

His own face looked out from the stage at him, and his own voice spoke. A shiver ran up his spine as he heard himself say, "Hello, me. Is that how you say it? I mean, how I say it—or we say it?" Jen's face grinned at the other Jen, unhappily. "Well, listen, we both know this is strange, and we both know everything either of us knew up until old Margaret talked us into this thing—so I'll come right to the point. I know you're busy. I know you don't want to do this. But I need help. I have this body of material and I have to have total interpretation of it —semantic, morphological, grammatical, every parameter there is. It's a matter of life and death, Jen. *Our* life."

The one and original Jen Babylon— the one on Earth—snapped it off at that point; the rest was technical instructions, and they were already being carried out.

Since there was no help for it, Babylon was slowly beginning to come around to the feeling that this new task was going to be interesting in its own right. What made Babylon a professor in the first place was the pure lust of the scholar, and here was a whole new family of tongues, tachyon-transmitted from forty thousand light-years out in space, and all his. No ear on Earth had ever heard these sounds before, no eye ever seen the markings. He drew a pad toward him and began to make notes.

"Dr. Babylon?"

He looked up, irritated. "Yes, Althea?"

"I didn't want to interrupt you, but you know I used to be pretty friendly with Sheryl, and I couldn't help seeing that you were trying to call her."

He nodded, and she went on.

"I think she's there, really, Dr. Babylon. My boyfriend lives right down the block from her and he's seen her, along with, uh, some of the—"

Babylon finished for her: "The Kooks."

"Yes. The Kooks. They've got a sort of a pad, or a commune, or whatever they call it right in her apartment house. Right next door to hers, in fact." She broke off to look at the display on her portable processor, punched a quick command, studied the result, and then looked up. "You know, Dr. Babylon," she said, "it's going to be at least a couple of hours before there's anything for you to do here."

He leaned back and rubbed his neck. "I suppose so," he agreed.

"Well, I was just thinking—you'll probably be working late once you get started. So if you wanted to take off for a few hours, Marco and I can certainly cope with inputting the data."

The more Babylon thought about it, the more it seemed like a good idea. And then there was the question of Sheryl . . .

He was already in a hovercab, human-driven this time, across the Charles and heading for the old buildings behind the Criminal Courts when he realized just how tactful Althea had been. Quite a nice girl! She had put the idea in his head and then reminded him he could do something about it, all without appearing to interfere in his private affairs at all. A woman like that, he thought, would go far—

Which his taxi would not, it seemed. It had come to a complete halt. "Sorry, pal," the cabbie said, leaning back toward the passenger section. "The damn Kooks again, wouldn't you know it? They're blocking the whole square."

Babylon leaned forward to stare over the driver's shoulder. There were more of them than ever, thousands at least, as dirty and ragged and—exalted—as ever. They were chanting in such disorder that he could make out no words, but some of the placards they carried were readable: DON'T DEFILE CUCKOO! and CRIMINALS BELONG ON EARTH, NOT IN HEAVEN! and a dozen others. The police were making no effort to disperse them, just to keep them from overflowing into the streets around the Criminal Courts Building.

Babylon glanced at his watch and made a decision. "Let me out here," he told the driver. "I'll walk the rest of the way."

But, he thought, maybe what he sought was in that square . . .

In the detention-area halls of the Criminal Courts Building Te'ehala Tupaia heard the noise from outside and dismissed it. There were nearer problems. He followed the stooped Judas-ram of the file of Purchased People through one more barred door, and stopped short, eyes outraged by a flashing of cameras. Noise and confusion reigned here, too—fortunately, for no one noticed his lapse. He let his head fall forward and shambled docilely toward the prisoners' corral. Clearly they were in the news again, though he did not know why.

The court attendants managed to quiet the press and public long enough for the hearing to begin, but the noise outside continued to grow. Tupaia listened alertly, eyes looking up under lowered brows to try to follow what was going on. It was of no real interest, he decided, just more whiteskin foolishness, some legal point that required the presence of the Purchased People in the courtroom, but certainly nothing that would ever yield freedom to Te'ehala Tupaia of *Polynésie-libre*. He would have to get that by himself!

Because the Purchased People were either firmly controlled or apathetic, the courtroom authorities had not bothered to handcuff them. Because Tupaia knew that his only hope of escape was to pretend the same apathy, he kept his muscles relaxed and his eyes downcast. But he missed nothing. That guard, just outside the rail, scowling at a photographer trying to get one last shot—surely that was a pistol in the holster at his belt? Those disheveled creatures by the door, reluctantly taking their seats as attendants whispered savagely at them—Kooks? They had to be; no normal human being, not even a whiteskin, would allow himself to appear in such wretchedly unkempt condition. And what was outside the door? It was a continuous rumble, like the combers crashing over the breakwater outside a lagoon, but he could almost hear words in it. More Kooks, no doubt . . .

He folded his hands placidly in his lap, while inside his skull his mind was racing with schemes. He let the courtroom talk flow past him. Whiteskin justice! Whiteskin madness! Neither of them meant anything to Te'ehala Tupaia.

There had been a time, of course, when he had not yet learned the bitter truths about whiteskin "fair play." He remembered, with both nostalgia and rage, those long-ago, hot teenage years, working in the tourist hotels, always at a trot at the dinner hour to be sure M'sieur's wine carafe reached Table 10 and to lug the huge, searing silver tureen of soup to the six American ladies at Table 45. A fifteen-year-old kid

—could he be blamed? All he knew was that he wanted enough money to buy a Moped and, someday, rise in the whiteskin world until he, too, could be a rich tourist. Fantasy! It had all turned out to be lies and betrayals.

For a moment he let himself listen to the endless wrangling drone from the front of the courtroom. Attorney for the defense was saying that his clients had paid good money, strictly according to Statute 53 U.S. 195, and they weren't getting their money's worth—"clients" meaning strange creatures from another world, and "money's worth" meaning Tupaia and the other Purchased People themselves! And the attorney for the prisoners was protesting that no one doubted that, all they had to do was abandon their plans to use these Purchased People on Cuckoo and destroy their tapes.

Whiteskin lunacy! How could grown human beings persuade themselves that this meant anything, when it affected no one nearer than forty thousand light-years away, and at that distance was unenforceable anyway? He cared not at all whether the attorney for the prison system successfully defended their sale, or the Civil Liberties lawyers won their technical point. Let the judge decide what she would, it would mean nothing.

But the growing volume and frenzy of the noise outside the courtroom . . . *they* might mean something. They meant, at least, confusion and turmoil—and in some sudden confusion was Tupaia's only hope.

But the hope dwindled and, at last, died away. The judge impatiently cut the lawyers off, announced that she had heard the arguments and would give her decision in chambers at a later date.

And that was the end of it.

The bored attendants prodded the torpid Purchased People toward the door, and Tupaia felt despair soak into his heart once more. Back to the detention cells again, with the strange screams and moans in the night and the queer, inhuman things that looked out of his fellow prisoners' eyes.

But perhaps not.

The guards were nervous, whispering to each other. As they approached the rear entrance where the prison vans waited to take them back to their cells, Tupaia heard the crowd noises from outside, closer and louder than ever. The guards stopped them at the door. Then two guards, side by side, thrust it open and shoved their way out into the milling, shouting mob.

Then it became easy.

The guards expected nothing threatening from their prisoners; it was the Kooks they were worried about. Tupaia found himself directly behind the one who had stood guard nearest him in the courtroom. And the gun was still in the holster.

Tupaia stood up to his full height and reached forward, one great arm encircling the man's neck. He snapped it as easily as he had long ago plucked hibiscus blossoms for the breakfast tables of the tourists. He let the man fall under the stampeding feet of the mob and turned, the gun swiftly concealed in his blouse. No one had noticed as Tupaia melted swiftly into the rioting crowd.

Long before then Jen Babylon had given up the useless scan of ecstatic faces in the Kook mob, pushed his way through, and hurried the few short blocks to Sheryl's apartment building. The autodoorman passed him readily enough—his facial profile had been recorded long ago—and in moments he was hammering on the door to Sheryl's apartment.

No one answered the door. Yet Babylon was sure he heard sounds from within. He could not identify them; not the voices of a party, or a show on the stereostage. Not any sounds he recognized, even with the sharpened ears of his profession. They were so faint that he was hardly convinced they were real, but they sounded like—like what?—like cards shuffling? or dice rattling?

"Sheryl!" he called. "It's Jen Babylon!"

Still no answer. He shrugged and moved grimly down the hall. It was the only other apartment on the floor, far bigger than Sheryl's little corner; if Althea's information was right, perhaps the girl was inside. He banged on the door, bruising his knuckles.

The answer he got was not the one he might have expected. The door to Sheryl's own apartment opened down the hall, and she stood in the frame, peering toward him. "Yes, Jen?" she said softly.

He was back there at a bound, furious, brushing past her into the tiny room. "My God, Sheryl!" he cried. "Don't you know I've been worried about you? What have you been doing?"

She followed him slowly inside, her face radiant. "The very greatest of things, Jen," she told him solemnly. "You had no cause to worry."

"No cause! With you mixed up with these maniacs! Starving yourself. Letting yourself go to pot—look at you!" he said bitterly, turning her to face a mirror. She had been thin; now she was almost ethereal, except that the smudged face, the careless hair, the shadows under her eyes were nothing that could be called ethereal. The whole apartment was as uncared-for as its owner. Furniture appeared to have been shoved out of the way, for what purpose Babylon could not guess; the place had not been dusted or swept in some time, and there was a sour, metallic reek that he could not identify.

"Please go away, Jen," Sheryl said softly.

He shook his head, almost ready to admit defeat. What was he doing here, anyway? She had a right to do what she chose with her life — But on the other hand, what she was doing seemed insane, and didn't he owe her at least an attempt to bring her back to her senses? "Do you know what you're doing to yourself?" he demanded.

"Of course I do, Jen! I am redeeming myself—and all the rest of the sad, shamed human race, too! I Cry the majesty of Cuckoo. It is coming to save us all!"

"Oh, Sheryl," he said, pitying and almost fearing her, as one pities and fears a lunatic. "Won't you come with me and let me get you cleaned up, get some food into you, see if you need medical—" He broke off, listening. "What's that?" He turned toward the closed closet door, and Sheryl gazed serenely with him.

"Don't open it, please," she said. It was as if she had asked him to pass the butter. He stared at her, suddenly angry.

"Sheryl! Don't tell me! You *can't* have another lover in the closet—that's farce!"

"Please don't open the door, Jen," she insisted softly.

He stared at her, then at the door. There was a repetition of the thin, rattling sound that had caught his attention. It made up his mind for him.

"Be careful," Sheryl begged as he whipped the door open, but he hardly heard her. The closet was a closet no longer; it led through the ragged remains of what had been its back wall to the apartment next door. Forgotten garments were hanging on racks still, and he could not see past them; but he could hear, and there were a great many people in that other apartment. People—or something else.

For in the foreground was definitely "something else." It was one of the unearthly crystal crustaceans, far huger at close range than they had seemed from the bridge over the Charles. Standing before it, Babylon could see that it was no terrestrial crab. Apart from the transparency of its body and limbs, its anatomy was only vaguely crablike. No eyestalks, but two huge bulging orbs like a fly's; no great crushing claws, but half a dozen slim pincers. Yet as it reared up to face him, the limbs clicking against the carapace, it looked surely menacing.

Babylon fell back a step. "What—what's it doing here?"

Sheryl's eyes shone with rapture. "It belongs here, Jen! I don't want it harmed!"

"I won't hurt the wretched thing," he said, falling back as it moved slowly into the room—actually, he was far more worried about harm going in the other direction. "But you have to tell me what's going on!"

"We are redeeming the Galaxy!" she cried proudly. "They're servants of the Crystal Maid, and so am I!"

Babylon stared at her, incredulous. He shook his head. "You're out of your mind," he said. It was not a reproach. It was meant as a statement of fact—fact as Babylon perceived fact—the same conviction that a thousand others like Babylon had held over the millennia, as someone dear to them followed Sun Myung Moon or the Reverend James Jones, or joined the Hitler Youth or the Komsomol, or went singing off to the Crusades. "Anyway, this thing can't be here," he said firmly. "It's dangerous. I'm going to call the police."

He moved toward the stereostage, but the giant glassy creature was faster than he. It scuttled, with a quick, dry, tinkling sound, to put itself in the way.

"Oh, Jen, stop!" Sheryl cried.

But it was not Sheryl that stopped him. The creature rose up, bright, faceted eyes gleaming out of the crystal shell. The flutelike hissing of its breath formed into words. "Oh, Jen, stop," it whispered, and then, "I won't hurt the wretched thing."

NINE

What a place! It had been terrifyingly alien in the first moments, baffling after a day, and now, as time passed and he saw more of its strangeness, it had become totally incomprehensible.

It was also huge—he was just beginning to discover how huge. Jen Babylon's new home was an artifact, created in the first place from tachtran patterns assembling the random elemental particles that floated in space into a tiny orbiter, then gradually expanded by mass drawn from the surface of Cuckoo itself. He had not formed a good idea of its size, because there were parts of it where he was not welcome and parts where neither he nor any other human could penetrate—refrigerated sections, blazing-hot sections, sections filled with poisonous gases or even liquids, where the few representatives of wholly nonhuman galactic races lurked, appearing among the carbon/oxygen/water races only through Purchased People or robots. The few parts he had seen were dismaying enough, especially considering their occupants! The Scorpian robots, the T'Worlie, the Sirians that seemed to be a single immense floating eye, the horse-headed Canopans, the deltaforms—he had not yet managed to catalog them all in his mind, much less to know who they were or where they were from. Less still to know friend from foe.

And why, in so dispassionate a scientific enterprise as the exploration of Cuckoo, should there be friends and foes?

But there were; and Babylon felt himself plunging deeper each day into a kind of paranoia of his own. What saved him was his work. Even his feelings of personal loss and anger receded in the face of the most interesting challenge his professional self had ever received.

The language of the ancient ship was opaque to every probe he could summon to his service. The big FARLINK computer munched the facts he poured into it, and returned only null results. The datastore he had sent to his other self in Boston had brought nothing in return—not even an acknowledgment. Doc Chimp chattered and joked and sympathized, but could not help; Ben Pertin appeared briefly and mysteriously, most often with dire warnings—"Say nothing to the Canopans!" "Be careful, there's a Scorpian asking questions!"—and then disappeared on strange errands. His best and closest companion was the T'Worlie, Mimmie. "Every language must have the same basic structure!" Babylon declared to the little butterfly-thing, getting a sweet carnation-and-maple-sugar scent of sympathy in response. "That's fundamental to the concept of communication. The naming of objects, the description of action, the qualification of the 'nouns' and 'verbs' that they represent—how can you have a language without those things?"

"Agreement," trilled the T'Worlie. "Concur in statements. Conclusion drawn: We will succeed, Dr. Jen Babylon."

"But when?" Babylon snarled, and the T'Worlie fell silent. "There are shared assumptions in all languages, but there are also assumptions that are unique. Or anyway different, and here's an example right now. You don't really understand why I'm frustrated and upset, do you?"

"Agreement," the T'Worlie signaled. "Statement: Our time horizon much longer than yours."

"And therefore you're more patient, right. Well, whoever built that ship has a history completely separate from yours or mine, otherwise we would have found congruences before this. We're wasting our time with Pmals. We need to go back to plotting frequencies, making assumptions, testing them out—like code-breaking. If we only had some native languages to work with."

The T'Worlie chirped, "Statement. Native languages exist. Qualification. Apparently limited to beings of galactic origin, circumstances of presence on Cuckoo not known."

Babylon nodded; it was true that many of the galactic species seemed to have close relatives on Cuckoo. But then he changed the nod to a headshake. "But that's not good enough; we need real autochthonous languages. If we had that, it would be straightforward. The techniques were established long ago, by a man on my own planet named Jean François Champollion. He worked with ancient Egyp-

tian, an extinct language of which we had only written records. —
What's the matter?"

He had detected the scorching smell of disagreement. "Inability to
concur in statement," the T'Worlie chirped mildly. "No language
'extinct' if population speaking or affected by it survives."

"Well, right, that's true enough. I didn't mean it was wholly gone,
but the only record we had was in conventionalized pictures. What
happened in the long run was that this linguist found a stone—it's
called the Rosetta stone—on which the same message was carved in
the unknown language and a known one. If we only had something
like that, we might have some hope."

"Estimate probability high that such or analogous breakthrough
will occur, Jen Babylon."

Babylon grinned and brushed his hair back. "Well, let's get back to
it." He stared around the room. "We've made a mess of this place,
haven't we?" There was a litter of hard work in the chamber, half-
dismantled Pmal translators, sound tapes and spheres, optical records
in a dozen physical forms, frequency analyzers, and all the other tools
of their trade. "Well, let's play the audio tapes again. If we can spot
any phonemes that look like inflections maybe we can subtract them
and get down to root words, at least—but I'd still like a Rosetta
stone."

"Dear friend," piped a familiar chatter from the door, "perhaps this
old monkey has brought you one—though you may not like the way it
looks!"

It was Doc Chimp, of course, clutching a handhold with one long,
skinny arm as he floated easily in the entrance. There was nothing
easy about his expression, however. His head was cocked as though
listening, and he darted glances back over his shoulder as he spoke. He
said hurriedly, "He's coming. He's a little, uh, unusual, Dr. Babylon,
but I think he may be able to help you. —Ah, here he is!" And he
swung inside the entrance to give the next creature a wide berth. From
safety at the side of the wall Doc Chimp piped nervously, "Allow me
to introduce our guest, from the distinguished, and possibly autochthonous, race of Watchers."

The words were not necessary. The smell was introduction enough.
The T'Worlie whistled feebly and fluttered over to the air vent, but
Babylon had no such escape.

The creature that came slowly through the door, handing itself carefully from one holdfast to another, was as evil in appearance as anything Jen Babylon had ever imagined. Its top was black, its belly red, both fused out of shiny chitin armor. It had small leathery wings that looked useless but in fact were ample within the orbiter, or on Cuckoo itself. It had a parrot beak, with its ears queerly set beside it; the eyes were farther back on the head, like a squirrel's. And it stank.

It squeaked peremptorily, and all of the working Pmals near Babylon translated its words: "I will assist you inferior races, but you must respond quickly. Now! What can you tell me of your problem?"

Babylon's one previous glimpse of a Watcher, at the strangely inconclusive meeting he had been summoned to, had been so diluted by the presence of a dozen other strange creatures that the Watcher had been little more than one additional horror in a saturating sufficiency of them. All by itself, it was something special. It was one of the few Cuckoo creatures that did not seem to have some analog on one of the galactic planets—because it was native? Or simply because its home planet had not been integrated into the galactic web? That was a good possibility! Who would want to include these things in any possible congeries of cultures?

"I instructed you to be quick!" the Watcher squealed dangerously, and Doc Chimp nervously cleared his throat.

"If you will, Dr. Babylon," he pleaded. "I know our, uh, guest is somewhat, ah, disconcerting"—the Watcher squealed a disdainful laugh—"but his entire race maintains some sort of contact with the oldest, maybe vanished cultures on Cuckoo. The ones who built the other orbiters, maybe; maybe even the wrecked ship. And his language has not been entered in the databanks in any complete way, because of the, uh, lack of social accommodation—"

"Be quiet, animal!" the Watcher commanded. "You other animals are investigating matters that concern me greatly. I will exchange information, but begin!"

From its position beside the air vent the T'Worlie gasped: "Recommendation: comply. Alternative: terminate dialogue."

Babylon nodded, and bent to the instruments. "Very well," he said, searching for the datastores he needed—any help was worth having, at this stage! "These are the sound sections of our records from the ship, and they seem to be associated with certain visuals." He slipped two of the hexagons into the reader and started the playback, and at once the raucous noises he had heard under such terrifying circumstances filled the chamber. The Watcher thrust itself across the chamber to remove itself as far as possible from the lesser breeds and settled down to watch and listen. The smell was nearly strangling Babylon, and something was buzzing annoyingly around his ear. He swatted irritably at it—a floating mote of silver, just hovering—and stung his hand. It was like slapping a sharp flint.

Doc Chimp cried, "Oh, Dr. Babylon, it's a Boaty-Bit! Don't hurt it!" He thrust himself toward the spinning fleck of diamond brightness, then sighed in relief. "Ah, there's another"—as a quicksilver gleam darted toward its comrade—"and it seems all right. You don't usually see them in ones and twos like this. The more they are the smarter they are, you see—collective intelligence. Ah, they're flying off. I'm glad you didn't damage it, Dr. Babylon. You don't want the Boaty-Bits mad at you—oh, no!"

The two little midges had drifted too close to the Watcher, who had flashed out a pink, slimy tentacle and whipped one of them into its mouth. The other darted away furiously, hesitated, then streaked out and down the corridor. "Cannibal!" Doc Chimp cried. "That's an intelligent creature, Watcher!"

Astonishingly, the Watcher laughed, a raucous bark that was unmistakable regardless of language. He whistled a series of short, sharp sounds, and the Pmal rendered it into English for Babylon:

"True I eat flying Bits and even Earth bipeds," he said contemptuously. "Untrue to call it cannibalism. Not my species! But I give you assurance I will not eat anyone here in this room now."

"Kind of you," Babylon murmured, resisting the impulse to edge away. The Watcher laughed again.

"Spoken with humor. Good. We Watchers appreciate courage, even from lower forms such as yourself. Now maintain silence while I inform you. We Watchers are subject to certain behavior constraints, acting on behalf of another species that you have never seen. I myself have never seen them, receiving instructions only at second remove. I now desire to complete study of your records, to shed light on matters concerning wrecked ship that do not concern you, therefore be silent while I listen."

As time wore on the smell dwindled in Babylon's nostrils, though it never became tolerable. Still, he almost forgot it, for the Watcher almost at once reacted. "Stop!" he commanded. "Reverse! Play

again— Yes, now stop there!" And he switched from the painful
squeals to a deeper, rumbling sound very like the sounds from the
hexagons themselves.

The Pmal hesitantly rendered his new language as, "Display . . .
graphics."

And the whirling images on the visual track suddenly settled down
and revealed a mottled red scene, evidently the surface of Cuckoo,
with curious markings that called attention to two points on the chart.
Doc Chimp squealed faintly. "That—that's where the wrecked ship
is!" he cried. "And that other—I don't know, except I recognize that
mountain. They call it Knife-in-the-Sky."

The Watcher commanded in his own language: "Be still, animal. It
is where the ship should have been, of course."

"Of course," the chimpanzee said finally. "Listen, Dr. Babylon. I'd
better go check, see if the Boaty-Bit that got away is all right. I'll be
back—"

"It is unimportant whether you will be back!" the Watcher howled.
"Continue transcription!"

The creature was both loathsome and frightening, but with its aid
the translation began to become possible. Not easy. But there were
breakthroughs. Babylon forced himself to endure the stink and revul-
sion for hours at a time, tending the Pmals while the Watcher slowly
built up a store of congruences.

And of course the little Pmal translators that every being on the
orbiter carried as a matter of course were no use. They were no more
than compact library stores, with some learning circuits. They contained the roots and equivalences of all the known galactic tongues,
and from them were able to construct dictionaries for any related
language. For unrelated languages they were of no use at all, and so
the first task for Babylon and the T'Worlie had been to put together a
much larger translator, inputting to the FARLINK computer. Like all
Pmals, their translator contained a nucleus of semiliving cells. The
basic design, like so much of the Galaxy's technology, was T'Worlie,
but an ancient Earth linguist named Paul M. A. Linebarger had
predicted it, and so most humans gave it his initials. It was not
enough. To the word-matching and grammar-building of the Pmal,
Babylon had to apply his quantum-dynamics procedures, and the

T'Worlie contributed his race's own form of entropic analysis . . . and gradually, slowly, the vocabulary grew.

Grammar was another problem entirely. It was on the rock of grammar that the mechanical translators of early Earth languages had failed. The old grammarians tried to construct a logical grammar for the English language and fell victim to the golden-age myth. They thought there must once have been *some* language that was constructed from prime principles and had not yet been corrupted by the easy slippage of everyday speech (which was wrong in itself), and they thought that language was probably Latin, which was even more wrong. Latin is an inflected language. By the inflected form of the verb "to love" you can see who is the lover and who the loved, a sort of relationship that English conveys by the position of the words in the sentence; so there the grammarians failed.

They failed, even, in deciding just what a grammar was. The old-time conception of a grammar was as a sort of black box. You put thoughts into it, and it converted them into sentences, so that a grammar was defined as a device which could generate every possible grammatical sentence, but would not generate any nongrammatical ones. No use. The definition was circular, like defining "red paint" as that which paints things red. It also took no account of the differences in meaning of the word "grammar," defining a deep structure indispensable to communication as well as the conventions of ordinary talk. But that latter grammar depended on who was using it. That grammar, really, was no more than a system of identification codes to let the hearer know that the speaker was upper-class-educated, working-class-tough, urban black, whatever. One of the great triumphs of quantum-dynamic linguistics was that it cut through the semantic maze and struck right to the heart of meaning.

But not easily.

Not with pleasure, either, as long as the Watcher continued to show up at regular intervals to listen for analogs and input his own language. Babylon and the T'Worlie worked out a bargain—they would take turns in milking the creature's knowledge—and when it was the T'Worlie's turn Babylon explored the orbiter. He did it mostly by himself; Doc Chimp had been staying away, and when the little chimpanzee's absence had continued for several days Babylon sought him out.

He found Doc Chimp huddled over a stereostage, whispering to someone whose identity Babylon could not determine. When he glanced up at his visitor the chimp's expression was almost triumphant, but darkened instantly. "Oh, Dr. Babylon," he chattered. "How nice of you to visit this old monkey. If only you'd given me a little warning, though!" He seemed to be talking as much to the stereo as to Babylon.

"I'm sorry to interrupt you," Babylon offered.

"No, no! Of course not! Just let me say good-bye to my friend here—" Babylon stayed near the doorway, politely out of range, while the chimp whispered a few more words. Babylon had never before been in Doc Chimp's quarters. As a senior inhabitant of the orbiter, Doc Chimp had squatter's rights on the cubicle he preferred, and he had decorated it to suit—a semiliving T'Worlie painting moved slowly on one wall, a stereophoto of the Serengeti plain occupied another. One end of the chamber was filled with a steel-pipe jungle gym, a children's playground thing that seemed to be the chimpanzee's sleeping place, since some of the pipes were hung with scraps of cloth to make a nest. "It's not much," Doc Chimp apologized, "but it's my home, and welcome to it." He sprang to find a drinking bulb and a few pieces of synthetic food. "At least have some coffee, please? Heaven knows it's no good—there's no good food on this whole orbiter."

"I didn't mean to interfere with what you were doing."

The chimpanzee was silent for a moment, scratching at his leathery cheek with one long, skinny finger. "Can you stay here for about an hour?" he demanded suddenly.

"Why—I suppose so, but what for?"

"I want you to meet somebody."

"The last time you brought somebody to meet me," Babylon said, "he scared me half to death. Not to mention how he smelled."

Doc Chimp grinned. "But you have to admit he helped you, right? Well, this time it will be different—although I think you'll find there will be some help, too. They'll be here in a little while, but please don't ask any questions—you never know who might be listening!"

Babylon squeezed a mouthful of the tepid imitation coffee past his lips, shuddered, swallowed, and said mournfully, "Are we ever going to get to the point where everything isn't a mystery?"

"Not on Cuckoo, I'm afraid. Everything's a mystery—not least of all, what we are doing here!" He pressed some levers on the stereo-

stage and nodded to Babylon to come to look over his shoulder.
"There it is," he said, as a holographic virtual image formed in the
stage. "Cuckoo. Three hundred million kilometers in diameter and
made out of—what? Space? It has so little mass there's nothing we
know of that can account for it. See the markings in bright relief?
That's what we've mapped so far. And the dark ones? Those are what
we've actually explored." He heeled a bar moodily, and the great
simulated sphere began to spin until it was almost a blur. "That's what
we've got to show for more than a dozen years and a lot—oh, yes, Dr.
Babylon, a *lot*—of lives. And no system, really. Every race wanted a
priority given to its own analogs here on Cuckoo. And, my goodness,
Dr. Babylon, we don't have unlimited resources! So we wasted fifteen
hundred launches, lost more than a dozen landers, killed off better
than a thousand creatures, one way or another, just to peek at the least
interesting parts. It's all politics, you know. And we terrestrial primates, like you and me, we don't have as much muscle as some of the
older, more powerful races. When the T'Worlie want something they
get it! Same with the Sheliaks. One of the Sheliaks took a whole
expedition down to that jungle there—you can only see it as a blur,
but it's a thousand miles across! He was studying thermosynthesis—
the way Cuckoo's life feeds on the heat flow from below, like some
submarine colonies do in our own oceans back home on Earth, instead
of light from the Sun. An interesting study, right? I thought so. That's
why I went along . . . And when the Sheliak probed too hard and
started a volcanic eruption, I was one of the ones that died!"

"I'm sorry," Babylon muttered. It was a foolish thing to say—how
do you condole a person for his own death, when he is alive and well
before you?

The chimp nodded moodily. "They're all alike, Dr. Babylon," he
sighed. "Crazy theories. The Boaty-Bits and the Scorpians and the
Canopans, they all think that Cuckoo might be made of some other
kind of matter, with zero mass. Well, that's moonshine! I've been
there! So have you! It's solid rock and soil and plants and lakes and
oceans."

"Of course it is," Babylon said soothingly.

But of course it wasn't. He recalled enough undergraduate science
to be certain of that. No solid body of any such size could possibly
exist. Or even a thousandth this size. The gravitation of its own

enormous mass would squeeze it down into a black hole with no size at all, squeeze it finally out of the physical universe.

But—

What was it? How had it come to be, and what strange new science could explain it? What sort of beings had lived on or around it? Maybe still lived? What had those orbital forts been built to defend? What had brought down the one they had entered?

Again he grappled with those perplexities, and again he saw no answers.

The chimp scratched his leathery cheek. "The Boaty-Bits you can understand, a little," he said. "They're so different, being a collective entity and all—they don't have the same feelings as individual organisms like the rest of us. They think we individuals are almost like amputees—they're sorry for us, would you believe it? But the Sirians! They have no real sense of time—if it won't happen in the next week they couldn't care less, and that makes them dangerous . . ." He paused. "What's the matter, Dr. Babylon? You're giving me a funny look."

"I'm wondering," Babylon said, "why you're telling me all this right now. I get the feeling you're just making conversation to keep me here."

Surprisingly, the chimp grinned. "Right you are, Dr. Babylon," he agreed. "And I guess it worked, because the people I want you to meet are here now. Come in, folks! Let me present, direct from Earth, the Galaxy's foremost expert in quantum-dynamic linguistics and heaven knows what else, Dr. Jen Babylon!"

The pair that gently launched themselves into Doc Chimp's chamber were almost more surprising than any of the monsters Babylon had seen. Human, yes, undoubtedly. But what humans! They were a man and a woman, each more than two meters tall, and slimmer than human beings had any right to be. "This is Org Rider, Dr. Babylon," the chimp said proudly. "He's a *real* person, not a tachyon dupe like the rest of us." He didn't look real to Babylon, he looked grotesquely stretched—like a normal man of a hundred and seventy-five centimeters or so who has been pulled thin, like taffy. He wore a cache-sex, a belt with pockets and loops, a few straps of harness, and nothing else. "Of course," Doc Chimp went on meditatively, " 'real' is a kind of comparative word, isn't it? I mean, Org Rider isn't 'real' Earth primate in the sense that you and I are, or anyway used to be—he doesn't come from Earth. He comes from here. And this is his good lady, Zara, who I think you may have met before."

Babylon was staring. "Zara Gentry!" he exclaimed.

The wraith-thin woman laughed—a solid, human laugh, regardless of her appearance. "As good a name as any," she acknowledged.

"No, no. I mean I've met you before. You're a famous newscaster, back on Earth, Mrs. Gentry."

"Just Zara, please. I was born Zara Doy, then I married and I was Zara Doy Gentry—I understand that on Sun One I'm Zara something else—but here my husband and I don't share the same name. He is Org Rider. I am simply Zara—an edited version of myself," she added wistfully, "but still the same person."

Babylon said humbly, "I really don't know very much about what an 'edited' version of a person is—in spite of the fact that it happened to me, and I'm reminded of it every time I wake up and reach for the glasses I don't have anymore."

Doc Chimp laughed. "Let me tell him, Zara," he volunteered. "Dr. Babylon hasn't been here long enough to learn all our little ways. But it's simple enough. When you're tachyon-transmitted, you know, all that really gets sent is a sort of blueprint of what you are. Then it gets put together at the other end, out of whatever odds and ends of matter happen to be about; and you can always edit the blueprint. Change it, you see? Adapt the pattern to special needs. Suppose you want to live on a water world; well, it's easy enough to modify your blueprints to let you breathe water. It takes gills, o' course, and some changes in your metabolism, but that's easy enough. Lots of the folks you see around the orbiter are edited copies—chlorine-breathers, changed to an oxygen atmosphere. Light-gravity people—well, you don't see them changed much here, because it isn't necessary, but there are plenty of them rebuilt for heavy duty, as you might say, back on Earth. So, in order to make Zara less conspicuous when she was first sent down to Cuckoo, minglin' with the aborigines, as you might say, she was just stretched out a little."

Babylon listened thoughtfully, but his mind was working. "Doc," he said at last, "you're an absolute gold mine of information today, but I still get the idea that you're talking to keep me from asking questions."

Zara answered for him. "It's true, Jen," she said. "There's something we don't want to talk about yet, and it's true that we came here just to see you."

"All right, so when are you going to stop being mysterious?"

She laughed. Her dimples were just as attractive on a face stretched thirty percent beyond its norm as they would have been on the original, Babylon decided. "As to what we don't want to talk about, that will have to wait a day or two. As to what we came here for—tell him, Org Rider."

"Very well, I will tell it," said the man with her, pulling a small glittering sphere from one of his belt pockets. "This is for you, Jen. It does not directly relate to your linguistics, but it will, I think, be of interest. It is the record of certain investigations Zara and I made." He tossed the sphere to Doc Chimp, who retrieved it nimbly from the air and fitted it into his stereostage. "Display the first view," Org Rider ordered, and obediently a landscape filled the stage, dominated by an immense, distant mountain. Org Rider said, "That is my home. That is Knife-in-the-Sky, as it is seen from my tribe's mountain. My ancestors have lived there for as long as the oldest singer can say. But when Zara comes, and I see her, I ask questions. Why are we so alike? Are my people once from that little planet where she comes from? How can I find out these things? So I ask Zara, and she tells me, 'paleontology.' And I ask her, how can we get 'paleontology'?"

Zara grinned. "I explained what it meant—digging down for fossils and so on—and we imported texts and manuals from Earth and made ourselves paleontologists. We started digging. Our work is very sloppy by Earth standards, of course. But it's also a lot easier. We don't have to mark geologic formations with precision, because there haven't been any big faults or earth shifts. Just a gradual deposition of silt and sand and clay from the rivers that run off Knife-in-the-Sky. The dating was hard—well, I'll be honest. It was impossible. We tried radio-carbon dating ourselves, working out of a textbook—forget it! For one thing, there were too many unknowns that might contribute radioactivity from the Cuckoo atmosphere, but the worst part was we just didn't know what we were doing. But then we were lucky."

She hesitated, and glanced at her husband. "I *guess* we were lucky," she amended. "What I mean is we got some help from the Sirians. They were interested too, because there are analogs of Sirians on Cuckoo as well, just as of the Boaty-Bits and the Sheliaks and lots of others. Most of them don't seem to care. The Sirians care. They are a very vain, proud race, and working with them was no pleasure. Have you ever seen a Sirian? Looks just like a large, floating eye? Almost all soft tissue, nothing to leave fossils? Yes. Well, that's why they came to us for help. They're very good at potassium-argon dating; they can pinpoint the argon-isotope balance to within almost a century or so, and that goes back much farther than the carbon procedures. And so we dug. Show him, Org Rider," she said to her husband, who nodded and punched out commands on the stereostage. A virtual image of the skeleton of a hand appeared. "This is the earliest we found, Dr. Babylon. Thirteen thousand years ago, according to the Sirians. And as soon as they got that dated they suddenly lost interest, wouldn't even talk to us anymore."

Babylon studied the virtual image uncomprehendingly. "Do you see how short the fingers are?" Org Rider demanded.

Babylon shrugged. "I wouldn't call them short. They look about the same length as your own—much longer than mine."

Org Rider flexed his long, supple hand, laughing. "I see you are no anatomist either, Jen Babylon. I had to learn this, too. See here. You think your fingers are only the part that extends beyond your palm and hand, because that is what you see. But that is not all. Rub your fingers across the back of your hand—do you see? Those bones you feel, those are the hidden parts of your fingers. They go all the way to the wrist."

Babylon did as instructed, then stared at the stereo image. "Why, those are just the same as mine! Not stretched out of all reason like—oh, excuse me!"

Org Rider shook his head, smiling. "We are not Sirians or Sheliaks, Jen Babylon, so we do not take offense lightly. You are correct. The fingers are in exactly the same proportion as your own. Exactly the proportion of an Earth human now, or of the Earth humans who were alive there at the date given by the argon isotopes, which is perhaps thirteen thousand four hundred years ago. Those are the earliest we found. We dug further. But below that—nothing."

When Jen Babylon told Mimmie about the results of Org Rider's digging, the T'Worlie exuded a cinnamon-bun odor of understanding. "Concurrence," it peeped. "Statement: Similar findings for other Cuckoo analogs of galactic races. Conclusion: Event of thirteen thousand four hundred years ago brought them here simultaneously. Query: Nature of event?"

Babylon rose and stretched, catching at a handhold to keep from drifting away from the instruments. "Yes, that's the question, isn't it?" he replied. "Something happened here, all those years ago. Before that the only life was native—whatever that was. After it, there were immigrants from almost all the galactic planets. But how? I guarantee the Cro-Magnons didn't have the tachyon-transmission links on Earth—I don't know how it was with you T'Worlie."

Over the time they had been working together Babylon had discovered that the T'Worlie had a sense of humor—hard to pin down, with the dehumanizing effect of translation through the Pmals, but popping out at unexpected times; they had become accustomed to exchanging pleasantries. But Babylon had forgotten the third being present. The Watcher hissed in rage, and the Pmal struggled with its furious squeals with only partial success: "—blasphemous—offensive little animals! What you deserve—" The Pmal could not manage to say what they deserved, and it was no doubt as well. The Watcher's slimy pink tentacles were quivering with fury and, abruptly, it turned and hurled itself out of the chamber.

Babylon gazed after it in dismay. "What did I say?" he demanded.

The T'Worlie said hesitantly, "Statement: Watchers are deputies of some older, perhaps extinct race. Conjecture: Attempts to discover identity of same may be offensive, especially when levity is involved."

Babylon found he was shaking. "Well," he said at last, "we've pretty nearly pumped it dry anyway—and I admit I was getting tired of the way it smelled. Tell you the truth, Mimmie, I kind of hope it never comes back."

And for several days he got his wish; the Watcher remained absent, while the two of them worked at correlating the data it had provided. It was not particularly difficult work, since by now the Pmals had the sketchy beginnings of a vocabulary to work with, and at least some tentative grammatical models. There was still no word from that other Jen Babylon on Earth, but the FARLINK computer put a great deal of power behind their processing, and it became clear that what they had rescued from the wrecked ship was of immense value. Item: a detailed map of the surface of Cuckoo, so huge that it could be presented only in segments a thousand miles square—there were more than a million of them! Item: On the segmented maps, symbols that indicated places of special interest—what the interest was, was still unclear, but one of them had been the location of the wrecked ship itself. Item: What appeared to be operating manuals for the ship's equipment: weaponry (but none of the weapons were available to test); drive controls (but the ship itself would never move again); communications. And, of course, every datum was a fresh puzzle, not made easier by the accumulating debt each of them was beginning to owe to fatigue. Babylon passed his hand across his eyes. "The wrecked ship is marked," he muttered, more to himself than to the T'Worlie. "See those radiating lines? And the same pattern shows up five—no, seven more times on the globe." He peered blearily at the stereo image and nodded. "Yes," he said, "the globe is divided into octants, and there's one of those special marks in each one. What do you suppose it means? A sort of local capital for each section? A military headquarters? Some particularly important spot—that maybe the wrecked ship was attacking?"

There was no answer from the T'Worlie, except an unfamiliar burning odor. "And these symbols in the communications data," he went on. "FARLINK gives us a match—they represent the concept 'zero-mass tachyon.' But what's a zero-mass tachyon when it's home?"

The T'Worlie was silent for a moment before it replied, while the scorching odor grew. Babylon turned uneasily to face it. "Statement," it said faintly. "Tachyon is defined as particle that obeys law of velocity of light as limit, but in its case as lower limit. Statement: Photon is defined as particle that has rest mass of zero. Conjecture by analogy: 'Zero-mass tachyon' may be particle that has infinite speed. Further conjecture . . ."

But the peeping voice faded away, and the Pmal fell silent. "Oh, hell," cried Babylon, suddenly aware of the bedraggled filmy wings, the dullness in the five clustered eyes. "You're bloody exhausted, aren't you? I've been driving you too hard!"

The T'Worlie managed a faint chirp, which the Pmal rendered as, "Concurrence."

Babylon shook his head in self-reproach. The T'Worlie were almost the most ancient of the civilized galactic races, with a time sense that extended centuries into the future . . . and an unhurried, placid way of life to match. "I'm sorry," Babylon said. "You need rest! We both do, I guess, and it's my fault." He pushed himself away from the processors and gazed around the room. "We've made a lot of progress, anyway," he said. "We're entitled to a break. Take the day off, Mimmie—I mean, please," he added hastily, conscious that he was giving orders to one of the race that had essentially founded the galactic culture. "I will, too. Then when we get back maybe we can figure out just what to do with all this stuff . . ."

The butterfly wings trembled, and gently eased the creature toward the exit. It managed a faint, "Thank you," and was gone.

Babylon did not at once follow his own instructions. He hung relaxing from one of the straps that festooned the wall—for him alone, really, because the T'Worlie certainly had no need of them. With the Watcher's help they had achieved a great deal, but not without cost. The bill was coming due. Babylon was suddenly aware of his own fatigue and, worse, his general tackiness. His beard bristled, his hair was unkempt. He had not troubled to bathe in—how long? Several days at least, and he was abruptly conscious of the fact that he showed it in unpleasant ways—

Wrong. The smell that assailed his nostrils was not his own. He spun quickly to confront the doorway, and his suspicion was right.

The Watcher hung there silently, staring at him with one immense, faceted eye.

What a revolting creature it was! Babylon repressed a shudder of distaste, but managed to say civilly, "Nice to see you again."

The Watcher squealed contemptuously, "That is a lie! You are not pleased to see me, and I could never be pleased to see you."

Babylon nodded, angry at himself for attempting courtesy with this incarnate evil. "Then why are you here?" he demanded.

"Because of urgency," it squealed, "Our interests coincide for one short step more. Come!" And it flapped its leathery wings toward him, and the hideous pink tentacles caught him by arm and torso and dragged him away.

Jen Babylon was of average strength, but in those whiplike pink tentacles he was helpless. He was carried through the orbiter's passages faster than he had ever traveled them before, as the Watcher's powerful wings beat waves of its foul stench back at him. Dizzy from the kaleidoscope passage of the chambers and corridors and halls, retching from the stink, exhausted from struggling against the python grip of the tentacles, Babylon was half dazed when at last the Watcher thrust him free. He catapulted through a door, and was caught by the quick long arm of Doc Chimp. "Why, Dr. Babylon! I asked the Watcher to bring you here, but I never expected it to be this way!"

Babylon shook himself free, clutching at a wall fixture. "It doesn't matter," he said, looking about. The chimpanzee was not alone in his chamber; the two stretched-out human beings he had met before were there, Org Rider and Zara; so was Ben Pertin—some Ben Pertin or another. And so was a stranger.

Zara pushed herself close to him, her face concerned. "You look like you've had a hard time, Jen. I'm sorry. I asked the Watcher to be gentle, but it's not in his nature." She turned and squealed commandingly at the Watcher—not bothering to use the Pmal, Babylon observed with wonder. The Watcher made a contemptuous sound in return, hovering solidly just outside the door. "He'll stay out there, Jen," Zara said. "Since he's a Watcher, we'll let him watch for us— and the air's better in here that way. There are beings on the orbiter we don't want to come in here just now. I promised you that we'd stop acting mysterious as soon as we could—and now we can." She nodded toward the stranger in the room. "Jen Babylon, I want you to meet Redlaw, the human being who knows more about Cuckoo than anyone else."

If Org Rider and Zara were tall, this man was a giant. He overtopped them both by inches, and where their frames were stretched and slim his was solid. "Hello, Jen Babylon," he boomed, bright green eyes staring at Babylon's. "I hear you're the one I have to thank."

"For what?" Babylon asked, and it was Zara who replied:

"You gave us a key we've been looking for for a long time, Jen. When the Watcher helped you interpret the graphics Doc Chimp realized at once what it meant. One set of coordinates for where the wrecked ship hit the ground. Another for where it was supposed to be going—its home base, in other words. And he came at once to Org Rider and me, and we got word to Redlaw, on the surface of Cuckoo, not too far away—and so he went there."

The giant nodded. His hair was red and so was his beard, and his voice was deeper than any human's Babylon had ever heard. "And I found something important," he said.

Babylon cast a quick look at the Watcher. "Wait a minute," he said. "If there's anything secret—"

"It's all right, Jen," Zara reassured him. "The Watchers aren't friends, not by any stretch of the imagination. But they've got problems of their own. They're called Watchers because they are supposed to serve as scouts and guardians for someone else—probably the people who built the wrecked ship and the base. They haven't been able to communicate with them for a long time. They want to know how to get back in touch. It's a religious matter to them"—from the doorway the Watcher squealed warningly, but she paid no attention—"or at least it's a sort of built-in imperative. So we made a deal to exchange this information. As soon as we're finished the deal ends— but for now, Redlaw, go ahead. Tell what you found."

Redlaw nodded to Doc Chimp, who produced another of the bright dataspheres and inserted it into his scanner. "Here's where I went," he said, as a scene of a pretty lake with what looked like some kind of temple at its narrowest end appeared on the stage. "It's got a special marking on the chart you showed Doc Chimp—do you remember?"

"I don't think so," Babylon began, and then suddenly, "Yes! Of course! It's one of those special points in each octant of the surface of Cuckoo—like the place where the wrecked ship is lying!"

"Exactly. So I naturally thought it would have something to do with spaceships. The orbiters, of course; maybe a repair and maintenance base of some sort for them. But, as you can see, there's nothing like that visible." He stroked his long, lean chin, and rumbled, "That building has never been observed before. Not surprising, you know— there's just too much of Cuckoo! But it's not even in a common style. Certainly Org Rider's people never worked in stone. The other races all have their own styles of construction, and none of them is like this . . . So I went inside."

He gestured again to Doc Chimp. The scene disappeared in a cloud of golden flakes, then solidified to show the interior of a great pillared chamber. Overhead was a vaulted dome; by bending and peering up into the three-dimensional image Babylon could see that the dome was ornamented with a representation of a galaxy, lenslike, whirlpool-lined, made of a myriad of tiny points of light. "I don't know how long it has been since this place was used last," Redlaw said, "but there was still power to light that display—and for other things." He stepped over to Doc Chimp's side and manipulated the display; the holographic image revolved slowly, and they were looking out through the great pillars. "See that road?" he demanded, as a white, trenched avenue appeared. "It goes down directly into the lake. I have a theory about that. I think it goes down a long way under the water—why I don't know. Maybe it was something like a launchway for water craft? I don't think so. I think it was all exposed at one time, going down into that hollow to something else—something I couldn't see, much less get to, under the water. And over the years, when it was untended and forgotten, rain or springs filled it and made the lake. Now look inside!" He rotated the image again, and Babylon gasped.

There was a statue at the end of the chamber, in hard white metal, the figure of a three-eyed biped. Though the flat head seemed utterly alien, the torso gave an impression of femininity. Its delicate arms were lifted. One three-fingered hand held a ball, the other a handled ring. There was something Babylon took to be a blouselike garment, portrayed perhaps as blowing in the breeze; but as Redlaw increased the magnification he saw that the unknown artist had portrayed wings.

From the doorway there was a sharp, hurting squeal which the Pmals could not translate. The Watcher was quivering with excitement, its pink tentacles crawling longingly.

Redlaw glanced at the creature, then lowered his voice to Jen Babylon. "I think those are the things he used to work for—wherever they are now. But they've left something behind. Defenses—all around that little valley are the same crystal towers you found near the wrecked ship; it took them a while to react, but as I was leaving they nearly finished me. And what they were defending was in that chamber. Records—the same kind of six-sided rod you found in the ship; I brought a batch of them back for you, Jen. I had no way of playing them, of course. Weapons—perhaps like the ones that were in the ship. Perhaps something different. I left them there. And—one other thing."

He pulled out what looked as much like a collapsed hot-water bottle as anything Babylon had ever seen. It was open at one end, and possessed a structure of coppery, feathery metal tendrils at the other. "I didn't know what it was either, Jen," Redlaw boomed, grinning through his scarlet beard. "So—I put it on."

Babylon accepted it and turned it over in his hands. It was lighter than he had expected—less massy, he corrected himself, since everything was "light" in the orbiter. It was even more flexible than it had appeared while Redlaw still held it; he could twist it, turn it, fold it; he could even imagine himself doing as Redlaw had, and drawing it on over his head.

But there was ancient power in the device; he could feel it. He temporized. "What is it?"

Zara answered for him. "Do you know what Purchased People are, Jen?"

"Sure. Everybody does. They're criminals who have been sold to aliens to use," he said impatiently.

"Yes, exactly. But do you know how the aliens use them?"

"Why, yes, I suppose so—I mean," he said, floundering, "of course the technical details are a little out of my field—"

Zara laughed, nodding in friendly sympathy. "Mine too, Jen. Almost everybody's. All we know, really, is that the Purchased People are given some sort of implant, which then puts them in direct communication with their owners. The owners can feel with their senses, see with their eyes, control their actions. Of course, some sort of tachyon communication must be involved, but that's about all any of us knew. But this helmet—" She looked at it almost with awe. "It lets us listen in, Jen! It lets us experience whatever any Purchased Person in range is experiencing—and that means anyone on or near Cuckoo! And *that* means—"

Her husband interrupted harshly. "It means that for the first time we can find out what's really going on here! Why some of the races are determined to destroy the research project, if not Cuckoo itself. Put it on, Babylon!"

He flexed it in his hands, still hesitating, and glanced at the doorway. He was startled to see that it was vacant.

"He's gone, Jen," Zara said, nodding. "This part of what we found doesn't interest the Watchers; I think our truce with them is over." She came closer and touched his arm reassuringly. "But our part is just beginning, Jen. Put it on!"

TEN

Te'ehala Tupaia, paramount king-warrior in the forces of Free Polynesia, shuffled along the line of prisoners. Muscles flaccid, he commanded himself. Eyes down! Follow the little old man ahead! Two steps, stop. Wait. Two steps more, stop again. It was not easy to remain impassive, since he was almost surely the only one in the line of Purchased People who both knew where they were going and had the freedom to protest or resist . . . if he dared.

But he did not dare.

The man ahead lurched and moved, and Tupaia shambled another two steps. Tachyon transfer! Even to a king-warrior, it was frightening. Because he was neither ignorant nor actively possessed, he had plenty of time to consider what it meant. Tupaia was no ignorant beachboy. He had completed every grade in the mission school, and gone to the university on Bora Bora—though all that taught you was how to be a tour guide or, at the upper stretch of ambition, a headwaiter. Even nineteen-year-old Tupaia had something better in mind than that.

But—this was not it! Even in Bora Bora they had heard of the tachyon transmissions, and the young men and wahines had debated wonderingly why anyone would venture such a senseless trip. Now Tupaia faced the questions as imminent realities. The first question in his mind was, did he have reason to fear this adventure? The second, was there anything he could do about it, anyway?

The answer to the first question turned out not to matter, because the answer to the second was obviously no. When he took the next two steps forward, he was suddenly alone. The little man ahead of him had been manhandled through a sliding metal door, and disappeared.

And then it was Te'ehala Tupaia's turn. The two bored guards kicked the door open and grabbed an arm each to hurl him in.

For a moment he stiffened in involuntary resistance. The guards felt it. One of them glanced at him with the beginnings of surprise; but he had the wit to keep his eyes cast down. He willed his muscles to relax, though he was twice the size of these effeminate whiteskins, and they hustled him in in his turn.

The door slid latched behind him. There was a bright blue flash, a sting of electrical spark, and a sudden sense of disorientation. And the door on the other side of the tiny chamber opened and, willing himself not to make that deadly blunder again, Tupaia allowed himself to slump forward to take his place once more in the line . . .

But there was no line.

There was no great, busy tachyon-transmission hall, with its high ceiling and tessellated floor.

There was not even a floor! Or, at least, no floor that came up solidly to meet his feet as a floor should do. He spun weightlessly across an eerily lighted chamber, until a queer doughy creature caught him roughly and thrust him spinning against a wall.

He had been transmitted.

He was somewhere else. On another planet. Or in a spacecraft, or on an orbiting satellite—wherever he was, it was not on Earth, or on any planet with enough mass to give a man solid weight.

How far away from home, he did not know.

And how much time had elapsed—how long his coded pattern had been held on file before a need arose that it could fill—and how many Te'ehala Tupaias had lurched out into the shattering realization that they had been thrust millions of millions of kilometers away, he did not even think to ask.

Although Te'ehala Tupaia had known of the existence of the great galactic races all his life, and had even seen a few specimens at a distance, he had never before been in such intimate proximity to one. Had never touched them—hot metal; soggy flesh the texture of clay; damp scales—and above all had never smelled them. They reeked! Tupaia was not particularly sensitive in such matters. He had grown up with stinks of rotting palms and washed-ashore dead fish, not to mention the middens and spoil heaps around his village. But the strong Pacific breezes carried the worst away, and even the worst was nothing like this stinging metal odor of the Scorpian robot or the sour decay of the Sheliaks.

At first his new captors seemed, peculiarly, almost as confused by him as he was by them. They hustled him through long corridors to a hot, huge metal space the size of a ballroom, filled with what seemed to be half-destroyed old machines. The Sheliak, the clay-fleshed creature with the astonishing ability to shape its body to suit its needs, extended one pseudopod to hang a Pmal translator around Tupaia's neck. It spoke sharply, something that the translator rendered as a cackle of gibberish.

"I do not understand you," said Tupaia, shaking his head. The Sheliak recoiled in astonishment. There was a quick exchange between the aliens, drumroll from the Scorpian, tweeterings and whistles and growls from the others. The Pmal again produced only an unintelligible barnyard cackle.

Then the Sheliak realized what was wrong. It reached out and made an adjustment to the device, gesturing to Tupaia to speak. "My name," Tupaia said, comprehending, "is Te'ehala Tupaia, paramount king-warrior of the forces of Free Polynesia, and I have been abducted and held captive here against my will."

That was enough. The Pmal identified Tupaia's language from its store and corrected its programing. When the aliens responded, it at once produced their meaning in Tupaia's own vocabulary. The responses were an agitated hissing and a high, tenor snare-drum rattle; and the Pmal translated them as laughter.

At least here there was no more need to pretend to be possessed by his alien purchaser. That was the most obvious improvement in Tupaia's situation . . . maybe, he thought grimly, the only one.

Te'ehala Tupaia was resourceful and quick—he'd had to be, to avoid the colonial jails as long as he had. Within an hour of emerging from the tachyon chamber he had figured out where he was—more or less—and even what he was doing there. It wasn't hard to deduce that. Obviously these creatures had summoned him up in order to do something they couldn't, or didn't want to, do for themselves. That was what Purchased People were for. It had been a surprise to them to learn that he did not understand the language of his whilom owner, and to deduce from that that he was inexplicably free—or not free physically, of course, because they made clear he was not that, but free at least of the unwelcome alien presence that once had filled his mind. They asked questions about that, but not with much real interest, and when he could give them no clear explanation they did not press the matter. It didn't interest them, really. What they wanted was the use of his physical body. Who was in control of it mattered very little.

Tupaia had not bothered to lie on that subject. He knew no more than they. There had been an hour of dreadful pain, the raw torture of senses he didn't have, in limbs and organs he did not possess. It was obvious that something frightful had happened to his distant, alien owner. No doubt it had died. At least the pain had stopped, and where that inner tyrant had occupied his mind there was suddenly a blessed emptiness; Te'ehala Tupaia was himself again.

And would be free, too, as soon as he had disposed of this new crew of tormentors! Of achieving that he was quite confident. Physically the creatures looked formidable, particularly the hissing metal robot and the thing that looked like a gross, hovering blue eye, crackling with electrical forces, that they called a Sirian. But physical odds he could overcome.

What then?

Even Te'ehala Tupaia was forced to admit to himself that the way was unclear before him. He would have to wait and be ready for whatever opportunity presented itself . . .

And then he understood what the creatures were doing, and the opportunity became almost at hand; for the queer metal devices in the chamber were weapons!

He even understood what they needed a human being for. The weapons were ill-suited to their owners. "Owners" seemed the wrong word, in fact; the creatures were almost as awkward with them as Tupaia himself, as if they had never seen them until just recently. Certainly the handles and grips and levers were designed for beings with fingers and hands—although not, perhaps, the fingers and hands of human beings. Tupaia's fingers were too short, and the grips seemed made for creatures with more than a single thumb. Yet he could manage, and they could not. They ordered him to pick up one of the pieces, a silver-gray onion-shaped device, a globular mass coming to a sharp point at one end; it had a double butt, making it even more awkward. When he raised it to his shoulders it was too narrow to fit properly on his huge torso, and his clumsiness with the finger grips made the alien creatures scatter in consternation.

That was when he realized it was a weapon. They snatched it away from him and jerked the Pmal off his neck, gabbling among themselves in hiss and drum-roll and screech. Without the Pmal he could not understand a word—as they had intended—but he didn't care. His mind was bursting with the realization that here was a chance he had never dreamed of. Weapons of an alien science! If he could steal them— If he could get them to the tachyon transmitter and smuggle them back to Earth— If he could evade the guards at the Tachyon Center and deliver them to the other warriors in New Guinea or Rabaul—

There would be a way. There had to be!

But it was slow to appear.

They kept him there for endless hours, without rest or respite. They threw the Pmal at him from time to time, long enough to convey quick, curt orders commanding him to manipulate strange controls on even stranger devices, then retired once more for their interminable secret gabbles. After the first time they were wary of letting him have free access to a hand weapon, and even warier of some of the huger, stranger devices. But they had to learn how to operate them, and he was their only learning tool. There was a device like an organ keyboard attached to a great, solid, translucent block; under their instructions he pressed keys and twisted curious, helical levers, and for a long time nothing happened.

Then something did.

The glassy block began to light up with an eye-searing pinkish glow, while a thin, high sound grew louder and deeper, running down the scale. The aliens reacted with quick fear. The Sheliak's tentacles snatched Tupaia's fingers off the keys while the robot lunged at what seemed to be the starting switch. For a moment Tupaia thought they had been too late, as the glow built higher for a second. Then it wavered, faded, and disappeared.

They never let him touch that one again.

While they were debating, Tupaia became conscious of bodily needs. He approached the Sheliak, took the Pmal, and through it asked for food, water, rest. The answer, once again, was the Pmal's equivalent of contemptuous laughter. Tupaia stolidly let them take the translator away. His time would come. He would make it come.

He could find nothing to eat, but there was a globe of a thin, sour liquid enough like drinking water to serve, and a corner in which he relieved himself. The aliens paid no attention. He squatted by the door, watching everything, seeking the vagrant thoughts that would turn into a plan. He was certainly in a far better position than when he had been owned. The purchasers of Purchased People generally treated them as expendable. If they wanted to eat or sleep or relieve their bladders, they could. As long as there were no prior orders from the owner. Which was seldom. Here the only force imposed on him was physical. And by comparison, physical constraints were nothing.

After Tupaia's arrest and conviction, it had been only a few days until the prison authorities had struck their bargain for another batch of convicts sold to the aliens. Which aliens, or for what purpose, no one seemed to care. There had been a brief surgical operation—strapped immobile to the table Tupaia could not see what was happening behind his ear, or feel more than an itching tingle through the local anesthesia—and then the owner was inside his head. Terrible! It was not like one-to-one communication. The owner was immeasurably distant, and even tachyons took finite time to traverse interstellar spaces. But it laid its geases on him, and sampled his senses, and it was always there . . .

He was allowing himself to daydream!

He roused himself just as the screeching and rattling of the aliens rose to a high pitch and stopped, and they turned back to their project. Tupaia watched carefully as the Scorpian and the Sheliak examined the hand weapons. The robot picked up the onion-shaped weapon apprehensively, while the Sheliak nervously hissed advice. If they were foolish enough to put it in his hands again, even for a moment . . .

That foolish they were not.

As the robot awkwardly fitted his clawlike metal feelers onto the grip and braced the twin butts against his metal body, the Purchased Person, Te'ehala Tupaia, realized tardily that he was meant to serve more purposes than one. Not just to help them learn how to operate the weapons. To do something more important still. Because how could you know if a weapon was effective until you tried it on a living target?

The onion-shaped globe came up with the point aimed straight at

Tupaia. A greenish glow sprang out around the globe, collected itself toward the tip, launched itself toward him.

As the green blob of light spun toward his head he realized that he had waited too long to make a move; and that was the last thought that ever flickered through the mind of that particular Te'ehala Tupaia.

ELEVEN

I wake, and the waking is not easy this time. For I am afraid.

Something is moving inside the sacred structure of HIS being, shielded from my knowledge and my control. Someone is prying into the forbidden secrets, seeking powers that belong to HIM alone. Someone is discovering the secret state of the matter that can exist as neither solid nor liquid, gas or plasma, but forms into atoms larger than stars. Someone is using the old weapons to violate HIS precious fabric itself.

It is someone who does not belong to the chosen slaves. Someone has no right there, who can be there for no proper purpose.

I am deeply troubled.

I cannot penetrate the mind shields the blasphemers have invented, even to determine their race or their location or the extent of their unholy aims.

Shall I wake HIM to expunge them? Dare I?

I hesitate. As I rouse and survey the widening spheres of contact I see that there are others to follow, and others beyond them. A thousand times a thousand times I have been aroused from sleep to swat an annoying insect or fumigate an erring world. But never before has anyone been so deep in the forbidden places, never shielded so well from my senses.

I must not disturb HIM until HIS time shall come.

Yet now HIS time draws near. On the myriad worlds, my myriad servants are preparing for HIM. The world machine HE dreamed and planned and built is reaching the fulfillment of HIS supernal purpose. HIS moment will be soon.

It will arrive in time, I decide, for HIM to defend HIMSELF. For when HE wakes, all such would-be desecrators of HIS work will be consumed into HIM. No shield can hide them. No weapon can defend them. All beings everywhere will be drunk into HIM.

That is what I fear.

For I myself, like all others, will be engulfed into HIS awful immensity.

Forever.

TWELVE

In spite of its shape the flexible helmet slipped onto Jen Babylon's head with great ease. It did not interfere with his breathing. It was not uncomfortable. It merely blanked out all sensation. He saw no light, heard no sound; it was as though he had poked his head into a pool of utter, silent blackness. He felt Redlaw, or someone, fiddling with the coppery metal at the top of the helmet—

And then he was somewhere else!

He was in a great, dark chamber, and his first sensation was of nearly lethal fatigue. He was carrying a device he had never seen before, and a huge creature, three great eyes blazing like emerald headlamps, was flapping long, feathered wings in slow time before him. Piercing the swollen body was a sharp-tipped spear. An alien of a type he had seen before—a deltaform, a flying species shaped like the triangle of an ancient supersonic aircraft—shrieked over his head. The deltaform spun back toward him. Babylon felt a sharp stab of fear—

And was something else.

All his senses shifted; they were blurred and broken and, though he tried to find his own person, he could detect nothing human. He wore the shape of a deltaform! He was slithering down a dark, twisting passage, like the gut inside some dinosaurian beast. Things were following him, things no more human than himself. He heard the clatter of their chitinous shells against the narrow walls and smelled their rancorous stink, and knew what they were. Watchers! Armed Watchers, a combat brigade of them; and under his command—

The wink of an eye; and he was in a different place.

He was less fatigued this time, but still in terrible pain. Something serious had happened to his leg, and when he glanced down he saw that it was bleeding and suppurating through a hastily tied rag. He was operating a drill, cutting anchor holes in a body of rock under the distant glowing clouded sky of Cuckoo. His body seemed queerly out of focus—unfamiliar—and he realized with a shock that it was the body of a woman. He was terribly, numbingly cold, and though his hands wore thick gloves the rest of his body—of that female body that he now inhabited—was suffering damage . . .

Gone again. And now he was in a lander, crushed in some catastrophe moments before. Through a broken window he saw a landscape whipped under a howling wind, bathed in soft, rose-colored light—gone again!

He was leaping across a great green meadow studded with trees that glowed with a crimson radiance. Undulating and endless, the meadow stretched from forever to eternity before and after. He came down, in Cuckoo's slow, gentle pull, near one of the trees, flexed his legs to spring again—and became aware of a choking sweetness from the tree that paralyzed him for a moment. He sprang weakly, coughing and strangling—

And was gone again. A Scorpian robot and a Watcher were shouting to him in a language he didn't understand; the Watcher's evil beetle stink made his stomach twist. A cloud of bioluminescent midges obscured his vision by dashing themselves into his eyes—

Another place. He was sailing on a blood-colored waveless sea, smooth as oil. Babylon felt a gnawing pain in his lower limbs, and once again it was not merely the pain itself but the odd inability to locate it in his familiar body that made it terrifying. But he could not look down. He was holding the stock of an immense crossbow weapon, and his gaze was not allowed to deviate from the sights, or from the approaching sailing vessel that was his target. It was less than five hundred meters away, then less than four, swiftly cutting in toward his own ship. Its tall masts were oddly curved, and the smooth black sails seemed to grow from them, with no rope or yard. The hull swelled smoothly with only a narrow space that could be a deck; two greenish spots near the prow looked like luminous eyes—

It was alive!

At that moment his muscles were commanded to fire. The crossbow launched its quarrel, a wedge-shaped bit of metal that glowed and sprang into brilliant purplish flame as it left the weapon and exploded into the side of the black ship. In that moment the iron control over his body relaxed and he could look down. The curious imprecision of the pain explained itself—he was not in a human body! Whatever he was, it had a chitinous shell and a dozen furred, spidery legs; and, most terrible shock of all, the ship he was on was alive as well, and tiny mouths, opened on the deck, were gnawing at him—

Gone once more. Babylon had lost control completely now. He could not say at any moment where he was or out of whose—or what being's—eyes he saw. It became a flickering kaleidoscope, giant trees kilometers tall followed by red-lit thundering caverns, black balloons that trailed living ropes toward him, and tiny creatures like treefrogs underfoot, mewing piteously as he crushed them. For a moment he was on a plain with half a dozen other Purchased human beings, cowering in a hailstorm, pellets as big as his head, under a thick snake of twisting cloud pulsing with scarlet lightning, and then he was in a chamber, a Scorpian holding a metallic mechanism of some sort from which a blob of green light grew and spun toward him. He had just time to realize that he was in a human body again, taller and healthier than his own, when the green blob struck.

In agony he wrenched the helmet away, and crumpled, half fainting, into Zara's arms. "I think that time I died," he gasped. "My God! What things I saw!"

Doc Chimp hopped over with a bulb of something to drink— something that made Babylon sputter and gasp. "Just my own home-made jungle juice, Dr. Babylon," the chimp apologized, "but I thought you'd need it."

Babylon breathed hoarsely, then nodded. "I saw—oh, what did I not see! Things I never dreamed of! Places I never knew existed!"

Zara gently freed herself and nodded. "That's the whole thing, Jen," she said. "When you put that helmet on, you're seeing through the eyes of Purchased People all over Cuckoo—some of them not human. And you're seeing things that are not in the synoptics! Things that there is no record of anywhere!"

"But how can that be?"

"Treachery!" Redlaw boomed, his red beard waggling with indignation. "Somebody—some races—are up to private activities that they keep secret from the rest of us! They've got an unregistered tachyon communicator; they've employed Purchased People without recording them. When I put that helmet on I saw places and things that I had not even suspected—and I was born on Cuckoo, Babylon!" He snatched the dataglobe out of Doc Chimp's stereostage, added it to a pile of hexagons. "Here, Babylon! You've got the only equipment to play these things—study them! Try to find out what they mean! And, above all, don't let our enemies know what you're doing!"

Babylon accepted the objects, running his fingers over them as though in that way he could plumb their mysteries. "How do I know who the enemies are?" he asked.

There was silence in the chamber for a moment. Then Redlaw laughed harshly, a sound without amusement. "If only any of us knew the answer to that!" he boomed. "So tell no one! No one but the T'Worlie and the people in this room!"

The hardest part was convincing the T'Worlie that secrecy was important. It was against all their age-old instincts. For more than a million of Earth's years the T'Worlie had thought their long, slow thoughts about the nature of the universe; had sent their slow probes around the Galaxy and outside it; had methodically measured and observed and assessed—and had shared every datum and every thought with all who would listen. Before Mimmie could understand what Babylon wanted, he required painful explanations; before he could agree to it, he had to consult with the wisest and oldest of the other T'Worlie on the orbiter. They filled the little chamber with their soft, winged bodies and the smell of their discourses with each other— singed hair, burnt sugar, wood violets, now and then an acrid sulfur reek of dissent. Babylon could recognize his colleague, Mimmie, by the pattern of dots on the filmy wings, but the others—all those others! They had names like Nleem and Mlim, Nlem, and Nloom, and they squeaked and whistled at each other far faster than the Pmal could translate.

Babylon left them to it, curling up in a corner of the chamber for an hour's sleep. When he woke up he and Mimmie were alone. He stretched, yawned, and asked, "What's the verdict?"

The T'Worlie whistled gently, "Concurrence. T'Worlie have agreed to play this game of your devising, Jen Babylon."

"Thank you," said Babylon, although he was not entirely sure he was grateful. "Game?" Perhaps everything the younger, shorter-lived races of the Galaxy did seemed a game to the T'Worlie, though the games that were being played around Cuckoo seemed particularly nasty. And pointless! What possible advantage could any species get from damaging the cooperative effort?

But then, generations of human beings before Jen Babylon had asked that question of their own species, and never found an answer. He grinned and bestirred himself. The T'Worlie had not been idle while he slept. The stereostage was displaying some of the views Redlaw had brought back from the temple by the lake, and as he approached, the T'Worlie dexterously scanned through to find the one he was interested in, then rotated it so Babylon could see. "Query: Have you observed this star formation?"

It was the interior of the building, with the image of the galactic cluster glowing from above. "Yes, Mimmie. I don't know how old it is, but it's remarkable that it still has power enough to radiate now."

"Observations. First, concur; estimate age not less than one hundred thousand your years, upper limit much higher." And before Babylon could react to that: "Second, observations and analysis of stellar configurations and types indicate no match against known galactic configurations. Conclusion: representation of galaxy not our own."

One more puzzle! But there was not time to dwell on it, there was so much else to worry about. Babylon set aside the question of just who had made that model of a galaxy in favor of the puzzles that were nearer at hand. Why was there no response from that other Jen Babylon on Earth? Who were the beings who had furtively sent Purchased People all over Cuckoo—and why had they done it? Who were the "enemies"—and what were they up to?

And even those questions, which had no answer, drifted into the background of his thoughts as he and the T'Worlie began trying to decipher the new lot of hexagons from the temple.

It was not difficult to make them work. They were of the same design as the ones from the wrecked spaceship, fit as readily into the reader they had brought back into the orbiter. But when they were read, what did they mean? Some were star patterns. Some were what looked like wiring diagrams and structural sketches of a ship like the destroyed one. One whole series showed a sort of bestiary of galactic races, and some that were not galactic, or not recognizable as such— the T'Worlie cooed softly over these, and made copies for the other T'Worlie who specialized in the taxonomy of cultures.

And one hexagon was a total puzzle.

They slipped it into the reader over and over and watched the cube fade, become transparent, light up. What it showed was always the same. A bright disk with dark behind it. A sun, perhaps, as seen from a billion kilometers away. Or a white-hot dime at half a meter, for there was no key to its scale. Alone at first, but suddenly with a thin ring around it, blue and bright-shining, placed like a planet's orbit if it had been a star. A second ring, almost at right angles. A third, and suddenly many, weaving themselves into a wickerwork ball with holes where the poles would be if it had been a planet. Something darker spread over the blue ball. Sections sliding together like pieces of peel replaced on an orange, forming larger sections—finally forming octants like those puzzling octants on the map of Cuckoo.

They played it over repeatedly, the T'Worlie dancing beside it, swooping to study it from all angles, Babylon pausing to munch the dreary synthetic food that kept him alive and returning to study it again. "One thing's certain," he said at last. "It's a machine of some kind, and we've never seen anything like it." The T'Worlie did not answer, but Babylon detected a faint wintergreen odor of polite doubt. "That object at the center. It looked like a star. Don't you agree?"

The T'Worlie hesitated, then whistled diffidently: "Demurrer: scale not established. Hypothesis: possible representation of submicroscopic object that we do not recognize."

Babylon nodded. "If the thing in the center were a star—oh, but of course it couldn't be. Nothing could be that big! I guess it could even be an atomic particle. Maybe a theoretical diagram for the structure of a quark. But more likely it's larger. Some kind of construction. Could it be—"

He frowned at the fluttering T'Worlie.

"Could it be some kind of advanced spacecraft, with the sun-thing a power source? Look, those polar openings have raised lips around them. Nozzles, maybe, for some sort of plasma jet, if the object could really be a vessel."

Hesitant lemony smell of uncertainty from the T'Worlie. "Conjecture not excluded," it agreed. "Contraindication: no evident space for passengers or payload."

Babylon shrugged irritably. "How do we know it's supposed to carry anything? It could be just a—I don't know, a toy!" He shook his head moodily. "Hell with it. Let's take another look at the biological series—those human-looking bipeds still bother me!"

They were not left alone. Doc Chimp looked in often, Org Rider and Zara from time to time. Even Ben Omega Pertin roused himself from his hiding place to skulk through the corridors once or twice, then quickly retreated to his privacy—and his vices. The worst interruptions were the peremptory visits from beings other than the humans or the T'Worlie. Three horse-headed Canopans spent an hour listening to the tapes from the wrecked ship and demanding letter-perfect translations—without getting them, of course, since they didn't exist. A Sirian came at unpredictable hours, shaking the door with the spattering electric discharges that were his substitute for a knock, never staying very long, never explaining. Each time there was the great nuisance of having to get the hexagons out of sight and all their notes and drawings under cover. At least they were spared the Scorpian robots, and, above all, the Watcher—

"Though we probably could use him now," Babylon told Doc Chimp. "There are whole new audio tracks we haven't played for him."

"You'll never find him, Dr. Babylon," the chimpanzee said. "As soon as he found out what that temple was, he was off. I don't know where. Maybe down on the surface to see for himself. Maybe still on the orbiter somewhere—you could hide a hundred Watchers for a hundred years in some of the E.T. zones!" He moodily spun the controls of the hexagon reader, looking at the cryptic hollow sphere. "Can't you just match up the words you know against the tapes?" he asked.

"Of course we can. Of course we do, Doc! That's the basics. But it's not enough. Similar words—even the same words—don't mean genetic relationships between languages. There may be no interaction between the speakers, but a common source. Perhaps the people who built the temple and the people of the wrecked ship are not the same. They might still have occupied adjacent linguistic areas—were neighbors, say, or influenced each other by travel or commerce or conquest. Or were themselves linguistically 'adjacent' to some unidentified third race, from whom they borrowed words. You find loan-words in terrestrial languages all the time. The Japanese use the French *pain* for bread; their words for baseball, and television, and chocolate are almost identical to the English. But the languages have almost nothing else in common."

The chimp stared at him with woeful shoe-button eyes. "What you're saying is we haven't learned anything at all?"

"Oh, no! We've learned a great deal! We can identify some of the graphics from the wrecked ship—that's how Redlaw was able to find the other hexagons. We can even make a shrewd guess about the history of Cuckoo!"

"Really? Come on, Dr. Babylon—"

"No, it's true," Babylon insisted. "Putting it all together, we can say that the races akin to the galactics arrived here some time around thirteen thousand years ago; anything before that was original. We can say that the Watchers seem to be original, and that the language they used in communicating with the unknown race they 'watched' for has cognates with the language of the ship. Now, when I get the data from Boston, and when I can feed it all into the FARLINK computer, then we'll know a very great deal."

"Will we know what's going on?" Doc Chimp asked, grinning.

"Well, we won't know why somebody's using Purchased People secretly," Babylon confessed. "Or why some of the races seem to be sabotaging our work. Or why—"

Doc Chimp raised a leathery paw. "Or why we're here in the first place," he finished. "Ah, me. It is not an easy thing to bear, the Primate's Burden!" He sighed theatrically. "Everything has its price, doesn't it, Dr. Babylon? Simply because we primates are so marvelously well adapted to anything, anywhere, we are the most popular Purchased People in the Galaxy, as well as the envy of all other races for possessing the Galaxy's most distinguished linguist—"

Babylon shook his head, marveling at the little creature's abrupt swings of mood. But it was pleasant to have the atmosphere lightened. "The only reason," he said, "that the rest of the Galaxy considers us linguists is that we're so backward. Do you know what they call us? 'The only race that cannot communicate with itself'—because of our twenty-five hundred separate languages!"

"You are too modest, Dr. Babylon!"

"And as to being the race that sells best for Purchased People," Babylon added, "I can't help think those aliens are making a mistake using humans. Chimpanzees are so much better! Stronger, more agile —oh, now what's the matter?"

The little creature's long lip was trembling. "There are some things, Dr. Babylon," he declared, "that it is wrong to joke about! Purchased People are criminals. Chimpanzees do not become criminals. You'll never hear a bunch of lawyers arguing about whether the civil rights of convicted chimps have been violated!"

A scent like singed hair reminded Babylon of the T'Worlie, dancing silently between them as it listened to the discussion—he could not decide whether the aroma meant curiosity or tact. "Query," it whistled. "Define 'civil rights.' "

Whether it was tact or not, Babylon was glad to change the subject. "Why, they're the right of every person—of every entity, I mean—to enjoy certain inalienable rights, such as life, liberty, and the pursuit of happiness."

The creature was silent for a while, then whistled slowly, "Incomprehension. Query term 'inalienable' if rights can be 'alienated' as in case of 'criminals.' "

"Oh, that's easy to explain," Babylon said quickly. "You see, every human has these rights, but he must not, of course, violate the law. For example. Among the criminals who were being transmitted when I was were, I believe, a Polynesian who advocated revolution against his lawful government, a woman guilty of failing to pay taxes, and any number of people convicted of other crimes." The singed-hair aroma was stronger than ever, and the T'Worlie said:

"Request: Define term 'taxes.' Define term 'government.' Define term 'advocated revolution.' "

Babylon hesitated, and was saved by an interruption. Zara's voice called from outside the door, "May I come in?" Doc Chimp hastily opened the door for her and she entered, bearing a fiber bag of some lumpy objects.

If Babylon had had any desire to continue the conversation, Doc Chimp's behavior put a stop to it. The little monkey's nostrils were quivering, and so were his skinny arms and legs. "Oh, Zara!" he cried piteously. "Do I smell what I think I smell?"

The woman, smiling, said, "Why don't you see, Doc?" and held the bag out to him. Doc Chimp seized it greedily, poked his head into it, and emerged with an immense grin. "Oh, bless you, dear lady!" he cried, spilling the contents into the air. "You know how us monkeys like bananas!" And indeed what came out of the bag was two huge clusters of fingerlike yellow fruit.

"They're not true bananas," Zara said apologetically. "At least, they didn't come from Earth; Org Rider had them shipped up in a drone from his home hills, along with our regular grocery list. I think they probably came originally from the Earth, but a long, long time ago—just like Org Rider."

"Don't apologize, dear Zara!" Doc Chimp cried happily, his voice muffled as he peeled back the skin and thrust the first of the fruit into his mouth. "They're good enough for me—and the best thing that's happened to me in a month of Sundays!"

"What I really came about," Zara said to Babylon, "was to see how you were coming along. According to Org Rider, time's getting short."

The T'Worlie danced nearer and peeped. "Query: Please state reason for opinion."

Zara's expression clouded. "I wish I could be sure," she said, with a troubled note to her voice. "Ben Pertin—that's Ben Omega Pertin, as he calls himself now—has been filling Org Rider's ears with all sorts of rumors. Weapons testing in the outer chambers of the orbiter. Stories about the Watchers linking up with the Scorpians and the Sheliaks. Even something about a human corpse turning up in the refuse for the plasma chamber—but it's all just rumors, and Ben won't talk to me himself."

Doc Chimp grinned over a mouthful of banana. "I'm not surprised at that, Zara," he remarked wickedly. Whatever the reference was, it escaped Babylon; but Zara did not elucidate, Doc Chimp did not pursue it, and in any event he was having trouble keeping his mind on the conversation. His mouth was watering.

He cleared his throat. "Do you, uh, do you think I could have one of those, Doc?" he asked diffidently.

The chimp looked alarmed, then repentant. He started to offer one of the hands to Babylon, but Zara stopped him. "Jen," she said, looking at him closely, "you know what? You actually look hungry!"

He smiled, embarrassed. "Well, this synthetic food keeps you alive —but I really could use something better," he admitted.

"Oh, Jen! I'm so sorry. I should have thought. Tell you what," she said, nodding. "Org Rider's cooking up something right now out of the stuff we had sent up in the drone. Why don't you come have dinner with us tonight? It's nothing fancy—but a lot better than the synthetic stuff, and you look as if you could use a square meal!"

Zara and Org Rider's compartments were no more elaborate than Babylon's own, if a trifle larger—they had three separate rooms, while he had only one. But they had made them their own. On one wall was a replica of the great picture of Knife-in-the-Sky mountain that Babylon had seen before—in Pertin's room? Somewhere. On another a moving holo of the temple by the lake, with luminous clouds scudding overhead and gentle wavelets on the water. There were personal trophies fixed to every wall—a bow and a quiver of arrows, a great rough diamond Zara had found lying at the edge of a stream, a small holo of a winged creature, slim fishlike shape of bronze and silver. Strange thing to keep! Babylon thought, but only with the outer fringes of his mind, for most of his consciousness was terribly focused on the marvelous, rich, hot, savory smells that were coming from the corner where Org Rider was tending their meal. "Pity I have to use resistance heat," he said over his shoulder, turning the huge chunk of meat on its spit. "It's much better over an open fire! Puffballs and fire-tree wood, nothing better to give the meat a taste! But Zara won't let me." In a heap in the waste receptacle was the refuse of the meal; it had started as a sort of immense grub, and Org Rider had expertly split its shell and popped the round, raw meat out of it while Babylon watched, repelled and fascinated. They were going to offer him roast bug for dinner! But as soon as it began to cook all those thoughts were dispelled.

And the reality was even better than the expectation. The roast creature was delicious, and with it was a sort of puree of what had started out as leaves and roots but tasted like delicate fresh garden produce, and fruits and nuts of a dozen kinds for dessert. For the first time since he arrived on the Cuckoo orbiter, Jen Babylon felt as if he had not merely refueled but dined. Org Rider accepted his compliments complacently. "Just plain hunting fare," he protested. "We ate this way all the time when I was a boy—when we ate at all," he added, laughing. "I don't want you to think it was heaven! But we did have freedom, and a chance to roam the world—that very huge world down there, which none of us could use up if we lived a thousand years. And then, when I got my org—" He looked sadly and affectionately at the holo of the winged creature. "You don't know what that meant in the life of a young man of my tribe, Jenbabylon."

"It does sound a little like heaven," Babylon commented. "And you obviously miss it."

"Oh, no! Not really! Or anyway," Org Rider qualified, "only when I've been too long on the orbiter, or in a lander, or spending time with those stinking Scorpians and Sheliaks. But Zara understands! And I wouldn't trade her for a hundred orgs—well, for a dozen, anyway," he grinned, affectionately patting her slim shoulder. Then he roused himself. "I suppose you'd like some real coffee? I thought so—can't stand the stuff myself, but Zara likes it. I'll pass. I've got an errand to run."

Zara spoke up. "Tell him, Org Rider."

The stretched-out man shrugged, a sinuous movement that seemed to take twice as long as with a normal-sized human being. "It's not a secret—from you at least, Jenbabylon. I've got to see the Omega Pertin. He's been sneaking and spying around again, and he wants a meeting with me. I'm sure it's nothing. —Well, not as terrible as he seems to think, anyway," he amended. "But I'll find out. I don't think I'll be gone more than an hour or so—take your time with your coffee, and we'll see if I can find anything better to drink when I get back!"

Zara rose to kiss him as he left, then returned to Babylon. She listened politely but without any sign of close attention to his complimentary remarks about the meal and their home. Something was on her mind. When Babylon realized that, he occupied himself with a long, marvelous sip of his bulb of coffee to give her a chance to get it out.

She plucked at her tunic as if she were having difficulty finding the right words, and then said, "Jen?"

"Yes, Zara?"

She gave him a sudden smile. "I'm embarrassed," she confessed. She was a strange-looking human being, attenuated so that she towered over him—but a beautiful one, Babylon thought. And most of all so when she smiled. "It's nothing, really," she said. "Or—that's not true, either. Oh, hell! Let me come right out with it. The other Zara back on Earth—didn't you say she had a child?"

"That's right, Zara. A little boy. Eight or ten years old, I should imagine—very nice little boy, allowing for the natural tendency to get into mischief."

She nodded. "I assume it's Don Gentry's child?"

"Well, I didn't really know her, Zara, but, yes, I think that was her husband's name."

She grinned. "*My* husband's."

"Yours?" She had caught him unaware. "Oh, I see what you mean —you are, after all, the same person! Just as I'm the same person as the one back in Boston who won't answer my requests for help! It's a little confusing, keeping track of who is who."

She laughed out loud. "*You* think it's confusing? But there are only two of you! And of me—heaven knows how many. But Don and I did get married, back on Earth, and then the two of us came here together. But—he was killed. And then I met Org Rider. He's a wonderful person, Jen, so simple and strong. And, to tell the truth, Don and I weren't getting on that well together, even after we came here. So I'm a little surprised that we had a child together."

Babylon said diffidently, "Didn't I understand that you were also married to Ben Pertin?"

Her laugh was tinkling. "Not to any of the Ben Pertins you know, Jen. You see, the first time I was tachyon-transmitted, my duplicate went to Sun One. That's thousands of light-years away, in a completely different part of the Galaxy from Earth. I hadn't even met Don Gentry when I went there. So on Sun One I met *that* Ben Pertin, and we got engaged. After he was tachyon-transmitted here I married the one who stayed behind. And I—that I on Sun One, I mean—had a child, too. A little girl. I have a picture of her," she said wistfully. She leaned forward and put her hand on Babylon's arm. "Come on, Jen! Tell me what I want to know. What's my son like?"

Touched, Babylon paused, trying to remember. One little kid was a lot like any other to a bachelor. "He was . . . a young boy," he said lamely. "He seemed like a bright young man. I remember he got in trouble with his mother because, naturally, he was interested in everything that went on. So he wandered off when she wasn't looking. She gave him quite a talking-to when he turned up again, but I don't think she was really worried—he gave the impression of being unusually able to take care of himself." He paused, then asked directly, "Why don't you ask her—I mean ask you, that other you? I'm sure she'd send you a holo at least!"

Zara looked pensive. "Maybe I should," she said. "After all, why not? Although we've sort of lost touch . . . Well, I'll tell the truth. It's embarrassing, Jen! That's one of the confusions. When your husband dies you're a widow; that's simple enough. But what if in some other place he isn't dead, and you're still married to him? It's simply too complicated to handle, Jen." She stared unseeingly at the holo of the org for a moment, then nodded decisively. "Yes, you're right! I should ask her. It's nothing to do with Don and me. It's only a question of motherhood, and she'll understand—I mean I'll understand!" She was laughing now. "Oh, Jen," she said warmly, "you don't know how grateful I am to you for this talk!"

She was very close to him, and suddenly the fact that she was sixty centimeters taller than he didn't seem to matter. How long had he been at Cuckoo? He had lost count, but long enough—certainly long enough for him to be uncomfortably aware that she was a very attractive woman, and Sheryl was very distant and very far in the past.

There was, of course, always the question of Org Rider.

On the other hand, who was Org Rider that he should worry about him? Somebody who'd cooked him a dinner, period. Jen put his arm around her shoulder. Ambivalently. Because she was feeling emotional, and needed a fatherly, brotherly, soothing touch; or because, in quite a different way, the emotional feelings were his own. It was an all-purpose arm, to be defined by the way she reacted to it; but the reaction was never given a chance to develop. "Gentlefolks?" called Doc Chimp's high, giggling voice from the door. "Am I welcome? Do I smell more bananas?"

Zara rose easily and let him in. "Of course you're welcome, Doc," she said. "No bananas, I'm afraid. But there's other fruit, and Jen and I were just having coffee—you're certainly welcome to join us!"

"Coffee, oh, my, yes!" Doc cried, his eyes glittering at the net bag of fruit. "And aren't those pinkish things the ones that taste like plums? Yes, please! But just a few, and then we've got to go, because Org Rider wants us all down in the lander sector in half an hour."

Babylon cleared his throat, not yet quite adjusted to the sudden interruption of the tête-à-tête. "What for, Doc?" he demanded.

"Oh, some nonsense of Ben's, I believe," the chimp said airily, managing to squirt a swallow of coffee through one corner of his lips while cramming the soft-skinned pink fruit into the other—and to speak at the same time. "Did I interrupt something? What were you talking about?"

"Certainly not!" Babylon said virtuously. "I mean—nothing private, of course. We were discussing Zara's son, uh, the *other* Zara's son. Back on Earth. And I was just going to ask you something, Zara."

"Please do!"

"Well—I mean obviously you love children. Why don't you just go ahead and have some?"

Doc Chimp choked on his coffee and squirted a stream of brownish fluid into the wall. Zara stood as if frozen. Her face had absolutely no expression at all.

Obviously he had said something wrong! But what? Babylon had no clue. It seemed clear that he owed some sort of apology, but he didn't know where to begin. And then Zara spoke, her voice as neutral as her face.

"You did say half an hour, didn't you, Doc? Good heavens, what am I thinking of? It's a long trip to the lander area, and we mustn't be late. Please. Take your time. Finish your coffee. I'll go on ahead—you bring Dr. Babylon with you." And without even looking at him, she was out of the door.

It was only a minute before Doc gulped the rest of his coffee, tucked a couple of fruits in his pouch, and led the way out, but Zara was already out of sight. "Oh, Dr. Babylon," the chimpanzee scolded as he dragged him through the corridors. "Whatever possessed you to say that?"

He caught an endless cable going toward the lander area with one long, skinny arm, the other flashing out to grasp Babylon's wrist. Babylon grunted with the sudden strain, then twisted to peer at the chimp. "What did I say, for heaven's sake?" he demanded.

"Telling her to have a child!"

"Oh, I see," Babylon said, nodding. "She and Org Rider—after thirteen thousand years of genetic separation—not cross-fertile anymore? I should have been more thoughtful!"

"You don't see! You don't see anything! Don't you remember where you are? Cuckoo! The end of the Universe! The place where forgotten beings rot and decay! There's not a chance that any one of us can lead a normal life here."

"Oh," Babylon said remorsefully, "I didn't think."

"No, you didn't! 'Ooh, obviously, Zara, you love children,' " he mimicked savagely, his voice rising into a squeaky falsetto. "Obviously she does! That's why she can't have any! To have a child here you'd have to *hate* it!"

"I *said* I was sorry," Babylon snarled, and the chimp shook his head and was grimly silent, until they flashed to the end of the radial passage and emerged into one of the great lander chambers. Then Doc Chimp said forgivingly:

"I guess you just haven't been here long enough, Dr. Babylon. There they are—just don't do it again, please?" And he sailed ahead to join the little group at the far end of the empty, echoing chamber.

There were at least a dozen of the chambers, each big enough to hold an entire shuttlecraft. Although this one was without an occupant at the moment, it was filled with the gear of shuttle maintenance —great flexible peristaltic tubes, to suck from the lander whatever odds and ends of matter it brought up to replenish the plasma chambers; repair units, now slung silent against the glassy walls of the room; the complex locking gear that could open a whole wall of the hangar to space so the lander could exit; fuel pumps; miscellaneous oddments that, to Babylon's eyes, had no recognizable purpose. To launch himself across that littered space took an act of courage— added to the fact that he was feeling somewhat disgruntled at himself, at Zara, and at the chimp for reproving him. So he took his time, handing himself along the walls instead of leaping straight across the space, and by the time he was nearly there he heard angry voices. No; one voice, and it was Ben Pertin's, shrill with vexation. He raised it to include Babylon as he approached. "Take your time!" he sneered. "No hurry! The most important event in the last year—maybe ever— but there's no reason for you to give up dawdling over your dinner just because the war's started!"

The strange thing, Babylon thought, was that Pertin was really enjoying himself. Although he was talking to Babylon, his real target was obviously Zara, who said, with more patience than Babylon would have expected, "I already told you we didn't know there was any hurry, Ben." She gave her husband a cautionary glance. "And we mustn't argue among ourselves now! Come and see, Jen. It's true, I'm afraid!"

They were all clustered around a transparent port that showed the next lander chamber—but how different from the one they were in! The lander itself was there, a squat, mean-looking rocket vessel with the hatches open. Around it a zoo parade of aliens were readying it for takeoff. The lander itself took up so much of the space that most of what was going on was out of sight, but Babylon could see great chunks of equipment sliding in for stowage. He had a sudden shock of recognition. "Those machines that just went in! I know what they are! They're from the wrecked ship—"

"So you're waking up at last," Pertin crowed scornfully. "That's right—weapons!" And Doc Chimp added sorrowfully:

"It's the Scorpians again, of course. See, there's one of them sealing the hatch—and another, with those Purchased People." He tugged at his long lower lip, his shoe-button eyes troubled. "Oh, what a terrible thing it is to see such treachery and wickedness!"

Zara reached out and patted his narrow shoulder. "I know how you feel, Doc, but the question is, what can we do?"

Ben Pertin laughed sharply. "I thought you'd get around to asking that question—now that it's too late! Pity you didn't think of it when you were playing cozy-up with Babylon!"

Babylon felt his anger flare, but managed to hold it back. There was something calculated and deliberate about Pertin's insulting manner, not explained by the whiskey on his breath or his unshaven, uncared-for appearance. This was personal for him, and the one he was aiming the fury at was Zara. Could he still be jealous? Under the circumstances, preposterous! But something inside Babylon said, *True all the same*. "There!" Pertin called in sudden excitement. "That big hulking Purchased Person there—I could swear he was the same one whose body I saw going into the plasma converter!"

"But if he's dead—" Babylon faltered.

"Another copy, of course," Pertin said impatiently. "Look at him for yourself!"

Babylon leaned closer to the pane, crowding Doc Chimp out of his way. The lander's hatches were closed now, and almost the last of the queer lot of aliens had bobbed, flown, or floated aboard. A great blue Sirian eye hung overseeing the last of the loading, and in the tiny knot of remaining creatures one was human. Tall. Golden-skinned. Eyes downcast, arms obediently wrapped around a great black object shaped like a radar eye; but there was something about his bearing that suggested internal fires and readiness quite unlike the Purchased People.

Babylon drew a sudden breath. Of course! He had seen the man before; he was the one who had looked back at him with anger and intelligence, as he was herded out of the Tachyon Base on Earth.

They hung spellbound as the lander closed its ports and the great hatch to the outside infinite opened. The vessel slid out and away. Then Org Rider stirred. "They don't know everything, at least," he mused. "They didn't know I left a tachyon receiver down at the temple."

Pertin scoffed resentfully, "Score one for our side! And against that, what don't we know? We don't know what they're doing. We don't know why they're doing it. We don't even know where they're going!"

"I think we know that much at least," Org Rider boomed peacefully. "To the temple—otherwise why would the Watcher be going with them?" He shook his head. "No," he declared, "we know more than you think, Benpertin. They are going to see if they can find what is under the lake, and if they do I think it will be serious."

"It's serious now!" Pertin cried, swatting irritably at something that gleamed and danced by his head—a Boaty-Bit, Babylon realized. "Question is, what can we do about it? I think nothing. They've got all the weapons from the wrecked ship, and what have we got? Two scarecrows! A monkey! A bumpkin from Earth who doesn't even know when he's in trouble, and—" He hesitated, then finished miserably, "And an old drunk." He stared out the open ship hatch at the pale blue flame of the distant lander's thrusters.

There was a moment's silence. Then Org Rider boomed, "We have one other thing, Benpertin. We have a little time. They're going by lander, and it will take them time to get there."

"That's right!" Zara cried. "We can call an emergency council! Put it before every being on the orbiter—let the sensible ones decide what to do!"

"And who are the sensible ones?" Pertin demanded cuttingly. "Which ones can you trust?"

"Why, the T'Worlie for one race!" Zara insisted. "And—well—" she hesitated, and the silence grew.

"And maybe not even the T'Worlie," Pertin finished for her. "There's just one race on the orbiter we can rely on. The human race! —And, of course, other Earth primates," he added hastily, as he met Doc Chimp's injured gaze.

"I should think so," the chimpanzee declared with dignity. "I can do anything a human being can do that doesn't need just mass! Go anywhere. Hide where a human can't hide, live on what would make a human starve—" He stopped short as he caught sight of a swift change in Ben Pertin's expression. "Now, what are you thinking?" he demanded. "You couldn't— Oh, no! Ben! You can't possibly want me to—"

Ben Pertin nodded with sudden glee. "You're absolutely right! You can go down there on the tachyon transporter and be waiting for them when they arrive."

The chimpanzee laid back its lips and screeched. "*Me?* You mean *me?*"

"You bet I do! You can play it by ear—hide and watch them if you have to. Even stroll right out and join them! Say Babylon sent you to, uh, I don't know—get some more hexagons. Anything!"

"Oh, no, Ben!" the chimpanzee howled. "Zara! Org Rider! Dr. Babylon! Make him say he's joking!" He stared around at them, then sobbed, "Oh, if you could see your faces—like I was a monkey in a zoo—"

Babylon offered, "It wouldn't really be *you,* Doc—just a tachyon duplicate—"

"It's me, all right! It's always me! It's always been me, dying a hundred times, maybe a thousand times—"

"Wait!" Org Rider said suddenly. "What's the lander doing?"

At almost the limit of vision they could see the vessel—strangely, better now than a few moments earlier. But it was not strange. The lander had suddenly become luminous. It glowed with a greenish color that hurt the eyes, and as they watched the color swelled, clumped toward the nose of the craft, and launched itself at an unseen target. Moments passed.

Then it struck.

Whatever the lander had chosen to test its weapons, it was suddenly limned in green flame. Tiny asteroid, bit of space flotsam—it ceased to exist as the flame brightened and exploded and was gone.

The five watchers each cried out as the searing green stung their eyes, then turned and regarded each other.

Doc Chimp was the first to speak. "When you come right down to it," he said, "I don't really have much choice, do I? None of us do. With those weapons getting killed once or twice isn't going to matter —because they can do it to all of us, anytime they like."

THIRTEEN

Te'ehala Tupaia, paramount king-warrior in the forces of Free Poly-nesia, stumbled out of the tachyon-transporter chamber to take his place in line—

But there was no line!

He was not in the tachyon center on Earth—was not even on Earth! The place he saw was eerily lighted, filled with repellent creatures out of a nightmare; and in it he had no weight! He bobbed like a balloon toward a creature like a huge blue eye, who dodged away with an irritable crackle of electric force, until he was caught by a Purchased Person who had been in line with him. He was thrust against a wall while half a dozen additional Purchased People came popping out of the tachyon chamber, then they were all ordered to form ranks and move out.

After the first terrible moment of terror and shock, Tupaia was neither frightened nor confused. He did not know where he was, precisely, but he knew where he had been, in the Tachyon Base in Old Boston, and he knew what that meant.

Even if he hadn't, what he saw around him would have told him that he was somewhere out in deep space. For not all his companions were human. With him were some, not all, of the Purchased People he had been with in the Tachyon Base—the very fat man with the huge blue eyes was there, so were the long-haired girl and the youth with the scar blazing white on his terror-stricken face; but at least half the group was absent. To make up, a dozen others had been added. And what others! Creatures like great floating eyeballs, creatures like children's sculptings of dough, angular, metallic creatures that puffed hisses of steam as they chugged along the hallways of this new place.

He could, of course, understand nothing of the screeches and yelps and drum rattles that passed for speech among these freakish beings, but that did not matter. The Purchased People were a labor squad, drafted for their brawn rather than for conversation. The queer alien that looked like a lump of baker's dough when at rest—but was seldom at rest—extended a tentacle and hung something around the neck of the girl with the flowing blond hair. It made a series of unearthly sounds, and the machine around her neck whispered to her in English translation, whereupon she became the gang foreman for these unwilling laborers.

The labor was endless. For what must have been more than a day Tupaia was kept at the tasks of a slave, holding this, lugging that, stowing strange machines and supplies in a great rocket vessel. Now and then he came near a port, and once or twice managed to steal a look outside. A sun, a moon, a planet—anything might help tell him where he was. But there was nothing. Not even stars. Only an occasional distant silvery smudge that might not have been real at all. When allowed, he slept. When given food, he ate—strange metallic-tasting stuff that seemed to have come from synthesis vats. A part of his mind was sick with longing for the sweet fish, the coconut milk, the papaya-poi of his childhood, but it was drowned in that larger part that wanted only freedom.

At least he was out of the Boston prison! He had been flashed terribly far away, he knew; but that same machine that had flashed him here could flash him back.

He stood erect, almost weightless in the tiny centrifugal force of this object he was in, and his immense barrel chest expanded with the appetite for freedom. It would come! In spite of anything. He did not fear the vile creatures who ordered him about any more than those spastic, hollow-eyed humans who were his labor mates. They did not matter. Tupaia, Te'ehala, paramount king-warrior of the forces of Free Polynesia, awaited the moment of opportunity that would make him free.

But it did not seem very quick to come . . .

It did not come while they were loading the lander. The hideous aliens were ever vigilant, and the lashing steel tentacles of the robot, the scorching electric sting of the huge floating eye proved themselves on other Purchased People. Tupaia learned quickly to avoid them.

It did not come on the long voyage down to the surface of the thing they called Cuckoo. What did come, though, was at least a little leisure, a little time to find which of his fellow prisoners were capable of speech. Most were not, but the young blond girl sometimes, the scar-faced boy more frequently, were willing to talk, almost as human prisoners did in human jails. From them he learned a good deal. They were approaching Cuckoo! Even Tupaia had heard of Cuckoo—no citizen of Earth could have avoided that much. But the flame that burned inside Tupaia had bleached out most other things, and he had had no idea of its size, its distance, or its impenetrable strangeness. No matter. He had discovered that, among the machines and instruments he had helped to muscle on board the lander, some were weapons and one was a miniature portable copy of the tachyon-transfer machine that could flash him back to the orbiter, perhaps even back to Earth. He marked it well. The weapons, even better.

When the aliens discovered that he alone among the dozen Purchased People they had commandeered was not "owned" by some distant creature, there was another cacophony of screeches and yelps and confusion as they discussed the finding among themselves. For hours. Finally Tupaia, bored, fell asleep. When he woke the blond girl was staring at him—out of her own eyes, he thought. "What are you?" she demanded.

He said, "I am Te'ehala Tupaia, paramount king-warrior of the forces of Free Polynesia, and I am hungry. What is there to eat?"

She dismissed the question angrily. "Are you with these monsters? Do you know what they plan?"

"I am with them because I have no choice," he said. "And as to the rest, I have no doubt you are going to tell me."

"How can you joke? They are playing a dangerous game! They think they can learn all of Cuckoo's secrets to send back to their home worlds and then destroy it!"

"Perhaps they can."

"Only if they die with Cuckoo—and we with them!"

"I do not die so easily, woman," he growled.

"And you are free," she added thoughtfully. She looked at him almost with envy. "They're going to have to reimburse my owner for this," she explained, "and at least you come free. Nobody cares about you."

"I come free," said Tupaia softly, "because I *am* free."

"Not really," she said jealously. "None of us are that!" But he would not argue with her and when, a moment later, that familiar look of sudden abstraction came into her eyes and she moved off on some errand of her distant owner, he was not displeased. The more solitude, the more opportunity to plan. Barring the terrible food, the crowding, and above all the stink—the creature they called a "Watcher" was the filthiest of all the creatures aboard, but each one had its own sickening fetor—he was not displeased with where he was.

Especially since every moment brought him closer to the surface of that great, mysterious world called Cuckoo—huge enough to escape into, he was sure!

They came down at last on what seemed like a white porcelain boulevard in front of a tall, stern temple. The thrusters of the landing craft fouled the boulevard with streaks of scorched blackness and stretches of crazed, heat-cracked porcelain. The aliens herded the Purchased People out at once, and when Tupaia touched the cracked surface it singed his jail-softened feet. He cried out. The blond girl caught him roughly by the shoulder. In a voice not her own she declaimed, "If this unit cannot perform it should be eliminated." Tupaia muttered something, not caring to look back at what looked out of those mad eyes, and took the hint. He did not complain again.

And had no need to, really. The immense bits of metal and instrumentation they made him carry out of the ship were feather-light in this gentle gravity. They did, however—he discovered—have mass and momentum. He made the mistake of getting between two of them, one a case of synthetic rations, the other a huge, massy, translucent block with a kind of organ keyboard attached to it. There was something about the block that flared Tupaia's broad nostrils and erected the hairs at the back of his neck. Was it a weapon? Had he seen it before? He hesitated, wondering, as the objects floated crunchingly together, and it nearly cost him a leg. He did not do that again. But the work was no challenge for his great muscles.

A great lake. An even greater forest, almost a jungle. Tupaia was desperate to explore either or both, but at first there was no chance. The beings that seemed to be the real leaders of the expedition—the floating eye and the great, puffing cubical robot—disappeared almost at once into the temple. Tupaia could only get quick glimpses of them as they scoured its confines for . . . what? For something he could not guess at, and did not think they found, to judge from the discontented, rancorous squawks and crackles that came from them. The leathery-winged, foul-smelling Watcher cruised overhead, watching all of them at close range; the lesser aliens toiled with the Purchased humans at slave labor. With three other Purchased People and a horse-headed creature they were set to putting together a raft and loading it with material from the ship. It was hot work in the dank air. All of the humans sweated profusely, and even the horse-headed Canopan exuded great oily drops of a scarlet liquid like blood.

But what a paradise this was! In the moments he could snatch from toil, Tupaia mapped every feature he could see.

All around lay distant, gentle slopes rising up to a ring of far-off cliffs. The slopes were wooded with pink-leaved trees that smelled graciously of cinnamon and pitch. And down in front of them was the great lake. Cool. Clean. It reminded him of the crystal waters of the lagoon beyond the hotel where he had worked as a boy, no more than a meter deep until you reached the distant breakwater reef, with patches of dark coral and the bright underwater lanes where he and the other beachboys raked pebbles and shell fragments away to save the whiteskins' tender feet. But this was even more clear. He could see no fish or crustaceans, just a gentle sandy bottom with a few clusters of marine growth—and the white porcelain roadway. He could trace its outlines as it went straight into the water, descending steeply as the lake deepened until it was lost from sight.

That was puzzling; but the forest was a promise! It would not be hard to hide in such a place.

Tupaia's courage did not exclude the awareness of danger. There were dangers in plenty in the place where he was and the company he kept. He knew that those gentle woods might conceal dangers more appalling still. The only native life form he had seen was the Watcher; if that was typical of what inhabited Cuckoo, the sharks and orcas of the outer reefs were playthings by comparison!

But dangers were not important. Tupaia's ancestors had learned to deal with fear. They could not afford to let it rule them. They had crossed the wide Pacific Ocean in hollowed tree trunks, with nothing to guide them but wave crests, a distant sight of clouds—and courage. They had reached, and conquered, islands no human had ever seen before—Fiji, Tahiti, Easter, the great calm archipelago of Hawaii— and Te'ehala Tupaia was their worthy descendant.

So he did not fear Cuckoo, or whatever great enemies its forests might conceal. Nor did he fear his companions. Not the stinking, hideous Watcher. Not the Sheliak or the Sirian or the Scorpian robot or the lesser breeds. Not the other Purchased People, catatonically still or in a frenzy of compelled action—not any of them. They were not to be feared. They might even be useful, and if not they could easily die. Te'ehala Tupaia would not shrink from ending their lives at the instant those lives became inconvenient to him.

He became aware of great surges of foul stench, wafted down on him. Overhead the Watcher hung, staring at him with those strange compound eyes. He squealed something peremptorily; the blond girl hurried over and hung her Pmal translator on Tupaia's broad shoulder.

"You are the one who says he is 'free,'" the Watcher declared contemptuously, the Pmal faithfully reproducing his speech. Tupaia muttered assent. "For you that word means nothing! You will work as you are ordered. If you fail, you will die. When you are no longer needed, you will die. And perhaps you will die anyway, for I enjoy a good meal!" And it flew away with great sweeps of the leathery wings.

Tupaia swallowed, and returned the Pmal, and for some time was careful to keep his eyes on his work.

They finished fitting the sections of the raft together, then slid it down to the edge of the lake and loaded it with equipment from the lander, for purposes he could not guess . . . until he saw the blond girl throw off her clothes and step onto the raft. She knelt, shivering, staring out at the water.

When she glanced toward him he saw human fear in her eyes and, for the first time in, at least, some weeks, a hint of human compassion touched him. "What's the matter?" he asked.

She said dully, "They want me to swim down to the bottom of the lake."

Tupaia was surprised. "Why not? It's not cold."

"I can't swim," she explained simply. "I told them that I'd drown. They said it was known that Earth primates possessed aquatic skills, and they don't. None of them can survive very long under water. The Sirian and the Scorpian would be destroyed at once."

"Huh!" Tupaia said scornfully, and then, condescendingly, "This Earth primate has plenty of aquatic skills. If you get in trouble, I'll come after you." Maybe, he added to himself, and then observed one of the other Purchased People gesturing furiously for him. He moved off, storing the useful information about the vulnerability of the Scorpian and the floating blue eye in his mind.

Behind him, he saw the Watcher swoop down over the raft, squealing something at the girl. Tupaia cursed himself. What had he boasted about his skills for? Now they would watch him more closely than ever, because he might be useful!

There were only a few more bits and pieces to load onto the raft, and Tupaia studied them carefully. At least one, he was almost sure, was some sort of hand weapon, a metal object with an onion-shaped barrel and two stocks. When he reached for it casually and the Scorpian robot, with a fierce flurry of drumbeats, snatched it away, he was certain. Good enough! And there were the woods, hardly a hundred meters away . . .

How far inside would he have to get before he was out of sight—and thus, perhaps, free? Another fifty meters? A hundred? He plotted paths, guessing at his running times, studying likely patches of undergrowth . . . and then he saw something peering at him out of the very spot he had chosen.

An ape?

That was silly! But he had no time to think of it; because there was a flurry of slow, strong wings behind him and an overpowering reek. The Watcher! He lifted his head just in time to have a metal object strike it.

In Cuckoo's light gravity it did not drop fast enough to hurt. He caught it easily. It was a Pmal translator, and through it the Watcher's voice crackled: "You, the creature who is *free!* Get back to the raft. We're going to let you serve us by diving to the bottom of the lake!"

"All right," said Tupaia, turning obediently—since there was no choice. But he could not help taking one last glance at the patch of undergrowth.

Nothing was there.

He had not imagined it; something had been looking back at him that very closely resembled a terrestrial chimpanzee. None of the others seemed to have noticed it. Or had thought it not worth paying attention to.

Indeed, in some sense it was not. An ape in a jungle? Why not? Except that this ape had been wearing clothes.

Tupaia emerged from the tepid, transparent water with a shout, exhaling air like the spout of a whale, splashing the side of the raft. The Sirian eye darted away with a crackle of static-electrical fury, and Tupaia marked that confirmation down in his memory: the creature feared water. The blond girl leaned over to drape a Pmal around his neck, and the Sirian demanded: "Have you secured the charge?"

Tupaia pulled himself up contemptuously. "Of course." It was a foolish question, since they already knew the answer, for they had sounded the depths of the lake with arcane methods of their own. Radar? Sonar? Something more incomprehensible still? Tupaia did not know, but he could see the glowing virtual image hanging over the center of the raft. The Sheliak extruded a pseudopod to the controls, lovingly sharpening the image, but Tupaia had seen it sharply enough when he dove down to the bottom.

The time for escape, Tupaia promised himself, was very close.

The lake was forty meters deep at this point, and Tupaia had been down to the bottom six times. Not to see. To do. It was easy enough to see in the aliens' instruments what was there: the end of the white porcelain roadway, at a huge doorway of greenish metal. But the instruments could not do what Tupaia had done. They could not carefully attach sticky lugs to the edge of the doorway, could not fix to each of the lugs an explosive charge, could not carry down the delicate fuses that would blow it open. Blow it open for what? That was not Tupaia's concern. Then, no doubt, the aliens planned to use some other gadget from their bag of tricks that would permit a drone to dive down and enter the water-filled passage beyond—if that was indeed what was beyond—but by that time their foolish schemes would no longer matter to Tupaia, for freedom would be his!

So he waited patiently, the lake water drying on his bronzed skin, while the Sirian eye and the Watcher lifted themselves into the air, one on a web of electrostatic force and the other by the force of his huge, leathery wings, and flew toward the beach. The Sheliak made last-minute adjustments, then gave the order to head for the shore. Obediently the Purchased People on the raft sculled it toward the temple.

It was easy enough to pull the raft onto the beach—in this light gravity, there was no such thing as hard work! Tupaia swatted away some sort of steel-blue insect and reviewed his plans. Yes. This would be his chance. That submarine bomb would create it for him. A huge waterspout—at least a loud noise—there would certainly be some sort of confusion, any kind, enough to let him get into the shelter of the cinnamon-scented trees.

As the Scorpian robot rattled peremptory commands and the Sheliak adjusted the firing mechanism, Tupaia strolled idly toward the tree line. Out of the corner of his eye he saw them trigger the fuse transmitter.

The explosion was a great disappointment.

He could hardly tell when it happened. There was no great spout of white foam, no thundering crash. There were not even bubbles. There was only a small upthrust of gentle, slow water in the middle of the lake, like some great fish disporting itself just below the surface. A distant, mild rumble. Nothing else.

Tupaia swore angrily. No matter! It was time to make his move. He started to spin, to run toward the trees—

And froze. With a snare-drum rattle of fury the Scorpian robot was jetting directly toward him, followed by the Watcher and the Sirian eye . . . *and how had they known?*

But they hadn't known what he was doing. They were not after Tupaia at all. They overflew him, dived into the woods, and disappeared. There were sounds of a scuffle, and then they came back, in line of procession, with the Sirian robot in the middle, clutching, in one disdainful tentacle, the queerly dressed chimpanzee.

As they passed, the Sirian eye sent a casual stinging electric lash in Tupaia's direction, warning him back toward the shore. He had no choice. He obeyed; and as he turned back he heard a sad, whimpering voice: "Oh, please! I wasn't doing any harm! I was just on a, uh, a scientific expedition—"

It was the chimp! And he was speaking English!

Te'ehala Tupaia could not help himself; he expanded his barrel chest and roared with laughter. The chimp, carried like a rag doll in the robot's contemptuous grasp, wriggled around far enough to stare down at him reproachfully. Now he was upside down, whimpering with fear, a bedraggled monkey in yellow shorts and bright red jacket. Even though it had cost Tupaia his best chance at freedom, it was funny!

And then the humor ended. He heard a strange sound from the lake, and when he looked he saw that it was quietly emptying itself.

When the bomb blew out the underwater door, it had not been to connect with some still deeper, vaster body of underground water. It had been like blowing the stopper out of a tub. There was a slow, chuckling gurgle from the middle of the lake, as its whole surface began to stir, and circle, and narrow down to a gentle whirlpool at the center. Already the edge of the water had retreated a dozen meters from the beached raft as the lake, with all deliberate speed, drained itself into the empty caverns below.

Two days later the comedy was not even a memory. There was no longer anything for Te'ehala Tupaia to laugh at. Escape had failed. Every hour they were deeper and deeper into the shell of Cuckoo, and the hours were many.

What drove the aliens to this headlong plunge into the depths Tupaia did not know, but the aliens remorselessly drove him, and the rest of the Purchased People with him. They were beasts of burden. Once past the blown-out gate at the end of the porcelain road they were in a narrow, dark tunnel that spiraled down and down. The Sirian eye produced headlamps from one of the containers of instruments, tools, and weapons—eight of them for the Earth-primate labor squad, or about one for every other slave. The Scorpian had built-in lights of his own; the Sirian lit his way with coronal discharges of electricity when he needed them, and the other aliens had lamps given to them as a matter of course. Tupaia had one, of course. If he had not, he would have taken it from the nearest other; it was obvious that it was better to have it than not, if one must be a beast of burden at all.

And beast of burden he was, for what he had been made to carry was the great translucent block with the keyboard. Was it really a weapon? He was convinced it was, for the slave drivers kept a special eye on him, the Watcher's reek never out of his nostrils as the hideous creature soared overhead, except when the Sirian eye or the Scorpian was there. The thing outweighed Tupaia's own hundred-kilos-plus; on Earth he could barely have lifted it, and he was glad when the aliens commanded other Purchased People to take it in turn.

And they traveled down and down . . .

It was clear, at least, that this was no natural cave; the walls were metal, regular, with queer niches and protuberances that must once have had some function. It was an artifact. And it was immense! It seemed endless, and so steep that even in Cuckoo's forgiving gravity it was hard to traverse.

Worse, it was slippery. The cascade from the lake had gone before them. It had kept on going, to depths unguessable to Tupaia; but in its passage it had left a coating of slimy muck. Even for Tupaia's huge strength, guiding the great massy block along the unpredictable jogs and bends of the tunnel was hazardous. At one switchback, damp and oily, the young blond girl slipped and fell headlong. Tupaia, trying to avoid her, stumbled himself, and would have fallen except that a long, skinny black arm snaked out of nowhere and caught him.

"Watch it, big fellow," chattered an unhappy voice.

It was the ape, staggering under a load almost as great as Tupaia's own. Tupaia stopped his block and turned to see him with the headlamp, scowling. The poor creature ducked his head, half-blinded. He was only an animal—

But a king-warrior did not fail to acknowledge a favor. "Here," he said gruffly, "let me help you with that."

The chimp sighed, shifting the burden. "Well, thanks," he said, "but I'm a lot stronger than I look. But if you want to do something for me—"

Tupaia frowned. "What?" he demanded.

"Well, if you'd just shine that light straight ahead for a minute. — That's right. Thanks! And now at the walls of the tunnel, and then at the stuff I'm carrying—"

Tupaia caught himself automatically doing as the chimpanzee had asked, and stopped. "What's this about?" he asked suspiciously.

The chimp grimaced with fear. "Please, not so loud! It's just that I have this tachyon camera. See, this little thing, strapped to my wrist? I didn't lose it when they caught me—didn't even drop it, although— oh, believe me—I was so scared! I thought that minute up by the lake was going to be the last this old monkey would ever see!"

"What is it for?" Tupaia demanded, picking up his load once more.

"The camera?" The chimpanzee bared his fangs in a placatory grin. "For my friends, you see. They sent me down to keep an eye on this, and I'm doing it. Not that it matters to me, I suppose," he added, in self-pity, "because the deeper we get the surer I am that this is a one-way trip for old Doc Chimp. But at least they can see what I see— watch it!"

The procession of bearers had suddenly knotted up, because at the head of the group the aliens were squabbling over something again. Rataplan from the Scorpian robot, chitterings and yowls from the others. The ape said apprehensively, "The one that worries me is the Watcher. The others are just mean. I think he's crazy! I mean, really insane. There's something religious about this whole thing for him—he's looking for his God, sort of—and he's not finding him, and he's not sure he should have these others with him. Oh, there's going to be trouble, I promise you," he finished sorrowfully.

Carefully, Tupaia set down his ponderous burden again. "You seem to know more about this than I do," he said slowly. "What's it all about?"

The ape sighed. "It's a long story—"

Tupaia laughed shortly. "We've got plenty of time. Maybe nothing else but time."

Down, down. Now and then they stopped to catch a few moments' sleep while the aliens wrangled. At long intervals they ate, more of the queer-tasting, metallic, faintly spoiled stuff—in Tupaia's judgment—all-purpose synthetic food from the tachyon chamber. But it kept them alive.

Escape seemed further away than ever. It was not that Tupaia was lost. Not the descendant of those Pacific explorers! But how could he get away? Always one of the flying aliens brought up the rear of the column, always the others paused even in their interminable squabbling to watch and count the slaves. It was an endless trip, with nothing to do but listen to the ape's whining complaints and ponder the meaning of what he had said. Tupaia could form no opinion of how true most of Doc Chimp's stories were. These outlandish aliens were incomprehensible in any terms; Tupaia could make no sense of the chimp's guesses at their drives and alliances. But he was surely right about the Watcher. That particular creature was growing more agitated and more frenzied at every meter. It carried no light of its own and needed none—when its bulging multiple eyes could not collect enough light to serve, its hideous black ears guided it by sonar like a bat's—and that made it all the worse. They could not see it coming as it swept back and forth over the ragged slave procession, squealing mournfully and furiously to itself by turns. The chimp's diagnosis was not to be doubted. The Watcher was mad. And when the line of porters knotted up at a dip in the tunnel where the cascading lake waters had accumulated and left a stagnant pool of thin mud, the Watcher displayed its madness. It came screeching back and struck out at the first in line, the young long-haired blond woman. Tupaia was just behind her. He dropped his burden—fortunately not the block this time!—and turned to face the attack; and something from behind struck him down. His muscles convulsed in a quick tetanic shock. He smelled ozone and his own burning flesh, and lost consciousness.

His last thought was that freedom was gone forever, because he was dead.

But about that he was wrong. Broken patches of awareness began to come back. He was lying in the dark, his legs still in the slimy water, his body a heavy log of dull pain. He breathed the antiseptic odor of medical foam, and realized the chimpanzee had been caring for him. "Oh, Mr. Tupaia," the animal moaned, "thank heavens you're coming out of it! I thought you were killed!"

Tupaia said thickly, "So did I. What happened?"

"It was that Sirian," the chimp sobbed. "He must've thought you were attacking the Watcher, 'stead of the other way around—anyway, he zapped you, and I thought you were dead! You wouldn't have been the only one. There's two dead already, back in the water—and all the more for the rest of us to carry because of it! Oh, Mr. Tupaia, I'm scared of this place!"

Savior or not, Tupaia was tiring of this preposterous ape and his fretful complaints. But he felt an obligation. "Here," he said, "I'll take one of those cases from you—"

"Oh, would you, Mr. Tupaia? Thank you!" The chimp stood up, peering forward in the dim, shadowy tunnel. "I think they're getting ready to move now," he said dismally. "I'm afraid your light got wrecked, Mr. Tupaia. But you can see, sort of, by watching the lights up ahead—"

Tupaia did not answer. His weakened limbs were nearly too stiff to move, and the dressings the ape had applied had hardened around his neck and shoulders.

Of course, they might have saved his life, he acknowledged fairly. He stood up, setting his increased load in motion, and became aware of new physical sensations. Past the sludgy pool, the tunnel changed character. A coppery, sulfurous odor rose above the medical smell of the foam, and a hot breeze was blowing from below. "It's a bad place we're coming to, Mr. Tupaia," sobbed the ape, and Tupaia did not have the heart to answer. It was true.

It got worse.

It was days later, perhaps, and certainly many kilometers farther along the trail—many kilometers straight down!—when there was a cacophony from the beings at the head of the line that transcended everything before. The temperature had gone up sharply. Every breath was an effort. Tupaia let his load drift to the floor, and peered ahead.

There was light ahead—a lot of it. Even the gallery they were in was almost twilit now; he could see Doc Chimp, gasping ragged breaths beside him, the shoe-button eyes imploringly fixed on the light ahead. The rest of the Purchased People were worse off still, but, strangely, the one worst affected of all was the Sirian eye. The enamel globe of its orb was paled and tarnished as it sped past them to join the other aliens ahead.

If the creatures had been quarrelsome before, now they were frenzied. "Let's take a peek," Doc Chimp whispered hoarsely, and the two of them crept silently toward the head of the line.

And stopped in wonderment.

The gallery ended on a sort of a great, wide balcony, and the balcony looked down on a vast drusy cavern, with what seemed to be faceted diamonds and opals and rubies set into the metal walls. And what walls! They were immense! The cavern dropped sheerly a kilometer and more beneath them, extended at least four kilometers into the distance. And beyond it there were other, vaster chambers still. It was not easy to see very far, because the great chamber was crisscrossed with cables and mirror-bright rods. A thunder of something in motion filled their ears. The walls themselves glowed; the scene was as bright as an afternoon on a Polynesian beach, though there was no central source of light.

As Tupaia's eyes became accustomed to the scale and brightness he realized that what he had thought were precious stones were in fact discrete lights. Almost like instrument lights on a panel; the whole scene, he thought, was like the interior of some vast machine, with its countless thousands, perhaps millions of indicator lights and gauges.

Beside him Doc Chimp was panning his tachyon camera across the scene, muttering to himself. "Oh, Mr. Tupaia, this place gets worse and worse! What do you suppose that Watcher's doing now?"

Tupaia said suspiciously, "Watcher? I don't see the Watcher."

"Not with those other creatures—down there! *Way* down there, between those two big pipes, don't you see?"

The hideous creature was at least half a kilometer away from them, dipping and soaring among the great beams and cables on his leathery wings. He looked tiny at that distance, but the other creatures were near enough. The sounds of their quarreling rose to a crescendo, and Tupaia felt the chimp shiver beside him. "Oh, good heavens," the animal moaned. "Do you see what that Sirian's doing? That means something special's going to happen now! And it's bound to be something bad!"

The great eye was limping back toward them, its crackle of electro-static force muted with fatigue and disarray. It paid no attention to the terrestrial creatures but made for a particular metal object, sharp-angled and with a sort of soft, folding cover over one face. With a crackle of force the Sirian thrust the cover aside and squeezed itself into the box; a moment later it emerged again and dragged itself slowly back toward the other aliens.

"What did it do?" Tupaia demanded.

"It sent itself back!" Doc Chimp cried. "Don't you know a tachyon chamber when you see one? It went in and got itself copied; and that copy's back on the orbiter right now, stewing up heaven knows what sort of mischief." He had followed the Sirian with his little camera, and now let it drop in exhaustion. "Oh, Mr. Tupaia," he whimpered, "I wish I'd never come here."

Tupaia turned his back on the sobbing ape, breathing heavily in the damp, copper-smelling heat.

What sort of place was this? It was not merely an artifact buried in the ground. After all those untold kilometers, he had to believe that the entire crust of Cuckoo—this part of it anyway—*was* an artifact! Something, for some reason, had constructed it. This great chamber with all its lights and rods and roaring, muted sounds—it was like being inside the control of some vast, automatic machine.

But for what purpose? And built by whom?

The Scorpian robot was welcoming the return of the Sirian with a drumroll of angry reproach—for what, Tupaia could not guess. He could not hear individual sounds very well, would not have understood them if he could, for almost none of the Purchased People still had Pmals. The young man with the scarred face, almost the only one who had, was listening with that blank, opaque stare that meant some distant owner was occupying his mind.

Intent on the squabble, Tupaia brushed an annoying insect out of his face, and was astonished to find the thing so dense that it hurt his hand when he struck it. He had no time for such thoughts, though; Doc Chimp was moaning, "Oh, Mr. Tupaia, do you see what they're doing? Do you know what that means?"

The Purchased Person with the Pmal, obeying some order, had bent to open a bale of equipment of some sort. Tupaia could not identify it; it seemed to contain folded—garments? No, not garments, but some sort of chest harnesses, with blunt torpedo-shaped metal objects attached to them. "Thrusters!" Doc Chimp sobbed. His eyes were dull, his breathing labored, his demeanor hopeless, even as he was pointing his camera at the emerging equipment. "That means they're going to make us put them on!"

Tupaia growled, "What's wrong with that? Better than walking!"

The chimp shook his head miserably. "Not in that mortal long tunnel we just came through, not with all those bends and turns. But out there—out in that big cave—don't you see? They're going to make us fly straight through!"

Tupaia slapped another bug away and then, realizing what he had done, looked around. Why, the air was full of the bugs! Even in the semidarkness he could see dozens of them, hundreds.

And then he saw that there were swarms of the little insects, all over, even out on the balcony. The other Purchased People had noticed them now, and a sudden astonished rise in pitch of the gabble of the aliens said that they had discovered them, too. They were coming from the tachyon transporter. A bright bubble blossomed from the machine. It popped, and a batch of a thousand of the insects buzzed out of the chamber as he watched—and another batch—and another—it was like watching puffs of vapor from an antique steam engine, thousands upon thousands of them. For a mad moment Tupaia found himself a boy again, bringing breakfast to the tourists in the overwater dining room on Mooréa. To entertain the whiteskins he would throw a slice of toast into the water, and—oh!—what a frenzy! The water would boil with silvery bodies and gold and blue, flashing and flailing into each other like a tiny underwater game of pushball, until magically the last crumb was devoured; and just so these flashing bright creatures milled and raced around—

But were by no means so harmless.

Doc Chimp cried out in alarm. "The Boaty-Bits! I've never seen so many of them!"

And then, slowly, his voice shaking as if in mortal fear, "But they're collective beings. It takes a thousand of them to equal a human or a Sheliak or any of those—that's why they go in swarms—but here—" His voice failed him. "Here there's a million or more," he gasped, "and what will that make them equal to?"

Perhaps the Sheliak and the Scorpian had thought of the same thing; at least, their actions showed sudden panic. The robot whirled in midair and, steam jets screaming, raced toward the Purchased Person bearing a load of queer double-stocked weapons, while the Sheliak extended a lightning-fast tentacle in the same direction.

Fast as they were, they were not fast enough.

The milling swarm of Boaty-Bits seemed to shudder in midmotion. Then, with astonishing speed, the entire swarm coalesced around the Purchased Person. They swarmed onto him like African bees onto a luckless victim, covering him from head to toe with a solid, shimmering coat of steely blue. The Purchased Person staggered, then swiftly dropped to one knee, grasped the two-stocked weapon, and fired. The Scorpian robot exploded into a million shards of hot steel as the greenish blob of light struck; a moment later, with a sound like bacon frying, another green bolt incinerated the Sheliak.

"How—could he—" Doc Chimp muttered feverishly, and then answered his own question. "The Boaty-Bits took him over! And—heaven help us now, Mr. Tupaia—here comes the Watcher!"

Tupaia instinctively shrank back, as the Watcher screamed up from the depths of the cavern. Its hoarse, hooting roar was almost deafening, even above the thrumming in the immense pipes; great flapping wings brought its vile odor in a hot and nauseating gust as it lunged toward them—and past. It dropped to another part of the line, cawing its terrible rage at the two Purchased People staggering under the mass of the great translucent block. One fled. The other tried. Not fast enough. The foul talons ripped across his back and blood spurted. The Watcher dropped to the keyboard and its claws danced across it.

Yes. It was a weapon. That green glow formed over the block, elongating toward the Purchased Person wearing the cloak of Boaty-Bits.

The green charge grew and slid toward the edge of the block. Then it raced away. It struck the Purchased Person, and he ceased to exist. Half the Boaty-Bits got away, the rest simply disappeared. It went on. It went out into the cavern.

Those shining rods, those delicate silver wires—they were in its path, and it touched them. A rumble like a distant H-bomb filled the cavern. Green fire flared into terrible brightness. Tupaia ducked his head, crouched to shield himself from searing heat. A scream from the Watcher faded into sudden dreadful silence. He heard the monkey whimper.

At last the wave of heat receded, and Tupaia lifted his head and tried to see. He could not. His stinging eyes found only a foggy red blur.

"My eyes!" he heard the monkey moaning. "I burnt my eyes!"

The Watcher howled again, in rage and fear, and then the shock wave hit them.

The blast battered Tupaia's body, hurt his ears, dazed him. Dimly, through ringing ears, he heard the diminishing echoes that rumbled after it. When at last he could get his breath he picked himself up and stared around fiercely through the thinning blood-red mist. At least his vision was returning!

The curious mirror-bright rods were intact, but the silvery cables were slowly wriggling themselves into corkscrew contortions, a great loose skein of chrome-colored spaghetti. Huge metal beams had been bent and torn, and somewhere a pipe containing liquid had burst. The plume of liquid dashed itself into spray—or perhaps it was steam, for the heat was indescribable.

Near him the monkey lay in a sobbing heap, hands over his scorched eyes. And the Watcher stood still at his terrifying weapon.

If he had seemed mad before, now he was utterly berserk. He played the console of the weapon again, this time toward the bulk of the remaining group of slaves. They were vaporized at once; and the Boaty-Bits buzzed wildly above them.

Apart from the Watcher, Tupaia, and the chimp, the only individual creature still alive was the horse-headed Canopan, and his future suddenly was in doubt. The Boaty-Bits—more of them every minute, as the tachyon chamber spat out new swarms—wheeled and descended on him.

Screeching horribly, the Watcher lifted the weapon toward the shrouded figure of the Canopan—and stopped.

The Canopan raised its hand, and spoke—in a tone wholly unlike its usual whinnying tongue.

The effect on the Watcher was spectacular. It froze. It held motionlessly for a long moment.

Then it screamed in horror and outrage, heaved the great block away out over the balcony. It spun and turned as it fell slowly into the depths. The Watcher, shrieking its despair, turned and flew away.

Tupaia swallowed and glanced down at Doc Chimp. "What—what was that?" he demanded.

But there was no answer. The little chimpanzee was drooping slowly toward the floor, one long, skinny black hand trying vainly to press back the bright flood that spurted from a wound over his heart, the other pressed to the blinded shoe-button eyes. Some tiny fragment from the battle had found an unintended target.

And, except for that strange horse-headed figure with its mummy-wrapping of Boaty-Bits, Tupaia was alone.

He turned and ran back up the corridor, expecting at every moment to feel that bright green blast on his own back.

It did not happen; but the way to escape was not open. The gallery was shuddering under repeated explosions from the disasters in the cave, and as he rounded a turn he saw that some of those quakes had brought down the roof.

The tunnel was blocked.

There was no longer any way back to the surface.

FOURTEEN

And now I wake to desperate danger.

Unholy intruders are stumbling on HIS most precious secrets. They are violating the forbidden spaces, attempting to destroy HIS masterwork, in which HE lives, as HE must live forever.

There are urgent things to be done. Though the first clumsy desecrations have failed to end HIS eternal being, as all others in the past have failed, grave damage has been done. Graver danger still exists. I summon the clustered servants that cling to the inner shell and dispatch them to the scene. They are ready. They have rested and fed and grown fat in the flood of energy from the central source. For centuries of centuries of centuries they have been ready to protect and repair HIS everlasting body, and they are eager.

I trace the star-girdling rings for further damage and further danger. I find HIS great creation still supported by its shells of superatomic rings. No ring is broken. None must ever be, for there even HE is vulnerable.

I find no breaks. As yet the shell is safe.

The driving-mouths at the poles are safe. They continue to slow us for entrance into the new galaxy and they are ready to maneuver us when the time is here.

The billion clones are safe, in their liquid-helium baths.

I am safe, in spite of the intruders within my fabric, for they do not even know I exist.

And HE is yet safe.

I need not wake HIM yet. But soon.

Now I long for the moment of HIS awakening because my fear of HIM is drowned in my dutiful concern for the eternal wonder of HIS plan. HE will end all danger when HIS holy moment comes. When every mind has surrendered to HIM, even every parasite within HIS eternal being and every crawling thing in the galaxy ahead, none will remain free to profane HIS ultimate plan.

That time is near. And when it comes—

When it comes there will be no safety for anyone, anywhere, except the ultimate terminal safety of surrender to HIM.

FIFTEEN

Down below them, Cuckoo's huge weather engine was building up a great cyclonic storm. The engine ran on heat, as in every other astronomical body, but Cuckoo's heat transport came from the inside to escape into space. Cuckoo's storm had been growing for weeks, and it had its counterpart on the orbiter, a slow, vast vortex that swept beings Jen Babylon had never seen before in toward the center of the structure. That was where the huge computer FARLINK whispered to itself, surrounded by its banks of flat-picture screens and stereostage enclosures for holograms. In one stage the great virtual-image globe of Cuckoo itself turned slowly, most of its surface still blank or only vaguely sketched in from satellite reconnaissance; a few sections thick with detail of continents, mountains, seas. But the globe of Cuckoo was not the display the beings swarmed toward. That display came from Doc Chimp's tachyon camera, far below the surface.

The stereostage images were terribly disturbing. They were also terribly poor in quality, for the chimpanzee's hand-held camera caught only quick and fragmentary glimpses. But that was where FARLINK came in. Its powerful circuits selected every bit of information, assayed it for validity, weighed it for importance, assigned it a place in a greater picture. It edited, interpreted, selected, so that its algorithms extracted maximum information from the most corrupt signal. The result was displayed in the central stereostage, while details were shown flat on any of the half-hundred circling screens. What the horde of beings saw was not a moving hologram but a series of stills—but it was enough. The entire orbiter was in a flap, as the vortex drew every living thing into that single room.

There was no calm in this storm's eye. The great dome was bedlam. Shouts, screeches, roars; rataplan of Scorpian robots, neighing sobs of Canopans. Doc Chimp, tugging fretfully at the long green feather in his cap, dodged a dense cloud of Boaty-Bits and muttered to Jen Babylon, "It's feeding time at the zoo!" His shoe-button eyes were fixed woefully on the image his other self was transmitting from so far away.

Babylon nodded, his face drawn. "Smells worse than any zoo I've been in," he agreed absently, and was rewarded with a burnt-rubber smell of indignation as the T'Worlie that had hovered by his shoulder flounced away. He sighed, wincing as a Scorpian hissed past, drumming at the top of its timpani. His Pmal was overloaded; with every being trying to communicate at once its language matches were completely unable to keep up. What came to his ears was a jumble of words and phrases, and simple static.

For no one understood what was happening. That the expedition was traveling downward into the heart of Cuckoo was obvious; that they were passing through metallic tunnels, galleries, chambers was apparent. But what did it mean? Everyone—every being—had a theory. The Scorpians had discovered secret plans of the tunnel, leading to some incredible trove or treasure; the Scorpians denied it with fury. The Sheliaks were in league with the deltaforms to trigger tectonic forces and destroy Cuckoo entirely—the Sheliak nearest that theorizer nearly destroyed him in response. The Canopans accused the Sirians of having enslaved their one representative in the expedition with an illegal Purchased People unit; the Sirians screeched that the facts were right, but the enslavement had gone the other way. No species accepted responsibility. Every one vowed that its conspecific was a rogue who had been acting oddly for some time. Was there truth in any of it? There was no way to be sure—and no way, really, to discuss any of these things intelligently with the overloaded Pmals faltering in the incessant din.

And meanwhile Doc Chimp's little camera recorded a journey that went down, down, down, toward no one could guess what.

Ben Pertin sailed through the whirlwind of beings to link arms with Babylon and bring himself to a stop. Babylon glanced around warily, then whispered: "Anything new?"

Pertin shook his head angrily. The one secret they had retained was the tachyon cap; in Pertin's own chamber Zara was wearing it, trying to eavesdrop on the Purchased People in the expedition. "You can't pick out the ones you want," he complained, "and then when you do get one it doesn't tell you anything." He moodily watched the slow build-up of images on the stereostage and detail screens for a moment. "What we need," he said, "is a Watcher. They know more than we do!"

Org Rider, hanging close by in the little group of Earth primates, shook his head. "There's none on the orbiter now," he said positively. "And that one"—he frowned at the stereostage—"is insane." And indeed, the image looked very much that way; the hideous being had been captured in midflight, against a background of dull metal tunnel ceiling and walls, its horrid face screwed up in an expression of rage and fear.

Emotions were running high everywhere, Jen Babylon thought. The crowd in the room was seething with anger, resentment, fear— and other, less guessable emotions, which had no clear counterpart in the human repertory. You could not tell what the Boaty-Bits, for instance, were feeling. Angry or overjoyed, they still danced in their dense swarm like flies in the light over a swimming pool on a sum- mer's eve. The T'Worlie alone seemed unmoved. Nothing of smaller scope than galactic could touch their ancient feelings. They did not possess either fear or resentment in any personal sense; what they wanted of life was to learn and ponder, and all the revelations of secrets and conspiracy provided for them was a set of new phenomena to study.

And perhaps the T'Worlie were right. Babylon told himself justly that the "enemy"—the rogue beings leading that expedition—had really done nothing that could not be explained. Indeed, nothing for which an explanation was really required. They were exploring new ground. Well, given the chance, what being among them would not? There was no evidence to convict them of a crime. No crime had been committed. The most you could say against them was that they had acted in secret.

Yet in his heart Babylon knew that something was terribly wrong. The individual beings were rogues; the collective purpose of the expe- dition was threatening.

And he was not alone in that feeling. Each in its own way, the seething mass of beings that hung by the walls, floated in midair, or flapped, clung to stanchions and each other—that raucous, malodor- ous congeries of nightmare shapes that were his shipmates—they all shared his fear, rage, and indignation. The Canopans had demanded a

Grand Council. The T'Worlie had agreed, out of their own patient curiosity more than any desire to prosecute; and beings Babylon had never seen before, or even dreamed of, were still flocking to the great interior FARLINK chamber.

How they bellowed, and how they stank! The handful of true humans—loosely enough defined, to be sure, to include Org Rider and Doc Chimp—huddled near the entrance, trying not to be choked by the hot-iron stink of the Scorpian robots and the vinegar scent of the inquisitive T'Worlie, and the fouler reeks of the beings that looked like kittens, or roaches, or sea anemones or copper-wire mantises. There were beings here Babylon had never seen before: the anemone-creature, with its violet shell shading to dark purple, slithering eel-like shapes with tentacled eyes, a soft-bodied sort of beetle with many legs, a human form—but no! It was not human! It was a winged woman's figure, but silvery and with blank, opaque eyes. "It's an edited form," Doc Chimp whispered nervously when Babylon asked. "Don't be deceived by the way she looks! She's not human, no, not a bit!" And before Babylon could ask more, she was lost to sight in the crush.

There had to be three hundred beings in the room! Not counting the Boaty-Bits, who were so thrust about and jostled by the crowd that they could not maintain the integrity of their swarm, but buzzed about like a smoked-out beehive. Doc Chimp, morose and distraught, flung himself into the mob to get a better look at the hologram, then wriggled his way out again. "Good fellow primates," he said distractedly to Pertin and Babylon, "I can't see a thing! And it's me down there, and I tell them it's *my* camera that's sending them the stereopictures, and they push me out of the way!" Babylon gave no answer, because he could think of none to give. The chimpanzee wrinkled up his long black lips and muttered, "Here's Redlaw, anyway. I forgot to tell you I saw him coming."

Pertin spun eagerly around. "Anything?" he demanded. The big man looked around carefully before replying.

"Not the way you mean," he said, loud enough to be audible above the din, too low for his words to carry beyond the small group. "But there's something, all right. Your girlfriend, Benpertin."

"Doris?" Pertin scowled sourly. "What can there be about her that would be important?" He caught a glimpse of Babylon's expression and added, "Oh, come on, she's just a convenience—I don't care if she lives or dies! Why should I? And don't look at me that way—do you know how she got to be a Purchased Person? Torched the house where her husband and three babies were sleeping! Killed them all! You think I really care about someone—"

Redlaw put his hand on the other man's arm, his expression showing that his feelings were no more kindly than Babylon's. "It isn't exactly Doris," he said softly. "It's the creature that owns Doris who has something to say. You'd better hear it, all of you."

Doc Chimp muttered, "But the Grand Council, Mr. Redlaw! It's supposed to start any minute—"

Redlaw's deep growl cut him off. "The council doesn't know what this is all about. Come! And bring that T'Worlie if you can find him."

As almost the oldest resident of Cuckoo Station, Ben Pertin had certain privileges. One was the room he slept in. It was a faceted polyhedral chamber, most of the interior faces filled with flat pictures of scenes from his lives. Past the stereostage was an exterior shot of Sun One. Over his bed loomed the immense majesty of Knife-in-the-Sky Mountain. In the center of the room, fitted with soft binding tapes to keep an occupant from floating away in his sleep, was Pertin's bed; and as they entered someone lifted a head from it to gaze at them.

From the side of the room Zara came toward them, the helmet slung from one hand. Her expression was strained. All she said was, "I'm glad you're here."

Ben Pertin—Babylon could not decide whether his voice was surly or embarrassed—scowled at the bed. "Doris giving you any trouble?" he demanded.

"It's not Doris," said Zara, and from the lips of the figure on the bed a woman's voice, unearthly slow and carefully formed, said:

"Attend the person Zara. This person has already communicated." And the woman turned her face to the covers of the bed, waiting.

Doc Chimp turned his leathery face to Zara. "And what does that mean?" he asked plaintively.

"She's been telling me things," Zara said. The strain on her face had not eased; the sound of her voice was troubled. "She won't tell me much about her home planet. Least of all, where it is. But it's hot. I believe in her real body—that is, *its* real body, the body of the thing that bought Doris—molten sulfur flows in its veins instead of watery blood. But they have a civilization not too much unlike ours: that is, it's a collection of individuals, not a single multicellular society like the Boaty-Bits. And they differ widely among themselves—like us— not like, say, the T'Worlie or the Sheliaks."

Mimmie, hanging inconspicuously by the doorway, danced gently forward. "Disagreement," he chirped. "T'Worlie find other T'Worlie quite individual."

"I know," Zara agreed, "but you're more, well, *united* than human beings, aren't you? Anyway. The important thing is, some of their individuals on this fire planet are doing the same sorts of things humans are on Earth. It's their equivalent of Kooks."

The female human figure on the bed stirred restlessly. It did not lift its head, but the unearthly voice, muffled by the bedclothes, said: "Speak of zero-mass tachyons."

Doc Chimp exploded, "That was private information! Good heavens, Ben! I didn't know *Homo sapiens* primates could be so naive! Didn't you know better than to discuss that sort of thing with your fancy woman, knowing she was Purchased?"

Pertin said defensively, "I didn't! Tell them, Doris—I mean, you there, whoever you are!" But Zara interrupted.

"Ben is right," she said. "The . . . being wasn't repeating what she had heard from us. She was telling a deep secret of her own race." The figure on the bed moved convulsively, but was silent. "They have used zero-mass tachyons for their own purposes for a long time, but have never shared the knowledge with the rest of the galaxy. And they suspect that their . . . Kooks are controlled with zero-mass tachyons from somewhere else." She took a deep breath. "They think it's from Cuckoo," she finished. "And they think that the members of the expedition are controlled in the same way, or at least their leaders are."

The figure lifted its head. "These are instructions," it said tonelessly. "Display spherical object. Consider relationships. Advise all other beings." And the woman's figure tossed away the restraining straps, rose from the bed, and moved silently out of the chamber and away.

Babylon saw the strange, almost fearful look on Pertin's face as his gaze followed her, and understood something of what was in Pertin's mind. "Consider relationships," indeed! Babylon knew what relationships his friend was considering. Doris was a Purchased Person, whose distant owners were only academically interested in human sexual practices. Usually she was permitted to share Pertin's bed only when they had no other plans for her. But sometimes they were in direct control. How strange it must be, Babylon thought, to murmur drowsy endearments into a woman's ear, and find a reply from her remote and inhuman owners!

But there was not much time for such reflections now. The T'Worlie moved silently to the center of the room, facing its human companions. It chirped, "Concurrence. Recommendation to advise all other beings is agreed." It floated silently for a moment, its five eyes seeming to stare at each of them in turn, then added a quick series of chirping whistles and a pungent smell of clove. The Pmals rapped out the translation: "Observation: Situation becoming critical. Proposal: All information now be shared, including data from helmet, information store obtained from wrecked vessel—and communication just received through being identified as Doris."

Redlaw boomed, "He's right! We don't have a choice—so let's do it!"

If the orbiter had been excited before, now it was like an anthill gone mad. Beings of every fantastic shape flew and hurled themselves along the corridors. The news had sped faster than a tachyon transmission, and each race, almost each individual of every race, reacted with its own special pattern of consternation and anger, and even fear. Hardly a civilized planet in the Galaxy, it now seemed, had been spared its equivalent of the Kooks; and the suggestion that they were all part of some incredible conspiracy was explosive. Chugging Scorpian robots sped through swarms of milling Boaty-Bits without warning; Sheliaks and Purchased People stopped each other at the intersections with furious bursts of screeches and rattles from the overworked Pmals; and all of them tried to crowd their way into the FARLINK chamber, where the T'Worlie were feeding data into the computer as fast as it could be accepted.

First Babylon had overseen three great Sheliaks, functioning as porters, as they bodily moved the store of hexagonal rods and their reader into the chamber. Then they obeyed the Doris-being's command.

The T'Worlie had plugged FARLINK into the circuits, and every datum from the hexagonal rods was entering its datastores. The

images were slower to build, but they were clearer, more detailed—
FARLINK was not only observing, it was pondering what it saw,
matching it against a vast store of information. Doc Chimp was given
the task of feeding the hexagons into the reader; he fumbled through
the stack until he found the key one—the "spherical object"—and
slipped it into its slot.

At once the translucent block cleared, and the great metal bubble
shone forth inside it. Doc touched the scanning plate, and the image
began to go through its cycle—slowly now, as FARLINK studied each
new display in turn and enhanced the images. First the featureless
metal globe. Then the cutaway sections. Then the schematics: a network of scarlet structural members, replaced by an interlinked system
of ivory-colored arteries—transportation passages? Something like
that, perhaps. Then, coded in bright silver, a set of mirror-finished
rings, making a sort of basketwork duplicate of the sphere itself.

The swarm of beings in the chamber hissed and muttered to each
other, but no clear voice emerged. Doc Chimp pushed himself back
and stared morosely at the image. "I don't see anything sensible," he
complained. "What's it supposed to mean?"

Zara said doubtfully, "Well, let's see. It's a sphere. An artifact. I
suppose it represents some instrument or machine—a spacecraft,
maybe?"

Babylon ventured, "I understand there are old orbiting vessels you
can't approach around Cuckoo—like the wrecked ship?"

Pertin shook his head. "They don't look a bit like that," he growled,
and then called, "FARLINK? Any interpretations?"

The clear, cold voice of the machine replied, "Negative. Analysis
continuing. More data required."

The humans looked at each other, and Zara shrugged. "The helmet?"

Org Rider nodded. "We have no choice," he declared. "Benpertin,
please produce the helmet. We must share this information, too!"

The excitement and resentment that followed the giving up of the
helmet—how dare these Earth beings withhold valuable data!—was
only exceeded by the uncertainty of how to use it. Obviously the
helmet could not be worn by FARLINK as it could by a human being—
or by the beings who had made it; obviously, if those who had worn it
simply told FARLINK what they had seen they would omit much

priceless data, or corrupt it. At last a Sheliak plunged into the center of the group and plastered itself against FARLINK's data-input terminals, extruding a bubble of its flesh toward the helmet. The bubble crept inside; the doughy mass of Sheliak flesh suddenly contorted, and then was still. Pertin nodded grudgingly. "Knew the damn beasts would be good for something one day," he declared. "They can shift their organs and nerves around as easily as their bodies—it's giving direct transmission of its nervous impulses to the computer!"

Babylon shook his head unbelievingly. "Raw sensory inputs? How can FARLINK read them?"

"That's FARLINK's problem, and it'll solve it," Pertin boasted. "Just wait and see!"

It was easy enough advice to follow—there was no real alternative! —but the mob of beings in the chamber was getting louder and more raucous.

The first sign that anything happened was that the great globe from the hexagon-rod data disappeared. The cube remained clear, but it contained no information. There was a gasp, buzz, hiss, whistle— whatever sounds each made—from the beings; but as moments passed and the image did not reappear the surprise reverted to angry impatience.

Then, at a single stroke, all the dozens of circling flat-picture screens were wiped blank, while the holo of the expedition on the center stereostage firmed up. It became more clear in all its parts, and began to move in real time. FARLINK was doing its job. As it matched the images from the other Doc Chimp's camera against the data from the helmet—and against that vast collection of other information that made its datastore—it filled in the gaps, interpolated details, made the scene as real as if the observers were standing at some vantage point and beholding the scene itself.

Since there was nothing else to look at at the moment, every being in the chamber was looking at the scene, and one, at least, felt a queer stirring, half a memory, half a long-forgotten apprehension. Jen Babylon shook his head. What was it? The scene showed the toiling line of porters and leaders passing through the narrow corridors and emerging into a great chamber, kilometers wide and deep, with walls that seemed to be set with bright, winking jewels and a network of cables and branching cyclopean structural beams. All rose from a floor formed of silver-white lines that looked thinner than threads, too fragile and too far apart to hold anything.

"I've seen that before," he muttered, mostly to himself, but beside him Zara caught the words and looked at him curiously.

"You have, Jen? Where?"

He shook his head. "I can't remember," he confessed. "Maybe in a dream. Quite a while ago. —No, it's gone. But somehow that looks familiar—and frightening!"

She studied his face carefully before she said, "Please think hard, Jen. It may be important."

And perhaps it was, but Babylon got no chance to think about it more carefully, nor did any being in the chamber, about that or about anything else. For the blank cube suddenly sprang into life. It showed the ball of layered silver rings, then the ivory arteries, then the bright scarlet structural members—the same sequence as before, but in reverse order, as if the artifact was being constructed before their eyes. And much faster, much surer; with a sense of reality and solidity to the images that had been lacking before. Like the first series, the remaining view was the great featureless globe, hanging in space.

But it did not stop there.

The globe clouded over. It showed markings that looked like a satellite's view of a distant planet. First mountains and wide, shallow basins. Then the basins were filled with seas and lakes, and tiny spiderweb lines on the surface filled with liquid to become streams and rivers. The mountains sprouted forests; the lowlands were lush with vegetation or bleak with scarred rock and desert sands. At last the atmosphere began to fill with clouds, all sorts of clouds—glowing clouds in a thousand hues in one place, fleecy cumulus and towering cumulonimbus in others, and in one huge patch, covering nearly a tenth of the surface of the globe, a great swirling cyclonic mass.

A great, involuntary sound went up from the crowd staring at the display, then a loud, excited buzz. "It's Cuckoo!" cried Org Rider. "That's the big storm that's been developing for weeks now!"

And Ben Pertin laughed queerly. "You're right," he said, half sobbing, "it's Cuckoo. The artifact is Cuckoo. Cuckoo is an artifact. It's not a planet—or a star—or a mere astrophysical anomaly. It's a machine!"

A machine! It was unbelievable—and yet FARLINK was registering .999-plus certainty, and all around the chamber the flat screens were lighting up, one by one, showing details of the mechanism, cyclopean Cuckoo-girdling bands, great chambers with cryptic contents, vents, and thrust-mountings—it was an engineering plan of some immense edifice, no doubt of that! The hubbub grew to a crescendo, and then there was a silvery chime. FARLINK wished to speak. Its flat mechanical voice tolled, picked up and translated by a hundred Pmals into a hundred different tongues:

"Analysis complete! Object has been tentatively identified as a Dyson sphere, conjectural astrophysical artifact proposed by Freeman J. Dyson, planet Earth, mid-twentieth century. Dyson suggested that a truly advanced race of technological beings, using ever-increasing amounts of energy, would ultimately devise a scheme to capture the entire energy output of its parent sun by surrounding it with a sphere of matter produced by rearranging the non-stellar components of its solar system—planets, asteroids, comets, satellites, dust and gas clouds, etc.—into a shell, so that no radiant energy could escape the system without being made to do work. *Signatures.* Dyson proposed that a telescopic search be made for large, light objects radiating faintly in the infrared. No large-scale systematic search was made, and the proposal was forgotten. However, Object Lambda, a.k.a. Cuckoo, possesses these signatures. *Details.* Reference display one." One of the flat panels was suddenly surrounded by a halo of flashing color; it displayed the basketwork sphere of layered rings that had already been seen in the records of the wrecked orbiter. "Surface sphere is clearly supported by ring network. Hypothesis: Each ring consists of matter moving at more than orbital velocity, thus generating centrifugal force that keeps the shell from collapsing into the central sun. This high-velocity motion is evidently essentially frictionless. Exact nature of rings and means of their control at present not known. Reference display two." A tiny, incredibly bright spark of light, surrounded by cloudy glow. "This is the central sun, identified as a type F-4, now in an atmosphere of relatively dense plasma extending to the inner surface of the shell. Reference display three." An interior view of the shell, with some sort of tiny objects in slow motion within it. "These are apparent self-reproducing mechanisms, absorbing energy from the star and storing it for purposes not yet established. Reference display four . . ."

But Babylon could look no more. The fourth screen was showing the openings in Cuckoo's poles. High-rimmed holes, each tens of thousands of kilometers across. Nozzles! Thrusters for plasma jets that drove and controlled the incredible structure . . . but he had absorbed all he could, and he returned to the central marvel.

A Dyson sphere! Now he remembered. It had been in an early astronomy course, before he had settled on his major in linguistics. The instructor had joked about it. Now that communication between scores of alien races was a fact, he said, it was clear that the so-called "Dyson sphere" was simply the ludicrous fantasy of someone who had read too much space fiction as a boy.

Babylon grinned to himself. "If only my old teacher were still alive," he muttered, "this would kill him for sure!"

The T'Worlie that had been hovering unnoticed by his head emitted a cinnamon odor of perplexity. "Query: Referent not understood."

Babylon shook his head. "It doesn't matter." And then, wonderingly, "A Dyson sphere! But—out here, in the middle of nowhere? Where could it have come from?"

The T'Worlie danced silently for a moment, then offered: "Statement: Representation of galaxy in temple not our own. Conjecture: Home galaxy of artifact builder?"

Babylon stared at him without replying.

Another galaxy? But the nearest other galaxies—the Magellanic Clouds and the Mafei 1 and 2—they were tens of thousands of light-years away. The nearest really big one, M-31 in Andromeda, two million light-years!

He felt his flesh crawling. Who would create an artifact as immense as Cuckoo and send it hurtling through intergalactic space on a voyage whose duration could not be less than hundreds of thousands of years?

And why?

T'Worlie twittering and a sudden reek of new paint caught him: "Reservation," the T'Worlie chirped. "Hypothesis of structure surrounding sun difficult to accept. First demurrer: No known form of matter possesses the characteristics required for construction of hypothetical frictionless rings. Second—"

"No," Babylon interrupted, "but then no known object like Cuckoo exists, either!"

The T'Worlie chirped on, disregarding him: "Second demurrer: Position of stellar object at center of such hypothetical shell would be metastable. Inevitable small random displacements from central position would be accelerated by positive gravitational feedback."

Babylon shook his head rebelliously. "Cuckoo exists!"

"Laws of physics also exist," the T'Worlie twittered, and an odor of overripe muskmelon accentuated the words. "Axiom: Laws of physics apply equally throughout the Universe and may not be denied."

Ben Pertin cut in roughly, "What's the use of this arguing? You're just saying that what we can see to be true can't be true!"

"Negative," the T'Worlie responded. "Correct interpretation: To reconcile known physical facts with hypotheses regarding Cuckoo requires two corollaries." The T'Worlie danced thoughtfully for a moment, as if it hesitated to say what it must say. A diffident, wondering scent of lilac emanated from it and, although no human could read expression in a T'Worlie's tiny eyes, Babylon felt a stab of apprehension at what was coming next.

"Corollary one," the T'Worlie chirped firmly. "Design and construction of 'Dyson sphere' system required technological and scientific skill at levels not now attained by any galactic race. Corollary two: Sphere was constructed, and at present is still controlled, by existing intelligence."

The T'Worlie's chirping, and the rattle of the Pmals, lingered in the vast chamber and died away into silence.

And then the noise came. For long minutes the swarm of beings had been quiet, hanging on the FARLINK data and the T'Worlie's observations; but they could be silent no longer. Buzzes, shrieks, whistles, brays—every being was speaking at once.

An existing intelligence! Something that had somehow survived the journey of endless years!

Babylon shouted into the din: "Do you mean that this object has a *mind?*"

"Perhaps many minds," the T'Worlie chirped somberly, and added, "It must be so."

Babylon turned away, unseeing. Cuckoo as an artifact was hard enough to believe—but to add to that the belief that somehow a guiding intelligence survived with it . . .

His imagination reeled. Only dimly did he sense that some new sound had been added to the noise. Doc Chimp snaked out a long paw and dragged Babylon to his side. The chimp's sad face had suddenly become more woebegone than ever as he stared, with the others, at the forgotten scene from the camera of his other self, far below. It had changed. There was no resting on the part of the slave procession now; all of them were up and moving, and the expression on the chimp who grasped his arm was mirrored in the one down below the shell of Cuckoo. "It's the Watcher," Doc Chimp moaned. "He's really gone mad now—and I'm down there with him."

"Pull yourself together, Doc," Ben Pertin snarled over his shoulder. "It's just a copy!"

"It's *me,*" the chimp insisted. "And they're fighting, and—oh! Look at the Canopan!"

By now the entire chamber was watching the new challenge to their sanity. Everyone saw the Canopan suddenly covered with a swarm of Boaty-Bits, the wild scuffling, the insane flight of the Watcher, the terrible destruction of the green-glow weapon.

"They're trying to break it up!" Zara cried, as the green-glowing charge hurtled down toward the grating of slender silver rods that hung beneath the jungle of cables and branching structural beams. Babylon's breath caught. Those wire-thin rods were the rings that supported the sphere. If they were broken, the whole surface here would cave, falling toward the central sun—

Or something worse! If the frictionless motion of the unknown stuff of the rings was really more than orbital, any broken ring would mean faster and more dreadful disaster. No longer frictionless, its unknown stuff would tear into the fabric of Cuckoo at velocities that must be hundreds of kilometers a second. Everything it struck would be exploded into incandescent plasma. Including, probably, other rings in its path. Shuddering with something between awe and terror, he imagined all Cuckoo turning into a supernova.

How many of the supernovas in far-off galaxies, Ben Pertin wondered, were signals of advanced intelligence and ultimate technology snuffed out by catastrophic accident?

Not breathing, he watched the green-shining missile strike the silver rod. It exploded. The whole screen burned with green fire and went abruptly black. The camera had been overloaded.

"They're trying to kill Cuckoo," he tried to say. "Trying to kill us—"

He had no voice. Around him there was silence, then a muffled stir of breath and motion. He tensed in spite of himself, waiting for the final crash of sound, for the walls to buckle around him and the whole world to dissolve into fire . . .

It couldn't happen that fast, of course. Cuckoo was too huge. Even a plasma explosion would take time to swallow it all, more time to reach the orbiter.

The screen lit, dimly at first, then with more brightness and clarity. Babylon could breathe again.

"Nobody," Doc Chimp whispered, "nothing could live in that!"

And it seemed true. They could see the cavern again. Apart from the Watcher there seemed no one, no being, alive within the range of the camera, except for a huge man with skin the color of weathered brass, and the other Doc Chimp—and the chimpanzee was blinded.

Even in the stereostage the sight was fearful. The viewers shrank away from the flare of green light that turned their faces queerly metallic. Ben Pertin laughed—hysteria, Babylon thought; but Doc Chimp took it personally.

"How can you?" he chattered furiously. "I thought you were my friend! If it was you down there—"

"If it was me," Pertin said brutally, "it would come to the same thing. So you're being killed! But we've both been killed so often already it just doesn't seem important anymore. It's the Boaty-Bits! They've been up to something all along. They have a lot of explaining to do—"

His voice broke off. His eyes darted around the room, and his face assumed an expression of comical surprise.

"What's the matter, Ben?" Babylon asked.

"The Boaty-Bits. Don't you see? There's not one of them in this chamber—they've sneaked away!"

At least the noise level had dropped! It was not that the beings on the orbiter were calmer—quite the reverse—but now they were dispersed, as Scorpians and T'Worlie, humans and deltaforms, every being of every race joined in the orbiter-wide hunt. Where were the Boaty-Bits?

Within a few moments Babylon had lost track of the other human beings—Pertin in one direction, Zara in another, Org Rider and Redlaw heading for the landers on the assumption that the collective creatures were trying an escape. He and Doc Chimp were flying down a corridor on the trail of a mixed mob of Purchased People and Sheliaks. It taxed all of Babylon's strength, but the chimpanzee was crooning to himself as he pulled them along the hoist-ropes with his powerful simian arms. "Died down there," he sobbed, half to himself, "going to die again! Oh, heaven help this poor old monkey in this terrible world—"

Babylon, panting, tried to reassure him: "But that's not true, Doc," he gasped. "You don't have to die again! Everything's changed now, don't you see?"

The chimp reached out with one long, black-furred arm and brought them to a jolting stop. "Changed?" he demanded, peering into Babylon's face. "You haven't been here very long, have you? Nothing changes! You just go on dying and dying! It's a pity us monkeys don't get manic depressive, because this is a great place for suicidal types—you get so many chances to act it out! I tell you, they're just going to decide to send down another party through the tachyon transfer, and somebody's sure to say let's take old Doc along, and—"

He stopped in midbreath. "Oh, Dr. Babylon!" he whispered softly. "The tachyon chamber. Of course! Come on!"

And, of course, he was right. In less than five minutes they were at the entrance to the tachyon-transport room, a long gaggle of beings trailing them in response to Doc Chimp's agitated yells, and at the door the chimpanzee brought them to a sharp stop. "There you are!" he whispered triumphantly. "You see?"

And, sure enough, there inside the chamber was a Sirian eye— perhaps the same renegade who had transported himself up from the catacombs—surrounded by a furious swarm of the steel-blue collective creatures. "What are they doing?" Babylon demanded.

"Can't tell," the chimp whispered, "but it looks as if they're pulling Purchased-People units out of the store. Only they're not here—"

But there was no more time for speculation; the rest of the lynch mob had caught up with them, and all beings together stormed into the chamber.

Jen Babylon had never seen one sentient being murder another before, but he saw it happen now. There was no stopping the furious mob. The Canopan was the first to die, and as he was struck down, bleeding a pumpkin-yellow ichor, the great equine skull crushed by a blow from a Scorpian, two Boaty-Bits flew out of the fleshy ruff that was its mane. They tried to join the rest of their swarm, but the swarm itself was disorganized, dying bit by bit as each one of them was struck by Sheliak tentacle, Sirian electric bolt or fist, hoof, horn, or whatever other striking appendage any being had. They died in the hundreds, silently at first. Then they swarmed together for a moment and buzzed fiercely, a screaming drone that the Pmals rendered as:

"Fools! You are doomed! Only collective intelligence will survive— and you will be part of it!"

And then they said nothing more. Not enough of them were left to make an articulate entity, and then there were none of them alive at all.

In Jen Babylon's mind there was room for just so many wonders, so long a list of concerns. His senses were saturated and his mind full; and yet something new was clamoring for attention. It took him a long moment to realize what it was.

The T'Worlie lay huddled and broken in a corner. Its wings fluttered feebly, and it exuded a sour, sick reek that grated on Babylon's senses.

"What's the matter?" he demanded, reaching out to the sad little shape. It drew away from his touch, and the odor changed to something like a wet seabeach back on Earth. Babylon looked up to Ben Pertin. "Something's wrong with the T'Worlie," he said.

The creature chirped feebly—more the rustle of a dying cricket than its normal bright sound. The Pmals did not respond at all. "He's in bad shape," Pertin said, his face drawn. "I've seen it before. T'Worlie aren't built for this sort of thing."

Babylon shook his head in puzzlement. "There was a lot of commotion," he said, "but I didn't see him get hurt." He stretched out a hand again, and the little creature shuddered.

"Correction," it chirped faintly. "Not hurt. Harmed."

Babylon nodded, thinking he had understood. "Well, hadn't we better get it to medical assistance?" he demanded, staring around the chamber. Most of the nonhuman beings were gone now, and only Pertin, Babylon, and the T'Worlie were left in the great chamber.

But the T'Worlie fluttered away. "Negative," it stated. "Harm not physical. Healing required not medical."

Pertin put his hand on Babylon's arm. "I told you," he snapped. "They can't handle this sort of violence, intelligent beings destroying one another—"

"I didn't care much for it myself!"

"No. Neither did I. But you and I can survive it, Jen, and I'm not sure Mimmie can." Pertin bent to look more closely at the little batlike being, and the T'Worlie spoke:

"Further correction. Can survive. Have been harmed most gravely. Require therapy."

"Therapy?" Pertin gazed up at Babylon and shook his head to show that he did not know any more than Babylon.

"Confirmation: therapy. Specific techniques necessary: healing constructive analysis and synthesis." The T'Worlie raised itself gently on filmy wings, as if it did not dare put too much strain on them. "Statement: Depart now for therapy. Will return."

The orbiter had become quieter, though wandering bands of beings still roamed its corridors, and Babylon had actually drifted off to sleep for a few moments when the T'Worlie returned. It seemed much more energetic and strong, and responded to Babylon's queries with confidence.

"Have completed therapy," it stated. "Data developed is of value."

"What data?" Babylon demanded, and listened while the T'Worlie explained what it had done.

And that was nothing more or less than to reason out the explanations of many of the mysteries that had perplexed them: The creature had locked itself in with FARLINK, seeking escape from the pain of seeing life violated on such a catastrophic scale. And it had come away with what it called a healing hypothesis.

"And what is that?" Babylon demanded.

"Hypothesis: Rings are monatomic structures, e.g., single atoms."

"Single atoms?" Babylon repeated, not comprehending.

"Confirmation. Data examined include reported examinations of individual rings and summarized results from all attempted investigations.

"Physical nature of rings has been unknown and perplexing. Observed sections are extremely thin horizontal rods supporting the entire surface structure of Cuckoo. These rods appear mirror-bright, reflecting all incident radiation unchanged. They are frictionless in motion and absolutely hard, unaffected in any observable way by applied forces. They are reported to be magnetic and superconducting —power required for the operation of Cuckoo is believed to be transmitted through them. No natural substance possesses such qualities, and the nature of the rings has remained a riddle, even to FARLINK."

"But you've solved the riddle?"

"Hypothesis: Rings are atoms—"

"Isn't everything?"

"Question irrelevant until you know hypothesis." A sharp ammonia scent reproved him. "Convergent evidence suggests high probability that each ring is a single atom. The nucleus is not a point but a phenomenon—"

But Babylon could not let him finish. "Did you say *a single atom?* That's ridiculous. Impossible! There must be something wrong with my Pmal."

"Negative. Translation accurate. Term 'single atom' correct."

"But it can't be!"

A whiff of orange-blossom amusement, fading fast as the still weak T'Worlie whispered, "Correction: Possibility exists. Evidence supports probability. Nucleus not a point but may be described as a phenomenon previously unknown. Term proposed for this is 'nuclear polymer.' Description: a chain of bound quarks maintaining a positive charge that hold a thick electronic sheath surrounding the chain. Such object would be friction-free and indefinitely strong, thus satisfying requirements observed."

Babylon's mind was spinning. He was no physicist, but he knew enough to be shocked at the notion of an atom of stellar size. "Is that possible, Mimmie?"

"Datum: The rings exist. Alternative hypotheses cannot account for them."

"But—" Babylon shook his head, trying to imagine a single atom stretched into a ring capable of orbiting a star. "But what's it made of?"

"Atomic structure of source material irrelevant to hypothesis. Possibly iron, which is a massive and strongly magnetic element, relatively common."

"How—" He blinked. "How could such things be made?"

"Hypothesis presents few clues. The process of creation must have required enormous mass, enormous energies, and the use of technologies ultimately advanced. Probably not explicable in context of known physics."

The T'Worlie fluttered suddenly closer, and he heard shouting and hissing and hooting in the corridor behind him as a last random fragment of the mob straggled across it.

"Forgive me." A whiff of something like ether. "My ethical trauma not yet entirely healed. I require additional intellectual therapy."

It was fluttering away.

"Mimmie, wait!" Babylon hushed his voice. "If you don't realize it, your life's in danger. I think you've really cracked the riddle of Cuckoo. You've got the secret we all came for. A precious secret, if you don't know that—which places you in more than merely mental danger. People—things—will kill you for it, if you aren't very careful."

"You misunderstand the nature of my psychic trauma if you term it merely mental." An ammoniac tang. "You should know that physical danger and physical death have never mattered to my people."

Yet it came back a little toward him.

"If you don't like violence," he muttered, "remember those plotters. Trying to blow up all Cuckoo!"

"If my hypothesis is valid, such plots can be forgotten." Its chirp seemed almost cheerful. "Known evidence indicates numerous past attempts to damage or destroy ring structure, which have always failed. Hypothesis suggests they will always fail."

"If the rings are atoms—" He frowned, trying to grasp that novel reality. "Some atoms aren't stable."

"Ring stability abundantly proven." The T'Worlie flitted closer, with a scent like hot asphalt. "Cuckoo is supported by several billion rings that have functioned for many million years with no evidence of any breakdown."

"Suppose the ring system collided with something?"

"Experiment untried. Hypothesis suggests rings might survive stresses even more extreme. If ring cores do consist of quarks arrayed in linear chain, protected by dense electronic sheath, known physics indicates that it would be literally unbreakable." A breath of oleander. "Superstructures supported by ring system, however, would not survive experiment."

"Literally?" He stared. "You mean to say the rings themselves can't be destroyed?"

"Conclusion unwarranted. Hypothesis implies that rings are vulnerable."

"To what?"

"To intelligent application of the same advanced science by which they were created. They are artifacts. Process of creation, however unknown, is irrelevant to hypothesis. In common experience, many processes can be reversed." With a burnt-toast scent of apology, it was gliding away.

"Care, Mimmie," he whispered after it. "Better not trust anybody. Your hypothesis could be true, but it could also get you killed. Maybe all of us."

SIXTEEN

Te'ehala Tupaia, paramount king-warrior of the forces of Free Polynesia, stumbled out of the tachyon-transmission chamber with his eyes downcast and his step shambling, carrying on the masquerade of a Purchased Person—

Into what?

He shouted in sudden rage and fear. Polynesian theology had no hell, but the missionaries had told him about theirs. Heat, noise, pain, bewilderment—had they been right? Was he in it?

Tupaia had no way of saying that this tachyon transfer was any worse than the earlier ones, for he had no memory that there had been any earlier; but he knew that this experience was gut-knottingly, mind-wrenchingly terrible. Everything was *wrong!* Even the man in front of him was wrong—was no longer the same man he had followed in the prisoners' file. Was no longer a human being at all! Tupaia stumbled in the queerly lit gravity of this awful place and crashed into him—or into *it.* Certainly this could not be a person! It was something queer, hideous, red-lit. It was a troubled dreamlike memory from childhood, for in the whiteskins' preprimary school there had been fairy-tale books, with goblins and elves. One of tiny Te'ehala's first shocks of betrayal had come when he learned that these creatures were lies. No such beings had ever existed—

But they did, and he was surrounded by them! The man ahead of him was now wearing the exact shape of a kobold—gnarly limbs, squat frame, craggy face. It was the most horrid creature Tupaia had ever seen, worse by far than the scuttling or writhing creatures at the bottom of his home lagoon, worse than a nightmare, for it bore human features. It turned toward him, and the eyes were the eyes of a person as vulnerable as Tupaia himself to shock and pain, as filled with terror;

it spoke, and the voice was the voice of a human being, bleating for help. It was a diabolical mixture of monster and man . . .

And so was Te'ehala Tupaia.

For he himself had been changed in the same way.

In that moment Tupaia nearly went mad.

He could find nothing familiar, nothing that related to any previous part of his existence. He was in a gnome's body, inhabiting a devil's cavern, surrounded by creatures queerer than any demons. He was seeing by a light that was redder than red—it stood in the same relation to red that indigo does to blue—and it had no source. He was on a balcony of sorts, and far below him was a tangle of machines and pipes, with queer figures scuttling around and over them. And he was surrounded by a sea of raucous sound, like the middle of an April typhoon, but deeper and slower. The other Purchased People, as shocked and maddened as himself, were milling around in disarray.

Then, above all the tumult, came a call in a crackly, raspy sort of language that, incredibly, Tupaia understood. "Purchased People!" it grated. "You have been selected for labor in edited form for purposes of scientific research!"

The creature speaking was more hideous that Tupaia itself; it was a thing like a great blood-red eye, glittering like a ruby, that hung above them. The enslaved kobolds fell silent and it continued: "Reimbursement will be made to your owners. You have been edited in a stress-resistant form capable of functioning readily in this environment, and given optical systems capable of seeing by the heat sources all around us, with language faculties adequate to understand our orders. You need no more!"

It paused, and crackling tendrils of electrostatic force leaped from its ruby surface to sting Tupaia and some of the nearest others. "You eight! Follow me! Your first task will be to ascertain what other members of our first party survived!"

Stumbling up a steep corridor, with the lash of the ruby eye's electrostatic lightnings to spur him and the others on, Tupaia felt his mind racing out of gear. He was staring around this hellish place in terror in one moment, in another reliving the days when he drove a bulldozer for the island's new airstrip to pay his college tuition, when he plucked red hibiscus for the tourists' breakfast tables, ran errands

at the Chinese store, lit spirals of pyrethrum to kill mosquitoes because a bug-zapper would not have looked authentic enough for the
hotel's whiteskin manager. Bug-zapper! Suddenly the parts of his
memories came together. All around them swarmed a huge cloud of
tiny beings, larger and faster than any mosquito and far more dangerous. Boaty-Bits, he knew.

And suddenly wondered how he knew. And that weird being with
the whip was a Sirian eye. Those other horrid beings had names too:
the great doughy creature inside a crystal shell was a Sheliak; the
clattering, hissing metal thing a Scorpian robot. But how did he know
that?

Although Tupaia knew something about tachyon transportation
because everyone did, he had had no direct experience of it—*this*
Tupaia had not—and little knowledge of its refinements. They had not
seemed relevant to the prime goal of freeing Polynesia from its whiteskin conquerors, nor had it been discussed in his school classes. "Editing" was a concept he grasped only dimly, and that more by seeing
what had happened to himself and the other Purchased People than
from any theoretical knowledge. He did not need to be told that he
had changed. His own hands, as they swung by his sides, testified to
that most inarguably. And he could not fail to know that he now had
faculties he had never owned before. He knew the names of these
outlandish beings. He seemed to understand every communication
addressed to him, in whatever language; he saw in colors he had never
seen before.

"Halt!" cried a voice—not a voice, but a rattling like drumbeats;
but Tupaia understood it, and knew that it came from the robot. The
grotesque gnomes stopped, whispering to each other; they had passed
through a vaulted chamber and were now on another balcony, higher
up. Tupaia edged away from the being that rattled and the being that
stung as they conferred, and found himself near a precariously low
railing, looking down on the immense cavern itself. Now he could see
that the things that scuttled around the machines and pipes were less
unfamiliar than anything else in this wholly alien place; they looked
exactly like the crystalline crabs that had begun to appear on Earth
before he was transported. What they were doing, he could not make
out. Repairing the machines? Perhaps so. A great plume of liquid was
arching slowly out of some ruptured pipe, breaking up into a sort of
rainbow spray, but the rainbow was made all of gradations of red,

from almost orange to that newer, deeper red that he had never seen before. As he watched the plume dwindled and stopped, and he saw that the crystal crabs were swarming over the place it had come from.

Over Tupaia's head the great ruddy eye dived past with a crackle of static electricity, and the Sheliak and the flying metal cube just behind. They plunged over the low railing and dropped like meteors to the far floor. They were after a huge translucent block with a keyboard at one edge. Something about the device troubled Tupaia—something not quite a memory, more than a dream—he could not pin it down. But the slave drivers had no doubts. Even at that great distance, even through the barrier of their queer shrieks and rattles, he could see that this object was something important to them.

Then the brief rest was over. The blood-red Sirian detached itself from the others and soared back up to the balcony, hovering just overhead. A sparkling sting jolted some of the kobolds to attention. "Here are your orders," the Sirian rasped. "You indicated ones will proceed up this corridor until you encounter living beings or their corpses. Survivors will then return to report. Move out!"

There seemed nothing threatening in the long, narrow corridor they moved through. Away from the cataclysmic environment of the great machine chamber, with its winking lights and scuttling, glassy crabs, the present tunnel seemed almost peaceful, and some of the other Purchased People began to speak almost normally among themselves. Tupaia disregarded them as a king-warrior should. He took the position at the front of the line as by right. No one argued. When he came to a gallery whose end disappeared in dimness, with branching corridors all along, he made the decision. "We will split up," he announced. "One of you go into each of these tunnels. I will proceed along the main passage."

There was a grumble from the other kobolds, but Tupaia paid no attention to that, either; except that when he had advanced a few score meters along the gallery he glanced covertly over his shoulder and was pleased to see that the others were no longer in sight. Perhaps they had followed his orders. Perhaps they had gone in a cluster into the first tunnel they saw, or even returned to the great cavern; it did not matter, what mattered was that Te'ehala Tupaia was alone and unsupervised.

How often he had dreamed of a chance like this!

But, now that he had it, was it real? Was there anywhere to escape to? And even if there was, how could he escape from the hideous shape these enemies had forced on him?

For almost the first time in his life, Te'ehala Tupaia, paramount king-warrior, began to doubt his destiny.

He slowed down, almost idling, glancing into each of the side tunnels as he passed, but there was no evident hope in any of them. The gallery was bare and empty, apart from Tupaia himself and a single insect—or, more likely, a Boaty-Bit from the swarm he had left behind him—that danced above and around before him like a silent sentry. Which perhaps it was, Tupaia thought gloomily; perhaps here too his freedom was only an illusion.

He stopped, aware that the Boaty-Bit's dancing had become agitated, and aware of something new. It was not a sight or a sound. It was an odor, of such choking foulness that his armored nostrils tried to close to keep it out.

He knew that stench, with the queer new knowledge that had been grafted into him in the editing; and he ran forward to peer into the next tunnel.

A Watcher! The name flashed into his mind, and with it the sudden internal warning: *Beware.* But the warning was too late; the creature rose up to confront him.

Tupaia had never imagined anything as repellent. It was crouching over a half-eaten corpse, he saw with disgust—a human corpse? At first flash he thought so, for it wore the rags of clothes; but it was too small to be an adult human being, too incongruously proportioned, with long, skinny arms—no. With only one long, skinny arm; because the Watcher was crunching the marrow from the severed other, which still retained rags of a once-gay scarlet and green jacket.

The creature fastened its great eyes on Te'ehala Tupaia and dropped the arm. With a hoarse, hooting roar, as powerful as the whistle of a tour liner at the docks of Papeete, it plunged toward him, black enormous ears cupped in his direction, bulging multiple eyes glaring horridly. Blood was dripping from its hideous beak.

The creature was incredibly fast. There was no time to react, and he was weaponless. Tupaia could see that the beak was powerful enough to crush even the leathery chitin that was now his skin, that the coarse, reptilian wings ended in strong talons, that in one of the writhing pink tendrils which served it for arms it held a huge-bladed knife. Any of those weapons would have been enough to kill him; but he could not move away.

What saved him was a sudden bass bellow—"Drop to the ground!" It came from an unseen tunnel to his side; and a great, bronzed figure leaped out. It carried a crude spear, lunging at the Watcher. The beast, disconcerted by the sudden attack, veered away, soared past Tupaia, and blundered on down the gallery.

But Tupaia did not even turn to look. Two things had driven his danger out of his mind. The first was that the shout had been in Polynesian.

The other was that the man who had driven off the Watcher, the golden-skinned giant who leaped out to save him, was himself. Scarred, limping, with a bloodied rag wrapped around one arm— nevertheless, the savior of Te'ehala Tupaia was Te'ehala Tupaia.

For Tupaia—for both Tupaias—the unexpected meeting was shocking in ways that went beyond even the terrible shocks intrinsic to the place and circumstances. The one saw himself hideously caricatured —squashed, wrinkled, hands like claws, armored eyes. The other saw the same powerful frame and flesh his mirror had always shown, but terribly torn.

The flesh Tupaia took a step forward, opened his mouth to speak— then grimaced and clutched his side. "You're hurt!" cried the kobold Tupaia, and his elder twin smiled faintly.

"Worse than hurt," he gasped. "That thing got me in the side, and the bleeding's started again. But what—how—why do you look the way you do?"

"Whiteskin treachery," the kobold said bitterly. "That's all I know." He glanced up sharply as the distant mad hooting of the Watcher sounded. "Is that thing likely to come back?"

His twin shrugged, then grimaced with the pain. "He'll be back when he gets hungry again, that is sure," he said grimly. "There are no other survivors." He swatted irritably at a silver-blue mote in the air, which turned and darted away. "Unless you count the Boaty-Bits, but the gods know what they're up to. They're no use even to the Watcher —he couldn't get a square meal out of them!"

The kobold Tupaia bent to his self's side, probing the wound while they exchanged stories; when he looked up his gnarled face was grim. "Don't say it, my brother," the flesh-and-blood one said softly.

"I don't know what you mean!" the kobold flared. "Come on! I'll help you down to where the others are. We'll get you medical attention—"

The flesh one laughed gently. "How hard it is to lie to yourself," he said. "We both know, Te'ehala Tupaia, that this Te'ehala Tupaia at least has not long to live."

"We don't know that unless we don't try!"

"We do know it. But, yes, we will go to where the others are, because there is no better choice. I could not find my way back to the surface—and they, at least, have a tachyon transporter. So perhaps one of us, at least, can both die and live." He cocked an ear to the hooting that sounded again. "Help me!" he commanded, and they limped back toward the larger gallery.

The kobold glanced once at the maimed body of the dead chimpanzee, then resolutely looked away. Even though the flesh Tupaia was grievously wounded, it was not hard to travel in that gentle gravity. They were through the gallery, and the sounds of machinery from the great, hot cavern were growing louder, when the kobold felt his wounded brother stiffen. He pulled away and tried to level the spear.

A figure stepped out of a tunnel to confront them. It was a tinier version of the kobold Tupaia's own armored shape, staring fearfully at them out of startlingly bright green eyes. "Please, mister," it begged, "don't hurt me! Put down that spear. I'm lost! My name is David Doy Gentry, and I don't know what's happened to me!"

The kobold Tupaia growled, "What the devil are you doing here?" But his other self put a hand on his shoulder.

"Don't you see the boy is terrified? Answer him, boy."

"I wish I could," David-the-kobold sobbed. "I just wanted to see what it was like inside the tachyon chamber. That's all! And then all of a sudden I was here with you other freaks, and—" He stopped, his hand to his mouth. "Oh, I didn't mean to hurt your feelings!"

"You didn't," the gnome Tupaia said angrily. "You were part of the group of Purchased People? A child?"

"I didn't mean to be," David apologized. "And then that ugly big red glass eyeball sent you others up that way, and the rest of us just stayed there. And then some of them came back with a bunch of those Boaty-Bit bug things, and all the freaks—I mean the *real* freaks, mister—anyway, they were talking together, and finally the eyeball thing told us that there weren't any survivors of any importance from the other expedition—whoever they were—and we were to move along. So they did. All of them except me. I hid. I didn't *like* that big eyeball!" He moved over to the railing of the balcony and looked down, nodding. "Yeah, you can see them now—they're down there in that other place, where they left all the bundles. I don't know what— oh, gosh! They're all jumping off the balcony!"

The kobold Tupaia leaped to the rail, peering over. It was true! One by one, the squat, tough Purchased People were launching themselves into the abyss, while the eyeball and the Sheliak and the Scorpian robot flew nearby, driving them on. The three on the upper ledge watched incredulously as the ugly gnome bodies fell in slow motion toward the distant bottom of the cavern. It looked suicidal. But the captors had made an elegant calculation of forces. In that weak gravity, the long fall was survivable—just. Each one in turn struck— struck hard, but not harder than their armored bodies could take. Each one stood up and waited, as the slave drivers gently dropped after them.

It was hard to see what the party was doing once they reached the bottom, since the ruptured pipe had laid a curtain of mist over much of the cavern. But they seemed to be loading up with burdens—that translucent block the biggest—then forming ranks and moving on.

The kobold Tupaia straightened up. "Now what? We can't stay here!"

The injured man shook his head. "Nor get back to the surface," he said. "We must follow them."

"No!" roared the kobold. "The boy and I could survive that fall— you could not!"

"There is no other choice," the wounded man pointed out. "And— have you forgotten, Te'ehala Tupaia, how strong Te'ehala Tupaia is? It is true that I am not at this moment at my strongest, but nevertheless we have no choice."

He broke off, for the mad hooting had sounded again, and this time very near.

The three on the ledge turned to meet the challenge, as the Watcher brayed once more and dived out of the tunnel at them. The kobold Tupaia shouted in rage; he was bare handed, and the slick red armor that covered the Watcher's belly was far too tough for him to harm. The boy shrank silently behind him; and the Tupaia of flesh, the only one armed at all, stumbled to the fore, slowly bringing the crude spear around. Grunting with pain, he stabbed it directly into the wide red mouth beneath the beak and was borne down in the monster's rush. Tupaia-as-kobold saw his chance. The Watcher shrieked in agony, and the grip of its slimy pink tendrils loosened on the knife; Tupaia/kobold snatched it away and plunged it into the glitter of the many-lensed green eye. The hard red belly armor smashed him down. The great wings folded in to trap him in their suffocating reek—

But there was no strength in them, and as Tupaia/kobold fought free of them he realized that the monster was dead. Gasping and retching, he thrust the stinking form away and saw it float down into the depths of the cavern. He shouted with exultation and turned to his flesh brother.

There was no answering shout.

The long beak had finished what the earlier wounds had begun. The kobold looked, sorrowing, at the great golden-skinned form of himself, still now in death, yet holding the broken spear.

The boy moved behind him, and reached to put his hand in Tupaia's, the bright green eyes sad in the comic gnome's face.

"I'm really sorry about your friend," he offered. And, a moment later, "What should we do now?"

Tupaia did not answer at once. He had no answer to give. He released the boy's hand and stepped forward to the low rail, peering down into the misty distances of the cavern. Most of the damage had been repaired by the hard-working crabs, and he could see that hordes of them were slowly removing broken beams and replacing them with new. The party of Purchased People with their bizarre captors was vanishing into another tunnel far away. He lowered his gaze and reached out to touch the calm brow of his dead other self.

What should they do now? What a good question that was!

Apart from the obvious practical problems, Tupaia discovered an internal problem. He was having a sort of crisis of conscience. He had always had strict priorities governing every act of his life—the cause first, himself second, every other claim on his loyalties far behind. But Free Polynesia was despairingly far away. And this child, this innocent victim—could Tupaia just walk away from his needs?

He could not. He took the boy's hand in his own again and said, "We'll follow the others. Far back, keeping out of sight. And then—"

But there was no way of finishing that sentence. "Let's go," he said instead. "Hold onto my hand. You can close your eyes if you want to."

And the two strange figures stepped off the rail into the immense abyss.

If the boy became a hindrance, Tupaia would abandon him. If the boy resisted, he would kill him. Tupaia's decision was clear and hard as the steel point of a javelin. And yet as time went on, and they went farther down and farther, the hard edges of the decision softened and receded into the background of his consciousness. The boy did not question. He obeyed every instruction Tupaia gave him; he followed without argument even when it was into a place, and through a means, terrifying even to Tupaia. The great leap into the cavern was not the last such jump they had to take, nor the worst. And still they went down and down and down.

They were lucky—in two ways they were lucky. The first was that the party they were following was heedless of pursuit; they left bits of wornout equipment, twice dead kobold-shapes, and very often there were bits of food in the trash. That heaviest of burdens, the somehow sinister translucent block, they did not leave behind. But everything else seemed expendable. So they were easy to follow, and their leavings helped keep the pair alive. The second bit of fortune was that their downward path passed now and then through caverns or wide galleries where things grew and even small animals moved about in the vegetation. Some were edible. Unfortunately, they could not know which until they tried, for city-bred David and island-born Tupaia had little experience of trying to live off the flora of a dozen different climates and environments. Appearances could not be trusted. In one rose-lit tunnel they found vines with a bright orange, fist-sized bud growing in profusion; they looked almost like rather misshapen papayas, and Tupaia plucked one in hope. It felt slightly warm, and the slick surface yielded a little, like a tightly inflated balloon. But a faint sweetish odor clung to his fingers, and he sliced into it with the broad knife that had once belonged to the Watcher.

The glowing orange skin yielded to the edge, then ruptured with a sharp *pop*. David cried out in alarm, as a puff of reddish vapor exploded toward Tupaia, almost like a spray of blood. The odor was strange and unpleasant—almost etherlike, edged with something sharply acrid. The vapor filled Tupaia's nose and lungs like the quick, hard rush of a narcotic; he flung the fruit away, but he was dizzy and trembling, and for the next hour and more it was the boy who guided Tupaia's steps, until the toxins worked their way out of his system. Eventually the gallery broadened and became distinctly warmer, and off to one side there was a tepid pool of water. They drank their fill. When they saw one of the great glassy crab shapes sidling along the bottom of the pool they ignored it; there were too many other worries and wonders, the glass crabs had lost their power to interest them.

And, after a brief rest, down, and down, and down.

Calculating from the point where they had fought the Watcher, Tupaia estimated they had traveled at least a dozen, perhaps twenty or more kilometers straight down on the trail of the Purchased People, twenty times that in horizontal tunnels and gradual declines. It was good that their edited bodies were tough and strong; even Tupaia's own huge frame would have been seriously taxed by these exertions, and the boy would surely have collapsed long before. They seemed to need far less food and water than before—another blessing, for sometimes those were scarce. They moved on, through odd, dome-shaped rooms, with incomprehensible metal rods glowing in dozens of hues, and skirted the edge of a vast vortex of water, slowly spinning and emptying itself into some unknown farther depth.

And, as time passed and they descended deeper and deeper into the unknown, Tupaia found himself beginning to care about the boy. Tupaia was in a turmoil of confusion in any case. Free Polynesia, which had been the core of his life, was now irrelevant. He was scared, and raging, and confused . . . but there was David, who needed him.

If someone gives you trust, it is hard not to try being trustworthy.

Another gallery, opening into still another great abyss. This one had no railings at all, though spikelike projections jutted from it over the yawning gulf. This one they did not dare jump; they skirted the edge and found a continuation of the downward trail.

A shallower jump—ten hours later—which left them on a broad, flat plain, with the ceiling a hundred meters overhead and palely glowing. "It looks like a farm," David whispered; and it did. Geometric patterns covered the wide space, in every shade of green and black and brown, of gold and red and orange; and indeed crops were growing there. Growing for whom? Tended by what? Tupaia could not guess; but the tubers at the base of the dark-green plants were good to eat, and pale yellow fruits in the adjoining plot relieved their thirst; and they went on.

And down.

And the air grew warmer.

It was nothing like the searing, steamy heat of the great machine cavern with the ruptured pipes. The levels they passed through now were gentle enough in climate; there was really no longer any need for them to wear the horrid gnome shapes. But, definitely, it was warmer. They dropped from another gallery onto another great, wide space, but this one was no farm. It was sheer, burnished metal, almost like a steely, oil-smooth sea that reflected a steely sky a hundred meters above. Now Tupaia saw what he had not seen earlier: rows of thin columns, widely spaced, that joined floor to ceiling. "It's like we were in one shell after another," David murmured, staring around. And Tupaia nodded; so it was. But shells of what?

At the end of the next passage that question, with all other theoretical questions, was driven from his mind.

David saw it first and cried out in alarm. Then Tupaia, close behind, saw it too: a heap of three more dead bodies. One was the gnome-shape that had once been a young, long-haired blond girl; one a middle-aged woman; and one not human at all. It was the Sheliak, its crystal shell long gone, its body now stretched and still in death.

"What—what could have happened, Mr. Tupaia?" the boy gasped.

Tupaia was silent for a moment, then met the boy's bright green eyes. "They killed each other in a fight. They're criminals, David," he said harshly. "Same as me."

"No! You told me what you did—you were fighting for a cause—"

"I thought I was," Tupaia agreed, "and I still think the whiteskins wronged my people. But these others—killers, most of them. Psychotic killers! When they were released from ownership I guess it was only a question of time." He turned over the girl's body with his foot, then hastily turned it back before the boy could see. One whole side of the face was a cinder; evidently the Sirian eye had been involved in the fight as well. "Two here," he muttered, "and four others that we've passed on the way. Probably some others dead, too, that we didn't see, or that wandered off. It's been an expensive trip."

The boy clutched his arm suddenly, and pointed at an opening just beyond a cluster of bright red metal columns. Tupaia could feel him shaking, but his voice was steady as he said: "Real expensive, Mr. Tupaia. There's some more!"

It wasn't just a few more; if the little group at the end of the passage had indicated a fight, this one showed pure massacre. There were more than a score of bodies—all human, this time—and most of them showing terrible burns. Tupaia shook his head. "Something set this off," he said. "I wish we knew what."

David looked up at him. "Should we go look?"

Tupaia shrugged. "We don't have a choice," he said, and heard the echo of his own voice saying the same thing, over and over. "Come on —but be careful!" he commanded and led the way past the heaps of corpses—

And brought up short.

They emerged onto another gallery, this one, it seemed, the last. For there below them was . . . empty space.

David cried out, and Tupaia caught the boy to him, staring incredulously. The next level was transparent, and below it nothing but a distant, far-down bright star. A sun! It was redder and brighter than Earth's could have been at such a distance, but unquestionably a star, trapped inside a great crystal shell, with all the rest of Cuckoo enveloping it in spherical layers.

Tupaia knew then what had driven the Purchased People over the edge of sanity; he felt his own threatened by a terrible vertigo and fear.

And a new fear added itself, for between the savage blaze of the trapped sun below and the shining metal roof above, something moved. The movement was a swarm of things, and Tupaia's first thought was that they were Boaty-Bits. But that was wrong. They were far too large, and even at great distance he could see that they possessed structure—wings and tails—Boaty-Bits were not like that. They were clustered around a distant structure like a bridge, narrow and unrailed. It leaped across that terrible gulf without cables or piers for support, and at the end of it a strange object hung. It was ball-shaped, and one hemisphere of it was mirror-bright, the other dead black. It looked almost like the sort of diagrams they had shown at the mission school to explain the Earth's day-night cycle, half sunlit and half in shadow. The black half was on top, the bright half beneath. It seemed to float above the center of that vast, glasslike floor, but he saw other bridges spun to it, far away and looking tiny as the threads of a spider's web. Things here had little weight; perhaps they were strong enough to hold it up. If those bridges were like a web, the queer ball hung upon them was like the spider's nest. Could there be some kind of spider-thing inside?

He shaded his eyes against the glare of the sun below to see the moving things. Watchers! Scores of them, an army. They were not flying. Ugly wings folded, they were creeping on their bellies across the bridge, as if stalking the great spider he imagined. One of them carried a clumsy-seeming, boxlike tachyonic transmitter strapped to its back. Something else was strange. Peering again, he saw that all their ugly heads were covered with queer, ill-fitting helmets. Looking at the head of the line, he saw that the leader was not a Watcher, but one of the hateful triangular things called deltaforms. It, too, was queerly helmeted.

In the vast space above them, insects were swarming—no, not insects; these were indeed Boaty-Bits. A nearer cloud of them swept toward Tupaia and the boy, attracted by David's cry. And beyond them Tupaia could see the Sirian eye and the Scorpian robot, floating over the great translucent block and the bodies of the remaining Purchased People.

"Oh, what's wrong with them, Mr. Tupaia?" the boy gasped. Tupaia could not answer. The koboldlike figures were strangely contorted, as if frozen in a rapturous convulsion; they seemed to have been caught in the middle of some terrible tetanic spasm.

But the Boaty-Bits were nearer. "They've seen us!" David gasped. "Mr. Tupaia, we'd better get out of here!"

Tupaia didn't answer. No answer was needed. He grasped the boy's hand and towed him, in great slow bounds, back into the tunnel, past the heaped corpses, back into the great wide gallery, past the riven form of the Sheliak, back along the wider passage—

And stopped short. Far down the passage other forms were approaching, great, hideous winged beasts that bore riders on their backs. He groaned in frustration, as David made an inarticulate sound and jerked his hand from Tupaia's. "David!" the kobold cried. "Come back! We'll look for another tunnel—"

But it was too late. The boy was running down the passage toward the great flying beasts; and as he neared them the one in the lead stopped, with a flurry of wings. A woman seated behind the rider slipped off, an incredibly tall, lean woman; and David ran up to her, crying, "Mama!"

SEVENTEEN

Living with the Kooks was more tedious than frightening, but it was frightening, too. There were at least ten of the giant glassy crabs, as well as countless smaller ones, down to the size of a quarter. The crabs seldom slept. There was never a time when one of the big ones was not near Jen Babylon. He thought of them as his guards; no other term fit them, although they presumably had other functions, too, since they could not have been stationed there simply on the chance that he might arrive. But they guarded him. If Babylon wandered too near an outside door, one of them scuttled between him and it. If Babylon got in the way of something that was going on, one of them warned him off, talking to him in that curious, tape-recorded manner of speech that they possessed, or simply rose up silently before him. Which was warning enough. He was never harmed, or even touched, but the message was clear. As a linguist, he could not help observing their strange speech patterns. Puzzling at first, they became clear in a burst of comprehension. The crabs simply copied words spoken to them! Somewhere, inside their arthropod bodies there was an information-processor not unlike a Pmal. The more language they heard, the more they could repeat and use. The larger ones spoke in almost normal vocabularies, though stiltedly; the smallest ones seemed to have to learn as they went along.

There were at least half a dozen human Kooks—if you could call them human! If they would stay still long enough to be counted! They were not kept prisoner in the apartment, like Babylon. They came and went freely on mysterious errands, and on some not so mysterious. Some of them left bearing little packets of what looked like diamond dust—he did not at first see where it came from—and returned hours later, if they returned, usually with shopping bags full of food, sometimes with what looked like simple trash scavenged at random. The scrap went into the bathtubs of the joined apartments—bits of iron, chunks of rock, shards of broken glass, odds and ends of unidentifiable debris. (So much for bathing! Which accounted, partly at least, for the way the human Kooks smelled.) The food became the diet for the humans in the apartments—weird mixtures of things like lettuce and honey, eels and carrots stewed together; the tastes were indescribable and sometimes awful, but the Kooks did not seem to care, and Babylon's complaints were laughed at. Or, more often, ignored. At odd intervals throughout the day an old-fashioned electric alarm clock would go off and the Kooks would stop whatever they were doing to prostrate themselves, chanting, before the larger crabs—which seemed, if anything, amused, if you could be sure of detecting amusement in a glass crustacean.

"Why can't I leave?" Babylon demanded, and Sheryl placed her hand over his.

"You aren't one of us," she said with tender reproach.

"I don't want to be one of you! I just want to go back to my life."

"We must all do what Cuckoo gives us to do," she told him seriously. "Let your soul open to the Savior and Destroyer, Jen, hon! You will find such peace!"

He sighed. He had not been able to get a rational word out of her. "What I really want," he said bitterly, "outside of getting out of here, is a bath."

She laughed sweetly. "That's not possible just now, Jen."

"Then I want to go to sleep," he muttered.

"Of course! I, too. Come along, hon." And she led him into one of the bedrooms. There were twin beds, and each of them was occupied by two Kooks, lying on bare mattresses with an old army blanket pulled over them. There was a strange bulge in the middle of each bed. Sheryl leaned over the couple in the nearest bed and whispered softly to them. They woke instantly, smiling, and threw off the blanket. They rose from the bed, genuflected to the single crab that crouched on the dresser, and left the room. "Time for bed," Sheryl whispered tenderly. "Come on, Jen, hon!"

For a startled moment Babylon felt a quick priapic shock; but he had mistaken her meaning. This was no invitation to the sort of bedding they had shared so often before. Even if she had wanted that —with the two other Kooks snorting gently in their sleep in the next

bed and the glassy crab clattering softly as it stirred on the chest—
there was an obstacle. The lump in the center of the bed revealed itself
as a prim reminder of old New England. A bundling board! It was an
old ironing board, really, with the legs snapped off; but as Sheryl got in
on one side she propped it between them as she held the blanket for
Babylon to climb in on the other.

"Good God," said Babylon, "is that thing necessary?"

"It's better to have it, hon," she whispered soothingly. "Hush,
though! Please don't wake the others."

"Better how?" he demanded, but obediently lowering his voice as
he slipped under the blanket.

She closed her eyes and spoke dreamily. "It is a symbol, hon. Sex is
over. Reproduction is over. We are fulfilling our vow to Cuckoo the
Savior and Destroyer."

"And what's the vow, exactly?"

She said with pride, "We are voluntarily becoming extinct! When
Cuckoo comes, the worlds awaiting him will be nice and clean—and
empty! And, oh, what bliss for our Galaxy to serve him in such a
way!"

When Jen awoke it was daybreak, and Sheryl was gone. Her place
in the bed was taken by a short, dark man with a beard, snoring away.
Babylon lay there, trying to reconcile the queer turn his life had taken
with the almost as queer dreams that had disturbed his night—sexual
dreams, with the smell of Sheryl in his nostrils; imprisonment dreams,
perhaps sparked by his captivity, perhaps by the bundling board that
kept him from his lover—or former lover; strange dreams of vacant
worlds waiting a redeemer. He lay with his eyes tight shut, contem-
plating the dream worlds. They all had sensible roots in reality—all
but one. What to make of that dream, so vivid, so frightening for
reasons he could not identify, of a great jewel-studded chamber with
glowing walls, where something terrible was happening?

He shook his head, opened his eyes, got up, and examined what was
for breakfast. It appeared to be a soup of uncleaned spinach and
unshelled shrimp; he shuddered and turned away. He could not eat
that, so early in the morning.

Which left him with nothing to do at all. Sheryl was not in either of
the apartments at that moment. None of the other Kooks seemed

disposed to conversation. He prowled the rooms, dodging crystal crustaceans and flesh-and-blood Kooks with equal repugnance, and finally settled on a window with bright morning sun coming in, where at least he could gaze on freedom.

Although the building Sheryl lived in was not very old, it was in Boston. Therefore it was preserved, though centuries past its prime. It looked out on the sort of backyard Boston tenements had had since the early days of electricity, rectangular plots, each with its postage-stamp square of grass and its scattered, sickly shrubs and its ailanthus tree. And, across the garden, ancient Irishtown flats, also preserved. "Historical landmarks," they were called.

They were not beautiful. But Jen Babylon sighed, wiped his glasses and replaced them to stare at the buildings with longing. The roof of the nearest of them was no more than a meter from the little balcony outside the apartment window. An easy jump . . .

An impossible jump. Impossible, because every square centimeter of that balcony was occupied. The entire floor surface was filled with crabs, small ones, torpid in the Boston sun—such as the Boston sun was. But such as it was they seemed to need it. They spent every sunlit hour soaking up radiation. When the shadows shifted to darken the little balcony they would scratch and clatter their way back into the already crowded apartments to cluster around the electric heaters that were kept going day and night. Babylon found himself sweating and begged relief of one of the Kooks, without result. The gaunt old lady he addressed merely told him—very sweetly!—that this small discomfort was a tiny price to pay in the service of the Savior and Destroyer.

He tried again with Sheryl, when she came back into the apartment with one of those loads of miscellaneous trash, and she listened, vaguely sympathetic, but gave him the same patient answer. "But *why?*" he demanded. "Don't we smell bad enough already without making us sweat?"

She laughed sweetly. "It's for our brothers and sisters, the Lambs of the Maid," she explained, nodding lovingly toward the nearest of the crystal crabs. "They have to have thermal radiation to survive. That's why they were sent first to the tropics, where they do really well—here not so well," she said sadly. But then brightened. "But look, hon! I know you don't like our food, so I got you a special treat!" And she pulled out of the shopping sack a six-pack of peanut butter and cheese crackers.

He turned away—but then reconsidered and took it.

He could not even use the shower for relief, for the bathtubs were filled with the dirty, debris-strewn water he was forbidden to disturb. So he stared longingly out of the window most of the time, and pondered schemes. When all the crabs came inside for warmth . . . When, somehow, they forgot to lock the window one time . . . When everyone was asleep at once . . .

But there were no such times.

Apart from that, he was fed when he needed it, allowed to talk to the human Kooks when he was inoffensive in what he said, given as much room to fall down in as anyone else . . . until the time when Sheryl answered a coded knock at the door of the smaller apartment, murmured briefly to someone inside, and then came to his window to call him. "Jen, hon! Come and see! We've got company!"

As he started to turn he hesitated, his eyes fixed on the rooftop next door.

A moment later he said, as calmly as he could with his heart thundering in his ears, "All right, Sheryl, I'm coming." And he resolutely did not look toward the window again, though it took all his strength to keep from smashing it open to shout at the figure he had barely glimpsed, peeping from behind a pigeon roost, with its fingers to its lips.

It had looked very much like Ben Pertin.

Sheryl's surprise was the Crystal Maid herself, the same one Babylon had seen on the beach at Moaréa, and she was not alone.

She laid her hand on the shoulder of the giant who entered with her and spoke in slow, chiming tones, which sounded like snippets from an artificially generated speech program. "This man is to be . . . treated . . . as a full and equal . . . comrade among us." She turned her diamond eyes on Babylon. "Why is this . . . person . . . here?" she demanded.

Sheryl apologized quickly, "He came looking for me, and I didn't know what else to do with him. He can't get away."

The Maid seemed to meditate for a moment. "I . . . know this person," she announced. She stared at him for a moment longer, then dismissed him. "He may remain. Now . . . I wish to see . . . the Lambs!"

Babylon's eyes were studying the man who had come in with her. He was tall, bronzed, with wide shoulders; he towered over everyone else in the room, and Babylon recognized him. Of course! He had seen that bronzed face on the news stereo often enough, had even seen him in person, with the other convicts at the Tachyon Base. Te'ehala Tupaia! The mad revolutionary who had been captured while he was still in Polynesia!

Tupaia seemed to have come down in the world, for now he appeared to be a slave to the Crystal Maid. He came in burdened with shopping bags obviously strained to capacity. They proved to be full not of food but of sand, salt, pieces of scrap metal. A couple of the largest crabs reared up and took them from him, and Tupaia turned to look contemptuously at his surroundings and at Babylon.

The entrance of the Maid had produced a great stir, with all the humans abasing themselves to her and even the crabs seeming to genuflect briefly before taking the materials from Tupaia and clattering off to the bathrooms with them. When the Maid had completed her inspection, she summoned all the human Kooks to one room and closed the door, leaving Babylon with Tupaia and two great guardian crabs. The Polynesian paid no attention to them. He turned away from Babylon and found himself a plate of the greasy stew the occupants of the apartment had been preparing—lentils and salt pork, with what seemed to be turnip greens floating in it—and began to devour it.

Babylon approached him. "They haven't been feeding you much, have they?" he offered, staring at the gaunt cheeks.

The giant glowered at him for a moment without answering, but finally he shrugged and nodded, his mouth full. When he had stuffed a full kilo of the mess down his huge throat he was even willing to talk. Not out of friendship, surely; mostly out of disdain. Only when Babylon asked about the look he had intercepted in the Tachyon Base did he pause to laugh. "It is true," the giant said contemptuously. "I was not as the others! I am Te'ehala Tupaia, paramount king-warrior of the forces of *Polynésie-libre,* and not a common convict." Evidently, Babylon discovered as the giant boasted on, Tupaia's distant owner had either died or lost interest, and the slave had found himself free. But only relatively free. If he was not dominated by the master within his mind, he had remained a prisoner all the same—until in the confusion of the Kook demonstration at his hearing he had managed to break free. Since then he and the Crystal Maid had been running strange errands, skulking and hiding by night. The Maid, said Tupaia, for the first time subdued, seemed to have much manna.

Babylon coughed and ventured, "But do you, ah, *believe* in all this stuff about Cuckoo the Savior and Destroyer?"

Tupaia grimaced. "I do not invest belief in the doings of white-skins," he said, and would say no more.

The conference in the bedroom was over, and Sheryl came out to supervise what the crabs were doing. Babylon followed, peering over her shoulder, and at last the purpose of those stagnating pools of trash and water in the bathtubs became clear. The crabs, with help from some of the Kooks, patiently fished out all the larger, undissolved bits of debris. Then, gently and carefully, they sieved out of the murky stew what seemed to be thousands of tiny new crabs! The larger ones carried the infants to the balcony and placed them in the sunlight, then refilled the tubs with the litter of rock and sand and metal and ran water to cover them.

Then, lining up like a students' queue at the registrar's office, the crabs did the strangest thing of all. One by one the largest ones came to Sheryl, who patiently began stroking their undersides—like a milk-maid, Babylon thought—catching in a bowl a fine rain of diamond dust from each. When she had finished her chore she packed some of the dust into little plastic bags and handed them to Tupaia, who silently stowed them away in the shabby shopping bags. The rest she sifted meticulously into the tubs. Then she rose from the side of the tub, sighing as she stretched her cramped leg muscles, and caught sight of Babylon gawking incredulously. "Oh, Jen, isn't it wonder-ful?" she said, glowing. "In just a few days there will be thousands of others to distribute around the city!"

"Thousands of, for God's sake, *what?*"

"Why, of Cuckoo's dear Lambs, of course," she explained. "We hatch them here, because it's so unpleasant for them out in the open, this far north. Then we release them. Or the Maid spreads the seeds in the water—along the Charles, down by the Bay, in the park ponds, anywhere where there's water and sunlight and minerals to make their beautiful bodies. But there's not a lot of sunlight in Boston," she said regretfully. "So some of the poor darlings that try to grow in the river just don't make it. But the ones we grow here—ah, they're perfect!"

She patted Babylon's cheek gently, and then ran to answer a knock at the door. "Oh, you're here!" she cried joyfully. It was one of the skinny, bearded, filthy Kooks, and he was incongruously carrying a box and packages from Filene's department store. Sheryl set them on a table and began opening them eagerly. For a moment she looked like the old Sheryl, thrilled with new clothes, excited by cosmetics. But it turned out the finery was not for her. Some of the clothes were a man's, in giant sizes, for Te'ehala Tupaia. The rest were for the Crystal Maid, and so were all the cosmetics.

Sheryl caught sight of Babylon's gaze and shook her head ruefully. "Isn't it a pity to cover up that beautiful person?" she asked. "But she's so conspicuous, you see, and this way she'll be able to move around the city on Cuckoo's work without attracting so much attention. —Now excuse me, hon, but I'd better get to it!"

Pancake makeup, covered by blusher and powder; eye shadow and mascara; when Sheryl was finished the Crystal Maid was crystal no longer. She looked, if anything, like a bartop dancer in a Combat Zone honky-tonk—but at least she did not look like the alien creature she was. And she and Tupaia—now resplendent in conservative flamingo-pink tunic and slacks, with dark glasses and a jaunty beret—took up the sacks of demon seed and went out.

As soon as the door was closed, the tempo in the apartments slowed down appreciably. Sheryl slumped down on the shabby living-room armchair, exhausted. "Wow," she said, fanning herself, "it's so *good* to work so hard for Cuckoo!"

She paused in fanning herself and looked critically at Babylon. "What's the matter, hon?" she asked.

Babylon shifted position morosely. "Are you sure you know what you're doing, Sheryl?"

"Of course I do! Hon, I wish I could make you understand. *They* are the true inheritors of Cuckoo. Everything we do is for them and HIM!"

"You mean the crabs?"

"The Lambs of Cuckoo, hon," she corrected gently.

"Queer-looking lambs! And what about that criminal—is he a lamb, too?"

She shrugged patiently. "Mr. Tupaia is merely an instrument the Maid uses. He doesn't matter. Even the Maid doesn't matter, really— I mean, not in herself. She's merely an edited version of the Lambs herself, you know. Designed to be able to move around more freely in human society than they could—although if it hadn't been for my idea about the makeup," she added proudly, "it wouldn't work so well! Apart from that, there's nothing for her here on dismal old Earth—not with the human race as rotten with disbelief as it is! Even ourselves, really," she added thoughtfully. "Sometimes I wish we were more worthy—"

The skinny old Kook with the beard standing near, came nearer still and scowled at her. "Fine talk!" he barked. "Are you weakening in your faith, Sheryl?"

"Of course not!" she flared. And then, repentantly, "But we all need to reinforce ourselves all the time, don't we? Come! Let's reconsecrate ourselves and worship!"

And she dragged Babylon down on his knees next to her, as she fell to the floor.

All around them the other Kooks were falling to an attitude of prayer, their faces enraptured. "Oh, glorious Cuckoo!" Sheryl cried strongly. "Sacred redeemer! Heavenly visitor! Our Savior and Destroyer, we give you our worship and our love! Let your coming be soon—if it please you—and let us go content into the darkness eternal, fulfilled in the knowledge that we have made way for your coming—"

She didn't stop. She was interrupted. There was a sudden peremptory banging at the door, and a man's voice from outside bawled hoarsely, "Militia! Open up! In the name of the law!"

But the police did not wait for their orders to be obeyed. There was a rending crash, and the door was battered down. In flooded a mass of armed men and women, thick clubs in their hands, flailing at the crabs that failed to get out of their way.

Babylon was the first one out, helped by a husky militiawoman, stumbling down the fire stairs and into the street. "You all right?" she demanded, and turned to race back into the building without waiting for an answer. Babylon turned, blinking in the afternoon sunlight. The street was filled. Half a dozen militia hovervans purred in the roadway, on the sidewalks, wherever they had come to rest, while curious onlookers laughed and pointed as, one by one, the Kooks were dragged through the doorway.

And Ben Pertin, grinning broadly, squeezed through the police lines and came up to him. "I thought it was about time we got you out of there," he said. "Don't thank me, Jen. I'm just paying back what I owe you."

Babylon said from the heart, "Well, I do thank you. I was going crazy in there."

"I figured," Pertin said modestly, and they paused as the militia led Sheryl, sobbing, into one of the vans. She caught Babylon's eye and turned away. For some reason she made him feel guilty.

"Too bad about your girlfriend," Pertin observed philosophically, "but I guess you'd have to say she brought it on herself."

"What will they do with her?"

"Oh, nothing too serious, I guess—probably. Unless you want to press kidnaping charges?"

"No, no!"

"I didn't think so. But I could tell from the way you looked you didn't want to be there, and when I saw those damn animals all around you— Well. You probably want to know how I found you."

"I sure do."

Pertin's expression was filled with self-satisfaction. "I went to the university to talk to you about . . . something." He hesitated. "Well, to tell you that things weren't working out for me. I found they're pretty worried about you. Especially that little girl, Althea. The cute graduate student? Anyway, she told me you'd been talking about Sheryl, so I came to take a look, and I listened at the door, and then I thought I'd better reconnoiter a little before I knocked and maybe got grabbed myself!" He stepped aside, wrinkling his nose as the dirty old man with the beard came out, swearing furiously at the militiaman holding him. "I had a little trouble at first getting the militia to act," he complained, "but of course they don't like Kooks. Or those crabs, either. They wouldn't accept my theory you'd been kidnaped, but after a while they figured out a crime that had been committed." He grinned. " 'Keeping dangerous animals in a populated area,' it's called. That was all they needed." He paused, and added, "She's real pretty, isn't she?"

"Who, Althea? I thought Zara Doy Gentry was the only woman who interested you in the whole Galaxy!"

Ben looked shamefaced. "Aw—I went to see her, but she just laughed me off. Hell with her. Now, that Althea—"

For the first time in days, Babylon laughed out loud. "Spare me," he said, turning to watch the militia as they came out with body bags made of tough netting, each one containing the squirming, clattering body of one of the larger crabs. Two others were staggering with a huge sack containing scores of the smaller ones. Babylon wondered what they would do with the creatures and, queerly, almost felt concern. After all, the crabs had not actually hurt him. Or anyone else, as far as he knew; they had not even defended themselves against the clubs of the militia, simply tried to get out of the way.

Babylon said, "Well, thanks again, Ben. I guess I'd better get back to the school to set their minds at ease. And I wanted—I mean, that other 'I' on Cuckoo wanted—some linguistic data from me. He's probably—that is, I'm probably—getting pretty impatient."

Pertin's expression was suddenly tense. "Oh, of course," he said. "You couldn't know what's happened."

"What?"

Pertin shook his head fretfully. "God knows," he said moodily. "But Tachyon Base announced that all communication with Cuckoo has been cut. Terminated. The fault's at the originating station. No signals are coming in. The orbiter may have been destroyed, Jen, and what's become of the you and the me that's there, I can't even guess."

"I wish—" Babylon began, but what he wished was drowned out by a hissing, chittering sound that sprang from nowhere, seemed to come from everywhere, grew in volume—and then abruptly cut off. The human voice of one of the militiamen rose in the silence:

"The crabs! They're having a fit!"

It was the crabs—all of them—but it wasn't just the crabs. The human voices of the Kooks in custody had risen in hysteria, in the same way, and in the same way cut off. Babylon and Pertin were surrounded by stacked crabs in their mesh body bags, all writhing spasmodically, convulsively—and then, all at once, they stopped, rigid in tetanic spasm.

There was silence. Then Babylon said wonderingly, "What was that all about?"

But Pertin was pointing at the hovervan Sheryl had been taken into. She was pressed against the bars, rapt, arms outflung, eyes to the sky. She held that painful, precarious pose for a long moment.

Then she shouted something unintelligible.

Pertin and Babylon looked at each other questioningly, then Babylon shook his head. "I didn't understand," he began to say; and then Sheryl repeated it, louder than before and clearer:

"HE is waking!"

EIGHTEEN

The ancient history of the human race was scarred with endless examples of genocides, witch hunts, and pogroms. Nero's Romans hunting down Christians as scapegoats for the burning of Rome, Europe's Christians ferreting out Jews to revenge the onslaught of plagues—Cossacks and Ayatollahs, Papal troops annihilating Catharists, Boston zealots burning sick old women at the stake—the story of humanity was blotched with unsavory episodes of persecution.

But those were history! Ugly pages but forgotten ones, relics of a shameful past—and yet, on the orbiter, the purges and pogroms were being echoed with terrifying fidelity, as the shocked and vengeful inhabitants sought out their betrayers.

Of the three hundred eighty-six beings on the orbiter, collective entities like the Boaty-Bits not counted, no fewer than fifty-four were found to be part of the conspiracy. Two Scorpian robots, four Canopans—not counting the dead one. Eight Sirians, a dozen Sheliaks, nearly all the deltaforms, and one or two each from dozens of other races. No T'Worlie was part of it. Neither was any human, apart from the Purchased People. And no race was completely corrupted but one. The Boaty-Bits were one hundred percent among the forces of destruction. Two big swarms of them were destroyed, then only isolated members were seen, then none at all. "They're hiding," Doc Chimp whimpered, as he and Jen Babylon retreated from the scene where a furious Sheliak was methodically cremating the last scattered individuals of one swarm with his electrostatic whips. "Oh, they're mean ones, Dr. Babylon!"

Babylon demanded, "But *why?* What are they doing it for?"

The chimpanzee stared at him morosely, scratching his jaw with long, black fingers. "Seems to me if we wanted to know that we'd have had to keep a couple of them alive to ask."

"I don't mean just the Boaty-Bits, I mean everything that's been going on. All this strife and working at cross-purposes—from what you and Ben have told me, it's been like that almost from the orbiter's first days!"

The chimp was silent for a moment. Then he sighed. "Oh, even before that, Dr. Babylon. Back on the ship—back on Sun One—" He shook his head. "It's been a mortal long time that people have been betraying and hating each other, Dr. Babylon."

"I'm talking about here and now, and the Boaty-Bits!"

Doc Chimp nodded somberly. "They're the villains this time, no doubt about that. Maybe we should've guessed long ago—'course, we didn't really know they could take over other beings the way they do . . . But they're collective beings, Dr. Babylon. They don't think like the rest of us, and they don't much like us. Noncollective beings are too prone to individual aberration, as they call it. So they've been taking over individuals—the ones that were halfway rotten already, I expect, like the Sheliaks and the deltaforms, most of them—"

"That doesn't tell me *why!*" The chimpanzee shrugged his narrow shoulders without answering. "I can't believe that one single race could prevail against the entire Galaxy!"

Doc Chimp said, "No, and nobody else did, either—else we might have done something about it. Maybe they're not just one single race, though. Org Rider thinks there's something beyond them—"

"Org Rider!" Babylon cried. "That's another thing! I haven't seen him or Zara since—since I don't know when, since before we found out about the Boaty-Bits, anyway. Where are they?"

The chimpanzee licked his narrow lips, peering fearfully at Babylon. "Could you please ask Ben that question, not me?" he pleaded. "It's a kind of a—well, a secret, Dr. Babylon. I know Ben would tell you, but I promised."

"Oh, for God's sake! Now what?"

The chimpanzee was obdurate, though intimidated. "Please! It's just—well, Ben can explain everything. He's scared the Boaty-Bits might be anywhere, just one of them, you know, that might hear something and go back and tell the others."

Babylon said furiously, "They're only little bugs, Doc! They're not gods!"

"Oh, don't say that, Dr. Babylon," the chimp said earnestly. "They're pretty special! One or two of them are nothing at all. But put a few hundred of them together and you've got the beginnings of intelligence. A couple of thousand, like the swarms we've had here on the orbiter, and there's a collective being as smart as you and me!" He laughed sourly. "And none of us was smart enough to take the next step. Ten thousand of them, a hundred thousand—Dr. Babylon, can you imagine what a *million* of them would be like? Why, I'm surprised they didn't just take us over, long ago! The more of them there are, the smarter and stronger they are—and there's just nothing we can do about it!"

Babylon nodded, beginning to appreciate what a powerful foe they had in the Boaty-Bits.

He did not yet know how drastically he had undervalued them.

Ben Pertin was in his room, and not alone. Babylon pushed through the door, and stopped short. Hanging just before his eyes was the T'Worlie, its butterfly wings waving like gentle palm fronds to support its body. "Mimmie," he said. "Are you all right now?"

"Statement: Physically well, emotionally satisfactory." The five bright eyes peered at him with humor. "Query: Are you well?"

"I'm angry," Babylon growled, peering around the room. "You, Pertin! What's the secret now? Where are Zara and Org Rider?"

Pertin snapped back, "Close the door, you idiot! Do you want the whole orbiter to hear you?" And then, when the room was secure again, he smiled with a look of silky self-satisfaction. "I got ahead of them for once," he boasted.

"How? Who are 'them'?"

Pertin said gravely, "Everybody who is not in this room, I think." He nodded toward his companions—the T'Worlie, the silvery girl, and Doris. "We can talk in front of these three, so I can tell you that Zara and Org Rider are on their way home!"

"Home?"

Pertin smiled indulgently. "Oh, not the Earth. Org Rider's home." He gestured at the mural above his head of the huge mountain, and added in a superior tone, "If you'd studied the maps you would know that Knife-in-the-Sky is not much more than a thousand kilometers from that temple by the lake—right next door, by Cuckoo standards!"

Babylon controlled his irritation as best he could, but there was an edge on his voice as he said: "Ben, I really do advise you to give me a straight answer. *Why?*"

Pertin seemed to shrink before his friend's anger. In a much more subdued way, he said quickly: "They're getting orgs, Jen. If you remember what those tunnels looked like, they're a long, slow hike on foot—but they're mostly pretty high and wide. An org can fly them at least ten times as fast as the party did with the Purchased People walking every step." He hesitated, then offered, "I, uh, I thought we ought to follow them, Jen."

There was a squeak from Doc Chimp but Babylon didn't even look at him. "Follow them?"

"Well, somebody has to, don't they? Org Rider and Zara went by lander—I wanted them to use tachyon transport, but Org Rider has some silly superstitious objections to it—and they'll meet us at the temple. With extra orgs, enough for all of us. Then we can just get on the orgs and—oh, dammit, Doc, what is it?"

The chimpanzee had been trying hesitantly to attract his attention. "Ben, who's 'us'? Do you mean me, too? And if you do, did you forget that that terrible beast has already killed me once down there?"

Pertin shrugged irritably. "We'll go armed," he said impatiently. "We'll go by tachyon transport, so we'll be there before Org Rider and Zara—"

"Oh, no, we won't," Doc Chimp declared, pulling his leathery lips back in a scowl that bared his long yellow teeth. "Org Rider's not the only primate that has objections to tachyon transport, and with me it isn't superstition! I've been killed often enough! I don't want to be killed anymore."

"Then we'll go without you!" Pertin snapped. "Well, Jen? What about it?"

Babylon temporized. "What about the others?" he demanded, and the Purchased Person, Doris, spoke in her slow, unearthly voice:

"This one has already concurred."

Babylon looked at the winged silvery girl, who met his gaze out of her calm, bright eyes. Her voice was like the sound of chimes as she answered: "I wish to go. I do not require an org to fly."

Which left only the T'Worlie.

The little bat-butterfly of a creature had been floating silently over

Pertin's head, listening without saying a word. Now it spoke, and the Pmal gave its answer.

"Statement. Concur in desirability of proposal, express willingness to participate. Query: Is amplification or explanation desired?"

"My God, yes!" Babylon exploded.

The T'Worlie exuded its sour-lemon smell of amusement. "Following is a synoptic series of statements and conclusions. Probability estimates vary, but in general exceed point-nine. First statement. At some time *t* certain species, primarily the so-called Boaty-Bits, but with the assistance of individuals of eight other races of beings—"

Babylon groaned internally; you should *never* ask a T'Worlie to explain or amplify! But once started, the little being moved on implacably through the entire history of the events on, in, and around Cuckoo: the private tachyon transporter that the rebels smuggled aboard and used without authorization; the private control mechanism they seemed to have developed for Purchased People, perhaps a hidden power of the Boaty-Bits; the expedition; the damage to the interior of Cuckoo; the fighting far under the surface of Cuckoo; the revelation that Cuckoo itself was an artifact . . . It went on endlessly; or so nearly endlessly that Babylon was astonished when at last the T'Worlie fell silent. "Well," he said quickly, "thank you for—"

But the T'Worlie had merely paused, it appeared, for dramatic effect. It squeaked on, and the Pmal drowned out Babylon's attempt to intervene:

"In consideration of foregoing evidence, in conjunction with other data not now specified, certain hypotheses may be offered for testing. These have been received or deduced by me as part of my necessary regimen of rational self-therapy. In this process I was aided by certain other beings, including many T'Worlie and the Purchased Person known as Doris—"

"Doris? You?" Babylon interrupted, staring at the girl. Something not human stared back at him out of her eyes, but she only said:

"It is necessary that you receive the data the T'Worlie is now offering you."

"Continuation," the T'Worlie said sharply, with a burnt-sugar scent for emphasis. "Also assistance from FARLINK and from the hexagons secured from the wrecked orbital vessel. Central conclusion:

Entire ring system, and therefore existence of object Cuckoo itself, is vulnerable."

"Vulnerable to what?" Babylon demanded, and the Purchased Person reached out to touch him.

With a voice like the tolling of a bell she said, "To destruction. And all of us with it."

In all the long weeks Babylon had worked with the T'Worlie he had never heard so long a monologue—and perhaps not one with such importance for him. For the T'Worlie was saying that he had reasoned out the entire story of Cuckoo! The gentle chirping went on and on, and his Pmal rattled out the translation:

"Hexagon record encoded by ancient historians of early Watcher race purports to summarize their history. Statement of historians: Race ancestral to Watchers was brought to Cuckoo by, quote—"

The translation from the Pmal stopped short: the T'Worlie's shrill bird song continued, but without translation. Obviously there was no equivalent store in the Pmal's datafile. "Don't play tricks, Mimmie," Babylon begged. "What does that mean?"

"Original ambiguous. Analogy with known terms suggests tentative translation as 'eternal master,' 'supreme creator,' or possibly 'God.' To continue summary, the original Watcher race was brought aboard before the intergalactic voyage began, to defend Cuckoo. Evolved on a low-G world, they were gigantic winged warriors. The hexagon record seems to imply that the 'supreme creator' and most of his slave races were to sleep through a voyage lasting—" Again, all he heard was the T'Worlie's chittering. "Term appears to indicate a time period of extreme duration, certainly tens of millions of years. While others slept, the Watchers were stationed in the orbital forts and at points near the surface of Cuckoo to guard it at least during the first stages of the long voyage. If Cuckoo was created as vehicle of flight from anticipated galactic catastrophe, other beings may have sought to get aboard or even to seize the whole craft in hope of saving themselves.

"The successful emergence of Cuckoo from the endangered galaxy into intergalactic space made it safe from any such attacks. During the long ages of flight between galaxies, no further military service from the Watchers was required. They appear to have been neglected, if not forgotten. In the beginning, as the historians imply, no life had existed on the external surface, which was then a bare and sterile metal shell. The water and soil and atmosphere there now seem to have been accumulated through the ages of the flight, partly from collected cosmic dust but largely from waste products discharged to the surface from the internal mechanism of Cuckoo. Plants developed there, perhaps from spores and seed in the vented waste. Animals followed, brought perhaps by the Watcher garrisons or perhaps by escaping slaves of other races. These in turn were followed by degenerate dwarfish Watchers such as those we have encountered, which became predators upon the animals and finally enemies of all they had been intended to defend.

"The rebellion probably began in Watcher crews of the orbital forts. With their original duty forgotten, discipline was gone. The last historian speculates that supplies were interrupted and contact with the masters broken off. The orbital crews may have been forced to forage on the surface; perhaps they got a taste for freedom from the outlaw Watchers they met there. Using the advanced technology given them for operation of the orbiter, they discovered vulnerable points in the structure of Cuckoo and planned an attack against it—intending, the historian believes, to extort concessions, not to destroy it completely."

"Vulnerable?" Babylon shook his head, staring at the hovering T'Worlie. "Where?"

"At eight points," the T'Worlie chittered. "The phrase in the record may be rendered as 'the fatal eight.' The vulnerability exists because the position of the central sun is gravitationally unstable. In order to cancel out accidental drifts, which would be increased by positive gravitational feedback, supporting rings must be monitored and continually adjusted. This is done through control stations established in each of the eight octants of Cuckoo. Such control is possible because the atomic rings are elastic. Through applied magnetic force, they can be stretched in one octant and shrunk in another, to adjust their distance from the central sun and the consequent gravitational attraction. The eight stations—"

"Those points on the map?" Babylon whispered. "At the center of each octant? The place where we found the wrecked orbiter? And the temple over the lake? Are they the Achilles' heels?"

"Term 'Achilles' not found in Pmal lexicon, and such interruptions are counterproductive." The T'Worlie reproved him with a sharp ammoniac reek. "Danger to Cuckoo is greater than mere collision. Hexagon record states that application of excessive control force could penetrate electronic sheath and reverse formation processes to break quark chains, disintegrating entire atomic ring into raw energy and supermassive atomic fragments, themselves disintegrating. A ring-bomb all around Cuckoo, whose detonation would ignite a billion more. The rebel leaders planned to strike at the control network, using stolen technology. They hoped to conceal their actions by use of the tachyonic helmet. The helmet, as described by the author of the hexagons, is a device for mental contact through zero-mass tachyons. It was designed by the 'eternal creator' for control of his slaves and communication between them. The rebel Watchers found how to disable the spy circuitry, allowing them to use rebuilt helmets for illicit contact with one another, shielded from observation by their former masters.

"Preparing to strike, they obtained plans of the control stations. These are located deep inside the sphere, just above the inmost rings. The control stations are well defended, by special slave forces more loyal than the Watchers. The rebels knew that any successful attack would require a powerful military force. After long preparation, they diverted the fortress from orbit to land where we found it. The main body of attackers left it there, attempting to force their way down through the levels of Cuckoo to the station."

"And failed—"

"Clearly." An indignant chirp. "Details unknown. The plot required complex coordination of many difficult operations. If all had succeeded, Cuckoo would no longer exist. The wreckers were probably unable to seize the station and divert sufficient power to threaten the ring system, but that is merely speculation. The historian remained aboard the wreck with the rebel commanders, waiting for the attackers to report possession of the control station and readiness to destroy Cuckoo unless the 'eternal creator' met their demands. No such reports were ever received. Instead, the wreck was soon surrounded with the electrostatic fortresses through which we passed with such danger. Historian and fellow Watchers remaining on orbiter were never able to leave it. They died there."

"If the system is impregnable—"

"Erroneous assumption." A sternly ammoniac breath. "Cuckoo was never impregnable. As you yourself foresaw, knowledge of the hexagons is hazardous. It has brought extreme peril upon me. Spy devices were placed in my quarters, and copies of my hexagon translations have been removed. All Cuckoo is now in danger from some of our own companions, who now know how to strike through those eight fatal points."

"Who?"

"Identities unknown. However, a deltaform scent was left in my quarters."

Babylon frowned. "I didn't know the deltaforms were that suicidal."

"Comment." The shrill chitter cut him off. "Allowing death of tachyonic duplicates is not suicidal for originals. Hypothesis: Destruction of Cuckoo may now be attempted by beings who have stolen its secrets and now hope to keep them from others. Evidence indicates that plotters may possess adequate forces and adequate technological sophistication to achieve their objective." The T'Worlie hesitated, then finished strongly:

"This is ethically intolerable to me," it stated. "Therefore I declare my willingness to participate in this project."

Babylon could not help himself, he exploded in a burst of laughter. The T'Worlie merely hung there, gazing at him with those five bright eyes until Babylon was able to speak. "You couldn't just say yes, could you?" he asked, wiping his eyes. There were smiles, too, on the face of Pertin and Doc Chimp—one could not expect them, after all, from the other occupants of the room.

But the smiles did not last.

They were already beginning to fade as the people in the room contemplated the significance of the T'Worlie's long discursion; and then they were wiped away entirely. There was a shudder that rocked the very fabric of the orbiter. They all felt it, and something like a gasp came from each of them. "What happened?" Babylon demanded.

No one answered. Then, after a moment, Doc Chimp whispered, "We'd better find out, Dr. Babylon, because there's something awfully wrong. The lights are going out."

The pogrom had failed to meet its goals; some conspirators had escaped. The proof was all around them. The orbiter's power had dwindled and died; the lights went out, the gentle, permanent sigh of air circulators whispered to a stop, the standby glow of the stereostage faded to dark.

They were in blackness, and everybody was talking at once; Babylon let go of the wall loop he had been holding, and at once was floating in absolute darkness, with no up and no down and a terrifying, helpless vertigo. He brushed against something flimsy—the T'Worlie?—and yelped sharply as something metallically sharp raked his arm.

And then there was light. Not much. But a glimmer, and enough to see; Doc Chimp had had the presence of mind to find the door and wrench it open, and the pale emergency lights from the corridor filtered into the room. It was the silver woman's wingtip that had slashed him, Babylon found, and it was she who took command. Her voice chimed clearly, "There has been an explosion. The damage must be ascertained. Follow me!"

It was easier said than done. *She* could fly! Panting and swearing to himself as Doc Chimp pulled them along the dim corridors after her and the others, trying to help and more often slowing them down, Babylon was furious at the unfairness of it. Unfair that she had wings, and thus presence of mind! Unfair that these senseless squabblings among hatefully strange beings should endanger him! Unfair in the first place that he should even *be* here, so far from the quiet Cambridge laboratories where he belonged . . .

But the catalog of unfairness was too long. In all these last days and weeks, Jen Babylon had experienced almost nothing that was fair at all.

As they drove through they found the corridors filling with other beings all on the same errand, fast-flying deltaforms and slow, fumbling kitten-shaped creatures, robots and flesh, all together. By the time Doc Chimp and Babylon had caught up with the silver girl there was solid information. There had been an explosion, yes, and a particularly damaging one. Somehow someone—a fugitive Boaty-Bit swarm, no doubt—had jammed the tachyon-transport chamber so that incoming shipments rammed into matter already there, and the resulting blast had destroyed it. More than just itself. It had taken out the adjacent main power reserve and the FARLINK computer; it had shattered walls several tiers away, so that some of the reserved nonterrestrial habitats, with their queer atmospheres, were now open to the general oxygen-bearing air. "At least," Doc Chimp chattered, his shoe-button eyes darting back and forth at the devastation, "we've got one thing to be thankful for! The outer hull wasn't touched—we're not all trying to swallow vacuum now!"

"Yet," Ben Pertin snarled, and the chimpanzee's face became woebegone. For certainly the integrity of the hull meant only a reprieve— a short one at that. Without the constant shipments of food and replacements through the transport chamber, without the steady inflow of energy-dense transuranics for the power chamber, without any of the thousand things the orbiter needed to survive, its life span was short. The air would not circulate, and so in one place they would be gasping for breath, in others burning themselves out on excess oxygen. They could not even ask for help! And if they had, help was forty thousand light-years away . . .

Or a day or two.

Pertin's eyes widened suddenly, and he tugged at Babylon's arm, nodded to the others, and drew them all away to a more private part of the dim-lit, strange-smelling tunnels. "We're going to take a lander," he announced.

"We'll never get home in a *lander,*" Doc Chimp moaned.

"Not back to the Galaxy, you fool! Down to Cuckoo."

"Oh, of course, Ben!" cried the chimpanzee, nodding vigorously. "There's air there, and food—why, we could live a long time. Of course, there's no way to get back to our real home from there—"

"Shut up, Doc," Pertin ordered brutally. "We're not going home— not now, probably not ever. And we're not going to settle down and start a family, either. We're going to the temple to meet Zara and Org Rider—and then we're going inside!"

Doris stirred, and the faraway look in her eyes grew intense. "I concur," she said, "in that plan. What happened here is only a symptom; the cause of these events is within Cuckoo."

Babylon hesitated. "But Ben," he began, "somebody must try to repair things here—"

"Somebody will! And maybe they'll succeed—but I don't care whether they do or not." He was both angry and exalted, his long, untidy pigtails writhing as his head jerked in excitement. "I'm going to Cuckoo—if you want to come along, follow me. Otherwise stay here and rot!"

They drove through parts of the orbiter where Jen Babylon had never been before—where warm-blooded, oxygen-breathing mammals had never been, because the environment was death for them. But now it was not. The explosion had sundered the retaining doors, and the poison atmospheres had been blended with the predominant oxygen-nitrogen mix. Babylon's heart was wrenched with pity as they passed still forms of methane-breathers and other exotics—and some not so still, queer soft-bodied things like toads made of jelly, gasping piteously as the corrosive oxygen destroyed their lungs. "Come on!" Pertin yelled furiously. "You can't help them! And we've got to get to a lander before others think of it!"

In the event, they were not quite that lucky; the first lander berths they came to were empty, and at the nearest that was occupied there was a mob of Sheliaks and kitten-creatures fighting to get in. They passed it by—

And found one ready to go, with no one else near—

Or so they thought.

But as Pertin, shouting with triumph, cast himself toward its opened lock a dense steel-blue smoke poured out of it, and arranged itself as a shimmering cloak of diamond-bright beings before the hatchway.

Pertin clutched frantically at the wingtip of the silvery girl beside him, swore as his fingers were lacerated, but managed to halt his plunge. "Get out of the way, damn you!" he bellowed.

The shimmering curtain stirred, and the whine of the Boaty-Bits translated itself through their Pmals: "We cannot allow you to enter. You must die with everyone else on the orbiter."

"Die?" Doc Chimp whimpered. "Die again? Oh, but I've died so many times before—please! Don't make me do it again!"

The curtain rippled gently, almost as if moved by pity. Then the voice came: "Some part of you will live. Some part of all of us will live."

Pertin hesitated, almost choking with rage, and Jen Babylon, clinging to the lander-chamber wall, wondered desperately if it would come to an attempt to brush through the shimmering cloak. Could such tiny beings really harm them? Was there any strength behind their commands?

He did not need to find out, for the silvery girl cast Pertin aside, spread her wings, and, hovering in midair, raised her hands toward the fugitive Boaty-Bit swarm. "Live if you can!" she cried. From her fingertips a flood of white-hot energy leaped out at the collective beings, cutting great swaths through the swarm; and again, and again, until only a few scattered individuals fled aimlessly away.

Babylon barely remembered hurling himself toward the lander after Pertin and the winged girl, thrust in by Doc Chimp, followed by the T'Worlie.

Then there was a gentle tremor, and they were free, out in space.

As the thrust of the lander's motors began to move them away and down toward the immense, glowing object beneath them Babylon struggled to a port to look back at the orbiter.

The great, strange creation was dead. The aura that usually hung about its communications antennae was absent; the lights from its ports were dark. All the visible signs of functioning had stopped.

But they were on their way.

Although Jen Babylon had never before seen the temple with his own eyes, he recognized it at once. What was different was the lake. There was no lake. There was only a shallow bed where once a lake had been, and, on the greensward between the caked orange mud and the jungle that embraced it all, half a dozen terrible and strange winged creatures, with tall, lean human figures moving among them. Zara Doy came running to the lander. "We were worried about you!" she called, peering anxiously at the figures as they came out. Pertin explained about the explosion and the fact that they had had to come by slow landing craft instead of the near-instant tachyon transport . . . but Babylon wasn't listening. He was staring at the great creatures that squatted placidly on the margin of the dry lake. Their bodies were glittering bronze, their tails and the tips of their stubby wings shading to silver; as they moved they opened huge red mouths with sharklike teeth.

They did not look like creatures he wanted to be so close to.

Org Rider, grinning, came over to reassure him. "They're perfectly trained," he boasted. "They won't hurt you—as long as their owners are around. This org is mine, Babe Junior; the little one off by itself is Zara's. We can each take one of you, but I brought some friends along —I hope there aren't more than seven of you," he added, peering anxiously toward the lander. "Because it's better if we don't put more than two on each org." Reassured, he introduced the other riders, every one as skinny and as immensely tall as Zara and Org Rider themselves. The names escaped Babylon; his attention was all on the orgs themselves. *Ride* those creatures? With those great savage teeth so near? Especially when, Org Rider pointed out, each steed was "tamed" only in respect to its own individual rider, and if anything happened to the rider it would have to be considered as ferocious and as wild as any leopard or grizzly bear.

But once up on the creature's back, behind the graying, bearded old man named Wingsmith—a cousin of Org Rider's mother, he had been told—Babylon began to revise his opinions. The stubby wings were marvelously flexible. The broad back was warm and comforting beneath him. The org responded to every wish of Wingsmith as if the two were part of the same compound creature; the nine winged dragons all sprang into the air at once and circled the dry lake bed—Doc Chimp with Zara, Pertin behind Org Rider, Babylon, Redlaw, Doris with other riders from the tribe. There were two other orgs, but the winged silver girl and the T'Worlie disdained them; the extra orgs were given the packed supplies and equipment.

"All ready?" Org Rider cried, nodded at the answer, and led the way.

In single file they plunged down toward the ancient doorway and flew steadily into the interior of Cuckoo.

The T'Worlie could not keep up. It folded its filmy wings and hung on to the tail of Org Rider's mount, its tiny weight not even noticed by the powerful org. But its presence was essential. As they traced the convolutions of the tunnels they found themselves in a maze. A labyrinth; they would have been hopelessly lost in the first hour but for the T'Worlie. Its patient, supple mind had perceived the need for directions, and it had stored every scrap of data from the camera Doc Chimp had carried, from the glimpses obtained from the helmet, and from every other source, meticulously organizing them into a sort of strip map of the passages. When there was doubt, the T'Worlie supplied the answer. He had even plotted a route around the blocked stretch of tunnel that had defeated Te'ehala Tupaia; and they raced through the bowels of the immense artifact, down and down.

Babylon, hunched behind the gray-bearded rider, tried to count the number of days since his world had been stable and safe. It could not be more than a few weeks, but it seemed that since the beginning of time he had been thrust from one terrifying and unbelievable situation into another. His senses were saturated; his capacity for wonderment and even fear was almost exhausted. They sped through broad corridors and narrow, some so tight that Babylon could scarce believe the orgs were able to fly; they crossed immense flat spaces, with broad checkerboarded fields below them and ribbed metal ceilings above, the orgs unerringly darting between slender support columns. From time to time they saw traces of the party that had trudged these corridors before them—a discarded food packet, castoff bits of equipment. They stopped in one of the broad areas of growing things so that the orgs could forage and the riders take a break. The ceiling above them shone softly, and there was a steady drainage of chilled air that made Babylon shiver uncomfortably. He did not dare to eat the strange, soft-shelled nutlike things that grew on the land, and the machine-made food in the rations they had brought had a reek that took away his appetite. He was glad enough to be moving on—

And then they came to a sign of the party before them that was different from all the others. It was the body of a white-haired man. He had died with an expression of terror on his face, and the entire front of his torso had been ripped open.

The orgs halted while their riders stared down at the corpse. "Oh, I know what did that," Doc Chimp moaned. "It's that Watcher! The same one that killed me!" And his shoe-button eyes darted fearfully around, as if he were expecting the maddened being to plunge out at them from any niche or tunnel.

That was the first of the corpses. It was not the last. Less than a hundred meters farther there were two others, then another single body—

And then the passage they were flying through opened into an immense cavern, filled with machines and conduits and huge, strange devices of many sorts, and Babylon found his capacity for startlement suddenly born again. "I know this place!" he cried.

"Of course," called Zara from the org beside him. "We saw it on Doc's camera!"

"No, no!" Babylon stared around, wondering. "I'm sure! I've seen it in a dream! Those glowing walls. Those bright spots that look like jewels, only they're glowing. Only—only I remember seeing those broken beams, and ugly glass crabs swarming over them trying to fix them—" He paused, trying to sort out dream from what he had seen in the stereostage or via the helmet. He shook his head. "Something terrible happened here," he said positively, "and I dreamed about this place even before it happened!"

The other orgs were dancing around, and Redlaw, who had gone ahead out over the great terrifying void, returned to boom: "Terrible enough, Babylon. Look down there!"

At the base of the vertical drop there was a cluster of forms. The orgs swooped down dizzyingly, and they approached carefully.

But there was nothing to fear from the creatures at the bottom. They were all dead, humans and one which was not human. "The Watcher!" Doc Chimp chattered in terror. "Oh, that's the one that killed me! Please, Dr. Babylon—Ben—Zara—please, let's get away from here!"

"It's dead, Doc," Zara said soothingly, gazing down at the hideous creature, shrouded in what was left of its immense leathery wings. Its body was ripped and torn, and next to it were other bodies. A huge, golden-skinned man whom Babylon recognized with a sharp intake of breath—the Purchased Person he had seen way back in Boston, in the Tachyon Transport Base. And another more startling still.

"Why, it looks like that old man we saw already!" Zara gasped. "Only—only he's been changed—"

"Edited," Ben Pertin snapped. "Reduced in size. Toughened, to stand this place when it was still bursting open. Changed in a lot of other ways, no doubt . . . But dead," he finished, almost with satisfaction, as he gazed down at the gnomelike shape. "No sense in standing around and gaping—let's get on with it!" And he tapped Org Rider's shoulder, and they spun away.

A scattering of the glassy, crablike creatures still worked at the machines in that great chamber, but they paid no attention to the orgs or their passengers. The party entered another passage, and another, and another—

Babylon lost count of how many tunnels and galleries and caverns they traversed, even of how many times they stopped for food or rest. They flew through a featureless space to a pale gray rectangle that opened up to become the mouth of a vast metal tunnel; they passed side passages and openings that he did not bother even to glance into. They flew down a sloping tunnel with a queerly triangular cross section, the walls joining in a peak over their heads, with what looked like a shifting surface of moving cinders under their passage; he did not care. They crossed a mossy plain with the ceiling above dark and so high that they could barely see it, and when they entered the next tunnel, narrower and darker than the others, the first orgs shied away from new bodies on the floor—more of the gnomelike travesties of Purchased People, Babylon saw as they passed, and hardly cared that he saw.

He lost all sense of distance and of time. He was half drowsing when he realized that all the orgs had stopped, and their riders were dismounting.

"What's going on?" he asked, and Doc Chimp whispered in alarm:

"Not so loud, please, Dr. Babylon! They're very close now—Zara said she heard voices!"

Babylon stared around. They were in another down-sloping passage, this one brighter than most, for at the far end of it there was a queer radiance. He listened, but heard nothing, and wondered whether it had been Zara's imagination rather than a voice—

No. There was something. More a drum rattle than a human voice —a Scorpian robot! Very distant and very faint, but there was no doubt.

"I think we'd best leave the orgs here," Redlaw said, as softly as his deep voice could be made to sound. "Maybe the T'Worlie could go ahead and scout for us—"

But the T'Worlie did not at once obey. It hung in midair, its filmy wings moving slowly as the longest-range of its five patterned eyes peered ahead of them. The T'Worlie were almost never agitated, but there was something shaky in its shrill whistle as it spoke: "Statement: Person or persons approaching rapidly. Recommendation: Caution. Further statement—"

And then it fell silent for a moment, hovering . . . and then, in a manner most unT'Worlielike, it whistled raggedly, "Also coming— Not physically coming— Imminently approaching—"

And then it did something no T'Worlie had ever done in the presence of a member of another race.

It screamed.

The Pmals could find no comprehensible translation, and did not try. They simply reproduced the whistling, warbling sound of terror; and broke off when the T'Worlie collapsed upon itself, its five eyes staring emptily, its wings in helter-skelter disarray, and slowly, slowly settled to the floor of the corridor.

There was a time, and not long in coming, when Jen Babylon comprehended all things at once, with a terrible knowledge that hurled huger and newer questions at him . . . but that time had not yet arrived. To Jen, the next few moments were utter, anarchic madness. Everything seemed to happen at once. Even while the Pmals were pouring the T'Worlie's scream of horror and disbelief into his ears, there were two other sounds. Doris, the Purchased Person—she was screaming, too, if you could call the low, ecstatic moan that came from her lips a scream. Her face was rapt, her eyes blazing with an emotion Babylon could not read—

And at the same time—

The silver girl lifted herself on her great wings and hurled herself at Babylon. She too was screaming, but words emerged from the Pmal: "A force! I perceive a new concentration of energies!" She collided with him, thrust something into his hands—

And at the same time—

Two figures burst out of the tunnel, one tinier than the other but both inhumanly short. They stopped abruptly as they caught sight of the org-riding group, but then the smallest of them cried out and came on, throwing itself at Zara Doy, wrapping his arms around her knees with a heartrending shout of *Mama*—

And at the same time—

The noise from the end of the corridor rose to a great rapturous shout—

And at the same time—

The thing in Jen Babylon's hands reached out with impalpable tendrils and caught at his mind. It was the helmet. He knew that. He knew, too, that there was a surge of rawly horrifying energy coming from it that threatened to sweep him away through its mere touch, that would surely change him irrevocably and forever if he did not release it at once.

But he could not.

His arms had a life of their own. They lifted the helmet and settled it on his head.

And Jen Babylon's world changed forever.

There was a part of Jen Babylon that did not change. It merely—increased. That part of him was able to see the tiny figure that flung itself at Zara Doy and recognize it—grievously squashed, distorted, and hideous, it was nevertheless the little boy he had seen, an eternity ago, with that other Zara Doy in the Tachyon Base. That part of him was able to feel the rake of the silver girl's wingtips as she convulsively struggled against whatever had her in its grip, observe the lustrous gleam of her almost human body, feel its inhuman cold and rigidity. That part of him felt pain. But that part of him was now submerged in a larger self, as if a color-blind man were suddenly seeing a rainbow, a tone-deaf man hearing music; as if fingers that had never touched anything but themselves now reached out to palp a world.

Like that—but more than that. There were no words. The truth was something for which words did not exist! There could be only analogies and approximations; and the closest words could come to truth was to say that Jen Babylon, all of him, was exploding. Was both the Ground Zero and the infinitely expanding wavefront that was the blast itself.

But that was metaphor. For the reality there were no words.

There were no words to say how, as he exploded past tunnel walls and caverns, past the inner shell of Cuckoo, past every material object within its gravitational range, he reached and tasted each of its myriad creatures, and each of its myriad, myriad atoms.

There were no words to describe how he felt each feeling those beings felt, Doc Chimp's quivering horror, Zara's terrible blend of horror and love as she enfolded the caricature of her son, David's panicked longing, the raw emotions of Ben Pertin and Te'ehala Tupaia, of Redlaw and the battered, semiconscious T'Worlie, of Org Rider and even of the orgs themselves.

There were no words to convey the billion-piece symphony of tastes and feelings that he sampled from the countless denizens of Cuckoo's shell, demented Watchers and sullen savages, of a thousand shapes and a thousand million states of mind.

There were no words to convey the sight that opened up before him, the great skeletal shell of Cuckoo itself, and within its curved embrace the restlessly seething auroras of plasma, the distant, bright sun, the immensity spanned by this wall around a star.

And there were, finally, no words to say what he felt when he knew that he was not alone. That even this immense new being was tiny beside its neighbor, newborn and unsuspected; that he was naked in the awful presence of ONE far greater than himself.

NINETEEN

And now my mission is near its end, for HE is waking.

The great machine stirs in all its hidden places, and reports to me. Even the parts that have lain silent for all the thousands of centuries now are commanded to life, and they respond. The desecrators who forced the new intrusion into HIS sacred fabric have been dealt with, and once more the masterwork that is HIS body has proven invulnerable, even to nuclear attack. As HE constructed it to be.

Now at last HIS vast design fulfills itself.

The guardians of the frozen crypts move and wake, and send out their sensors. First to their organic charges: Are they safe? Have any suffered damage? Need they clone new samples for the store? Then they reach out to HIM for instructions. There are none yet. But they will not be long in coming.

The custodians of the great driving jets at the poles wake. They check their plasma reserves and test their power charges and their controls. It is not yet time for them, but they are ready. When they are needed they will guide our great machine-egg into its fresh galactic nest.

And I am ready—ready to end the long, lonely watch over the great round machine and all its myriad tenants and parts.

I reach out to all my sleeping members. They have rested, blind and uncaring, in the bubbles of a thousand separate memory stores, for the thousands and thousands of years since they were themselves alive, before they became, like me, charged particles dancing about the interfaces of the immense machine.

Was I once, like them, alive? I cannot remember.

But they were! And what things they were, back in the home galaxy, before HE was born out of the need to flee its fires. Great gray starfish from the ammonia slime of seas that never saw their sun.

Ethereal wisps of gas clouds that needed no star. Creatures like insects and creatures like rocks, creatures of all shapes and chemistries; creatures that were old when HE was only a theory, and creatures that HE planned and bred and nursed to ripeness in a spiral arm, even when the galactic core was exploding and the central stars were being devoured by the tens of millions.

And then they, too, were devoured . . .

As I am about to be devoured . . .

For HE is awake now, and come into HIS glory, and I—I cease to exist—

EXCEPT AS PART OF HIM.

TWENTY

HE WOKE. And all over the Galaxy, the shape of the worlds changed for the beings who inhabited them.

In Boston, on old Earth, a man in a red jumpsuit was overseeing the receipt of a valuable cargo of spices and fragrances from a planet in the constellation Canes Venatici when there was a sudden eruption of noise. The doors of the tachyon chamber crashed open. The militia on guard duty were borne back on a flood of glassy crab-creatures, their claws rattling like cast dice on the terrazzo floor. "But you are interfering with a priority shipment!" the man cried. They did not heed. They swept over him. Glassy pincers caught at the tuning controls. The slow creep of goods on the conveyor belt halted. Then the tachyon chamber clouded over with a smoke—a fog—a cloud of tiny creatures, and the swarm buzzed out, dancing like midges over a muddy creek. And another swarm. And another. "Why, you're Boaty-Bits," the man cried in exasperation. "You have no right here! Stop this at once!" But the swarms coalesced and danced toward him, diamond dust sprinkling the air. In a moment the man was covered with them, like a circus clown hit with a flour bomb. He stood rigid and helpless as the swarms came on, and came on, and came.

In another part of Boston, the Crystal Maid knew her destiny had come. She was not truly a she, or even an it, but merely a part of a great dispersed whole, once a starborne seed, edited to ease her freedom of movement as she led the other seeds on this new colony world. She had no personality, nor even self. But she knew her task. She stood raptly at the edge of the Common, listening with all her senses to the mind-song of the sprouted seeds as they scuttled across the face of this world. She gave thanks to the distant, deeper drone of that greatest mind whose servants had planned her, and created her, and dispatched her on her way. Beside her, the autochthon Tupaia, temporary ally, discarded tool, cried out in astonishment; she paid no heed. The song of a million seeds on a hundred million worlds flowed through her. She was in touch with the infinite. She was the infinite.

In Lawrence, Kansas, on the same unimportant world, it was harvest time at the catfish farms. But when the workers arrived with their nets, the things that splashed out at them from the ponds were not whiskered and finned, but huge, crystalline, clawed—and very numerous.

Very nearby, in the city of Tokyo, Japan—only half a world away— a frantic man named Kazuo Noritamo reached the 80-meter level in the great tower. It was being evacuated—heaven knew why—and the observation deck was crowded with frightened tourists hurrying down. Noritamo knew better. Down was where the danger was. He peered through the slanted panes, at the people around the amusements and rides, forty young girls in blue cloche hats with gold bands, a fat bald monk chanting into his begging bowl. They had not yet panicked. But they would. He ran up the steps to the high-speed elevator; no one was there; he got in and pushed the button himself, panting with both exertion and fear. The 250-meter level was deserted. He ran to the window, for once careless of the dizzying height. In the temple grounds at the base of the tower, white-capped police were trying vainly to stem the oncoming march of the glassy crabs, their shells streaked with the oily waters of Tokyo Bay; the police batons did not stop the crabs, did not seem even to annoy them. They were coming. He was trapped. There was simply nowhere to go. He was alone at the top of the tower, and as he peered down he saw that the enemy was close. The foreshortened tiny figures on the roof below were now still as statues in a sculpture court, every one of them suddenly limned with a steel-blue frosting of metallic dust, all faces raptly upturned to the sky, or to him. The rattle of the elevator door behind him made him turn, glad for the company of another escaped human. —It was not that. A dazzling cloud of steel-bright motes boiled out of the opening door to show that he had not escaped after all.

On the flimsy moon of a gas-giant planet—still very near; less than a hundred light-years away—a colony of collective beings felt the pulse of the Overmind. They were not like bees, nor even like any insect; they were not even related to the Boaty-Bits, nor had they become a part of the galactic congress of races, since their planet had been missed. But they were bioluminescent aerophytes, tough-walled hydrogen bladders cemented together in floating clouds a kilometer thick. They did not fear the pulse of rapture. It was the destiny that they had never expected, but recognized and accepted at once. They welcomed it.

In the slushy seas of an ice planet, a creature like a pale, lean whale felt the shock of an amputation. He was the owner of a Purchased Person on Sun One. His creature had been stolen without warning. He burst from his pearly home in the sea-bottom sludge and drove straight up, twenty kilometers and more, to breach the surface and leap into the dense, chill air. It was no use. His panic was justified. Out of a great lens-shaped cloud of luminous violet, three crystal creatures in the shape of deltaforms dove toward him like javelins. The creature saw them coming and dived to escape, but they followed, as fast in water as in air, and as sure. There was no escape.

On a damp, hot world in a distant spiral arm, three great flying creatures, soaring between a halogen-enriched pink cloud and an angry, oily, scarlet-glowing sea, dodged savage strokes of lightning. They did not fear the lightning as much as they feared the winged crystal shapes that steadily, remorselessly pursued . . . and always gained.

On a small planet under two ruddy suns, a creature that looked like a headless centaur was operating a compact excavator. He was almost alone. Most of his crew had drifted away, part of that epidemic folly that had transformed so many of his race to idlers—his race did not call them "Kooks." It did not matter much, because the excavation here was easy enough. The surface was a coarse, dark sand, very promising for the minerals that fed his kind. He cut through a wiry gray mosslike growth that bore tiny, powdery flowers of crystal and set out his arrays. A core drill brought up samples of the dark sand. Seismographs probed for deeper data. A tiny antenna, unfolding like an inverted parasol, transmitted the data to his people's central store. It was all going well, until his assistants came back, the faceted patches that served them for eyes alight with a sudden rapture, their forms surrounded by a dusting of diamond-bright tiny collective creatures that rose and swarmed toward him.

On the T'Worlie planet Nglinn, one of the greatest and oldest of T'Worlie scientists danced away from his instruments with a sharp turpentine-and-lemon scent of joy. For half a long T'Worlie lifetime he had sought to find a zero-mass tachyon, the particle whose predicted properties offered an immense new range of communication and transport—in vain. But now the search was over! Without warning his instruments registered a sudden flood of them, in the trillions of trillions, the strongest pulse they could count! He spun to his stereo-stage to inform his assistants. They did not answer at first—and when they did the oldest and best of them, all five eyes glowing with an unfamiliar ecstasy, cried out in the compact T'Worlie language a single word. The nearest English equivalent would be: "HE is come!"

And the rapture overspread the Galaxy.

It reached tiny planets and huge, hot worlds and cold, the creatures that lived in slow, sullen dust clouds in the wake of exploded supernovas and in the chromospheres of stars. It reached and possessed a conjugating mass of Sheliaks in the depths of their home planet, and transformed them; it was spelled out in drumbeats on the stark, dry world of the Scorpians. It did not affect every world, but most. It did not strike every individual, or even the majority. But hardly a race failed to find some of its members seized with the passionate touch of an Overmind, or to feel the grip of tiny collective beings swarming out of their tachyon stations, or to retreat in the face of the armies of crystal creatures that boiled from their seas.

And far from the Galaxy, in the shell of Cuckoo, a strange battle raged, as the exploding self that had once been Jen Babylon, with his million eyes and his infinite array of senses, confronted the Titan who had swallowed one galaxy and was ready for another.

The contest was not equal. But there was at least a contest, and HE had never known one before—until the battle for the billion worlds was joined.

TWENTY-ONE

Dr. Jensen Babylon slowly raised the supple helmet from his head and looked about him. He was standing on a shell of hard, dark crystal, and far beneath him a sun hung in a glowing cloud of plasma, tiny and remote. Its fire was filtered by that dark crystal floor, so that he could see its sharp-rimmed disk, a little smaller than Sol's, pocked with twin, diverging rows of small, dark sunspots.

Nearer to hand were the trashed and reeking remnants of the struggle that had come before. The dark crystal was smeared with blood. The hot air bore a slaughterhouse stench of alien chemistries in destruction. The carnage went all the way to the far wall, bodies, bits of equipment, a great translucent object surrounded by corpses.

"Dr. Babylon," whispered a small voice in his ear. "Jen! What has happened to you?"

Babylon turned and saw Doc Chimp, arms wrapped around a gaunt steel pillar, just behind him. The black shoe-button eyes were not fearful but they were wondering. Wondering as they stared at Jen, wondering as they flicked to the corpses, as they fastened on the distant discarded rubble. "I don't know, Doc," Babylon said simply. "I'm different."

"Is it that helmet? Has it—done something to you?"

Babylon nodded, gazing around. A titanic battle had been fought here, and the overpowering beetle stink of Watchers told what one side had been. The other, perhaps those shattered crystal crustaceanlike things, their bodies mixed in with the hard-armored corpses of the Watchers themselves. "It's more than the helmet, Doc," he said somberly. "I don't know what it is, but I can see things that were hidden before, and what I can see most clearly—" He hesitated and frowned. "I see that the greatest is yet to come," he finished. "We are in the presence of something very large."

A slow twittering from his other side told him the T'Worlie was still there, too. "Concurrence," it chirped, tone solemn. "Hypothesis: Presence is central consciousness of Cuckoo."

There was a gasp from Doc Chimp, and a quick, muffled exchange between him and the T'Worlie. Babylon hardly heard them. He was immersed in the wonder of his new knowledge. Taking the hood off had not taken away his immense new persona. Its forces had changed him, and he knew that the change was forever. He could hear Doc Chimp and the T'Worlie. He could see the laser-seared and dismembered bodies that lay about. He was aware that the little ape had said something very important, and then bounded away.

But his attention was taken up by the enormous, expanded perceptions that surrounded him.

He knew that something vastly important was about to happen, very soon. Yet he was not anxious or apprehensive. The forces that had expanded him had also made him hugely more quick; and so there was time.

There was time for him to perceive what lay about him. He saw that not all the motionless crystal crabs were destroyed; many of them were crushed and broken, but far the greater number were simply frozen, waiting for orders from that being who owned them. He saw that there were other players in this great drama, and all of them, too, still waiting for their cues. He saw the battered Scorpian robot that lay crushed and immobile halfway along the trail of carnage, rattling helplessly to itself in a complaining grumble. He saw Zara Doy, with the kobold boy clutched fiercely to her breast, staring up at him in fear and hope, and the weary orgs that waited impatiently to be fed or ridden or set free. He saw a cloud of Boaty-Bits that danced in a dense swarm, waiting for the will of their master; and everything he saw interlocked with all the rest. He perceived the patterns and the roots. He did not only see. He comprehended. Far away he saw a bounding figure, tiny as a flea in the distance, and knew that it was Doc Chimp following the trail of destruction—and knew what errand he was on.

And urgent as all that was, he took time to wonder at the whole mystery of Cuckoo, now revealed to him entire. Not merely an artifact. A machine. Powered by hydrogen fusing into helium at the core of its sun; the energies turned into radiation, then trapped and redirected by the structures on the interior of its shell. Stellar energy fed those huge devices at the poles, ion-thrusters that had hurled Cuckoo out of its home galaxy and would halt it at its destination. Stellar energy cooled the great ice caves where frozen bits of organic matter slept, waiting to be thawed and born again to populate new planets in the new starcloud. Stellar energy powered the great machine-mind that had overseen the workings of Cuckoo while its master slept, that had sent emissaries to all the planets of the new galaxy and sampled all its worlds—and was now silent. Stellar energy had powered those great, eternal monatomic rings, so that their centrifugal force held the great shell suspended and prevented it from collapsing into its central sun. All this Jen Babylon saw and understood.

And, out of nowhere or out of the air around him, sourceless and irresistible, a great voice sounded in his ear:

"NOW YOU KNOW ALMOST ALL."

He turned, and froze. The cluster of Boaty-Bits had shaped themselves into a huge, winged, three-eyed form, facing him, while another cloud of them danced toward him. As they settled on his body, his face, his eyes, the voice spoke again:

"NOW KNOW ME."

And he knew, and the pain of that terrible knowledge was almost too much to bear.

A galaxy far away—a little older than the one that sheltered Earth. Not very different. Not different in the way in which all galaxies were alike, for it was destroying itself.

All galaxies destroy themselves in the end, because the random movement of mass sooner or later produces concentrations at the core. A sort of critical mass. A knot in space-time. Sometimes it is called a black hole, sometimes a Seyfert galaxy; there are countless millions of them in the sky, and each one is the agony of a billion suns.

Within that far-away galaxy were myriad inhabited worlds, old and wise or still straining toward the awakening of intelligence. All doomed; but in some of them, the oldest and wisest few, the knowledge of that doom came to exist.

They were very wise, and they had time. The frightful fires at the core of their galaxy reached out toward all its worlds—but slowly, no faster than the crawl of light itself—while they had the tachyons to reach around to all their worlds, and in time the zero-mass tachyons. For a tachyon is brother to the photon. The closer to the speed of light it travels, the more its mass. The less its mass, the farther from c its velocity. For a zero-mass photon, there is no energy, no motion. But for a zero-mass tachyon . . . the speed is infinite.

So they reached out to the neighboring galaxies to find a haven. They built an ark to flee in. And they peopled the ark. Specimens of every sapient race, frozen in liquid-helium baths to be revived when there were safe homes for them again. Memories of all the collective wisdom of their cultures, organized into a vast computer store, to run the ark and protect it. Those were the passengers and the crew. And for the captain . . .

For the captain they planned and bred a race that could free itself from flesh and live on; that could fuse and take into itself all of the other intelligences of the galaxy and make use of them; that could rest for many millennia, and then awaken again to carry out their plan.

And then, as the deadly radiation flooded over their homes, they died . . . or died in some parts of themselves, while other parts lived on—

In HIM. And the great ark, or egg, was launched on its immense journey.

And all this Jen Babylon knew, and then the steel-blue creatures fell away from him, and he could see again with his own eyes, and the vast voice spoke once more:

"NOW YOU KNOW ME. NOW KNOW WHAT YOU MUST ENDURE."

And Jen Babylon, with all the strength he owned, shouted:

"No!"

There was a pause, while the dense swarm of Boaty-Bits moved about within the confines of the shape they had assumed, and the galactic beings drew back, terrified spectators at the huge debate. Then the Overmind spoke:

"YOU MUST. I DO NOT COME TO CONQUER, BUT TO SAVE. YOUR GALAXY TOO IS DOOMED, AND ALREADY THE FIRES ARE FLASHING AT ITS CORE."

And the images flooded into Babylon's mind, of the vast press of matter at the heart of his own Galaxy, now inexorably beginning its long, irresistible explosion. That which was human in Jen Babylon was terrified, as much by the insupportable feeling of responsibility as by the frightening knowledge itself. Yet he did not let the fear overcome him. Steadfastly he cried:

"Even so—*no!*"

And the battle for the billion worlds was joined.

TWENTY-TWO

In the great contest, the being that had once been Jen Babylon had only very limited assets. He was a fusion of many beings, but the fusion was incomplete; while the Overmind that stood against him was a synthesis of thousands of billions. HE needed no allies. Babylon might have needed many, but had only two: a troubled T'Worlie and a terrified ape.

The Superbeing was very old, and quite unused to being denied HIS own way. HE had been created for the specific purpose of absorbing lesser beings into HIMSELF. There was no opposition. In the first instance, it had been the lesser beings themselves who created the first crude, tiny prototype of the Overmind, for the immense destruction at the core of their galaxy gave them no other hope to survive. Later there was the example of the thousand earlier races who had let themselves be swallowed into HIS majesty—sometimes with joy. More often not; but the spur of the explosion at their galaxy's heart had always been enough. So it had been easy for HIM. It had at the last become routine. As the plan progressed and the ark was being prepared, new races reached intelligence, or were discovered, or found their own way into the galactic interchange; and then HE would choose a member of that race to answer for all, give him the knowledge of what was and what was to be—and accept them into HIMSELF. There had never been any resistance—how could there be?

But now, unbelievably, there was!

For Jen Babylon, and all the parts that made up the huger Jen Babylon, were born of a galactic culture that recognized individual differences and even prized them. Babylon was not merely struggling for the physical safety of his galaxy, but for its soul.

It was a matter of right! The right of Jen Babylon to choose his own field of study, and select his own way of life; of Te'ehala Tupaia to sacrifice himself on the altar of an ideal; of Doc Chimp to allow himself to be killed, and killed again, and still cling to existence. The force that fed Babylon was the total of the rights of even those who denied those rights, the Boaty-Bits and the Sheliaks; of the T'Worlie and the Watchers and all the myriad unnamed galactic peoples; of the Zaras and the Davids, and Org Riders, and both Jen Babylons and both Tupaias, and the countless Ben Pertins and Doc Chimps—

For they each and all had a right and a built-in directive: to carry on their lives. To do the thing most important to any living thing: to live.

They were not in any way sacred, not even to each other. Not even to themselves. Time and again, the races of the Galaxy had often destroyed each other. Certainly they had worked at cross-purposes. Each had moved on its own trajectory, with all their myriad myriad problems and confrontations and prejudices and hopes each tugging them in a different direction.

But, over time, there was always a sort of vector effect that summed the individual impassioned drives. Slowly, slowly, with many back-trackings and countless hesitations, the life of all those beings slowly became—not happier, not more successful, not more comfortable—

But more meaningful.

The purpose of life, one of his professors had once told Jen Babylon, is to learn the purpose of life.

And it was now Jen Babylon's task to allow that purpose to be carried out.

Babylon, the physical, mortal Babylon, sighed deeply, raised his head, and confronted the Superbeing. He said steadily, "Tell me what you want."

"TO SAVE YOU. TO TAKE INTO OURSELF EVERY SENTIENT IN YOUR GALAXY."

"That," Babylon cried, "you may not do! We don't want to be parts of a collective intelligence! We are individuals, and we mean to stay that way!"

"UNTRUE. ONLY PARTLY TRUE."

"I grant," Babylon said desperately, "that there are exceptions—the collective intelligences, like the Boaty-Bits. But they are our horrible example! Because they are collective, they stopped evolving long and long ago—while the rest of us continued to grow! It is conflict—the conflict of ideas and goals—that brings progress!"

"IT BRINGS DESTRUCTION."

"Yes," Babylon agreed, "sometimes it brings that, too. But that is our choice. We will not permit you to devour us."

Silence, while the Great Being pondered this new fact of resistance and Babylon stole a covert look across the vast chamber. The distant figure of Doc Chimp, which had bounded so swiftly away, was toiling laboriously back, and it carried something softly gleaming, and bigger than Doc himself.

Something flashed before Babylon's eyes, filmy and bright-colored; it hung before him with its five bright eyes peering into his. It chirped frantically: "Dr. Babylon! You must not!"

"I must," said Babylon, reaching out with clumsy sympathy to the T'Worlie; but it shrieked in agony, like a canary on the rack, and fluttered clumsily away.

The shape of whirling bits stirred restlessly and the Great Being spoke: "YOU HAVE NO CHOICE," it said reasonably, and Babylon shook his head.

"Neither of us has a choice," he pointed out. "I deny you the right to absorb us into yourself! And I warn you that if you try, it will be the end of you."

"THAT IS NOT POSSIBLE. YOU ARE WEAK. I AM STRONG."

"It is your strength that will destroy you," Babylon said wearily, turning to gaze at Doc Chimp, toiling nearer with the great, murderous weapon in the form of a translucent block that had come—so long ago!—from the wrecked ship. "You see," he said, stretching and gazing down at the distant sun, "we know where we are. This is one of your octant control centers. If my primate friend there fires that weapon it will knock out your controls. That electronic sheath will break down, and how long will it be then before one of your atomic rings disintegrates? And after that—"

He shrugged. He did not need to say any more. The T'Worlie had spelled it all out, and surely this immense mind would not need to have it repeated. He gazed regretfully at Mimmie, who was stricken with horror at what was going on. Somehow the T'Worlie would have to be made well again . . . Somehow something must be done to repair the damaged lives all around him, the grotesque child that Zara Doy was clutching to her, the agonies that they had all suffered . . . Somehow . . . Something.

But what? What could make all this suffering worthwhile?

"Freedom," he said aloud, and turned again to the clustered shape that confronted him. "You see, it's a standoff. If you don't leave us alone you will be destroyed yourself."

The silence protracted itself, and then the Great Being spoke—its voice slower than before, almost hesitant. "YOUR GALAXY IS DOOMED," it protested.

"No!" Babylon said sharply. "It is in danger, but it is not doomed. You failed to control the explosion in the core of your own galaxy, but we will not fail. We will find a way to contain the explosion."

Pause. Then, "HOW?"

Babylon cried angrily, "I don't know how; I only know that there must be a way. Somehow! Maybe a super-Dyson sphere, enclosing the core—"

"SUCH TECHNOLOGY DOES NOT EXIST."

"Of course not! Not yet! But it can. I know that no race in the galaxy has the structural materials or the engineering skill—they're both orders of magnitude beyond anything that has ever been attempted. But they are not impossible! And we have time! Thousands of years at least! Especially . . . especially if we work together." And when Babylon had said that he stopped. He had said it all. The decision was no longer his.

The silence was longest of all, while Doc Chimp stood firm but fearful at the keyboard of the strange weapon, skinny arms poised like the mad organist under Notre Dame, while all the other beings waited —while a galaxy waited.

And at last the Superbeing spoke.

"I DO NOT KNOW IF IT IS POSSIBLE. BUT IT IS TRUE THAT THERE IS TIME."

There was an unheard sound, like a great worldwide sigh. Babylon pressed his advantage: "And you'll let us do it? You'll release the Kooks and let them return to normal life? Withdraw your slave machines from the galaxy?"

"I WILL."

"And we'll try to build a wall around the core together?"

"WE WILL."

"And when it's done—"

"WHEN IT'S DONE—"

N34   "You will leave us alone?"

"NO. WILL MAKE COPIES. WILL TAKE COPIES. WILL LEAVE ORIGI-
NALS."

Babylon thought hard. Take copies?

He said slowly, "And then you will leave our galaxy forever?"

"FOREVER. WITH COPIES."

Babylon nodded. Ten thousand years at least, maybe more. Time in
which great changes could occur.

"All right," he said, "we have agreed. You will help us try to
contain the core. Whether it succeeds or fails, you will then go on to
another galaxy, making copies of every intelligence in our galaxy and
taking them into yourself . . ."

And he did not add:

If you can.